KILLING MARY JANE

AMARIE AVANT
NICOLE DUNLAP

Edited by
JULIETTE CROSS

Edited by
JULIE DEATON

ISBN-13:

978-1725874183

ISBN-10:

1725874180

❀ Created with Vellum

VOLUME I

What is life?
A Frenzy.
What is life?
An illusion, a shadow, a fiction.
And the greatest good is trivial;
for all life is a dream and all dreams are dreams...

Pedro Calderon de la Barca

PROLOGUE

THE GOLDEN BEAUTY TREMBLED LIKE A LEAF AS SHE STOOD center stage. A neon sign reading *The Petting Zoo* hung behind her but her feeble attempt to shield her face from the floodlight and cover her ample curves did nothing. Before her, every seat of the strip club was taken. An endless sea of men had come to see *her*. Those who often favored the bar had left their rickety barstools to stand and get a closer look; their gazes locked on her lace outfit as they waited for her to dance. Yet the wolves were kept at bay as three armed men stood at pivotal locations in front of the stage.

"Give 'em a lil' something, sugar," a man said, giving off an aura of importance. He was huge, almost as wide as he was tall, and in a double-breasted suit. He sat front and center, plump lips pursed against a Cuban cigar. He slammed his hand down onto the tiny tabletop. A glass of whiskey trembled as much as the heavenly beauty before him. "Twirl, Mary Jane. Bitch, give 'em a lil' taste!"

The woman on the stage took a hesitant step back. *Who is Mary Jane?* she thought, almost losing her balance in spiky heels. Her head pounded as all her thoughts moved in slow motion.

"I'm Beasley," the man said, climbing up the steps of the stage. "But you've probably forgotten that by now, haven't you?"

Before she could ask why she was there—*who exactly she was*—Beasley shouted, "I told you to shake that ass!" Sprays of his saliva accosted her face with each word.

She slapped his face with all of her might. This was truly a nightmare. Moreover, the bastard didn't budge. He only continued to clamp his hand across her mouth while his fingernails chewed into her cheeks.

"Fuck!" she screeched from the sting. She bit down on the inside of his palm. Beasley instantly let her mouth go but then he coiled his fingers through her hair, grabbed a handful of thick strands and yanked her down to the floor before him.

Mary Jane didn't scream. Though she wasn't aware of much, intuition told her that he wasn't a man you could bargain with to keep your life. Besides, something in her was broken, as if she'd done enough begging to survive for a lifetime already.

Her thick lips spread into a line.

He wrapped his hands around her throat, further challenging her with a hard squeeze.

Her glare never wavered as she dared Beasley to take her out.

The light began to dance before Mary Jane's eyes and her lungs screamed as he choked her. She had no idea what else there was to live for. She knew nothing about herself – not even if her name really was Mary Jane. *Why live?* How would she even know if there was anything to live for? But, deep down, Mary Jane felt a seed of courage brewing and an innate need to know more about this place, about herself. She started to reach out to slap him again. In. a split second, decision, she went for his eyes instead—they'd go out together. "Beasley, if you kill her, she won't dance!" another voice boomed beside them. It was one of Beasley's strong guards who had been posted against the stage earlier to keep the horny hounds at bay.

The fat man let go of her throat. Mary Jane jumped up, gasping for air. She rubbed a hand across her neck. The large room hushed.

"Jake, I could kill you for thinking you have the right to even speak to me without being asked to," Beasley replied as he wrenched his tie away from his triple chin. "But...you're correct."

She looked Jake over, concentrating on her unlikely savior in this den of sin. The guy with tanned skin and curly hair was the most beautiful man she'd ever laid her eyes on, scar included—and not because she had no recollection of the past either. His muscles strained against a V-neck shirt that clung to well-defined muscles.

His eyes were the same complementing gold as his skin tone, offering a fleeting sense of comfort as he looked her over. Not leering, but with compassion.

"Do you want her tonight?" Beasley grinned.

Mary Jane took a stand. "Let me go. I don't belong here!"

Jake said nothing.

Beasley ignored her. "Yeah, you want her, Jake. Just looking at her makes my cock stand at attention." He nodded with a sneer, this time addressing her again. "Mary Jane, you'll be my most-prized possession at The Petting Zoo, until I grow tired of you. *Because there isn't a single soul in this world searching for you.* I'll work that little ass of yours, and then I'm going to squeeze that scrawny little neck again.

Next time I do it, the trashcan out back is where you're going."

Mary Jane's chest puffed up as her lungs filled with air. She leaned back and hawked a loogie. The spit landed on Beasley's nose. He backhanded her harsh enough to send her sprawling onto the floor again.

This time the crowd of men heckled, some of them arguing about how they'd paid good money to see her dance. *Finally,* dance. Beasley knew how to advertise his new meat with just a pet here, a paw there. However, he was ruining the very thing they craved.

Jake went to her side. He held out a hand but she turned away from him in shame. His deep voice was comforting, strong, and smooth, "Come with me, darlin'."

"*No!*" she screamed at him, sobbing so hard her vision blurred. "No! You *abducted* me. I *don't* belong here. I'll kill all of you!"

"Didn't I tell you she had a mouth?" Beasley shook his head.

"You stole me!" she screamed, although she couldn't recall anything beyond the past few minutes. As she shouted at Jake, he scooped her into his arms. She unfolded her body backward, hoping the dead weight would cause Jake to struggle and drop her but he tossed her over his shoulder with ease and carried her toward the steps leading off the stage as the crowd booed.

"Tame the little animal," Beasley called after them.

Upside down, she'd been frightened and searching her surroundings for an escape route as Jake moved toward the side of the building and started up another set of stairs. The murky air burned her eyes as they ascended to the second level of a square-shaped building.

Below, strippers began to flood the stage. Some sort of

hype man yelled, "Mary Jane will return to The Petting Zoo soon enough, but for now..."

Jake stopped before a dingy, yellow door and opened it. She felt sick as he rapidly turned around with her, closing the door behind him.

Her teeth sunk down into his shoulder as he attempted to reposition her. She braced herself for pain. The tightening in her heart loosened when Jake placed her onto a bed with meticulous care. The walls of the room were white, not a picture or personal note anywhere. She glanced around for some sort of weapon. Something pointy, sharp. The only thing available was a copper ashtray on the nightstand at the opposite side of the room.

"This is my room, MJ. But don't you worry about me touching you," Jake murmured. His demeanor had changed. The sympathetic look was gone. Instead of ogling her, his façade was emotionless making the scar on his cheek appear menacing. It was thick and aligned almost from eye to jaw. She wondered if someone had marred his glorious face to warn others away from him.

No more wondering, Mary J – she paused. The name was too awkward to complete. It couldn't have been the name she'd had her entire life. *No more wondering,* she told herself, *find a weapon.*

She scurried to the farthest side of the bed, trying to get closer to the ashtray. It really wasn't much of a weapon, but it'd come in handy if she needed to slam it across Jake's head. She didn't trust anything he said, or his kind gestures. Putting a single ounce of trust in another person was far from her mind—she couldn't even trust herself—she didn't know herself enough yet.

"I will not let you touch me. I said I'd die fighting before I let you place a single finger on me."

"I know," Jake replied.

She glanced around. The only weapon available was the ashtray. "I swear, if you come near me, I'll kill you." *I'll die trying.*

"Well, MJ, I highly doubt that. I done murdered a good number of people in my life." His head cocked as if he was in thought. "Probably killed more people than the years of your life. You don't know that either, do you? How old you are?"

She sat in silence. There was no need to answer. Jake's question had to be rhetorical. She didn't know anything. He did, though. She just had to read between the lines.

"But if *you* don't touch *me* or bite me, I promise to return the favor." He turned away from her and went to the dresser, his broad shoulders on display. After he rummaged around, Jake pulled out a flannel shirt and tossed it in her direction.

"What do you want from me?" She looked at the blue-green shirt then back at him.

"Nothin'." Jake shrugged, keeping the distance. "I reckon you're not as free and as wild as they'd like you to be—yet. So get dressed, MJ."

While picking up the shirt, Mary Jane sighed. It felt like home to her. Home? It had the fragrance of fresh linen and woodsy cologne, like him. Her eyes burned.

She waited, but now blurred memories accompanied the sensations.

Tuning out the nostalgic feeling, she continued to take in the simple room. No pictures, no TV, nothing to indicate where she was or why or how. When had she arrived? They'd abducted her from somewhere. She didn't have a shred of memory pointing to family or friends or even an attempt to call the police when she was taken.

She had a life somewhere. An accomplished life. It had

to be true, she felt it in her bones. She wasn't a cracked-out stripper.

Somewhere, someone had to be looking for her.

Somewhere, someone loved her enough to search without ceasing. She knew this to be true, even without the memories of her past.

"MJ, stop trying to figure things out for now, and just put on the shirt." Jake started to take off his snakeskin boots. "This is my bed. As long as you stay on your side, I'll stay on mine. If you bite me again, I'll have to bite you. A blow for a blow." Then he smiled. "A kiss for a kiss."

"Don't try me," she growled, shoving one arm after the other into the shirt. She'd argue and tell him that Mary Jane wasn't her name, but what was the use? "Look, can you just tell me what you know about me?"

"All right. You don't belong here. I saved you from Beasley tonight. And I ain't one for a skittish broad. That shit makes me nervous." He glanced down at himself as he began to unbuckle his belt. "Get comfortable, or I'm gonna have to kick your ass out. I need rest to keep my paychecks comin'."

She tried to relax but couldn't. He tugged out of his jeans. Boxer briefs accentuated a heavy package and thick thigh muscles.

He rubbed at the bristles along his chiseled jaw. He was a man that didn't talk much.

She leaned back at the edge of the bed, trying to appear comfortable. She gave Jake her full attention, believing he had something to tell her.

Reluctantly, Jake spoke, "I saved you from Beasley, Mary Jane. This ain't the first time."

Hadn't he already said as much? She licked her lips in apprehension. "Have I...has Beasley slept with—?"

"He ain't the type to bone his premium product. And I won't allow you to follow the course of how shit happens here."

She thought of asking about the other girls but, with Jake speaking, she became mute and concentrated on how to find her own way out of this horror story.

Jake forked his fingers through his hair. "I just keep thinking; I've saved you so many damn times from him deciding that you weren't worth that mouth of yours. I bet you don't even recall. Different night, same story." Jake reached over, opened the top drawer of the nightstand, and grabbed a glossy photo.

Lips tensed, she tried to remember her past with Jake. No. She didn't recall him or Beasley, but instincts, more than the words coming out of Jake's mouth, told her that they'd played this game before.

Still confused about the history they had and not wanting to irritate Jake with too many questions, she instead looked at the high-resolution flyer. There was a picture of three women: two busty blondes with a golden beauty in the center. The trio wore lingerie, but the focal point was dead center, a captivating woman.

"That's you, MJ," he indicated, pointing to the beauty. Before she could ask for a mirror to confirm, he continued, "It's all about losing status and position here. It's only a matter of time before another girl with big baby-blue eyes will capture Beasley's attention again, then one of these girls on the sidelines will be removed, and you'll get their spot. There's only one place to go when you're at the top."

He was saying something about the not-so-lucky girl being repositioned elsewhere. She didn't catch the sinister note in his voice because she was stuck on the fact that she was the chick dead center. She lifted her hand. She had the same skin tone, but was this woman really her?

Why can't I recall my own face? I'm not a vain woman, but it doesn't take much education to be aware of something so simple! And why would they be advertising abducted women for the world to see?

He finished his statement by rubbing a hand at the back of his neck. "I'm so fucking tired of saving you from him."

"Then let him kill me, or you kill me," she blurted, carelessly. "If you were just implying that everything gets worse, I'd rather get it over with. Beasley becomes tired of his human chattel and does away with them? Let's get to the good part."

"That mouth of yours," Jake mumbled to himself. He reached over, his knuckles caressing her jaw. "I've only known you a few weeks. During this time, you've reminded me of...of this good time I had in my life—when I was a man and not yet a monster. But you can't go popping off at the mouth. Pick your battles and make it easy for me to help you. I'd save you a thousand times more, so I wasn't saying I didn't want to save you."

"Okay," she murmured, still confused. "I've been here for weeks?"

"Yup. And I wanna save you. Once. And. For. All. I haven't felt anything in years, but I fucking hurt every time I see you here, in this shitty-ass Petting Zoo."

Her mouth tensed. Her stomach dropped. This was not a life she'd chosen. Even if she couldn't remember who she was before, she'd never want this life.

She hoped that her past wasn't plagued with something that would warrant this karma.

This bad karma.

But then a tiny voice within her brain begged her to ask Jake how he could save her . . .

Jake spoke the very words she grew anxious over, saying, "I would save you. I'd come up with a plan, but you'll just keep forgetting." His teeth gritted in frustration. "We've gotta get you to stop forgetting," he mumbled, more to himself than her.

"Come with me," she murmured, deciding that bargaining with the devil was just as good as living with a slew of demons. "Save us both."

Jake shook his head. "Nah, darlin', ain't no saving me. This is hell. I love hell."

1
_____

DYLAN WULF HAD A LINEBACKER'S BODY SQUEEZED INTO THE space of a full-sized bed. His broad shoulders engulfed much of the space, and his muscular, long limbs draped over the edge. To make matters worse, he'd fallen asleep wearing his steel-toe boots. The Samoan gave a hard grunt as he lurched himself into a seated position. He rubbed at the stubble on his jaw. The old him would've had a rigid plan for the day. Saving the world started better with a clean-cut and shaven face. All of that didn't matter now.

Not here.

Dylan Wulf had already condemned himself straight to hell. He hated it, but he deserved it.

"Yeah, you made up for being a punk. Climbed the ladder of the LAPD, lived a respected life, then you shot it all down. Bang. Bang," he mumbled the reminder, while rubbing the tension at the back of his neck. "Now, here goes another day in hell."

Wulf arose from bed. In half of a stride, he was at the dresser, picking up his badge for the Santo Cruces Police Department. He'd traded in a position as head of the Gang

Unit in Los Angeles for a small-town police department in Arizona. He tossed it back onto the dresser and decided to at least take a shower before heading out. Just as he started to turn around, his cell phone vibrated on the countertop.

There could only be one of three people calling him. His adoptive mother, adoptive sister, or...

He glanced at the screen. It was his old partner from the LAPD.

"You on your way home?" Quincy spoke as soon as he answered.

"You are aware that I have a nine-to-five, right?"

"Good ol' Dylan Wulf, by the book. How many DV situations can one tiny ass town have?"

He tried to add a little *give a damn* to his tone while asking, "Hey, Quincy, how's it going?"

"*Dylan*, what are you doing with yourself? You saved lives. You took badass little kids out of gangs before they could jump in graves. You cleaned streets. Now, you're arguing with saggy-tit Dixie about pressing charges after toothless Bubba knocks the stank from her mouth."

"Ha," Wulf replied sarcastically. He glanced around. The sun hadn't risen yet but even the dim light couldn't shield how awful a home he'd made for himself here. Really, he could've just called in to work and hit the road. There was no action in Santo Cruces City. No lives to save, no people to help. Just domestic violence situations like Quincy joked about—and the dreaded paperwork that accompanied them. "Not funny."

"Oh, so I'm not funny enough? I could do funny if I weren't shaking in fear. Shelly's just gotten off work, those nurse hours, and now she's upstairs in our bedroom packing and repacking things for our trip."

"I talked to Shelly yesterday and told her I would be in

there bright and earlier tomorrow morning to watch my nephews and baby niece." Wulf almost cracked a smile at the thought of kids and having a carefree life for a moment. "See what happens when you marry your partner's adoptive sister?"

"Shit, who you telling? Wait, Dylan, did you just call me your partner? So, you're done sulking? Ready to come back home for good?"

Wulf disregarded his question. "I've got a case of energy drinks. I'll be there by morning, just like I promised, ready to entertain."

"For good?"

"For a week. By the way, who goes on a Disney cruise without their kids?" Wulf asked, although he knew the answer very well. Shelly was a Minnie Mouse junkie, and her argument was that their children hadn't acquired a taste for Disney yet. But he knew very well, once the kids showed interest, they'd all be going on Disney cruises. His little sister would probably force him to go too.

THE SUN WAS A BLISTERING ORB OF LAVA IN A CLOUDLESS SKY. All around her blew tumbleweed after tumbleweed. She glanced at the man near the sliding glass door of the gas station.

Have I lost my mind? He can't be talking to me?

It would be just her luck if the guy with sun-kissed skin and dark curly hair was addressing her. But, he was just *too* handsome to be crazy. Again, she turned around to see a lonely highway. Then her eyes stopped, glued onto the luxury trailer parked in the last gas port.

She gawked at the side of it. A sleek, caramel-coated woman with dark brown hair dominated the scene in a hot-pink matching bra and panty set. The smoky paint of the woman's captivating, glittery eyes complemented the airbrushed words, "The Petting Zoo."

"MJ, c'mon." The man stepped off the curb and took her arm. "It's too damn hot out here, and it ain't even nine in the morning."

As if the heat didn't already singe her skin enough, warmth crept up her cheeks. She quickly turned away from the trailer and looked forward. The hot guy placed a hand on her shoulder. His arms bulged, and the jeans that ripped across his athletic legs left nothing to the imagination.

"Excuse me, uh—"

"I'm Jake; you're Mary Jane," he replied. The left side of his lips turned upward. "C'mon, MJ, now is not the time. I need you to remember. You had to take that damn medication which is fucking with your mind even more. I know it set our plan back, but, baby, you've gotta remember something."

I'm Mary Jane? I know you?

"Let's get you a drink of water and aspirin, hopefully, it counteracts the shit Beasley gives you. So come with me, darling. Don't look back."

He was easy on the eyes, except for the scar traveling down his chiseled cheekbone toward a strong chin. They walked through the door of the gas station convenience store and Jake's hand grabbed hers. In her mind, she could hear him saying, *"I haven't felt anything in years, but I fucking hurt every time I see you here, in this shitty-ass Petting Zoo. I wanna save you. Once. And. For. All."*

Jake's warm and callused hand engulfed hers. His large fingers wove through her tinier ones and she relaxed. They walked down the aisle lined with junk food on each side and stopped at a refrigerated display of drinks. When Jake opened the glass door, Mary Jane saw her reflection. She had the same plush lips as the sexy woman dominating the center billboard on the trailer. And the same sultry eyes—sans the makeup. A faint handprint at her neck made her gasp.

"The Petting Zoo." She mumbled the words scribbled on the side of the trailer outside, aware that hell had a physical location.

"Forget about that place, MJ." Jake tossed a few one-liter bottles of water into her hands.

She jumped and fumbled with the last one.

With quick hands, he helped her cradle them in her arms. "Didn't mean to scare you."

"Jake, am I drunk?"

"No, sweetheart. You don't drink, smoke, nothing. You're too good for that shit." He winked at her.

Mary Jane rubbed her head. "There's something wrong with me."

He bit his lip and nodded. "We can't talk here."

She followed him to the row with the medication and first-aid kits, watching as he grabbed generic aspirin. Then they made their way towards the cash register. He tossed the bottle on the counter and tapped his hand rather impatiently.

"Anything else?" the clerk stuttered, keeping his eyes averted to the countertop, while scanning the barcodes of her items.

"Gimme a pack of cigarettes and a fifth of Jack." Jake pulled a wallet out of his back pocket.

The clerk scanned the extra items and slid everything over with a plastic bag as if he didn't want their business but was too afraid to say so. After a moment of awkward silence, the clerk asked, "Anything else, Jake?"

"Do you want anything else, MJ?"

She shook her head, no. What else could she want? Why did it seem like Jake was stalling? It frustrated her to no end that she didn't know what to want. There were words at the tip of her tongue, questions to debate and ask, but Jake had just said they couldn't chat here. She was now beginning to feel uncomfortable with herself.

My mind is a crutch.

"Mary-*fuckin'*-Jane, we don't see you 'round town much!"

They all turned toward the door as two men walked inside wearing tattered jeans and wife beaters. The one who'd called her name had a cigarette carelessly held between thin, blistered lips. He pulled out his wallet. "MJ, how about a private dance?"

Mary Jane's eyes widened. She shook her head so hard her ponytail hit her neck with a hard sting. She didn't want to go anywhere with the two men. Instinctively, she inched closer toward Jake, but the next step would have to be in his arms.

"Y'all know Beasley doesn't let MJ do any private dances without me or Lyle," Jake interjected. "Gus is in the trailer. He'll run snitching to Beasley. And y'all know the new girls don't dance outside of The Petting Zoo."

"I won't ever dance." Mary Jane heard herself speaking.

"We heard about how Beasley did you last night," the man said, "let's make you feel better."

She gasped as the man tossed a few dollars at her feet.

"Jake, there's money in it for you too." He pulled a few more twenties out of his pocket. "Gus won't know. Beasley won't know. It seems to me that Lyle ain't around either."

"Well, all right then. Let's take this party to the back," Jake replied. He glared at the clerk. "Do you mind?"

The clerk, looking more afraid than Mary Jane, shook his head then turned around to rearrange a liquor case.

"Jake, please don't," Mary Jane whispered. She gripped the plastic bag, taking quick uneven breaths.

"Don't worry, MJ," Jake whispered low so the men couldn't hear. The warmth of his minty, liquored mouth began to settle her nerves. "I'd never hurt you. Beasley doesn't let me leave a place with you unless another one of the men are around. Gus is on the bus. Remember the plan. These idiots are your diversion."

"I don't remember," she quickly murmured.

As they started toward the back, a heaviness clutched around her heart with each step. They walked down an aisle of canned goods as he whispered something about a car and luggage in the trunk.

Jake opened a door with a sign reading, "Staff Only." She gulped as he flicked the lights on. The tiny storage room held cardboard boxes. A moldy mop hanging on the wall dripped into a yellow bucket. Stepping inside, Mary Jane sneezed and looked at the men as they shut the door. Their leering glances crawled over her skin.

"Y'all are in for a treat." Jake grinned. He winked at her when she gulped.

"Don't I know it." The other guy clapped his hands to his knees. "That little taste we got at The Petting Zoo ain't do nothing but piss me off—"

Before Mary Jane could blink, she saw perfect holes between the eyes of each man. The sound of gunfire made her ears ring. She turned wide-eyed toward Jake as he lowered a nine-millimeter to his side. The bag with the aspirin and water bottles fell from her hands onto the floor.

"Now, you have to go, MJ. Fuck these dead rednecks."

Jake pushed her toward the back door. She tripped over an empty crate. He hoisted Mary Jane under her arms, helping her reclaim an even stance.

"Take these keys. There's an '86 Corolla right outside with a stack of cash under the dash. Get into it and get the hell out of town. Don't look back. Not even for me, sweetheart. Go. *Now!*"

She took the keys thrust into her hand. At the sound of

gunfire coming from the front of the store, she ran out the back door.

As the door was closing, she heard Jake say, "MJ shot them and escaped."

Mary Jane ducked, gunshots popping off behind her. Keeping a hurried pace, she sprinted toward a gray, box-shaped four-door. It wasn't locked. She slid onto a matted seat. Hands shaking, it took a few attempts, but she finally got the key in the ignition.

A bullet blazed through the back window. The glass shattered, spraying the passenger headrest. Specks of fluff clouded her vision after a few slugs went out the other side and into the dash. Glancing in the rearview window, she saw Jake with three other men. He was arguing with one, while the rest of them had guns pointed in her direction.

With the engine sputtering and steering wheel shaking, Mary Jane ramped her foot onto the gas. The car bounced as it went over the sidewalk and off the curb. She jerked the wheel and turned down a one-lane highway. Joshua trees and cacti zipped by. The left tires hit a pothole. Two hands on the steering wheel, she worked hard to make sure it didn't veer off the road. From the corner of her eye, she saw a piece of paper in the passenger seat. She grabbed it.

"MJ, DO NOT go to the police station! Head NORTH. There'll be more directions in the trunk, clothes, food—Jake"

Forcing out a deep breath, Mary Jane silently thanked Jake for saving her life.

A glance through the rearview showed a red Ford-250 hot on her tail. With the long stretch of one-lane highway ahead, it was only a matter of time before they caught up to her. Her foot slammed down harder. The engine groaned in response but the car picked up speed.

Her eyes connected to a sign ahead that indicated "North." Mary Jane gave a psychotic chuckle. Her luck had changed—it was minuscule at best, but something. She was headed in the direction Jake had advised and away from the cops...

***

Two girls walked down a residential street, out of place in the neighborhood with white picket fences and manicured lawns. With thick hair in ponytails, their clothes were so worn that the cotton felt like sandpaper against their skin.

"The police are in front of uncle's, again," the younger one with two buck teeth said as they neared a three-level Victorian-style home. Her pace faltered. "I don't want to go home."

The older sister took her hand. "Don't worry. The police will help..."

***

". . . *The police will help*." Pulled out of the image, Mary Jane's body jolted forward. Before she could dissect that vivid memory, Jake's sidekick rammed the back of the Corolla.

Jarring her brain, the memory solidified the fact that she just had a premonition contradicting everything a man she hardly knew had told her. Jake had risked his life to free her. Mary Jane's hands tightened around the steering wheel, knuckles tensing at the thought of having faith in herself and trusting a split-second memory. This feeling of not knowing a single thing about herself was like being buried with red-hot ants. *C'mon, Mary Jane, you have to analyze everything. Don't trust anyone.*

Her hands shook as she raked one through her hair, realizing that even trusting herself wasn't wise. She'd need to second guess everything until her memories returned.

Hopefully, they'd return.

The truck was already catching up. Jake sat in the passenger seat, shaking his head in what appeared to be disappointment. The guy in the driver's seat had a crazed look on his red-blistered face.

Her heart stopped. Were they playing a game of chicken? *Well, you've messed with the wrong girl.* Mary Jane pressed harder on the gas, ready for a head-on collision. She was getting to the police station in this life or . . .

Her chest slammed against the belt again as the truck rammed the back of the car. In an instant, she removed her foot from the gas and gave the brake a hard push. Mary Jane yanked the wheel. "C'mon," she growled, praying the car would stay on the road as she made a U-turn.

As the truck sailed past her, still going North, Mary Jane's eyes connected with Jake's. Regret flooded over his gaze. She winced, heading South.

The steering wheel shook as the Corolla's engine caught back up to a steady ninety miles per hour. Mary Jane passed the gas station again, when the truck finally made a U-turn a few yards back.

Up ahead was a sign displaying the direction to the police station. A half mile ahead, a sign at the Y in the road pointed again to the police station. The car bounced over the dicey gravel as Mary Jane took the turn. A cinderblock building came into view with three police cars parked in front. Two officers stood just outside of the middle cruiser.

She pressed harder on the gas and gave another glance in the mirror. The Ford missed the turn. The officers scattered when she didn't appear to slow down. The car jumped the curb of the parking lot. In ample time, she pressed her foot on the brake but there was no traction because the Corolla continued at top speed.

3

MARY JANE'S JAW CLENCHED IN THE TEETH-CHATTERING COLD. Her brain boomed against her skull. She peeled her face away from the steel desk and sat up. *Fuck.* She glanced down at the chains around her wrists.

"Good afternoon, Mary Jane."

"Mary Jane?" Again, she'd forgotten her name and everything else about herself due to the medication Jake was forced to give her this morning. She looked around, eyes stopping on her reflection in the one-sided mirror to see her tousled hair.

"I read you your Miranda rights already. Maybe you were coming down from a high when you *hit* my cruiser. So here it goes again."

She blinked at the man. He was muscular and tall. His hair was chocolate brown, wavy, and shortly cropped. His skin was a deep golden brown which was a sign of some sort of islander heritage that coupled well with his beefy frame. His police uniform coasted over hard planes of muscle at his chest and thick-as-hell biceps. While she blinked, she imagined him on a sandy beach, surrounded by turquoise water, completing a hypnotic ritual dance which included herself ending up in bed with him for an all-weekend sexcapade.

Dwayne Johnson. The thought popped into her head. Who the fuck was Dwayne Johnson, and why did this cop remind her of him? She shoved aside thoughts of Dwayne Johnson, the cop, and screwing either one of them in Hawaii. Firstly, she didn't even know her own name, let alone the cop or who Dwayne Johnson was. Second, the officer glared straight through her as he continued to spout words of monotony. And third, *why am I here?*

"Could you shut up, please?"

The officer rolled his eyes and continued with, "Since I don't have the right—as of yet—to search your car, why don't you tell me more about why you were joyriding next to the police station?"

Mary Jane stretched her weak muscles, wishing her jeans weren't so tight. "Um...sir, what the hell are you talking about?"

"Wulf," he replied, leaning against the table. "Call me Officer Wulf. I've heard a lot about you, but I'm surprised they allowed you to leave The Petting Zoo. What's your full name, Mary Jane? Do you have identification?"

Her hard gaze slid away from his. *Good question. Where's my identification?* Mary Jane rubbed her hands over her jean pockets and laughed nervously. The clothing was too tight to hide anything. "No ID. I don't—"

"I can help you." His jaw tensed. "But before I can help, you must want to help yourself. Would you like to leave Beasley?"

Her eyes widened. She didn't know what he meant. "Who? What?"

Planting his hands back on the table as he stared down at her, she gawked in fear of his football player physique. "It's all fun and games with you girls, huh? No self-worth? What's his little harem of women up to?"

She clutched at her forehead, hoping the drumming would cease. "I don't like your attitude, Officer Wulf. I'll speak with someone else."

"Oh, you'd like special treatment?" Wulf sneered, "How does this sound? You tell me about the fingerprints on your neck. We can proceed from there."

Again she glanced at the mirror and gaped at the faint wounds. Flashes of memories came to her mind, of being knocked to the ground and choked.

"Oh, I get it. You don't know how that happened." Wulf pointed to her. "This is a warning. We are *not* at The Petting Zoo. I'll be back with a glass of water, then you can give me the dirt on Beasley. Big tip, you'd be wise to do so."

Mary Jane closed her eyes, needing to remember. Once she formulated the truth in her brain, the officer would have to listen to her without judgement.

Am I dreaming? This is a nightmare. No, this is real. I awoke this morning, and...nope. I don't remember a damn thing. Her hands drummed the table. *Jake!* She recalled them entering a gas station and how he'd put his life in jeopardy to save hers—he he was a beast with a gun.

***

Wulf refused to feel guilty about his callous treatment of Mary Jane. He couldn't afford to get distracted by her beauty even if it meant some asshole saw her as easy prey.

He rubbed the back of his neck and took a deep breath while standing outside of the interrogation room. The epitome of any man's dream girl was broken, and he wanted to save her. He wanted to help her, but she wasn't taking him seriously. Still, there was a determination in her eyes that he respected. She opened her mouth and in that sultry voice of hers, lied. She feigned confusion when he asked about the choking she'd endured.

He started down the hallway to the front of the station. There were six desks in two rows, one of which was occupied by a large woman named Patsy with pinkish, puffy hair. The rest of the seats were empty.

"Where is everyone?"

"Garland is at the Miller's. Patrick jumped on his old lady again. Keller and the rest of 'em were out before the poor thing hit your cruiser."

He sat down at his desk, which was directly across from hers. She was the secretary, and he was the newest on the force. Wulf swiveled around; the incessant creaking of his chair helped him concentrate. He knew nothing about the girl.

Don't think too hard, Wulf. She doesn't want help.

He immediately began to condemn himself for that thought. A few years ago, LAPD had intensive sex trafficking training, and he understood the type of mentality abused women like her had—extreme loyalty, even to the detriment of her own life. Her desire for help did not matter, she *needed it.*

This isn't no fucking Pretty Woman. He chuckled to himself. His little sister Shelly always got her way; needless to say, he was tortured by being forced to watch all of her romance movies.

Wulf stopped moving and the sound ceased. "Do you know the girl's full name? She won't tell me."

"No." Patsy shook her head.

He bit his lip for a moment. There were no other women in the office except for Patsy. She was too 'nice' and did not have the proper training to communicate with a victim of sex trafficking.

"You mind talking to her? Just a short chat to see if she has any family. Sometimes women feel more comfortable speaking to other women."

"Um..." Patsy's pale gaze flitted back and forth nervously.

"You know what, never mind. I'll get her a cup of water and start over."

The tension in her shoulders faded away as he stood up and went to the water cooler.

"Oh, Wulf. Keller replied," Patsy said as he started back toward the hallway. "He said to let the girl go. Beasley should be on his way to pick her up soon. Just give her a ticket."

"When did he—?"

"I just noticed a text from him. Keller said there's no reason to hold her. Beasley probably told her she could have a little fun. She's joyriding. You know how these young, pretty girls are. Rule the town."

He stared at Patsy. If she was this comfortable at talking, Wulf had a hunch she'd say a little more than usual. Like what really was going on.

"Officer Wulf, Beasley doesn't let his girls do drugs. She's not on anything. Just young, dumb, pretty. Give her a ticket, send her on her way. If Beasley has the funds to bail her, you know... small town, we could use the funds." She smiled, reinforcing his notion of their small town.

Patsy was right about one thing. Mary Jane didn't appear to be under the influence of any substance. There were no track marks on her arms. Her cuticles didn't look like a secret place to shoot up drugs. Besides, it only took a week as a rookie cop with the LAPD to learn the signs. Maybe they weren't doing anything illegal here, aside from having Beasley pay financially for the screw-ups of his beautiful women. Women Wulf rarely saw around town. *Something isn't right.* Wulf waited for her to continue chattering, but she just offered a smile.

"All right." Wulf shrugged. He'd feign disinterest, which wasn't hard to do since he'd started the job.

He continued down the hall, taking out his cell phone to dial Keller. He had a hunch, and even if he'd condemned himself to this place, he would put Mary Jane's life over his own and hope it did not end like last time.

Just as the call began to beep, Patsy shouted out, "Beasley pulled up. Get the girl ready and write out her ticket."

He ignored her, waiting for Keller to answer. But the call went to voicemail.

***

The door opened. Officer Wulf walked in with a glass of water and slid it across the table. Even though it chilled Mary Jane's teeth to the core, she gulped it down. When she looked up to thank him, the edges of his mouth were turned up. She breathed a tad easier. *Maybe he'll help after all.*

The smile turned into a sneer. "This is your lucky day."

"Thank you, Officer Wulf," she replied. "Thank you. Do you know who I—"

He cocked a grin. "Sure thing. Beasley's here. Don't be too happy."

"Please don't take me to Beasley!"

"Oh, a few minutes ago, you pretended not to know Beasley then you wanted to brush off the domestic violence incident. Now, you sound a little worried." He rubbed the stubble on his chin. "I offered to help in hopes that you'd want to change your ways, but all this back and forth—it gets ridiculous. If you wanted *out*, you should have *walked* into the station like a law-abiding citizen. When you've had enough mistreatment from Beasley, that's when I will be here for you."

Mary Jane stood, refusing to cry. She grew angrier by the second. Her throat burned as she stared at the headstrong officer, and then she followed him as they walked down a long corridor to another room.

A shiver of insanity rippled through her as the secretary stopped typing to offer her a look of empathy. *Beasley.* The name evoked a violent tremble in her gut.

Finally, MJ's eyes flitted to the opposite side of the front counter. A balding man in a suit, who probably hadn't seen his feet in years due to his bubble gut, smiled at her. Next to him, and a head taller, stood Jake. The fat man tracked Mary Jane as she moved toward the front of the station.

"Officer Wulf," she whispered.

Ignoring her, Wulf stopped near the waist-high wooden gate next to the counter and took his key ring off his utility belt.

"Please, Officer Wulf," she whimpered as he unleashed her cuffs, "don't make me go with them."

He said nothing. She sniffled and rubbed her wrists.

"Mary Jane, I hope these good officers have been treating you well," Beasley said.

"Cut the fucking bull, Beasley. You could've let her stay overnight, get a little rest first," Wulf retorted.

"Beasley!" Mary Jane screeched.

She bit her lip as Wulf unlatched the wooden door separating them. Her eyes went to the Glock in the holster at his side. She couldn't go back to Beasley or Jake.

Mary Jane froze for a second.

"Harder, harder," a man's voice wove into her mind, *"toss that elbow like you're not only breaking a nose, but dislocating a fucking jaw. Toss it harder!"*

A split-second flashback provided her with the fundamentals of how to react. She grabbed Wulf's gun from its holster. It was positioned to the side of his temple in the second that she realized how natural she felt toting a gun.

"Oh my Lord," yelped Patsy.

"What are you doing, Mary Jane?" Wulf's voice was tempered.

She unclasped the safety. His demeanor stayed the same. Mary Jane's mouth tensed. Resting her eyes on Patsy, Mary Jane snapped in a surprisingly calm voice, "Wulf is coming with me. If I hear a noise from any of you, I'll pull the trigger! Let's go."

The lady nodded, cheeks jiggling.

Mary Jane pressed the gun harder against the side of Wulf's skull when he didn't walk. Guilt gnawed at her gut, but she held steady.

"It will be a cold day in hell before I'm afraid of you," Wulf retorted.

"I will pull the trigger." She glared at him. "I *swear*. Beasley, *Jake*, lie down!"

"MJ, let me help you." Beasley's Southern drawl was soft, inviting.

She gave him just enough of a glare.

He grunted, breaths shallow, and kneeled to the vinyl floor.

Again, she nudged Wulf's temple. He sighed before moving with her at his heels.

"You don't want to do this," exclaimed Patsy from behind her.

Mary Jane growled, "I thought I said not a peep. Try me. Go ahead and fucking *try me!*"

"C'mon," Wulf said in a calm whisper. "Give me the gun, Mary Jane. We'll retract the last couple of minutes. You don't want to do this. I'm a police officer."

"I am *not* going with Beasley, or *you*." She glared at Jake. An imaginary fist clutched at her throat, reminding her not to trust anyone.

Jake lay on the floor, nonchalant as ever. Only the sparkle of his eyes hinted at something different. Amusement? Pride?

"Open it, Wulf," she ordered. As they went through, she noticed the only cruiser had a crazy concave bumper. The engine had to be sitting in the back seat. "Um, take me to your personal car."

"Flaws in your strategy?" Wulf gave an unamused grin.

"Do you feel the gun at your head?" She nudged harder.

"Pull the trigger." Voice calm, Wulf took even steps toward the side of the building where the police officers' off-duty vehicles were parked.

She remained silent. To her horror, he led her to a Datsun truck that had seen almost as many years as the Corolla. She knew there was only a matter of time before the police *and* Beasley were on her tail. She wouldn't be able to escape in the rattrap he unlocked.

"Are you serious? *This* is your car?"

"Oh, the junkie has high expectations."

"Let's keep the name calling to a minimum or die." She slid inside and over, with the gun never leaving her target.

"I call 'em as I see 'em." He got inside and turned the key in the ignition.

She chortled. "Maybe you don't *see* correctly, because I'm not who you think I am!"

"Then who are you?" He turned toward Mary Jane, gaze locking onto hers.

And Mary Jane knew that his name calling was a trick. He wanted to get a rise out of her.

"Drive!" she ordered.

4

For almost an hour, Mary Jane tracked Wulf and the dusty road, all the while wondering, *who am I?* The balmy air from the evening sun battered her face.

"Wulf, it's too damn silent in here," she grumbled. "How do you get around without a radio? I need some mellow music to calm my nerves."

No response. After the longest silence, she would've assumed he'd nodded off had she been the one driving.

She continued, "You have this demeanor about you."

He finally glanced over, and damn, his arched eyebrow was the most beautiful thing she'd ever seen. Just the sarcastic look on his face brought life to her body. Mary Jane smirked. "Granted, broody is a good look on you, but I'm still learning about you. So I need more than a Neanderthal shrug. Where are you from?"

He finally spoke, baritone voice filled with power, even though it hardly rose above a whisper. "How about you tell me more about you?"

She cocked her head sideways and ignored his request. "Humph. Broody and hard of hearing. Except when it comes to rules and regulations. You chewed me out at Shit City Police Station because I hit your cruiser. I wonder if you would've been standing on that soapbox, regurgitating the Miranda, had I not hit your car."

He scratched at the scruff on his angular jaw. "Thought I was correcting a woman who had almost killed herself for driving crazy. Forgive me for that."

"Ha!"

The conversation died again. Mary Jane began to count Joshua trees and tumbleweeds.

"There's a roadblock ahead," Wulf warned.

He had a deep voice, but either he had spoken softly or she was still semi-lost in her own thoughts. Straightening up, she told herself to be in the moment, every single second of it. She recalled how her mulling had ended last time— with Lyle ramming the Corolla. Since she wouldn't dream of taking the gun away from targeting his midsection, Mary Jane silently looked ahead. The same bright red F-250, and a black one, and a blue one were parked zigzag next to a sign headed out of town which she presumed read, "Bye-bye now. You've made it out of this hellhole."

"Um, take this turn," she perked up. The upcoming T in the road was the last one before the three big trucks. When Wulf didn't slow down to prepare for it, she exclaimed, "Take it or we both die!"

He'd be shot. She wouldn't make it out of a crash in an old truck. With no time left, he jerked the wheel. It skidded, drudging sand. He yanked the wheel back to the right side of the road, with effortless precision.

"Turn there," she ordered, noticing a leaning street post.

"That road leads to *nowhere*."

"Turn, Wulf, or die," she replied simply.

"Oh, I see. 'Or die' is how you end every sentence while

holding that gun," he argued, tugging at the wheel to right the tires on the uneven pavement.

They hit a pothole. *Bang!* The gun went off. Her eyes closed in shock. The car whipped toward the sandy side before lurching to a stop.

"You could've shot me!"

She opened her eyes. A hole pierced the seat two inches away from where his abdomen had been before they hit the pothole.

Oh, shit, what have I done?

"I – I wasn't gonna...give you the opportunity to *screw* me over. That was a warning. I'm giving you a last chance. Go before I have to wipe your brain matter from these super-skinny jeans!"

Tense-jawed, he pulled back into the lane. "As I said, this street leads to a blocked-off bridge. A *corroded,* blocked-off bridge."

"Mmhmm." She almost smiled, not trusting a single word.

Twenty minutes later, the setting sun cast a glow over the alleged "blocked-off bridge." She shook her head as he drove over the perfectly safe pavement, overlooking a dry lake. "Wulf, you have some balls, don't you? Deceiving a desperate woman holding a gun. I could shoot you and toss you over onto the sandy riverbed below."

His jaw tensed as she chuckled hard. After a few moments, he asked, "Are you done?"

"Yes." She wiped the tears from her eyes, allowing her laugh to die with a sigh. "I haven't laughed like that in...a while. We've been stuck in this truck for almost two hours. Let's play nice. Tell me more about yourself, Officer Wulf. What's your first name? What exactly are you? Polynesian, Hawaiian?"

"Samoan. Dylan. Tell me about you."

"Tsk tsk. We're learning about you, Dylan Wulf, who so happens to be Samoan. I detected a hint of a fresh island accent, but a little edgy—street edginess. Where are you from?"

He grumbled a minute later when the tip of the gun nudged his rib cage. "Los Angeles."

"L.A." Her eyes narrowed slightly as the place became familiar in her mind. Oh, yes. She'd seen the city in many movies—a big city with gangs, smog, traffic. "What did you do?"

"What do you mean?"

"Why are you . . ."

"In Santo Cruces City?"

Santo Cruces City, Arizona! She wracked her brain but couldn't imagine growing up here or seeing it in a movie. The place was virtually foreign to her. Mary Jane continued to operate under the guise that no one, not even herself, could be trusted. She'd allow Wulf to feed her small bits of information, then weed through those. "Yes, why leave L.A. for Santo Cruces City? I'm not even certain this place *qualifies* as a *city*."

"Change of scenery," he mumbled.

Hmmm, can I get more out of him?

"I'm sure you know more about me than I know about you. What did my police file read when you pulled me up in the system?"

His sexy groan warmed her insides, but she gave a triumphant grin, and again gave him the gun-to-rib push he'd need to proceed.

"If you must know," he began in an irritated voice. "Keller processed your file before leaving the office."

She grumbled, fixating on dissecting his information. "C'mon, Wulf. What do you know about—"

Before Mary Jane could blink, Wulf yanked the wheel in a harsh right. They swerved into a ditch. The gun flew out of her fingers. Mary Jane hit the side of her head against the passenger doorframe. Wulf's seat belt pulled so tight against him, it snatched his heavy frame against the seat.

The gun ping-ponged, only to nestle on the floor in between them. In her peripheral vision, she saw Wulf breaking the weak, spiraled material of the old-matted seat belt with a quick snap and bulging biceps.

He was going for the gun.

With no time for an axe-splitting headache, she pushed herself forward but was instantly tossed back.

She unlatched her seat belt.

He reached down to the floor between them and gripped the gun.

Mouth wide, she bit down on his forearm.

He yanked at her hair, but her canines held on.

His skin broke; she tasted copper.

His shout pierced her ears, but he wouldn't let go of the hair on her crown.

Extracting her teeth, she snatched up the gun.

In a split second, she had the passenger door opened and jumped out. Mary Jane scurried and trudged up the sandy ditch. Collecting her breath, she looked down as smoke fizzled from the hood that was smashed in like an accordion. Wulf made his way out of the driver's side, already calculating the best way up the slope.

"Stay back!" She waved the gun and gritted her teeth through the pain of a headache. She shot in his general direction then ran into an onion field behind her. Heart pounding, lungs raw, she ran toward a dilapidated barn about a quarter of a mile ahead.

Her boots sunk into the rich soil with each step and she risked a glance back. He'd just climbed up the slope but he wasn't chasing her down, not like Lyle and Jake had, which made her feel like drowning in worry. Wulf was going to return her to Beasley at the police station. Now, he was treating her like a lion to a mouse, leisurely gaining on her. Or maybe he was waiting for orders from his boss. Beasley had to be his boss. Mouth dry, she stretched her legs to the limit and continued to run.

The evening took the last bit of scorching heat. Gnats gnawed at her sweaty skin.

Mary Jane ran over ashes and a charred foundation that she assumed had been where a house once stood. At the barn, she pulled open one of the wooden doors and winced as splinters nicked her fingers. It was dark. The dust made her sneeze. The person who once owned the house must've abandoned the barn. Eyes narrowing, she barely discerned scattered hay. She closed the door.

Picking up a half-bent rake, Mary Jane wedged it between the two handles. As the sweat began to dry on her body, she speedily surveyed the barn. While her eyes adjusted to the dark, she gazed at the loft-style area above and started for the ladder. This would be her best vantage point. If her paranoia were true and Wulf worked for Beasley, then this was the end.

Today, I'm not dying without taking a motherfucker with me.
***

Officer Wulf wriggled his tensed jaw. Mary Jane was the bane of his existence. She was by far the most attractive offender he had encountered, but he wasn't sure how criminal the girl really was.

Shit. Stop it, Dylan. That bitch is off the market.

Blood seeped through the bandana around his forearm as another reminder. The lovely lunatic had chomped at his arm like it was her last meal. Boots kicking in the dust, he cursed her very existence.

"Damn Keller. All this waiting is ridiculous," he mumbled to himself.

He could go inside and apprehend her in less than a second. Mary Jane needed to be locked up so she could do no harm to anyone or herself.

He stood outside the barn and peered at the sliver of moon. Pulling out his walkie-talkie, he connected with Patsy for the second time. Their first conversation had been more about him calming her down and assuring her that he was alive. Now, he needed to make sure the ditz did her job.

"What's the ETA on Keller?"

"He and the guys are a few minutes out."

"You did well, Patsy." He hoped the compliment would calm the remainder of her jitters. Even if nothing ever happened in Santo Cruces City, she wasn't cut out for the job, but she was Chief Keller's second cousin. "Tell me more about Mary Jane. Does she have a record?"

"Just a sec, Wulf."

Earlier, when Keller told him to let Mary Jane go, he'd been so angry about Beasley's arrival that he hadn't asked any pertinent questions. Keller had been in a rush, but Wulf knew he should've forced his boss's response.

Now, he attempted to jog Patsy's memory of protocol. "Since I've been gone, has Garland returned to give you the processing file?"

Garland had been the other officer at the station, along with Patsy and himself, when Mary Jane had crashed into his cruiser. Garland had left for another incident, but surely should have returned by now. Probably with crazy, old Patrick.

"No, Garland told me to do it. I'm looking into it as we speak. Just one more sec."

Shit. Okay, so it's been a busy day, but I need a criminal breakdown on Mary Jane. How the heck did she grab my gun?

His thoughts slammed through his brain as a storm of F-250 engines roared. Beasley's men were riding over the onion field.

"Patsy, tell Keller I need him ASAP. Beasley's minions are coming."

Wulf paused. Rowdy men standing in the truck beds shot off rounds from their guns. His stomach coiled at the thought of the law-bending Beasley. Wulf darted to the side of the barn.

Engines off, doors slammed, and men jumped down.

Beasley hopped out of the blue truck. The shooting instantly ceased. In his obese, breathy voice, he gave an order. "Boys, don't touch *my* MJ! But by all means have some fun with the officer!"

Wulf grimaced. He leaned back against the wooden wall as he thought about a plan of action while Beasley's men cackled. A smaller, more compact engine sounded nearby. Keller? Wulf peeped around the side of the farmhouse as Keller and three other Santo Cruces City officers pulled up. All of Beasley's men were looking toward the two police cruisers, heading their way.

Wulf watched as Beasley shook hands with Chief of Police Kirk Keller, a lanky man. Standing together, they resembled the number ten. Keller had a cul-de-sac for a hairline and pipe arms.

"Beasley, how can I help?" Keller asked as he and the other officers huddled together.

"I don't know how you can *help*, Kirk," Beasley mocked. "That fucking newbie cop is in there with *my* Mary Jane. I'm not sure how much she *told* him! Now, he has to be dealt with."

"Let me go in and talk to 'em." Kirk held up his hands in a manner to keep the fat one from blowing a heart gasket. "I didn't witness the altercation, remember? I had to step out and call *you* when I learned of Mary Jane's arrival. I couldn't get a hold of *you*, so we left the station half-staffed to come lookin' for you!"

"Keller, watch yourself," Beasley began in a warning tone, lighting a cigar. He puffed and blew in Keller's face.

Keller coughed and turned his head toward the dusty ground. "Wulf is a good cop. He's too smart to let himself be taken so easily. There's no funny business going on with him and the gal. Trust me. From the accolades he received by the LAPD—he won't believe anything your little bitch has said."

Wulf turned to the wall and finally noticed a side door. He pulled a utility knife out of his pocket and, as quietly as possible, hacked open the deadbolt on the door. Slowly, he entered the room, checking all the corners. He was in the middle stall. He could hear Keller attempting to enter through the front; the little minx had hoisted a useless rake through the door handle without even a consideration for other points-of-entry.

5

MARY JANE'S BLOOD PRESSURE SKYROCKETED AT THE SOUND of gunshots and roaring engines. Every sound the men made in their attempts to get the door open increased her anxiety a hundredfold.

A callused hand covered her mouth. Before she could scream, she was pulled back against a muscular body. She tried to open her mouth to bite down, but her lips were pulled tight.

"Do not scream, MJ."

"You!" It came out muffled, but that's what Mary Jane wanted to say as Jake removed his hand from her mouth. He took the gun from her shaking hand.

"Why didn't you read the note in the car?" he whispered in pure irritation. "You could be in San Bernardino by now if you had driven a lil' *faster*."

She froze, watching her gun—technically Wulf's gun—being placed in his waistband. Biting her lip, she whispered one of the million-dollar questions that had been swarming in her head all day long for the man she did not trust. "Who are you?"

"There's no time for that, MJ. I'm a nobody, trying to save your hardheaded ass." When she opened her mouth, he placed a finger over his lips. "Shhh. Come this way."

He cocked his head toward the window behind her. She hadn't noticed it because the wooden shutters had been drawn and she had mistaken it for a back wall in the darkness. That's how Jake must've gotten inside. She tiptoed over corroded planks. Then her heart dropped. They both turned as the farm door opened and a figure stepped inside. She froze, and Jake placed a finger to his lips. The shouting and commotion faded as the door closed. She searched Jake's eyes, as hers semi-adjusted to the darkness. She had to trust him.

Downstairs, a sound of what only could be compared to a sack of potatoes falling, propelled her to move. She cautiously hoisted her right leg over the windowsill. For reassurance, she looked back at Jake. His hand went to her shoulder, a silent cue to continue. A clear case of vertigo had Mary Jane's vision swimming.

Jake pointed to a small hill of leaves that *might* break her fall. "Someone is here. Move your ass."

With a shallow breath, she hoisted her other leg over and was now seated in the windowsill. Her hands gripped at the splintered wooden frame, knuckles taut in fear of falling.

"Mary Jane?" another voice whispered.

She got ready to leap—

"MJ, it's me, Wulf. Come out. Beasley's here to kill you." There was a sincerity in his voice, begging for her to believe in him. "He even had Keller try to kill me."

She wanted to retort the obvious to the beefy overzealous cop, but she sat frozen in the window frame, legs dangling. She cringed, hearing Jake head toward the ladder. It sounded as if Wulf had come up, but she couldn't move.

Jake and Wulf's voices were muffled, but hard with anger as they argued.

"Well, *right now*," Jake continued, "you both have to trust me."

"Thanks to the dumb kid," Wulf retorted, "you're the only one with a gun."

Mary Jane thought to argue, but her vision was becoming blurry as she looked two story's down. Her eyes darted back towards them. The men had been glaring at each other for what seemed like forever.

Wulf's voice came closer in the darkness. "Keller works with Beasley. It's only a matter of time before the idiots see her dangling in the windowsill because she's too afraid to jump."

Inwardly agreeing, she almost fell as she leaned back. In a split second, Jake hoisted her up.

Wulf appeared at the landing. "We're going to have to find another way out."

On safe footing, she gave him the once-over. Did he really want to help? Wulf's chiseled face held the same confusion she clung to all day. Maybe they want to kill him too. But why? Easy. Wulf is an outsider.

One by one, they all went down the ladder. As soon as she turned around, she noticed a police officer lying on the floor. He must've been the "sack of potatoes" noise she'd heard. Mary Jane breathed a little easier, aware Wulf had protected her.

Mary Jane jumped at the sound of Keller's unconscious grunting. Jake's steel-toe boot came down on his cranium so swiftly that the crack reverberated in the quiet barn.

"Dirty or not, he was a fucking cop." Wulf squared up before Jake.

"Yup," Jake sneered. "We don't have time to bitch up. This area is known for underground passageways that lead to old mining companies. Let's check the stall floors. No time for talking. Everyone works for Beasley."

Jake's demeanor never changed as he turned toward the stalls but Wulf seemed momentarily conflicted before he started for another stall.

She tried not to let curiosity take hold as she started into a third dingy, old stall. A chill trickled down her spine at how easily Jake could hurt someone without a pause in emotion. But then she recalled the nanosecond of an image she saw and how she was trained enough to take Wulf's gun. Was she more like Jake than she was aware of?

A minute later, with them quietly yet frantically pacing around, they heard a squeak from a wooden board in one of the stalls. Wulf pushed hay around with his boot and found a latch.

Since the commotion hadn't stopped outside, Jake took the butt of his shotgun and jabbed the latch until it broke. Sand and hay gusted through the air when Wulf opened it.

Mary Jane stared down into the pitch-black space. Caught off guard, Jake's lips seized hers in a hard kiss. There was a hint of passion as he tasted her mouth.

"Good luck, Mary Jane."

Mary Jane was speechless. For once, she didn't contemplate conspiracies and Jake in the same thought. She asked wistfully, "Aren't you coming?"

"Nah, I'll go back through the window, trample your trail. Tell them you escaped."

He smiled as she descended the rickety steps. Then he locked eyes with Wulf, firmly handed him a flashlight and returned the cop's gun. Unspoken words of trust and murder flashed into Jake's eyes. "Keep MJ safe, and get the hell out of Santo Cruces City."

Wulf nodded. Ducking his head, the tall man descended the uneven wooden steps as the latch clasped overhead. Mary Jane stared at him as he made the last step onto the dirt pavement. She'd assumed they were in a basement, but the area was too narrow and led in one direction. So Jake had to be on to something when he'd mentioned mining companies and underground passageways.

At the faint sound of movement above, she could only assume Jake had scattered hay back over the door. Something in her spirit was unsettled about Wulf. She imagined every type of entrapment while alone with the police officer. Somehow, she trusted Jake more than the cop.

Leery of this new escort, she didn't move until Wulf began walking. When he turned the flashlight in front of him, she took in the scenery. They were in a narrow wooden pathway, littered with cobwebs. The wooden-beamed structure wouldn't stand much longer. Wulf had to keep ducking because the reinforced wood hung low in the underground tunnel that seemed to lead on to the edge of forever.

After five minutes of power walking, Wulf flashed the light in her face. "How trustworthy is that boyfriend of yours?"

Her lids shaded at the bright light. "I don't know him. Now, get that thing out of my face."

"That's odd." Wulf paused, turning the light back toward the constricted pathway. In an edgy tone, he added, "Jake seems to care a great deal about you. I've heard about him. Bad stuff. Sociopathic tendencies and he doesn't really like women. So what? Your lap dance must have really beat him into submission."

"I do not dance, Wulf. You can wonder about my character all you want, but I didn't sign up for a Q and A—so expect no answers. I don't trust him, and I'll be damned if I trust you." She started off in a jog.

He easily kept up with her as the circular light bobbed in front of them.

After almost an hour in the underground passageway, Wulf's breathing became slightly shallow. Almost six inches shorter, she wondered why the brawny man couldn't keep up.

"What time is it?" she asked as the narrowed pathway had yet to display a neon "Exit" sign. Their flashlight had begun to dim.

Wulf pressed the side of his durable watch. "Just after ten. But keep close to me. I know Jake said this passageway was once used for miners, but we don't know if it's still a good means for drug running."

"It'd just be my luck if we cross paths with a cartel down here," she scoffed and continued on into a jog...

Green foliage was all around. The sun was warm against her skin. Mary Jane jogged, wearing a sports bra and tiny running shorts. She glanced over her shoulder, offering a coy smile. The man behind her was total, utter perfection—square jaw, chiseled cheeks. His runner pants clung to slim muscles, and the hair on his chest always made her nose tickle when she laid down with him at night.

"I'll race you," she quipped.

"I'd rather lose." His smile was hypnotic as his gaze zeroed in on her ass.

"Oh, you always lose." She leaped over a fallen tree branch and took off in a massive sprint.

***

WULF GRUMBLED TO HIMSELF, "I shouldn't have slacked off."

Mary Jane was running at top speed. There was a day he could run her into the ground, but this wasn't one of them. After leaving home, he'd grown lazy. He was now paying dearly for it as he watched her. Running. Smiling. Running harder.

"I win!" Mary Jane stopped moving instantly.

If it wasn't for the glorious grin on her face, he would've had a hard time stopping too. He glanced at her. "What?"

"What?" she repeated. The sexy curve of her lips died instantly.

"What do you mean, what? You started off in a sprint, smiling and running," he stated the obvious. "Like we were racing. Like we were good friends."

She forked a hand in her hair. "We've been down here too long. Where's the damn exit?"

He stared at her in bewilderment.

She licked her lips, killing his curiosity and stirring his lust. "Wulf, I'm thirsty."

"I know, Mary Jane. I don't know anything about this underground pathway. Should we rest, then continue in the morning? The flashlight battery isn't going to last much longer. We can start fresh and early."

"No." She looked determined. She wasn't at all as he had previously assumed; not some ditsy woman who wasn't aware of her beauty and allowed herself to be taken advantage of. Not at all. At least that was his current observation. Women like that didn't have resolve.

He started walking again. "All right, let's pace ourselves."

A little while later, the flashlight began to fade and their passageway grew even bleaker, but the good news was they finally found a short door to the left side of the tunnel. The wooden planks were so haggard they almost missed it. Mary Jane looked ready to throw herself at the door as Wulf started to kick it. It took a few tries, but the boards caved in.

With just Mary Jane's luck, her first line of vision was the barrel of a shotgun. Her world faded into black.

6

WULF GRABBED HER BY THE WAIST AS SHE FAINTED. MARY Jane had already endured two bashes to the cranium during two car crashes. In fear of her having a concussion, he swept her up into his arms, but what he feared most was the faint desk lamp illuminating an *armed,* bearded man standing before them in long johns. He put his other hand up to indicate that they weren't a threat—even though he'd just beaten through what appeared to be the angry old man's basement office.

Wulf quickly introduced himself, noticing the cross dangling around the older man's neck. "I'm Officer Dylan Wulf. I understand that this might seem odd. A cop—"

"And a stripper breaking into my basement. Yes, I've seen the billboards. This is very odd. I'm Reverend Tobias," the man said, putting his shotgun on to stacks of handwritten papers cluttering the wooden oak desk behind him. "But more peculiar things have happened than someone using PGF Miner's passageway for the first time in, uh, let's say fifty years. That's the last time my brother and I played in those abandoned tunnels. What happened to the girl, officer?"

"She's dehydrated and most likely has a concussion." Wulf breathed easy, recalling being invited to Tobias's church during one domestic violence situation with a woman and her husband.

Wulf gingerly hoisted Mary Jane into his arms as Tobias led the way up some cemented stairs speaking over his shoulder as he went, "My family has owned this plot of land for ages. The house and the adjourning church, or should I say the church, first?" He chuckled and continued in a slow gait, holding on to the rail. "When I was a boy, my brother and I would use the miner tunnels to get to the dairy. It'd be over 100 degrees outside, and we only liked warm milk at night. I reckon it was hot today, and you were using this tunnel for...?"

"Because of Beasley," Wulf said.

"Oh, yes, I've heard of him. I've extended an invitation to my church countless times. Well, this is sanctuary. Let's lay her on the bed upstairs," Tobias suggested as they made it to the first floor of his home. They rounded the landing and the next flight became carpeted stairs.

"Toby, what's going on?" A pale woman in a flowery robe came out of the second room on the right.

"Officer Wulf broke through that old PGF Miner's door; you know, the one you wanted to have plastered over in my study while I was finishing Sunday's sermon."

"Glory be to God!" She opened the farthest door. "You always finish your sermon so early. There's a reason it took so long."

"Hilda, pull back the sheets so we can lay her down," Tobias ordered as they made their way into a modest room with a cross of Jesus on the pale-yellow wall.

"I'll go get a bucket of warm water and wash her up."
Hilda fretted as she pulled back the sheets. "Or should I call
the doctor? It's after midnight, but she—"

"Just clean her up, Hilda," Tobias grumbled about his
wife, while he and Wulf lowered Mary Jane onto the bed. He
nodded his head as Hilda rushed out. "That wife of mine
can go on forever with questions."

Wulf nodded and brushed the hair out of Mary Jane's
face as Tobias flicked on a lamp. Hilda gasped as she re-
entered the room with a large bowl of steaming water.

"I *know* this child." Hilda's cheeks flamed red.

"I was just saying that," her husband replied in a manner
meant for her to calm or maybe even stop talking so much.

"God bless her soul. She's in the right place," Hilda
murmured as she sat at the edge of the bed. She wrung out a
washcloth and began to cleanse Mary Jane's face. With a
tender hand, she dabbed at the crusted blood against her
temple. "Toby, go get more blankets."

When he left, her worried eyes turned to Wulf and
another gasp escaped her thin lips. "I've seen you in the
newspaper," she started.

Wulf gave Hilda all his attention. In a nanosecond, he
had assessed where this conversation was going and would
rather head the other direction. Away from Hilda, and most
definitely away from the beauty before him. He acknowl-
edged Hilda with, "That so?"

"You're *the* cop...from the LAPD."

"Yes, ma'am." Wulf clung to the appropriate amount of
distance he'd become accustomed to since leaving Los
Angeles. Everyone who knew of him admired him.

He didn't fucking deserve any admiration.

Hilda didn't understand his desire to be unknown, to be
just a small-town deputy. With her knowledge of Wulf's

past, she mentioned a few of the wonderful statements in the *L.A. Times* about him. "Something 'round here ain't right. You know that, don't you?"

He gave a subtle nod.

"God sent you to save these young women." She sounded so sure.

His worst fears had unfolded in Hilda's eyes. Wulf's only desire was to mend his broken spirit in a place where no one knew him. A place he'd closed his eyes and picked off a U.S. map.

Wulf hadn't done much police fieldwork in some time, as evidenced by how easily Mary Jane had outrun him earlier.

Tobias entered with the blankets. Hilda's hopeful eyes turned back to Mary Jane. She unfolded the knit blankets slowly and placed them around the girl in a loving manner.

After Hilda helped Mary Jane settle in, Wulf ate a cold ham sandwich and sat in the chair, listening to her pray over the young woman. *Hilda said I'm Mary Jane's saving grace. This town's saving grace.* He wondered if she was right.

He washed dinner down with a glass of water, but it still lodged in his throat. He leaned back in the rocking chair and nodded off to the sound of Hilda reciting Psalms. She seemed comfortable praying well into the night and waking up every so often to pray more.

***

"Our Father, who art in heaven...."

Mary Jane's eyes popped open.

"Thy kingdom come, thy will—oh, she's awake!" A woman with warm eyes smiled and stifled a yawn. Sunlight streamed into the large window and made her appear like a grandmother angel.

"Who are you? Where am I? What—" Mary Jane

jumped into a seated position in the twin-size bed, all the while keeping her eye on the old lady in the rocking chair.

"I – I ..." The woman was at a loss for words.

Mary Jane noticed her shoes on the floor. She scurried to grab them and noticed Officer Wulf awakening from the rocking chair next to her.

Slipping her feet into the boots, she ran for the door before he could get up. She had remembered the first night she'd met Jake. He'd saved her from Beasley. Before falling asleep with pillows wedged between them, he told her not to trust the police—that was if she got away.

Her eyes adjusted to the light of day as she scurried downstairs with Wulf calling her name. She headed for the screen door, noticing a white-haired man in overalls. He held a steaming mug of coffee—a potential weapon. Skidding in her boots, Mary Jane did an about-face and ran in the other direction, just as Wulf jumped the last couple of steps. She sprinted down a long hallway toward double doors.

Bursting through the doors, she stopped quickly to see a giant Jesus on a cross to her left and rows of pews to her right leading to the church's main entrance. Rainbows of sunlight transfixed the sanctuary in an ethereal glow from the long, multicolored glass windows above. Before her, on the opposite side of the church, was another set of double doors, but her eyes were transfixed on that of the Christ's spellbound by the pain.

"Mary Jane, wait!" Wulf called as she froze before the altar.

"Hold it, Mary Jane, we can help," came an ancient voice that she assumed was the old man's.

Before she could continue to the exit at the opposite side, the doors at the back of the church exploded. Bits and pieces of wood soared through the air. In a flash, she remembered Jake's sidekick, Lyle, speeding in a Ford.

Lyle, Beasley, Jake, and five other men entered the back of the church. They started firing shots at Wulf as he ran from the side door. Bullets riddled Jesus. Wood splinters broke from the front row of pews.

Wulf dove for Mary Jane and pushed her down at the front pew on the left side of the church. Her knees took it the worst. They crouched, staring at the exit only a few yards away, but they couldn't continue because two men were headed up the side of each row of aisles.

"*What in the world?*" The bullets stopped as Reverend Tobias entered the room.

"Well, sir," came Beasley's heavy, breathy voice. "All we want is the girl. Mary Jane, I have—"

Tobias cut in, entering the front right side of the church, "Not in my church."

Thump!

Mary Jane's eyes widened as life exited the old man's eyes. A single buckshot sent sprays of bullets in his chest. The exit wound splattered crimson at Jesus' feet. Tobias dropped to his knees in the middle of the sanctuary.

The old woman who'd leaned over Mary Jane mere minutes ago ran through the double doors on the right. She was instantly shot down, her body jerking as her chest and abdomen were rapidly pierced with bullets. She crumpled next to her husband. Eyes wide with tears, Mary Jane knew she'd never be able to get the image out of her head.

"Now that y'all know we're serious," Lyle said, starting up the middle aisle as Wulf again pointed to the left-side door. He and Mary Jane crawled toward it as Lyle continued. "Wulf, c'mon out. Santo Cruces City needs a new...What was Keller, a chief? Oh, hell, I don't know. But that could be you." Lyle rounded the first row of pews from the right and shot at the officer.

A bullet grazed Wulf's shoulder as he pushed the door open. He cursed. Mary Jane took his hand, and they descended the stone steps. On the freshly cut grass, they ran toward a carport off in the distance, hurrying past a small, empty, dirt parking area for parishioners.

"You're hurt," Mary Jane exclaimed as she hastily opened the carport side door. "Where's your gun?"

"On the nightstand," he grumbled, going inside.

He tried the truck door as she grabbed a dusty, old .22 caliber hunting rifle off a rack just a few feet away. Her finger looped inside of the trigger guard, and she pressed the butt plate into perfect formation. Lips tensed, Mary Jane pressed against the wall of the carport, peeked around, and aimed for Lyle since he came charging out of the church first. Blood and bits of flesh gushed from Lyle's leg. He yelped and crumpled to the floor. Glancing at Wulf as he searched the visor of the truck she asked, "Are the keys inside?"

"Gimme a sec," Wulf grimaced, bending down in the driver's seat.

She turned to see another man charge out in front of Jake. She aimed and shot, but the man continued to run. In fear of hitting Jake, she took a deep breath to try again, but the man fell to the ground. She sighed. Jake must've shot him. He winked at her. With a rush of relief, she smiled and wiped her brow. "Can I get an update, Wulf?"

"You asked me three seconds ago, MJ. Guess what? I'm not finished hot-wiring this truck!" he snapped.

"Okay, Wulf. I'm sure it *hurts your heart* to break the law—"

The air emptied from her lungs as a bullet blasted

through the doorframe inches from her nose. Sighing deeply, she trained her vision on the important task and fired at the Popeye lookalike. The bullet moved in slow motion and punctured straight between the man's eyes.

Oh, shit. He's dead!

Mary Jane didn't know if she should pat her back on such beautiful marksmanship or condemn herself for murder. After all she'd been through, a little self-praise didn't hurt. She grinned and continued. To her surprise, six men were sprawled on the ground. All but Jake.

She was aiming for the squirming Lyle when she noticed Beasley peer from the church door.

Come on out, you fat fuck. There's one here for you too.

She pulled the trigger. It clicked. She turned around toward the gun rack and grabbed a shotgun, just as the Nissan started up. Mary Jane grabbed the shotgun and in a few swift paces she was at the door to the truck. "Slide over. You're hurt."

Wulf did. Mary Jane hopped in, tossed him the gun, and yanked the stick shift into reverse.

"What the fuck!" he exclaimed as the truck screeched backward and through the rear wall. Boards of wood broke in their wake.

"I'm saving our asses!" Mary Jane jerked the truck into drive, going over fragments of wood. She turned the wheel sharply, and it sped down the dirt driveway as Jake, the lone, sneaky ranger, headed back to the church to grab fat Beasley.

"What if there was something behind the wall, blocking our path?" When she gave him an incredulous look, he elaborated, "Like a tractor, or fuck it, something else solid."

"Just wrap up your shoulder," she argued. "Which damn road leads out of Shit City?"

7

IN AN AREA RIDDLED WITH SMALL TOWNS, THEY DROVE UNTIL the gas light clicked on before Wulf decided it was time to fill up. He continued to watch the woman beside him. Either he'd become delirious or she was more than a hot piece of ass. He was attracted to her. He watched her freely while she drove.

How did she shoot all of those men? In twenty-four hours, she'd transformed from lying about her association to Beasley to having amazing marksmanship.

"Hello? Hey, Dylan?" She flashed a hand in his face. "Are you still alive over there or have you bled out? I'm starving."

He tuned in. She'd never called him by his given name, which led Wulf back to his original question. "Who are you?"

"What?" She pulled over to the side of the road. "Uh-oh, your overgrown muscles must be starving too. Your snobbish ass refused to eat those oranges from the orchard earlier. Your sugar level is lowering." Eyes narrowed, she looked into his. "Wulf, your pupils are dilated."

Wulf blinked at himself in the mirror. His usual tan skin

had paled. Before he could reassess the moment, she flicked on the left blinker and merged back onto the lonely highway. They zipped past tumbleweeds then Mary Jane merged off at the next exit and stopped at the first motel, which happened to be a one-level L-shaped building. The lobby was disconnected from the rooms and on the opposite side of the parking lot.

From the passenger seat, he watched her go into the one-room building that housed the lobby. A slight glare from the descending sun hampered his view through the glass window, but he noticed her leaning over the table, most likely sweet-talking the young attendant. Fuck, he was hypnotized by the thick curve of her ass and hadn't noticed what was transpiring between the two of them.

Mary Jane had just slid something on the counter, and the clerk, still wet behind the ears, took it. *Contraband*? Seconds later, the guy tossed keys to a smiling Mary Jane. Her curvaceous hips swayed, and she sauntered out.

"What just happened?" His eyes narrowed, much better at sticking to his guns while staring into her beautiful face.

She leaned into the open passenger window. "What?"

"Mary Jane, we barely have enough money for gas to L.A. How'd you get the room?"

"Why are you looking at me like that, Wulf? You were whining about getting to Los Angeles ASAP, but you need rest. Tomorrow, we can head for your friend."

"How'd you pay for the room? I am *not* sticking around if you're pushing drugs." He gritted his teeth, feeling the dull ache in his shoulder. Garland, the officer who had been chatting outside with Wulf when Mary Jane had crashed into his cruiser, had spoken to her when she awoke. He could only assume that all the officers at SCPD were crooked, and Garland hadn't confiscated Mary Jane's items.

How could he help this woman if she continued to break the law?

"Thanks for being an asshole, *Wulf*." Mary Jane folded her arms. "FYI, I am not a drug dealer or user. The guy was reading a magic book when I stepped inside. These types of places are never without a vacancy, and I bet him that I could do a trick. I pulled out a gold coin – and not from *my hoo-ha* if that's your next question! Sleep in the car, because I don't care at all."

Tensed with frustration, he watched the sexy nuisance stalk to the second-to-last room. After an hour and three more calls to Quincy, Wulf saw Mary Jane exit the last room, furthest from the lot. Her hair was wet and in tight coils as if she'd taken a shower. Through the side mirror, his eyes tracked her across the street and into a diner. Arms folded and lips taut, he watched through the rearview mirror until she came out toward him. She tossed a brown bag through the window. It landed on his lap.

"The waitress wanted to have a girl talk. Her husband, to whom she's been married for ages, is an asshole. I didn't have to lie *too much* for your meal. I said I was on my honeymoon, and the dumbass—being you—brought me to this hell hole. So, I'm sure you'll take that into consideration before eating. Oh, it's liver and onions. Hope you like." Before walking away, she winked. "I had a T-bone and eggs, mmmm."

He sat stunned as the beauty sauntered toward the motel room. Twenty minutes after having tricked himself into thinking liver was half as good as a juicy steak, Wulf hopped out of the truck with a full stomach. They'd replaced the license on the Nissan with an old one on the wall of the first gas station they'd come by earlier. Stalking toward Mary Jane's hotel room, he knocked on the door.

The sound of *Wheel of Fortune* met him as she opened the door and rolled her eyes.

"Mary Jane," he said as she jumped back onto the full-sized mattress. *Great, there's only one bed.*

She lay on her belly at the foot of the bed, her shapely legs up in the air. He stopped himself from looking at how the T-shirt she must have gotten at the diner ended just short of more glorious curves. His hands itched, and his cock was harder than ever.

Not paying him any attention, Mary Jane started calling out letters and making phrase predictions. *Shit, she's actually good at this game.* There'd only been five letters and a surplus of spaces as she came up with the right answer. He clicked off the television and turned back to the beautiful creature.

"Who are you?"

She moved into a seated position. For a few moments, she was quiet. "Well, I wasn't going to tell you, Wulf, but if I do, can you keep it a secret until we make it to California?"

"Who could I possibly tell?" He took a seat at the wooden chair by the door. Mary Jane's face contorted with mistrust. He sighed. "All right, I promise."

"The meds Beasley forced me to take are wearing off. I'm a secret agent, and some of my memory is returning."

Mary Jane blinked as Wulf chuckled, choked, and chuckled a bit more. He tried his best to keep a straight face, waving her on to continue.

"Damn it, Wulf, I'm providing you with highly classified information. Do you remember when Beasley told me he had Asia?"

"Where at? The station or the church?"

She grumbled. "We were at the church. While his armed men were coming up the aisles, he stayed in the back, shouting that he had Asia."

Wulf's eyebrows knitted. "Mary Jane, I don't recall any of this. Are you sure it wasn't your imagination?"

"Listen to me." She stood. He stood. She placed her hand on his arm and all the pain he felt vanished, leaving only desire. She looked him in the eyes and said, "What I'm about to tell you is G-4 classified material."

Fuck me, I'm attracted to a deranged woman. "All . . . right." He couldn't help but smile in disbelief.

"Asia is the codename for a prototype," she paused and placed her hand on her hip. Her shirt crept up more. Though she did well at irritating him, she was fucking gorgeous. "There's a new lethal weapon that can block every form of tactical defense in the USA. I was sent in to apprehend Asia, but my cover was blown. Beasley and his team attempted to erase my memory."

"Fatso?" Wulf folded his buff arms. *Keep your face straight. This chick has lost it.*

"Yes!"

"Mary Jane, the easiest way to shut someone up is to kill them." His voice was calming but he gave her a stern look.

"Can you literally just take the cop hat off for a second? I have more training than you do," she said, glaring at him.

He nodded for her to continue, not feeling the slightest sting at her attempt to insult him.

"Beasley works for a corporation that pilfered the Asia files to not only ruin our livelihoods as fellow Americans, but possibly even the entire world."

"Take over the world. Haven't I heard that one enough?" Wulf rubbed a hand over his face in an attempt to be serious. "All right, so I apologize about calling you a junkie. But—"

"Wulf," she began, "you will *not* make me out for an idiot. Didn't you see all those men on the ground outside of the church? *I* shot them. How can you justify your gun being confiscated at the Santo Cruces City jailhouse, by me, a little *drug addict*?"

"I—"

"You're the one who got shot at the church. I stealthily—"

"You're a commodity. I'm expendable." Wulf glanced at her breasts as she folded her arms.

"I could kill you," she said, stepping closer to him. Her vision trained on the pulsating veins at his neck. "With my bare hands, Wulf, *I can kill you.*"

"You couldn't." He gave a cocky smile.

Fist balled, she jabbed at his nose, but he sidestepped it. A surprise roundhouse kick to his gut made Wulf bump into the nightstand. The clay lamp jarred. He stopped the Native American artifact from falling. She elbowed him in the ribs while he placed it back.

When she went to knee him in the groin, he blocked it. Hand as stiff as a board, she did a judo chop into his wound. Wulf grimaced in pain.

In a wide-legged stance, she beckoned him. "Aren't you going to fight for your life?"

"I won't hit a woman, so I'll let you tire yourself out." He yawned.

Fighting dirty, she targeted his shoulder again. Wulf's forearm blocked it. He stepped behind her in seconds, holding her in a bear hug. Silky and deep, he whispered in her ear, "Are you finished, *angry little junkie*?"

"Grrr." She untwisted her arms and kicked him onto the bed then leapt on top of him with her hands around his neck.

He appeared unfazed.

She squeezed.

He did a forearm swipe and flipped her over, pinning her wrists down. "Are we done playing games?"

"We're done when I say so!" Mary Jane struggled to get up from her pinned position. Her eyes widened, and Wulf knew she felt him growing stiff.

"See where this game takes you?" Wulf shrugged.

Her voice was breathy and more assertive than she anticipated. "Get that sneaky snake away from me!"

"If you relax, I'll let you go," he ordered.

She tried to bite him, but he held her by the arms.

What the fuck are you doing? he asked himself as he descended down to her lush mouth. The instant his lips met hers the kiss became rougher, harder, as he bruised her mouth with his. She moaned and nibbled on his bottom lip a little too hard before her tongue took charge.

Her legs wrapped around his waist, pulling Wulf closer. He could never be close enough. Mary Jane moaned in his mouth as his hand reached under her shirt. The warm, roughness of his fingers against the silky skin of her abdomen and breasts had her purring as he pulled off her shirt and unsnapped her bra.

His mouth felt like satin over her erect nipples, and she gasped. He pulled her pants off, doing a double-take at her large panties.

"I-I stole a pack of them from one of the gas stations. *Okay*?" she snapped.

Her cheeks warmed with embarrassment as he pulled off the granny panties and tossed them over his shoulder. Dark coils were neatly shaven into a V, and so fucking pretty against her golden skin. His thick finger glided across her soft, moist lips.

Mary Jane gasped as he screwed her softly with his finger.

Her wetness made him ravenous.

When he removed his hand to grip her thigh, Mary Jane quickly flipped and straddled him. With swift, shaky fingers, she helped him pull off his uniform top and then his undershirt. A heavy, deep sigh escaped her starving lips. Her hands sailed over caramel-coated, washboard abs as she leaned over for another kiss. She unzipped his pants. His cock popped out like a large elephant's tusk, making her gasp yet again.

Her tongue flicked out and glided against the smooth hardness. His dick was perfect in every way. Slight curve that extended to a cockhead up top and two fat balls way down below. Her tonsils purred, sending an extra wet, tight pulsing along his crown. He gripped the hair at the base of her neck, coaxing her warm mouth further down his shaft. Her mouth hungrily sucked him like a vacuum.

"Fuck, I'm gonna come."

With gritted teeth, Wulf pulled at the nape of her neck. Mary Jane climbed up and planted soft kisses along his chest. Their mouths locked. He flipped her until her sweet tits sunk into the bed and she knelt with her ass up in the air. Mary Jane looked back at him, unresisting. He slammed his hand down on her ass cheek, causing her back to arch in perfection. The lips of her pussy beckoned from between her thighs.

"Ohhhh...*Wulf*!" Mary Jane yelped as his tongue dove straight inside her from behind.

Her soft, silky inner labia offered a sugary treat as Wulf surveyed deeper. He reached up and grabbed her hair, forcing her to arch more. This action created a divine reaction as his tongue slammed deeply into her tight core. The sticky, sweet cream was intoxicating against his mouth and tasted better than anything he'd ever eaten. He ate her frantically. Mary Jane clawed at the headboard.

"Wulllllllffffffff!" she screamed, as a mist slicked her skin when an orgasm slammed through her. Her back sagged. Once her legs shook uncontrollably, and no amount of spankings would force her to stay in position, Wulf let her body sink into the bed. She laughed, and it was contagious.

She laid on her back, a jolt of giggles taking over her. She looked delightfully tipsy. "You were..." Mary Jane paused, her tone no less than intoxicated from the way he'd made her come. "You were good, Wulf. I'll give you that. Damn, I have never laughed while orgasming before. At least, I don't think."

His face hardened. "You don't think?"

"Oh, don't get all stuffy on me, Wulf. Besides, I'll get you back."

"You'll get me back." He leaned on his knees and massaged his hard cock.

Mary Jane came up to her knees, still a head shorter than him. She reached up and kissed him. "Now, I'm on top."

He smiled. She assumed being on top gave her power. He'd allow it.

***

Wulf lay back as Mary Jane climbed on top of him. He'd eaten her like the grand opening of a Southern Comfort buffet. Her insides tingled. Her entire body felt light, and she had to stop herself from wondering if she had ever been this happy in life.

Didn't need to know. As long as this current bliss lasted, she'd be content.

The man with his hands comfortably positioned behind his head was panty-wetter fine, and lucky for her, she wasn't wearing any. There had to have been a gazillion folks on this bed over the decades, but Mary Jane couldn't imagine any man owning this bed nearly as well as him.

"Wulf," she purred in his ear as she slid onto every last inch of him. Her pussy expanded for his thick girth, only made possible by how super wet he'd made her. Damn, he'd been large in her mouth, but his cock seemed endless as she sank down on that slight curve.

"MJ, fuck me." He reached out one hand and cupped her tit, callused thumb flicking over her nipple. "Fuck me hard," he growled against her earlobe, giving it a little nip, "bad girl."

"I'm your bad girl," she panted.

"Yeah, you're my bad girl." His hand skimmed down her waist to her pussy. Now his thumb flicked at her clit until Mary Jane trembled, making it hard to keep herself upright. "And this is my pussy, Mary Jane."

"Fu . . . fuck." She leaned back, placing her hands on his knees while she rode him. As his thumb and index finger tweaked her tiny bulb, Mary Jane's pussy coasted up and down on his cock. "Fuck, Wulf. Oh my God, oh my...fuck me!"

He chuckled softly, leaning up somewhat. "I thought you were fucking me, sweetheart," he said, biting at her lip.

Mary Jane pushed at his chest until he fell back onto the pillows. "I am fucking you." Her pace sped up. She was so wet now; each stroke came easy and with it brought tiny orgasmic waves.

"You're fucking me, MJ?" His island tone had become thicker, making her slam down on him harder.

She ground down on his length. "We'll see who's boss when you come."

Wulf's hands took hold of her hips, guiding her to a

rhythm of his own tune. She gave a sly grin, doing a few Kegels on his manhood to let him know who was in charge.

The glazed look in Wulf's eyes from Mary Jane's walls clinging tighter to him made her go buck wild. Now she switched from cowgirl to positioning herself on her feet, crouching down, made it easier to pop her ass, and screw him like a piston gun. Her tits bounced as she gave a triumphant smile.

He reached up, gently grabbing her by the neck and kissing her, hard. Mary Jane didn't know it until she was beneath him. Her mouth hungered for his neck and she sucked on his pulse as hard as she could, and then bit into the soft flesh. That still didn't offer her control but the reaction made Wulf sigh.

"You're so fucking tight," he growled in awe.

For a second, he slowed down. She grumbled, needing him more than she needed power. "Fuck me. Harder!"

In response, Wulf's teeth sank into her skin as he pushed her legs up and to the sides.

He steadied her calves over his shoulders, gripping the headboard. Wulf plunged deeper and harder. Each thrust sent her moaning and bucking.

"Yes, yes!" she panted. A staccato series of moans were his stamp of approval, and he went hard, pulling out just to drive in again, deeper and harder. Mary Jane's soul shook.

The climax slammed into her body. Sensations rushed through her, beginning at their sweet, wet connection, speeding through her veins. It took all of her strength to drag her fingers along his short, silky brown hair, clasping the back of his neck. He kissed her tenderly but fucked her with primitive desire.

Wave upon wave rolled over her, offering multiple orgasms. Wet tears streamed down her cheeks.

How could he do this? Mary Jane couldn't recall much of her past, but she'd never had sex this great. Never cried out happy, elated, and ecstatic. All she knew was this could not end.

She couldn't speak as the giant huffed, falling to a spent position beside her. Her body was weak and trembling, but by hell, fire, or storm, this could not end.

8

THEIR LEGS WERE ENTANGLED. THE SUN WASHED OVER THEM through the weak, cheap draping the next morning. Wulf sighed as he watched Mary Jane's sleeping body. She was drop-dead gorgeous. Literally. She was the type of woman who men fought for, killed for. She was so soft in his arms. He mumbled to himself, "You have finally lost your fucking mind, Dylan."

The sex had been maddening, almost barbaric. Having always been the type of person who didn't understand relationships without trust, he couldn't fathom how they'd ended up in bed together. He recalled their many sexual trysts. Three times last night. Each time was like being with a different woman. Except the same addictive pussy. Somewhere deep within his gut, he didn't feel ashamed. He grumbled at the thought of no protection and said a quick prayer for the safety of his manhood and health. He imagined, that with his luck, she'd kill him one way or another. He chuckled at himself.

Wulf wiggled free from Mary Jane's hold. Even in sleep, she was a dominating force. She'd been so powerful with her emotions. She wanted it hard. She wanted it slow. She just wanted. Now, after a full night's sleep, he was still tired. He grabbed the cell phone from his uniform pants and went to the bathroom. Closing the door, he turned on the hot water for a shower then dialed Quincy again. Why hadn't his ex-partner responded already? He'd always been reliable. You wouldn't get far on the force with a partner that wasn't dependable. Besides, this morning he should've been home. They had to be leaving for San Diego where the ports were at any given moment. Shelly should've called and chewed his head off already by now.

"Quincy, call me ASAP. I have a girl with me who thinks she's some type of special agent. She doesn't even know her own last name. I fucked up." He finished off the call quickly, letting Quincy know that the station he worked for was crooked.

He hung up. Wulf was a pro at alienating himself from family after resigning from the head of the Gang Unit. Growing up as a foster kid, ghosting people and hitting the road was ingrained in his psyche. That was until Shelly's foster mother took him in. He was a teenager by the time he learned the real meaning of family. Where the fuck was his family?

Wulf chewed on his lip, knowing that Shelly would wreak havoc over his safety, and she was the younger sibling. His mother would too. But he told himself not to call his adoptive mother and worry her. Maybe they're still asleep? But that didn't account for his calls yesterday.

Placing the phone on the counter, Wulf tested the water with a touch and hopped in, telling himself to focus on Mary Jane. Nothing was going on at home. He tried to believe that, since he trusted Quincy with his family. Quincy *was* his family.

While using the soap, he contemplated the various shades of MJ. Who was Mary Jane? A drug addict? A stripper? A gunfighter? A great debater? He considered retracting the drug addict tag as he rubbed more soap onto the rough, overused face towel. Maybe Beasley had forced the drugs on her. As for stripper, well, her photo was all over town. Even Hilda became embarrassed by mentioning it. He'd remembered staring at a billboard the first day they were designed. He'd thought it was airbrushed. Now he knew the truth.

Clean and refreshed, he turned the faucet off. He pulled the large towel from over the lime-stained glass door and wrapped it around his frame before getting out. He snatched up his boxers. Mary Jane had to have washed them in the sink last night and placed them on the shower door to dry.

Wearing his now stiff boxers, he opened the bathroom door to see the sheets pulled back. Empty. He stepped onto the carpet. "Mary Jane?"

Senses piqued, Wulf heard a rustling to his side. Before he could react, pain seared through the left side of his temple. He dropped to the grungy carpet in an unconscious heap.

9

Music streamed from the speakers of the gazebo. With eyes closed, Beasley lay back on the jets of the hot tub as Diamond, the current queen of his mansion, massaged his temples.

"You have an unknown text," said the dark beauty with a short-cropped afro.

Beasley licked his lips as she handed him a plush towel from the side of the jacuzzi. He held it up and wiped his hands. When they were dry, she then handed over the iPhone.

UNKNOWN: *How is my girl?*

Chewing hard on his bottom lip, Beasley considered how to answer. *She's good. She's okay.* Fuck, what should he say? Mary Jane was gone!

BEASLEY: *OK.*

UNKNOWN: *Comfortable in her cage? Waiting for me to come save her. (Smile Emoji)*

His jaw tightened. He glanced around. Diamond's gaze found the ground. She was aware of her owner's discomfort.

Beasley continued to consider what to tell the man. Mary Jane wasn't like the others. She wasn't given to Beasley to work at The Petting Zoo. But when Beasley laid eyes on Mary Jane, she did things to him, like made his cock salute her. No, he'd never touched her. Touching her sexually or inflicting too much pain would be his death. He still regretted choking her out two days ago. That was the most pain he'd ever inflicted on her. Fuck no, he wouldn't allow anyone besides Jake to place a hand on her. Despite all the threats to her life, she was worth too much. She wasn't his whore.

BEASLEY: *She's not in the cage. It hasn't been a full month.*

His breathing came in sharp pants as he awaited a response. The man who owned Mary Jane had not one, but two islands, a slew of mansions around the world, and exotic cars. She was just one of his expensive toys; but Beasley knew he loved each of his toys.

UNKNOWN: *You're right. See you next week then.*

Beasley's lungs began to work right again. He handed his iPhone back to Diamond. She reached over and placed it away from the ledge of the jacuzzi. He controlled his nerves as he lay back into position for her to rub his temples again.

I must find this woman and bring her back, Beasley thought.

His heartbeat skyrocketed. With one flick of the wrist, the magic Diamond worked into his psyche stopped. His swim trunks puffed up like a blimp from the force of the jets as he stood.

He looked at Diamond. Mary Jane should've taken her spot at The Petting Zoo tonight. He had been given both girls around the same time; Diamond had come a little over a month ago and he owned her. Mary Jane arrived about a week after. She was owned by another. She wasn't supposed to be in his club, but what was the use of having such a beautiful woman rotting away in a cage?

His plans were to have Mary Jane strut her pussy around his club. He could just let the boys get a good sniff, make some money, and then lock her ass in the cage before her owner arrived. Diamond would once again return to The Petting Zoo and follow the normal rotation in Beasley's operation. After all, his clientele had a diverse palate, so what was the trouble with having Mary Jane at the club for a few days? No touching, just looking. Shit, that mindset had gotten him into this mess. He was already going to be in hot water for using Mary Jane for advertisement, if her owner only knew.

He should have prepared her and then placed her in the cage like he'd been told. Forget the good following at The Petting Zoo. His club was a fairly lucrative side hobby compared to the money coming in from his real job.

"I have business to attend to," he said. "Diamond, you do too. While we're waiting on MJ to come home, you head to The Petting Zoo and keep the guys satisfied."

Before he could turn away and climb the steps, he noticed the annoyance smeared across her face. His spine tingled. He waded back over. His fingers went to the beautiful bone structure of her cheek. He rubbed it softly, knowing she didn't want to strip. Diamond had a good life here. He had a fondness for Diamond, and with Mary Jane in her position for a few shows—while Mary Jane's owner was away—Diamond had gotten comfortable playing house. She stayed in the fifteen-hundred-square-foot bedroom and could purchase any designer item she fancied. Little did she know, that even when Mary Jane returned to her cage, Diamond would have to return to The Petting Zoo.

It was a no-brainer. He shuffled his whores when needed. Beasley had only wanted MJ as a trophy for the first few weeks of the month, then he planned to keep her locked up for her owner.

His fingernails dug into Diamond's cheeks until pinpricks of blood dripped from around his nails and mixed with the water on her chocolate-colored skin. "Are you going to take the prime-time shift at The Petting Zoo this evening?"

"Yes." She nodded as her breath escaped through gritted teeth.

"You know I love you, Diamond, because I *asked,* right?" His hand slipped from her raw skin where he'd scraped his nails into her. Can't ruin that pretty face. They call her "The Diamond in the Rough," such an innocent young woman. His hand stopped on her neck, but then he thought better of squeezing the life source.

Knowing her error, she spoke meekly. "Yes, you love me."

"That's right." His hand rested at his side. "Get ready, then rally up the men. Grab my box, and y'all join me in the meeting room in twenty minutes. Oh, and have them situated with a glass of Dom. We'll have ourselves a little pep talk—and give them a good reason to search harder for MJ —before you head over to the club."

She nodded and rushed past him to pick up the towel draped over the handrail. He watched her pretty, slender feet as she scurried down the stairs of the gazebo. She was cautious around his two beloved Rottweilers. Knight and King growled, their muscles bulging as they stood in a wide-legged stance, pulling at their restraints. The sound of chains being tugged from the stucco building made her pretty feet move faster.

Beasley smiled, thinking of the time the chains had

broken. He'd lost his moneymaker that night, but the sight of her death had left him excited for days. Flesh ripping from bones, blood squirting all over the patio.

10

HANDS ON TOP OF HER HEAD, MARY JANE MENTALLY COUNTED backward from twenty. Just ruminating about breaking every limb of Wulf's body had her nerve endings on fire. She'd start with dislocating his extremities—pecker included. Yeah, that was a pretty image.

An almost naked, unconscious Wulf sat in a wooden chair, tied with torn linen straps around the waist and ankles. It had been a feat to get the stocky man onto the seat. His arms were bound behind his back, and the smelly sock he'd worn yesterday was lodged in his mouth. Head cast downward, blood traveled from his forehead to his cheek, and dripped onto his masculine chest. It all made her feel good when she just wanted to be bad.

She should've gotten him dressed. Mary Jane's eyes locked on his face. After cold-cocking him when he exited the bathroom, she'd tied him up without dressing him. Her eyes flickered away from his washboard abs in anger. Even the dumbest cop knew rule number one. While undercover or running away from psychos like Beasley, no phone calls. The call could be traced.

"So you tried to double-cross me while taking a shower?" she mumbled.

Eyes narrowed, Mary Jane knew that she'd given him the best time of his entire life last night. Soon as he awakened, she'd serve the officer his balls on a platter. No other bloody mess. No other broken body parts—just his two wee friends decorating the top of a simple plate.

Looking around the room, she noticed that this option would not work, as there were no platters in sight. Her eyes stopped on the dreamcatcher artistically displayed over the bed. Hmmm, dangling balls, that's a thought. He thought he'd use her. Well, she'd use him.

Holding a straight razor that she'd nabbed from a trucker eating breakfast at the diner, Mary Jane patiently waited for Wulf to awaken. Then the carving party could commence.

"Grmmm," Wulf mumbled.

She glared at him. Standing up from the foot of the bed, she sauntered over. Placing the razor at his throat, she caressed the flat part of the blade against his carotid artery. In a soft voice, she said, "Wulf, I thought we were friends. I don't give myself away freely, but it seems you've been a bad boy."

"*Grrr*," he growled.

"Calm down." She paced back and forth and told him the rules. "Now, when I take the sock away, all I want to know is who you contacted. If you decide to insult me, as you've done so many times, I will slit your throat. If you decide to talk about anything other than what I'm inquiring about, I will slit your throat. And, because I desire to spare the life of the man I've been most intimate with, I will be kind enough to also add that if you scream, I will, of course, only be obliged to *slit your motherfucking throat*." She stopped right in front of him and again taunted him with the razor. "Got it?"

She removed the straight razor from his throat and he nodded.

"I thought so, Wulf. You seem to thrive on *rules and regulations*. Now, let's get started." She pulled the sock from his mouth.

He gagged and gulped.

"C'mon, Wulf, my time is precious. What happened to the man I met last night? That's the last time I sleep with the enemy. Get to talking!"

"Okay, okay," he sputtered as she gave his neck a prick. Blood instantly pooled in the quarter-inch slit. "I called my old partner from the LAPD, Quincy Jones."

Her eyebrows furrowed. The name sounded familiar.

"Don't look at me like that. It's not a joke. And he's not Quincy Jones, the producer." He spoke quickly. "Just check my cell phone."

How cute and innocent he looked when he was scared. "Not necessary, Wulf. I heard your entire call through the paper-thin walls." She closed the straight razor. "I also destroyed your phone."

Before he could protest, she shoved the sock back into his mouth.

"Beasley may have the means to track your cell phone." She gave him an incredulous look. "You're *only* a small-town cop, so I don't expect you to have the same training as I do. Fortunately, I checked it prior to disposal."

Irritation was written all over that gorgeous face of his.

"Wulf, I *am* a secret agent. When my mission is complete, you can bet your ass that you will be thoroughly dealt with." She pulled on a diner T-shirt much larger than the one she'd worn the day before and the same skintight jeans. After slipping on her boots, she walked out, slamming the door behind her.

In the sweltering air outside, Mary Jane placed a cowgirl hat on her head. She lingered at the door, reluctant to go.

"Adiós, Wulf," Mary Jane mumbled, mentally forcing herself not to feel a thing for him. Leaving him alone was good enough for her sanity.

While walking to the diner last night, she'd checked through her pockets and clothing, finding a phone number slipped into the crevice of her left boot heel. She slipped inside the stuffy lobby and sauntered toward some pimple-faced attendant.

He instantly perked up and placed his Spider-Man collector's comic book on the table. "MJ, we have a continental breakfast. It's not really continental, because all of it comes from this continent. This crummy town really, but we have hot chocolate," he jabbered, opening the partition that separated them to walk over to the table. She put her hand up, and he instantly stopped mentioning the menu, shamefully reclosed the latch.

Mary Jane smiled, glancing at his nametag. "Hi, Glenn."

"You remembered my name!" he exclaimed.

"Yes, Glenn." Mary Jane nodded, slipping the phone number out of her pocket and onto the table. "How could I forget about you? I need to use your phone."

Glenn pepped up at her comment and went back to chattering. "Mary Jane, you're like the *baddest* chick ever. I'm kinda supposed to call the police on you, though."

Her eyes widened. "Come again?"

"I'll show you," Glenn said.

With hands on her hips, she waited. Watching his every move, she had no qualms with beating up a kid who couldn't even vote for the president yet. But instead of picking up the phone, Glenn's hands went to the tiny television on the counter. He slowly turned it around.

"The sound keeps going out," Glenn said. "So I have it muted."

Mary Jane read the tiny stream of words at the bottom of the news station. On the screen was a photo of Wulf in his standard uniform and a camcorder high angle close-up shot of Mary Jane from the jailhouse. It had to have been a cropped frame from when Wulf was escorting her to the exit prior to her taking his gun. On the bottom of the screen the newsfeed read:

Santo Cruces City cop goes on shooting rampage with stripper, murdering the pastor and first lady of Santo Cruces City Friendship Church and five other parishioners. The current total dead count is seven.

Her mouth tensed. *The pastor and his wife didn't deserve to die.* It took her a moment to calm her frazzled nerves, then Mary Jane looked Glenn square in the eyes. "That's not me."

Glenn's head cocked to the side. "That's not you?"

When she reiterated, his head cocked to the exit. Through the sun's glare against the window, she noticed a man headed toward the door. Glenn motioned for her to come behind the counter. She hurried through. On her tiptoes, she pivoted inside the door that read *Employees Only* and flicked on the light as Glenn closed the door. In two seconds, she'd taken in her surroundings—an old couch and an out-of-order vending machine. To her side, a hallway led toward the restroom.

Mary Jane's ear went to the cool, chip-painted door.

"Mornin'." The voice on the other side was deep and strong.

"Good morning, sir." The soft, nervous voice had to belong to Glenn. "Do you need a room today? We usually don't open for check-in until the afternoon."

"What do we have here? Hmmm. Have you seen the woman on this television?"

"Yes."

Mary Jane's eyes widened. *I could have snapped your scrawny neck with ease!*

"Where is she?" the deep voice asked.

"On the TV." Glenn laughed.

The left side of her lip curved toward the dust-bunny ceiling. At the sound of a fist pounding the counter, Mary Jane jerked slightly.

"Are you alone, boy?"

Glenn didn't miss a beat. "Yes."

Moments passed. "Are you lying to me, *boy*?"

"No, sir."

Mary Jane stepped away from the door. She panted heavily, but she couldn't save Glenn. She jogged down the hall and into the unisex, one-stall bathroom. It smelled of piss and mild disinfectant. Stepping past a mirror smeared with dust and dotted with water spots, she found a rectangular window. Pushing up the glass, she climbed out.

On the side of the building, she waited for the man to exit. There were no shots fired or Glenn's high-pitched voice, so she assumed the stranger had either dealt cleanly with him or left him alive.

She watched the man dressed in leather studs and with a thick beard walk out of the lobby door. He stalked toward the driver's side of a blue *F-250*.

She turned around to go in the opposite direction, but a

man blocked her way. A thin, tall man with the same features as the stranger who had just asked about her in the lobby. Before she could sidestep him, she was cold-cocked on her temple.

Karma.

11

WULF SLOWLY PULLED HIMSELF TO HIS FEET AND RAMMED THE chair backward into the wall. Again, he pushed back against the wall. the top of the chair slamming into his shoulders with each hit. The legs finally snapped at the seat base. Still confined at the arms, Wulf cursed himself for giving into Mary Jane's bedroom eyes. He cursed her existence while he freed himself and kicked away the piece of wood.

His tense lips twitched as he pulled a splinter of wood from his left forearm. He slipped on his undershirt then pulled on his uniform pants and shirt. In the bathroom, he yanked his boots out of the toilet bowl.

"I'm going to kill her," he muttered, turning the boots over and watching the water pour out. The minion could no more be a secret agent than a menace to society.

Seated on the bed, Wulf put on his socks. The one she'd stuffed in his mouth was soggy. The boots squeaked as he pulled into them. On his way out of the room, Wulf mulled over his move from Los Angeles. *Only a woman.* He cursed his luck.

The second he turned around, it seemed his luck may

have changed. About sixty yards away, Mary Jane was climbing out of a tiny window. He opened his mouth to curse, but the words lodged in his throat. A male, approximately six and a half feet tall, wearing overalls, pistol-whipped Mary Jane on the temple. Every nerve in his body set on fire.

"Get the fuck away from her!" Wulf shouted, sprinting at top speed.

The thin man tossed Mary Jane over his shoulder so quickly that her head bounced on the back of his leather vest. She lolled, unconscious, as he ran to a waiting truck. A Ford. *Beasley!*

Mary Jane was tossed into the bed of the truck, and the man hopped into the passenger seat. Just as the door closed, Wulf lunged himself toward the truck. But there was another huge man in the driver's seat. Wulf breathed in the putrid exhaust smoke as the truck skirted off, over the curb and into oncoming traffic.

"MJ!" he yelled, but she didn't get up. If they were in an accident, she'd be tossed from the back and killed.

Wulf backtracked toward Tobias's truck.

"Keys! Shit, I hot-wired it."

He bent down to look at the mess. Mary Jane or maybe her abductors had cut all the wires. The colorful coiled wires were spaghetti heaped on the floor.

"Sir?" The soft voice made Wulf glare. "If you, um, come with me, we can save Mary Jane."

Wulf eyed the attendant. "Magic boy?"

"Uh, Glenn. Just come with me. *All right*?"

Wulf stood up, slammed the door, and they ran toward a souped-up Grand National. Instead of wondering why Glenn drove such a muscle car, Wulf hopped in the passenger seat.

His body jerked forward as Glenn slammed on the gas, going into reverse. Then his body went backward, the seat belt barely holding him as Glenn began to drive. Jet fast.

"Where the hell did you learn how to drive?" Wulf felt inches away from puking as they tore down the highway.

"Grand Theft Auto." Glenn smiled. "I beat *all* of the games."

Wulf nodded. His mouth tensed, considering a strategy to get her back. If Mary Jane's abductors took her to The Petting Zoo, there would be more men for him to fight in order to save her life.

Save her life. Damn! Isn't this like déjà vu?

Mary Jane reminded him of another misguided young woman who got mixed up in a bad world.

The other girl died.

He noticed the F-250 about a block ahead. "There they are. Slow down."

"Why?" Glenn turned to him again.

Instead of telling Glenn to keep his eye on the road, he said, "Mary Jane is in the bed of the truck. Those guys are ruthless. No matter how fast you can drive, if they see us following, they'll drive *crazy*."

12

In a cream suit and Italian loafers, Beasley walked down the hall between marble statues of Greek goddesses. He stopped in front of the door to his meeting room. A maid in a white-and-gray uniform opened it. Beasley stepped in the yellow room, rimmed with white painted French windows.

A breath of fresh air, Diamond wore tights and a flowing blouse at the opposite end of a long marble table. He smiled at her with pride.

Yes, she was so fucking innocent. The Zoo loves her. Too bad she wouldn't retain that innocence when The Petting Zoo became her permanent home.

Sunlight streamed through the open shutters, playing off the flutes of vintage Dom Perignon set before thirty men. The men sat with their eyes glossed in fear—except for his trusted second, Jake. Jake's glass was empty. The rest of them sat there as if Diamond had topped off the champagne with gasoline. Diamond sat at the head of the table with the black tin box and the bottle of Dom. Noticing Beasley, she began to pour his drink.

"Give Jake a refill, w-won't you?" Beasley stopped talking as anxiety clawed at his lungs. He forced himself to breathe.

Concern brimmed Diamond's beautiful eyes.

So innocent. She cares about my pain, no matter how I treat her.

Beasley gripped the back of a chair placed at the middle of the table. His heavy breathing slowed as he thought about his benefactor. The man who owned Mary Jane had gifted the other women to him. And this operation was just the tip of the iceberg. The scientist had a knack for brainwashing folks. The most beautiful, Beasley bought and used until he consumed every ounce of their looks. Truth be told, he spent more on having his women trained than he made off of them.

He loved playing God and he was a god to Diamond and the others. They did his bidding. Mary Jane, well, he did not own her. Once her brain was totally erased, the scientist would give her a new identity. Beasley could only presume that Mary Jane would be more agreeable. He was unaware of exactly why the scientist had given him the girl, because the scientist had taught Lyle, Beasley's most trusted, to clear their brains within a month.

And when their brains were fully erased from the past, they got to the good part. The women were given a new identity, one that guaranteed allegiance. However, Mary Jane was more important than all the whores in The Petting Zoo put together. He had no idea why the mad scientist didn't do the deed himself.

Beasley continued toward his pet. Diamond hastened out of the head chair and Beasley claimed the seat. She placed the box in front of him and slowly opened it with delicate, manicured hands.

"I'm sure you're wondering why we're celebrating, since

Mary Jane has gotten away." Beasley tried not to become riled. His doctor advised against it. "Whose idea was it to place her name in the local news?"

No one spoke up.

Beasley looked to Diamond as she stood next to his chair. "You're dismissed, Diamond. Now, you need to head to The Petting Zoo." He nodded toward the man to the left. "Gus, escort her."

Catching the slight roll of her eyes as she walked away, he pressed the timer on his Armani watch. His hand slipped inside the black box and onto the trigger of the forty-five-caliber gun. He pulled it out and shot.

The hydro-bullet rippled through the back of Diamond's silk blouse.

The force propelled her forward.

Her body slid across the marble floor, leaving a bloodied trail.

He smiled, having always loved the effect of hydro-shock bullets. Such a magnificent slug made an entry wound smaller than a marble and an exit wound larger than a grapefruit. He knew those precious breasts were all but blown to smithereens. *Oh, well.*

The time continued to click on his watch as he fed off the fear in his goons' eyes. With a grunt, Beasley stood, side-stepping the smeared blood. His soulless eyes glared at the lifeless body.

Five maids hurried in, three of whom got bloodstains on their uniform dresses as they hefted the body and carted it away. He glanced at the other two, who knowingly came in, toting buckets of warm, soapy water. They knelt on the floor and cleaned the marble. A flurry of pink suds mixed into the bucket as the maids rinsed their sponges and finished cleaning up the red, goopy mess. Their pace reminded him of a NASCAR pit crew.

When the process ended, Beasley pressed the stop button on his watch. "See how effortlessly that little bitch has been disposed of? Yet, seven dead bodies made it in the news! This process took one minute, thirty seconds. Seven dead bodies." He calculated the number. "Ten minutes, thirty seconds. That's the time it should've taken for the other trash to be disposed of!"

His hand went to his chest. Two men hastened out of his way in the expensive leather, rollaway chairs, giving him room to lean against the Cherrywood table.

"Local only, sir," one of the men spoke up as the wrenching in his heart decreased.

Fire overtook his eyes as he looked around. "Who said that?"

"I did." Jake stood up.

Beasley's eyes narrowed, and he stood up straight. Jake had always been his right-hand man. He didn't want to think about having to murder and replace him.

He mentally recited his ten favorite brews of beer like his doctor had instructed. By the time he got to one, Beasley had had a moment to collect his thoughts. "Hmmm. You're correct. Mary Jane's 'victims' only made it on the local news."

Though Beasley didn't want to think the worst of the man who kept his whole operation in check, he had to ask. "Jake, did you allow this to happen?"

"Nah, sir. I'm only mentioning that those deaths appeared on the local news. People don't talk. I reckon you'd rather it not have happened. It's impossible to erase the broadcast, but don't go having a heart attack over it."

Thick silence ensued.

A minute later, the left side of Beasley's mouth curved upward. He walked toward Jake. Stopped behind the man's chair and slapped his wingman on the back. "Touché, my friend."

Beasley turned back to the quiet crowd of men with a genuine grin, as always impressed by Jake.

"As I've said, we observed how easy it is to clean up one dead body. Seven's not much more, but there are a lot of you, so I assumed you could handle it. Now, who's the one who allowed the news coverage?"

"I did." Lyle stood slowly, using a cane. "Th-the news reporter came while I was waiting for more men. I was the only one there, being fixed up in the back of an ambulance. The EMTs begged to take me to the hospital, bu-but I waited for more men like your protocol calls far. You had left. Jake had to round up the girls for the night. There wasn't enough time to clean up all them bodies *outside* of the church."

Beasley nodded, mulling over his words.

Lyle's sunburned face brightened. He pointed to his leg. "The doctor said, if the shot was an inch—"

Beasley raised a hand, putting an end to Lyle's ramblings. He went to the head of the table and sipped from his glass of champagne. Lyle sat slowly. On cue, everyone else drank, believing he was satisfied with Lyle's excuse. He poured another glass. The bubbly stopped half-way. Beasley slammed the bottom of the empty bottle on the edge of the table. It sent shards across the marble tabletop and floor. Tight-fisting the neck of the bottle, Beasley watched as maids again entered with brooms and dustpans. He'd trained the maids well, but the men had yet to learn.

Lyle began to sob on key.

Beasley walked past the maids, his alligator shoes crunching over fragments of glass.

"I-I-I fucked up, Beasley," Lyle blubbered.

Snot ran down Lyle's mustache and crusted mouth as he begged for forgiveness. Beasley sighed, stopping behind Lyle, tuning out his pleading, crying, and sniffling.

"The anticipation of death is growing, ain't it?" Beasley began. Lyle immediately closed his mouth, whimpering in silence. Beasley continued with a mere monologue of ideas. "I suppose if I had a choice, I'd rather know when and how I was going to die. Lyle, my friend, I present you with that gift."

On Beasley's signal, the two men sitting on either side of Lyle held his arms down. He rammed the jagged edge of the broken champagne bottle into Lyle's neck, twisting it and turning it, tuning out the shrill, gurgling cry coming from Lyle's mouth as he wriggled in his seat.

Blood spurted on the table, Beasley's hands, and ruined the arms of his suit and cufflinks. The warm, sticky wetness gushed on Beasley as he worked the bottle tip deeper into Lyle's neck. Lyle's screaming dimmed. The two men let go of his noodle arms. Beasley, in a state of total euphoria, didn't notice.

Finally, feeling a prickle on his knuckles from a shaving of glass, Beasley took the bottle from Lyle's neck. The man instantly slumped forward in his seat.

Lyle's skin had been pulled through a human meat grinder.

Blood dripped from Beasley's hands as he watched the maids re-enter. He recalled each of their startled appearances on their first day of work for him. The money they received trumped their disgust, and more importantly, their fear. Now, they poured the contents of the broken glass into a nearby trashcan and again scurried around with buckets of sudsy water. A few hauled out Lyle's body. Their swift movement—how remarkable.

The Rottweilers would eat well today.

Beasley touched one of the women's shoulders as she began cleaning the leather chair.

"Just toss it," he said with a smile. "Order a new one and tell Diamond, uh...tell Sugarland to get dressed. She needs to work the prime shift at The Petting Zoo tonight."

The maid nodded and bustled toward the door.

Beasley began to loosen his cufflinks. "What are we going to do about Mary Jane?"

"Wyatt and Cody left a text while you were dealing with Lyle." Jake glared at the seat being carted away. "*They have her.*"

13

FOAM FROM TURQUOISE WATERS RECEDED OUT TO SEA BEFORE *rushing to shore again. Anya laughed as the salty water swished around her legs. She wore a bikini with a colorful ankle-length skirt that was drenched with salt water. Her feet were caked with sand and the gold ankle bracelet around her leg stuck to her skin. She picked up the length of her olive-green skirt and moved away from the water.*

The setting sun trailed the waters and sent a glint in Trent's gray eyes as the handsome biracial man handed her a fruity drink with a cute, little umbrella.

"No, thank you," Anya said.

Trent's lips curved into a devilish smile. "You don't trust me?"

"You can regain my trust." Her full lips turned into a wide grin.

"C'mon, Anya." Anger flashed in his eyes but, just as quickly as the waves coasted, his angular face softened. Anya was overcome by his movie-star good looks as he said, "There are no extradition laws here, Anya. You can't take me back, sweetheart."

"True. But I also can't be intoxicated while attempting to escort you back to America. I had high hopes that you'd come

willingly." She hid the flustered feeling that always consumed her as his hands trailed up her bare arm to the nape of her neck.

Slowly, he pulled her into him. "Remember those sprints we would go on? I would always let you win."

"Oh, you let me win under the guise that you couldn't keep your eyes off my ass." She tried to be nostalgic but worry still consumed her.

He pawed at that ass. "Yes, beautiful. I always let you win."

Trent's lips claimed hers with a kiss so familiar he made her forget that they were on a tourist island with families and lovers surrounding them. All of the training, all of the ranting she'd done to her superiors to bring Trent Winehouse back to America —unharmed, because she loved him—every thought faded away as she was kissed for the first time in ages. Thinking of Trent, thinking of the bad man before her, overcoming her, Anya pulled away.

"Damn it, Randolph!"

"Damn, Trent, you only use my last name when pissed." Anya smiled. Instantly, the smile fizzled. This wasn't really a laughing matter. "I guess, since we're on formalities, allow me to tell you how things are going to proceed."

"No." Trent turned away from her.

The rogue federal agent trudged through the sand toward the beachfront hotel, leaving her to watch the soft curls at the nape of his neck and his ruggedly strong shoulders as he walked away.

Her head tilted somewhat, but Trent didn't stop walking. She called after him, "I can help you clear your name, Trent!"

"No, thank you, Randolph," he tossed over his shoulder.

She winced. His use of her surname twice indicated that he was livid. A slight breeze flowed through her wavy hair as she watched him pass through exotic plants and onto an open balcony.

Licking the kiss off her lips, she reminded herself of the vows she'd made to the Agency, and to herself, as she followed. *Vibrant colored toucans chirped in the palm trees as she passed. She stepped up onto the balcony. Sheer curtains swayed in the wind. Cautiously, she peered through them.*

She wasn't dressed properly to conceal a gun. Wouldn't think of it. She'd bring Trent in willingly. Her ex-partner deserved as much respect, especially since he had been her best friend in college. So many hours of strip poker while they studied, and he prompted her toward grades that the FBI would surely be interested in. And then they'd been sought after by the Agency. She'd known he'd get in, yet they'd wanted her too.

After years of secret missions, something had changed. The years were sweet to them, romantically. However, she'd felt a pull, a slight tug, an ebb, before the Agency indicated Trent Winehouse had gone rogue. They wanted her allegiance, which she'd spent ten years proving.

The day he disappeared, her heart had stopped beating. Anya had agreed to take down the man she loved, if only to talk some sense into him or to see if he was being coerced. Today, three years later, she'd found him. Fortunately, she could breathe again. Her heart began to beat once more. Now, all she needed to do was set her heart on autopilot, bring him in, and...hope for the best.

Only her breath slowed as she slipped through the sliding glass door and into an ultra-luxurious living area with plush, white couches and silver accents.

Shoulders tensed, she jumped as he called, "I'm in here."

Slowly, she stepped inside. The air in her lungs expelled.

On the center of the king-size bed, amongst the feather duvet and plush pillows, Trent lay. His tanned body etched with muscles. So beautiful.

"How am I going to take you in like this?" she murmured.

"Come again?" Trent asked, eyebrow cocked, ever so sexy. "Come as many times as you like."

She took a step back and averted her eyes away from the tent in his pants. Every angle of his thick, fat cock was engrained in her memory. And she'd be damned if sex would weaken her resolve. Trent had fucked her over. Anya's heart was stitched up tight and would stay that way.

"Tell me why you went rogue, Trent," Anya begged. "I have to know. We were working the diamond heist and you...did you betray me for money? Money?"

He climbed out of bed as tears streamed down her cheeks. He stood in front of her. She felt the warmth and remembered the feeling, even before his calloused thumb touched her cheek. Trent caressed the tears, not allowing one drop to fall onto the floor.

"I love you, Anya Randolph," he whispered into the top of her hair as he inhaled her.

Even though she wouldn't say it, they both knew just how much she loved him.

She loved him more than he could ever love her.

***

Mary Jane's body went airborne from the bed of the F-250 before slamming back down. She rolled over and looked out the back of the truck. She reached out her hand. She could've sworn she ...no, it wasn't Trent, the man she'd imagined twice now: one on a run through the forest, and the other just now. It wasn't him, but the *snake*. Wulf! Either she was hallucinating, or the uptight cop sat in the passenger seat with Glenn.

Her head snapped forward as her body continued to jerk inside of the black frame. She turned around to see two creepy rednecks inside. The driver had incredibly large shoulders. The passengers were comparatively minuscule. She looked to the left and her eyes damn near popped out of their sockets.

A train.

Physics implied that they would not make it.

I'm not even in a seat belt. At least I'll die knowing who I am.

I am Anya Randolph, aka Mary Jane.

I am a secret agent.

***

Toggling with the stick shift, Glenn's skater shoe slammed on the brake. The Grand National skidded on the unpaved road. The rear of the car lifted in the air as it came to a halt, so close to the passing train that tiny bits of gravel ping-ponged against the hood of the car. The back tires slammed back down on the pavement.

"*What the fuck, Glenn! Drive!*" Wulf commanded, his body finally settling back in the seat as burnt rubber swished in the dust around them.

"W-we wouldn't have made it," Glenn said, gripping the steering wheel.

"They made it. We could have too!" Wulf stopped ranting, knowing they would have been flesh and confetti if Glenn had pushed it to the limit. Quincy's goading permeated his brain, warning Wulf that he'd gotten too close with another woman.

Glenn stuttered, "I-I think I know them."

Wulf was already in too deep. Dammit, he cared about her. He'd save her, and maybe take her over his knee before he had her body again. He gritted out. "You *think?*"

"I'm positive! They live on the same street as my ex." Glenn seemed confident, but then stuttered, "We c-c-can t-t-try their place first, that's if-if they took her home instead of to Beasley's."

"Then get us there before they kill her!" Wulf didn't even want to consider the firepower he'd have to deal with in going to Beasley's home.

Each lost in their own thoughts, they watched the dust

settle around them. Wulf couldn't breathe. Not with the sheer horror in Mary Jane's eyes that haunted him. She looked petrified. *She reached a hand out to me!*

Just as the truck passed, it was whisked out of sight by the train. He was numb to the train's blaring horn. The image of Mary Jane dashed before his eyes. He prayed her "dumb luck" would continue.

"We *have* to save her." Wulf tracked the train cars as far as the eye could see. He slammed his hand onto the dashboard. "They're headed into Santo Cruces City. If they get to Beasley first, I'm going to have a shitload of men to fight! I don't even have a fucking gun."

"I-I-I'm," Glenn sputtered, visibly shaken. The booming of Wulf's voice and the powerful train jarred his heart. "I'm sorry."

"It's too damn late for apologies," Wulf retorted, glaring at the red blinking lights as the last car of the train finally passed. "*Now, drive!*"

Glenn moved over the train tracks nice and slow as he revved the engine, then the muscle car darted along the paved road.

14

MARY JANE HEARD THE SOUND OF WYATT AND CODY'S BOOTS trudging through sand. She'd awoken when the truck came to a jolting stop. With not much time to react, she peered through hooded lenses, hoping they thought she was asleep. The hairy giants' faces looked just alike, but their bodies were the before-and-after pictures of a long stint at the gym. Wyatt had tons of jagged muscles, Cody did not. She knew who was which as they'd argued with each other when speeding away from the motel and apparently nobody had told these idiots not to use code names while abducting someone.

Wyatt whistled.

"Wyatt, I don't know about this," Cody stammered. He rubbed the sweat that ran down the furry skin of his neck. "Mary Jane looks damn near dead if'n you ask me."

"I didn't ask you!" Wyatt seemed older, or at least his bulky frame allowed him to call the shots. He leaned his hand over the rail and touched Mary Jane's bloodied temple. She forced herself not to tense. Her caramel skin had lost its glow. Her hair was matted with dried blood and she'd taken a hit to the head from when they went over the tracks.

His hand trailed down her soft neck, and he pulled up the large diner shirt and licked his lips. "Well, she ain't dead, still warm. C'mon, let's have fun with her while she's out. We can tell Beasley the cop kept tryna get her, so it took a while. Help me heft her out, and you can have a few minutes with her too."

Cody grabbed her legs as Wyatt grabbed under her arms. They carried her, careful of the upturned planks on the porch, and entered a dark, dusty house. Mary Jane bit her lip as Wyatt abruptly dropped her on the low, matted couch in the living room. He knelt on the floor in front of her seemingly unconscious body.

She mentally calculated that his face was perched just over hers as he argued, "Go on, bro. Uh, call your fat ass ol' lady and check in like you usually do while I have a little fun. It only takes you a minute or two anyway."

"Don't call my girl fat!" Cody frowned. Catching the anger in Wyatt's squared shoulders, he backed away.

From Mary Jane's peripheral vision, she peered through her eyelashes and saw him pull the Swiss Army knife out of his utility belt. She tapered her breathing, waiting for him to place the knife down in order to have a better chance at self-defense. He slit the collar of her shirt down the "Diner 24/7" words, and then tossed the blade onto the coffee table. It clattered and landed between empty beer bottles.

"Mmmm." Wyatt rubbed her lace bra. His large hands couldn't grab enough of her soft skin. His clammy hands trembled as they glided down her waist and she forced herself to wait for the perfect time. Breathing heavily, he popped the button of her jeans. Hastily, he bunched his pants and boxers around his ankles, too lazy to fully

undress. Bingo, with his pants down, she'd have some lever-
age. As Wyatt leaned in to kiss her, Mary Jane reared back
and busted the creep in the nose with her forehead.

Wyatt's vision instantly blurred. Shrieking, he fell back
on the coffee table. It caved in as he tried to get up, but his
bunched jeans made it difficult for him to move. To his
horror, he grimaced as Mary Jane leaned down before him.

She grabbed the knife from the floor and wrapped her
fingers firmly around his limp penis. He shrieked as she
rammed the knife into the base of his scrotum.

"*No, no!*"

"Oh, yes," Mary Jane affirmed. Lips taut, she swiveled
the knife, and the rubbery dick disconnected from Wyatt's
body just as Cody came running into the room.

"Are you crazy?" Cody screeched. She could barely hear
him above Wyatt's scream of agony.

In one swift movement, Mary Jane tossed the rubbery
stick at Cody's face. Wyatt screamed like a scalded cat,
holding his private area, blood spurting. He choked on the
blood coming from his nose, and the ear-shattering screech
transformed into gurgling coughs.

I am Anya Randolph!

She jumped over the table and jabbed at Cody's mouth.

Finally, sucked out of the traumatizing moment, the
lanky man ducked. Cody attempted to connect his elbow
with her ribs. She moved to the side. In the tight confines of
the small living room, she couldn't power-kick him. Pain
prickled through her knuckles as she connected with
Cody's pointy, strong jaw. His head snapped back at the very
moment the front door burst open. Cody froze. Mary Jane
rammed his frail body into the wall. Her forearm slammed
against his chin, this time forcing it in the opposite direction of her other hand, holding his temple. His neck

cracked, and a second later his dead body slid to the floor. She did an about-face in a nanosecond. Fingertips poised on the knife base, she was ready to throw it toward the intruder.

Every fiber in her body heightened to the max as sunlight streamed into the darkened living room. Wrist cocked, she peered through the bright glare of sunlight. All the air in her chest exploded.

Mary Jane dropped the knife, and it clattered to the hardwood floor. Her hands went to her hips. Wulf stood there, his gaze sparkling with relief. Glenn stopped just at his side, gawking at her.

"Glenn, take your eyes off my bra or I'll kill you."

"Oh, I . . ." He glanced down.

She glanced at the liar and turned away. Taking in the small home with the long hallway, she went into the bathroom first. The sink was riddled with old hair shavings and mucked to the rim with dirt. She grimaced as she touched the knob to rinse the blood off her hands, then she walked back into the hall and headed to the next door, which led into a tiny bedroom. Going to a dresser, checkered with missing drawers, she rummaged through the first one and grabbed a wife beater. It must have belonged to the skinnier one, because it went taut against her chest and abs as she pulled it on.

Back in the living room, she greeted Glenn with a back pat as he stood frozen, gazing at the crime scene. "You all right, Glenn?"

"I . . ." he stuttered, face a greenish hue. Glenn started running down the hall, holding a hand over his mouth.

"The bathroom is the second on the right," she called after him. Shaking her head, she glared at Wulf's chuckle. "What?"

"What do you mean *what*? We crossed three hick towns to save you!"

"Save me?" she asked, arms wide. She looked around at the creepy twins. "I think I've done an impeccable job, if I do say so myself."

Wulf's eyes warmed to a comforting chocolate brown as his hand went to the dried blood on her temple. He seemed worried, but she had no time for men in her life. Trent Winehouse had taught her to put work first. It was just a shame that she fucked Officer Dylan Wulf before she recalled who she was and how all men are the same— varying levels of the same "no good."

"Not too fast." Mary Jane sidestepped his gentle touch. She did her best not to look into his seemingly sincere gaze. Coupled with that accent, it reminded her of submerging into the ocean on a sunny day. This wasn't the time for a tropical vacation, and that's all Wulf meant to her. He was just a sexy momentary reprieve from life. "Wulf, I hope you haven't forgotten how we ended off hours ago. The sex from last night saved your life, by the way. You're still on my shit-list."

He didn't budge. So maybe she couldn't hate Wulf for the stunt he pulled this morning—he hadn't screwed her over like Trent. She hadn't known Wulf nearly as long, and she had no intention of repeating history. Mary Jane rubbed a hand along her kinky, tangled tresses. She had to wonder how long she'd felt so alone in the world before allowing her heart to numb its way back to normal. Now, she shoved those thoughts away for a more pertinent situation. "Wulf, I have a mission to concentrate on."

"A mission?" His eyes narrowed. "Do you know it's luck and Glenn that got us here? You need to be grateful that they didn't take you to Beasley's." He stopped arguing. She didn't appear to be listening. "What are you thinking, Mary Jane?"

"Look, you and Glenn went out of your way. Thanks. But my name isn't Mary Jane." She turned away from him, bent down to Wyatt, and checked his pulse. Dead. She walked to Cody. This entire scenario seemed a little too surreal for her, so she checked his gnarled, twisted neck. Dead.

"What's your aim, MJ?"

She stood up and stepped before the dominating man, bypassed all those muscles that held her close and safe last night. Her eyes locked onto his. "My mission is to apprehend the Asia prototype. I won't cease until I've completed it."

"Mary—"

"*Not* Mary Jane!"

"Hey, guys." Glenn pulled the wash cloth from his face. "Can we argue about this somewhere...*there ain't dead bodies*?"

She watched as he stopped before the doorframe, afraid of Cody's body leaning against the wall, less than a foot away. Smiling, she went to Glenn, took his hands, and told him to close his eyes. She walked him out of the front door with Wulf in tow.

"Thanks." Glenn gave a wan grin as she let him go. They hustled down the steps.

Mary Jane stepped toward the Grand National. Whistling, she sauntered around the muscle car. "Wow, is this yours, Glenn?"

"Yeah." He nodded, cracking a genuine grin.

"Nice!" She clapped her hands together, heart warmed at how Glenn set aside his nerves to help save her. "Okay. You guys, get out of here. I'm heading to The Petting Zoo."

"The place you used to strip?" The setting sun made Glenn's red cheeks more obvious.

"I did *not* strip there." Mary Jane felt Wulf staring at her, but she addressed Glenn. "Tell me all that you know about Beasley and the club. I'm going to go kill Beasley and apprehend the Asia prototype."

"No, you won't. Not by yourself." Glenn shook his head. "It'll be dark soon. Do you know how many men Beasley has? How many guys visit the strip club? That they'd do anything for him?"

"That's what you're going to tell me."

"All right, Mary Jane," Wulf growled. "Enough with the story. The two of us are headed to L.A!" he bellowed, standing in her line of vision. As thick and tall as his frame was, he stole the blaring sun from her gaze.

Mary Jane held her chin high. "I *am* going to The Petting Zoo."

Glenn added, "You would have better luck sneaking into his house, waiting for him to come home."

Her brows crinkled at Glenn's advice. "How do you know this?"

Glenn sighed, "Beasley ruins women. Once a female works for Beasley, it's usually the end of her. She starts at the mansion, if she's pretty enough. Beasley flaunts her around for a while, getting all the men hot and bothered. It's his way of advertising for his club. She eventually has her reign at The Petting Zoo as the night's star attraction for a while. When they've grown tired of her, or he has new girls, she disappears or becomes a prostitute."

"How do you know this?" Wulf asked.

"I've lived in the area my entire life. My family owns the motel where lots of the prostitutes do business," he said hesitantly. "I keep my eyes open."

"Keep going," Mary Jane interjected. "Can you tell me more about the women?" she asked, having remembered her wish to return and save them as well.

"They're crazy. And these girls are loyal to Beasley. Ridiculously loyal. Jake drops them off at the motel—"

"Jake?" Mary Jane asked. She held in her newfound hatred of him.

"Yes, the creepy buff guy." Glenn squirmed in disgust. "Jake drops the girls off in the neighboring towns—the ones who haven't disappeared yet. They like the rooms at the motel because we keep 'em clean."

"Tell me more about Beasley," she redirected.

"Okay, to take out a man like Beasley, it would be best that you wait until he finished checking on The Petting Zoo and goes home drunk. Most of his men stay at the club to keep the girls in line."

"All right, that's what I'll do." Mary Jane nodded.

"Glenn, no more humoring her," Wulf barked.

Mary Jane got ready to move, but Wulf's hands went to her slim waist. Her legs dangled as he pulled her up to his level. "There is no such thing as an Asia prototype, MJ. You aren't a secret agent. And you're listening to Glenn, who you've only known for twenty-four hours. I was literally waiting for you to question him during half of his story, you did not."

"I don't report to you, Wulf. And I don't know you either." She pressed at his chest trying to get him to let her go.

"Well, I'm learning about you, Mary Jane. And I plan to stick around until I do."

Her arms squirmed around, and she tried to grab his thick neck, but he held her just out of reach. "Put me down!"

"It's not safe. You're severely concussed. You were in two

car accidents yesterday! And then you go and get tossed around by those twins in their truck. You're delusional."

"I can prove it," she stressed.

When her eyes began to plead with him, Wulf growled. "How?"

"I have a contact. A phone number to call during shit-storms like this."

Wulf slowly lowered her.

Mary Jane's hands dug into her tight jeans pocket. There was nothing there. "Dammit, I left the paper at the motel. Remember, Glenn? When I came inside this morning, needing to use the phone?"

"I remember," Glenn mumbled as Wulf's smoldering glower intimidated him.

"Mary Jane," Wulf began, "it's illogical for you to have something signifying that you're working a case while undercover."

"*Dammit*, Wulf. My name is Anya Randolph! Why can't you believe me?"

Her voice quivered as she made her appeal, and she tried with all of her might to believe it too. Mary Jane took a deep breath, no longer wanting to accept that she couldn't trust herself as she once did when Jake saved her from Beasley. "You come out here to risk yourself to save me, but you refuse to consider what I have to say?"

"*Gracie, just stop it!*" Wulf's voice boomed so loud she jumped. Everyone was stunned silent for a moment. Even the big officer hung his head low, rubbing a hand at the back of his neck.

"Wulf, who's Gracie?" Mary Jane's light brown orbs darkened as she studied his shuttered expression. She knew the look...she'd seen it in her own reflection. "Wulf, please, who is Gracie?"

Wulf's chest puffed in and out as he breathed. "It doesn't matter."

Mary Jane ignored the stinging in her eyes. "I told you everything I know about myself last night."

"She's nobody, MJ."

She wanted to know his story, but she could be just as stubborn. She wouldn't beg. It was bipolar as hell, but the secret agent was submerged in a dysfunctional-ass world. "Whatever, asshole. I've been real with you but you can't be real with me. Glenn, take us back to the motel so I can get my note. His sorry ass can fall off the edge of the earth for all I care."

"*My* sorry ass?" Wulf pointed a stiff finger to his chest.

Without a word, she opened the front passenger door and slid into the seat.

"All I do is try to keep her safe, and this is the thanks I get."

Mary Jane heard Wulf grumble through the open window and stiffened in her seat.

Glenn quickly came to her defense. "Well, you could try placing yourself in Anya's shoes—"

"*Glenn*, her name is not Anya. It's Mary Jane."

Mary Jane laid her head back against the headrest as she chewed on her lip.

"Does it hurt to give MJ the benefit of the doubt? All you have to do is wait 'til she calls the number," Glenn tried.

She continued chewing on her lip till she tasted blood. Why had she slept with the infuriating Dylan Wulf?

15

DYLAN HAD GROWN UP IN THE SYSTEM. WHEN HE WAS A toddler, his father left his mother in Samoa and took Dylan to the States. Ironically, his dad didn't really want a son but a buddy in crime. Dylan had always been as smart as he was a badass. When he was little, his father had him sneak through windows of homes. When he was around nine, he became the lookout.

Under his father's wing, Dylan learned more about sex, drugs, and illegal weapon sales than obtaining an education. When he was eleven, social services detained him. His father rotted in jail without so much as mentioning Dylan's mother's name or how to find her. For the first few years, Dylan was kicked out of foster home after foster home for his behavior.

He eventually met Brenda Miller. She, and his new foster sister, Shelly, did one thing everyone else was incapable of. The two chose not to give up on him, regardless of his faults. They forced him to hone in on his intelligence at school while redirecting his misbehavior at home. As an adolescent, Brenda kept him from the target of the LAPD until he attended the academy and completed a total three-sixty. Now Wulf had a position in the Gang Unit but the goal-oriented man wasn't finished there. He became the leading agent.

"Gracie was a kid," Wulf began looking off into the distance, "stuck with the wrong cards in life. She had a boyfriend in the Gunner Gang—"

"The Gunner Gang?" Glenn screeched. "I've seen a few documentaries about them in the past. They're putting the Bloods to shame."

"Yup, then you get the gist. But there's no such thing as monogamy in those types of Gangs, Glenn. She was foster, like I was. Only, she didn't have a good family—the system had given up on even offering her a *family*. She was in a group home facility." He stopped to let the guilt sink in again. Wulf knew he would've been in the same situation as Gracie, had Brenda not been his last placement.

The social worker had threatened a young Dylan on the way to Brenda's home. *"Dylan, if you screw up with Ms. Miller, I'm starting the paperwork for group home, and I know you know what that means. No cell phone, no calls, no sneaking out. And check this, I won't even be your social worker anymore. You'll get a group home social worker that doesn't give a damn about you either."*

"She was a misunderstood group home kid, where the county pays out of the ass just to keep kids that they deem the worst of the worst safe. The group home she stayed at was no better than juvie."

"Wow."

"She'd come to see me, feed me a little information about the gang, ask if I'd help get her boyfriend out of the gang."

"That doesn't sound promising." Glenn leaned against

the car, his demeanor just as anxious and worry-filled as he was when they chased after Mary Jane.

Wulf paused to look into the back seat but the woman who was just as courageous and bullheaded as Gracie didn't seem to be listening.

"Even less promising since her boyfriend was one of the main honchos and she was blinded by love. I offered her witness protection, to change her identity, send her somewhere so that she could have a better life, but Gracie kept saying she wanted to wait for that piece of crap to wise up." He bit at his bottom lip, recalling the intuition he'd had. Gracie had almost seemed ready to leave the life she led, to give it all up and start over.

Glenn sighed. "But the Gunners went to jail, right? Like a year ago?"

Wulf nodded. "A year ago, Gracie came up missing. But she left me a note. I guess she was just smart enough to leave all the details before going to her boyfriend and asking if he wanted to leave. She had it wrapped into her mind that I'd give him a deal, and that they'd be free together. That wasn't the case. Her note held names and locations and ties to a cartel organization that the Gunners worked for. About a week later, the streets were clean, and we found her body."

***

Mary Jane's eyebrows crinkled as newspapers and reports flooded her memory of the gang's fall less than a year ago. Wulf had been hailed as a hero. She knew more about Los Angeles than she initially thought. She wondered if she'd been there on assignment, perhaps.

She looked at Glenn who was visibly shaken after Gracie's story. The agent in her required a tough skin, but Mary Jane offered Glenn a wan smile as he opened his door and she tried to make eye contact with him when he got into the back seat. She needed to show sympathy. Wulf'd been frozen as ice as he told the story. Now, he didn't even glance in her direction.

Who was she kidding? Wulf is a savior cop who doesn't want to be bothered. She was on a mission. Though she couldn't quite insert herself in Anya Randolph's mind, Mary Jane felt that if she truly were the agent, a mission had to take precedence over everything. Even though Wulf's story compelled her to comfort him, Mary Jane gulped down that need.

"C'mon, Glenn. I need to return to the motel," she said, finally looking at the fireball of a desert sun off in the distance. She looked back into the rearview mirror at Wulf who finally looked at her. Her gaze held as much apology as she was capable of and something inside of Mary Jane told her that Wulf didn't do well with sorrow. "I need the phone number. I must report to the Agency about the Asia prototype." *That is if, there truly is an agency and I'm Anya Randolph.*

As Glenn drove, she wrapped her mind around the few precious memories she had as Anya. Something didn't click.

***

The meeting adjourned with no more dead bodies. Jake watched as the rest of his crew walked stiff-legged out of the room.

He turned to Beasley. "Wyatt and Cody haven't texted me back. I should go check on them." Jake's face was stone-cold with disinterest. At least, he hoped.

"Not necessary. I've anticipated as such. Those idiots probably tied her up for a good time before dropping her off," Beasley said, leaning back in the leather seat.

That's what I'm afraid of. That weak-ass officer couldn't keep her safe! "Shouldn't I—"

Beasley chuckled. "I have a surprise for them. They think they can touch my girl. I've told one of the maids to awaken Hurricane. Jake, you have more pertinent matters to attend to. Round up the girls for the night. It's about that time."

Jake hid his grimace as he walked out. Once Hurricane caught up with them, everybody was dead. The seven-foot-two cannibal, Hurricane, was the only man Jake feared—if he could be called a man. Before Mary Jane entered his life, Jake had never crossed Beasley. He could always kill when he was unable to be loyal, but Hurricane was a different story.

Did Mary Jane mean so much as to ruin the connections he'd made? Just as he began to ruminate over it, another thought popped into his head. A thought so consuming, Jake knew exactly who he'd choose.

In the courtyard of the mansion, Jake called out to Steward, the newest member. "Come with me."

Standing next to the red F-250 with three other guys, Steward pointed to himself and then looked around at the other hooligans in astonishment. "Me?"

"Yes!" Jake's hand went to the back of the guy's neck, and like a dog, he pulled him toward the trailer. The bus he'd used to help Mary Jane escape. He'd barely gotten Gus to agree to let her ride along while they went to fill up the tank.

Jake got into the driver's side, and Steward hopped into the passenger seat. While pulling past a Ferrari and out of the U-shaped driveway, Jake said, "Listen here, Stew, you're gonna get the girls ready for tonight and take them into the neighboring towns. They know what street or which motel they should be dropped off. Got that, Steward?"

"But Beasley doesn't let any of the new guys escort—"

"Steward," Jake's voice hardened, "I get it, you're afraid.

There's repercussions for you screwing over Beasley. Shit, I don't even want to finish thinking about it."

"Yeah...me neither."

"We've all gotta be afraid of something, Stew. So, I feel you on that. Keep your eyes open."

On key, Steward glanced out across the wilderness as if he expected the king of the jungle to come bulldozing toward them.

Jake turned the large wheel and the big bus lurched onto the highway. "Steward, fear Beasley all you want. He's almost at the top of the food chain. Right above him? *Me*."

"Okay."

"When we get to The Petting Zoo, the girls will be ready, like I said. You'll transport them in this bus to their destinations for the evening. Do not touch the girls."

Jake pressed on the brake at the stop sign. Usually, he wouldn't stop, but he felt the need to give the guy a hard stare when saying, "This is our little secret."

"Okay."

Jake gave him a reassuring smile. Although Steward's agreement did not matter; come morning, Jake would cover up what he'd done, and that meant a bullet to Steward's brain. When he gave a shaky smile in return, Jake pressed on the gas. He needed to save Mary Jane before Hurricane forgot to *keep her alive* prior to his order of returning her to Beasley.

Jake had to kill Hurricane. He gulped down the lump in his throat. It would be a hard night.

16

"WULF, THIS IS WHERE WE PART WAYS." MARY JANE LOOKED up at him as they stood in the staff room back at the motel where Glenn worked. During the long ride, she'd kept quiet, not saying a word to him, and he hadn't said a single thing to her. It was as if the night they'd shared occurred ages ago. But for her, there was a longing to make a connection.

Wulf glared down at her. "That's a negative. You and I are headed to Los Angeles where we will connect with a friend—"

"I don't need—"

"—who will look into this situation," his voice boomed, "then I will personally escort you to a safe rehabilitation center, where you'll forget these delusions of prototype China, and sometime later, not now, you'll thank me for getting you away."

She tugged away from his touch but it was no use. She bit her bottom lip hard to stave off the need to cry. How could he not trust her?

Wulf's stone face didn't move a twitch. "I'm helping you, Mary Jane. *One day*, you'll understand that."

Her hard glare turned wide-eyed at the sound of a click. The sparkle in her brown eyes disappeared as she looked down to see her left wrist in handcuffs, followed by her right.

"Take these off," Mary Jane ordered, jiggling her confined wrists. "I'm not under arrest!"

"Um, Wulf, that's not something I would do, if I were you." Glenn spoke so quietly that Wulf could barely hear him. "You did see how she murdered those twins."

Ignoring the warning, Wulf said, "I regret to inform you, Mary Jane, that you indeed are under arrest for assault on a police officer."

"Oh, I assaulted you! Well, I think we're even, Wulf." She struggled against his clutch.

"This entire town doesn't make sense, MJ. I'm doing what's best for you and taking you to a friend at the LAPD."

"Los Angeles has no jurisdiction in Santo Cruces City, *Arizona!*" Mary Jane tried to turn to Glenn for help, but Wulf had yanked the front door open. "Wait, wait. Can't I at least call that number to confirm if someone competent can prove who I am?"

"No," he growled. He gripped her bicep firmly.

"*Please*, Dylan." Her tone held a note of sincerity. They both knew she didn't use his first name but it sounded so good coming out of her mouth.

"Listen, I know your scrawny ass listened when I spoke about the foster kid Gracie," he said, his gaze connecting with her. "I didn't save her, Mary Jane. I'm saving you."

She bit her lip and murmured, "I think you did your best."

"I didn't. Before Gracie was even moved to group homes she was coming and snitching to me. She had this foster mom that didn't give a damn about her. They had cup-of-noodle soup and other crap for dinner all the time, and I even went to her social worker about it, but the worker didn't care. Asked me if I wanted to begin the process of caring for her."

Mary Jane's lips trembled into a slight smile. However, they both knew how the story ended. She whispered, "Wulf, you tried, I know you did."

"MJ, my meddling got her put into a group home. The more calls I made to the social worker had her, in return, contacting the foster mom; and then that damn lady lied on Gracie. Lied about Gracie trying to shock her. It was either me or a group home...I should've taken her in."

"We can't change the past," Mary Jane whimpered. "Please, please, you've gotta let me figure out who I am. I keep thinking that I'm Anya but . . . but the memories are too short, and almost like watching TV, not as if I'm invested in that life. So, Wulf, you have to let me know just who I am. It's the most important thing to me in this entire world. Help me."

Slowly, Wulf stepped back inside the lobby and decreased the pressure on her forearm. After a few more moments, he let her go.

"Thanks," she said.

He looked away from her innocent gaze. Rubbing the back of his neck, Wulf nodded. He went to the continental breakfast stand and grabbed a package of instant coffee.

"Wulf, please take these off so I can make the call?" Mary Jane asked.

"No," he replied, pouring the contents into a Styrofoam cup. At the sound of her deep sigh, he picked up the electric hot-water carafe.

Knowing that Wulf had caved just about as much as a stubborn man like him was willing to, Mary Jane let it go.

With her wrists still confined, she found the piece of paper and Glenn went to grab the wireless phone from the lobby. She scanned the phone number and huffed. "No, this can't be right."

"What's wrong?" Wulf asked.

The relief on his face made her want to cram the paper down his throat. But she gave an infuriating grumble instead. "There are only *six* numbers!"

"All right, let's go."

Mary Jane yanked her clasped wrists closer to her abdomen. "No, Wulf. You just want to illegally force me into rehab! I'm not...." A lump formed in her throat and her voice decreased an octave. "I am *not* a drug addict. If you'd just believe me...we...we had something last night, so I just don't understand why you'd do this!"

"I'm saving you, MJ," Wulf's voice slammed into her chest. She could tell his patience was winding down to zero. "We are getting the fuck out of Arizona. My old partner, Jones, is going to look into this mess. We will collaborate with the proper authorities regarding the SCPD."

Mary Jane stopped speaking.

"Glenn." Wulf's eyes stopped on him, and Glenn stood to attention. "Thank you for the use of your car. You've been an invaluable asset. I will be confiscating your Grand National, but I will have it sent back to you once we are in Los Angeles."

Glenn's bottom lip dropped. "No – no, you can't take my car!"

"I can, and I am. Police business."

"But, well..." Glenn began, disregarding Wulf squirming around to keep Mary Jane in check. "My mom's car is in the lot. She never leaves, and she drives a Honda Accord."

"Okay, harder to spot car, less gas," Wulf agreed.

"This is ridiculous," Mary Jane cut in. "There have to be roadblocks in every direction, and our mug shots will be all over the place."

"I'll think of something," Wulf said.

***

The heat faded as the sun disappeared over the horizon. The sky transitioned from lilac to a deep indigo as Mary Jane stretched her legs in the back seat of the Honda Accord. They'd been driving for about thirty minutes, and she'd felt Wulf's gaze off and on. Her lips curved into a genuine smile as she remembered last night.

"Dylan, can't I sit in the front seat with you?"

His eyes sparkled. "I detect a hint of manipulation. You use my first name for self-gain."

Her eyes shaded slightly. She winked and in a seductive voice said, "C'mon, you love it when I say your first name. Let me out of these cuffs, and I'll hum it like I did last night."

"No, thanks." He glanced through the rearview mirror, back at the road, and then at her again. The way her pink tongue slowly came out and licked her lips chipped at his rigid demeanor. "MJ, I'll never forget you screaming out '*Oh, Wulf*' all night long. That's priceless. After we figure everything out, you and I can celebrate."

Yeah, right, you already think I'm crazy.

"Hmmm, I didn't say it like that, I said it like this..." She said his name in a sultry voice.

His dark eyes melted her insides through the mirror. Every part of her body tingled with a primitive craving. Her initial plan was to play nice, then disappear at one of the truck stops along the way. She had to return to Santo Cruces City and put the pieces of the puzzle together. For her sanity.

"Can't L.A. wait, *Dylan*?" She extended his name in a lengthy whisper. "It's a very long ride."

He continued to glance through the rearview mirror. Mary Jane unbuckled her seat belt. Who was she kidding, this one last fuck would hit it out of the ballpark for the two of them. Then she'd leave him before he could 'save her' and send her on her way.

His deep voice seemed to be weakening with desire by the second. "MJ, your safety is important, please put—"

Bam!

The car had been T-boned from the passenger side. The impact sent them flipping over and over.

17

THE TIRES LEFT RUBBER MARKS ON THE ASPHALT. JAKE slammed the door to his Camaro and stepped onto the curb at the crappy motel. It had taken *hours* to get Cody and Wyatt's neighbors to talk.

Still in a state of unrest, he wondered if Hurricane had caught up with Mary Jane yet. Jake pulled the cap lower over his face. It wouldn't do for Steward to see him since the girls should be moonlighting in the area already. Just before he gripped the door to the lobby, his cell phone went off.

The tune was different.

Only one person had this tune.

Intuition told him to just fuck it, not answer. But this was the boss of all bosses. "Hello," Jake gritted out.

"How is my pet?" the scientist asked in a calm voice.

Call Mary Jane your pet again and I'll take my sawed-off shotgun, press it into your motherfucking mouth, and watch your brains spray. "Good."

"You hesitated, Jake. When I hire a person and that person proves incompetent, they are expired," he said, tone never fluctuating. "Then another man is vetted and more is expected of him. You are that other man, Jake."

"She is fine," Jake growled.

Finally, a soft chuckle came through the line. "Good. Always recall who you work for. Beasley is replaceable. Everyone is replaceable, except for my...what's that silly name she was given again? I would've never thought to call her—"

Jake cut him off, "I have business to attend to, sir. Beasley is doing his job. Your woman is safe."

"Good."

The call disconnected. He hated men like his boss. Richer than Satan, they thought they were always one step ahead. Jake was a gift from the scientist to Beasley. At least, that's how the fat man saw it. His boss didn't trust anyone, and Jake reported back to his boss. However, this was the first time in years that Jake hadn't been honest.

Glenn was gulping a can of Pepsi. Noticing Jake, he choked on soda bubbles. Jake leaned over the table and patted him rather roughly as Glenn continued to cough. After a few more seconds, Jake had to repeatedly remind himself not to kill this one.

"Are you all right?" he asked in a condescending tone, whacking Glenn's back once more.

"I – *ouch*!" Glenn coughed. "Just don't help me. That hurts."

"Where's Mary Jane?"

"My dad's at the house. If you want some mary-juana, you know where to get it."

"Don't fuck with me, Glenn." Jake poked him in the chest. "You were with MJ today at Wyatt and Cody's place."

"Who?"

"The twins. Big guy, got his pecker sliced off. Little-big

guy, got his neck snapped. I was gonna beat the info out of you, but since you're helping Mary Jane, I will restrain myself. Where is she?"

"What's it to you if I'm helping her?"

Jake's eyes brightened as Glenn didn't back down. "I reckon you've grown a pair. Good for you, boy. There is a beast coming to eat—and I do mean *eat*—her. Nobody can stop him." Jake stepped closer and pulled out his gun. He aimed it at Glenn's nose, bugging the pimply schmoozer. "Where is she?"

"Beast? If anything, you're the beast!"

Jake tilted the gun slightly upward and popped off a round. White dust danced down from the ceiling. In a snap of a finger, Jake snaked a hand around Glenn's throat, and they commenced to familiar territory, with the skinny one shaking like a spindle. Jake yanked him so hard, Glenn almost fell over the counter. After a few moments of Glenn pulling at Jake's hands while he was being choked, Jake squeezed tighter. Still Glenn refused to talk. Letting up a little on the choking, Jake whispered, cold as ice, "You've heard the bedtime stories. I know that cunt who raised you got kicks out of scaring and telling you all about Hurricane."

Jake grinned as Glenn's eyes flickered with horror. Glenn's fingers shook as he tried to pry Jake's fingers from his neck. Once a bluish hue crept up his face, Jake stopped squeezing his neck, and instead pushed him back.

Glenn said not a word as he massaged the reddened skin on his throat. Stiff and thin-framed, his chest rose and fell, yet he refused to speak.

Sighing heavily, Jake noticed the flicker of manliness in Glenn's eyes. "Glenn, I'm going to *save* Mary Jane. I don't have much time."

"Why?" he snapped. "You don't care about anyone but yourself."

This very question had Jake speechless. That three-letter word, *"Why"* had been his only thought for the past few weeks. It had started one day. For no reason he could come up with. If Mary Jane had truly belonged to Beasley, he probably would've put a bullet to her skull by now for her behavior. They both knew he couldn't hurt her, but Jake had saved her.

Jake just kept telling himself that the scientist owned her and he was being loyal by saving Mary Jane from Beasley. That fat fuck wanted to use her. But what was he fooling himself for? The doc had used her first, probably even the worst. And he remembered just how Mary Jane reminded him of his past. Before greed and lust consumed him. When it came to her, he just couldn't be loyal.

He had to screw over everyone for her. Protecting her was an innate craving. A driving force charged through his psyche on repeat.

Save Mary Jane.
Save Mary Jane.
Save Mary Jane.
Save Mary Jane.
Save Mary Jane.
Save Mary Jane.

It's like I'm going out of my fucking mind! I have to save her. And I have to let her go . . .

That part hurt. For a man who felt no pain, knowing that Mary Jane had to survive and live free, away from him, cut to his core.

"Why, Jake?" Glenn asked again. "Why would you help her?"

"Because I must!" Jake snapped, returning to the present.

That very question had roamed through his mind far too many times to count. Every woman in the entire world had one use. If they crossed him, and he wanted them, they served him one way or another. In life or in death, they served their purpose.

Not Mary Jane. She was different.

Jake was different the moment he laid eyes on her, because something in his brain had switched. *Why?* The thought consumed him momentarily, because in the next instance, a driving force moved him again.

Save Mary Jane.

Save Mary Jane.

18

THIRTY MINUTES AGO...

SPITTING BLOOD AND SAND FROM HER MOUTH, MARY JANE pushed her face up and away from the cool, desert sand. Turning over onto her back, she took in the spray of stars and a full moon and gave a weak groan.

With care, she sat up to see the Accord tilted on its driver's side about fifty yards away. Every time she blinked, the image of the car being T-boned and flipping like the world's deadliest rollercoaster flashed through her mind.

Slowly, she started to stand, but her legs wobbled. She needed to save Wulf. He had his seat belt on so he had to be unconscious, and maybe, trapped. Alive and confined, unable to get out, or else he would've saved *her*.

The deep gash in her calf made Mary Jane crumble down. Her eyes widened, locking on a figure heading toward the car. She glanced down at the ground before her. There was a trail leading away into the desert. She must've been taken out, dragged to safety. She sighed hoping the stranger was being cautious and now about to help Wulf.

Mary Jane looked back toward the man reaching into the car and thought to thank him for—

Pop. Pop.

She watched the tall, burly figure as orange firelight flashed in the dark. The bastard had just shot off a few rounds.

The ringing in her ears stopped.

All noises gone.

Mary Jane's fused lips ripped apart. "Nooooo!"

A sob crashed through her body as the man turned toward her. Even larger than the twins, he moved toward her like a grizzly bear to a mouse, the smaller creature catching his attention with little fascination, but enough to taunt the beast.

A beast so scary her throat constricted as he stooped down before her. The darkness shrouded his face in shadow for a moment, before her eyes adjusted to the shocking reality. There were masses of grooves and ridges in his skin.

"They call me Hurricane." His unnatural, steely voice sent a tremor of fear down the nape of her neck. His breath reeked of rot. The kind of smell that, once you breathed it in, there's no forgetting. His callused hands claimed Mary Jane's cheek, so rough and abrasive.

"I'd love," he began in an observatory manner, "to peel off this velvety skin, but my master wants you *alive*. But he told me once he's done with you, I'll have you all to myself."

His mouth opened wide displaying jagged, shark-like teeth. Hurricane's tongue snaked out of his mouth. She trembled in terror as his bumpy tongue burned from her chin to her high cheekbone.

Hurricane lifted her up from the ground and over his shoulder. She jerked her arms and legs in one last attempt to get away, but it was no use. In her upside-down line of vision, Hurricane took her farther and farther away from the man who should have been her hero.

Her heart was crushed to smithereens.

Now Wulf was probably dead.

She'd be taken.

Her impending death didn't stop her from ruminating over memories of being Special Agent Anya Randolph. *Am I her?*

Hurricane neither bound nor gagged her during the long, quiet ride. His truck had been reinforced with an extra steel cage, which had been the reason the Honda summersaulted across the desert earlier.

Numb beyond belief, this moment dwarfed any of the feelings she'd had of Agent Trent Winehouse going rogue. Wulf had always had her interest at the forefront of his mind. Even when he'd mistaken her for a drug addict, he'd only wanted the best for her. Wulf cared for her.

She didn't move a muscle at Huricane's side. Nonetheless, her heart continued its relentless beat. Wulf's blood was on her hands.

Hurricane turned off the desolate freeway onto a one-lane road, ascending toward a lone mansion. It dangled against sheetrock. The truck climbed and climbed the hill until they came upon the open land of Beasley's home. An extravagant "B" on the wrought-iron gate gave the façade of wealth. He pulled through the gate, down a long lane with manicured cacti on either side, and headed toward a large U-shaped driveway. There were three red imported sports cars and those ominous F-250s in red, blue, and white—so very patriotic. Sensor lights turned on as Hurricane stopped between the Ferrari and a blue Ford.

Hurricane's voice broke through the pitch blackness as he removed the key from the ignition. "You ready to die?"

She nodded. *I can't take any more of this world.* Closing her eyes, the back of her head slumped against the headrest.

She heard rummaging, then the door slammed, indicating that the beast was out of the car. Seconds later, her door opened. Blood, sweat, and bad hygiene assaulted her before Hurricane pulled her from the seat. Orange tones burned her closed eyelids as the sensor lights flipped on as he walked.

Hurricane knocked at the door. It opened.

Mary Jane's eyes finally opened as she was flung into the foyer. She sailed across the waxed black-and-white-checkered tile. The blood from her leaking calf smeared until she landed near a marble décor table next to the left side of the double staircase.

"Mary Jane has returned!" Beasley's heavy, breathy voice rose as he neared. With a grunt, his fat thighs weakened as he bent to touch her clammy cheek. "Hmmm, I remembered you being more outspoken."

"She wants to die." Hurricane's voice was a life-shocking volt against her heart.

"A shame," Beasley sighed. "I rather enjoy torturing the reluctant. Return Mary Jane to her cage."

Hurricane's prickly, bearded face turned upward into a harsh smile. His long, thick hands went through her unruly tresses. "This will be mine," he said, pulling until she glided against the waxed floors by the roots of her hair.

A few minutes later, toward the back of the house, Hurricane finally hefted Mary Jane over his shoulder to carry her up the stairs to the servants' quarters.

He opened a door at the top of the landing and tossed her into a dark room, then flipped on the lights. The walls and floors were black, the only furnishing a five-by-five-foot cage along one wall.

She slowly took in the scent of bleach that almost masked others—blood, urine, death.

"Lock her in there, for now," Beasley ordered.

Hurricane's fists balled. "*Why wait?* She's bleeding. I can almost taste it."

Beasley's eyes narrowed at Hurricane's aggressive stance. "Will you disrespect *your* master?"

Hurricane's chest deflated. His eyes cast to the floor.

Beasley glanced at Mary Jane and took a step closer to Hurricane to whisper in his ear.

The beast of a man didn't appear too happy about Beasley's comment, but he was obedient. He held the cage open for her.

"Cuff your hands and ankles," he growled.

No amount of self-defense would save her from him. Mary Jane crouched into the cage, took a seat, and did as told. Hurricane locked the padlock on the door, reinforcing the truth. She wasn't leaving anytime soon. Then they left her in the room.

Tongue thick and stuck to the roof of her mouth, Mary Jane stared at the closed door. She refused to drink out of the doggy bowl near her bare feet.

There was nothing left to do but wallow in self-pity.

I got Wulf killed for nothing.

With no reason to live, she waited for death. Welcomed it.

I'm not a secret agent. I only have one memory. I'm nothing.

If she could fade into the black walls around her and become one with everyone who'd been tortured in this room, she would.

***

"I don't want to go home," the younger one begged, her bottom lip protruding.

The older sister stopped next to a Victorian-style home and turned in front of her. She placed a hand on the younger sister's shoulder. "Then what are we gonna do?"

"We can—"

"We can't con people into taking care of us if our own mother can't! Look, I know the kids laughed at our clothes today. They do it every day. All they remember is that we wore the same outfit a few days in a row," the older sister huffed. They weren't used to living in a good neighborhood. At most of the other schools, they blended in for a while until their mother moved onto a new man.

But her little sister wasn't to be consoled. "You can do your magic tricks like you did when Mother forced us to come out here. We drove so long, and you got us all kinds of food and stuff. We can find Dad."

"It wasn't just magic tricks." She bit her lip to force the bile from rising. "Should Child Protective Services split us up? Is that what you want?"

"No," the little sister whimpered. "I want to stay with you, Ma—"

***

Mary Jane's eyes popped open as she heard the doorknob turn. Hurricane's head dipped as he passed through the six-foot doorway. His eyes took her in like a piece of Kobe beef.

Mary Jane stared at the disfigured man. She took in the lumps on his face more clearly in the light, the jagged scars on his alligator arms and hands. Quietly, she took in every inch of Hurricane's disfigurement, ready and waiting to be killed.

At the sound of a voice behind him, Hurricane backed out of the room and shut the door.

She leaned back against the cage wall as her heavy eyes closed again. She fell into another lucid dream.

***

Sunlight danced along the gauzy drapes that rustled in the wind. The tropical island life outside beckoned Anya, proving that she could just stay here in paradise. She could just go rogue too.

The illumination highlighting Trent's light brown abdominals, his legs, and the biceps of his arms. It was all so romantic, almost dream like.

"Come here," he said.

She smiled groggily, but was surprised he stayed. After a wild night of lovemaking, she'd anticipated that the hotel room would be void of any remnants of the man. If Trent wanted to, he could make it look like he'd never been there.

Her heart lurched. She had hoped he'd left. After all the talk. The oath to the Agency. She sought the best for Trent. If it meant him disappearing in the night, so be it. As she maneuvered into the thick ropes of his arms, he spoke her very thoughts.

"I wouldn't leave without saying goodbye, Randolph." He kissed her softly on the forehead. "I'm not that cruel."

"But you have in the past," Anya replied. Though women's intuition screamed, she snuggled in the crook of his shoulder. Emotions clogged her throat and made the embarrassing words even harder to divulge. "You did leave me without saying goodbye."

His thumb brushed at the tears trailing down her cheeks. "I said goodbye, Anya. You just didn't understand."

Her nose crinkled and she thought back. Three years had passed. The memories weren't exactly easy to think about. Trent had never been an "assignment." She'd always cared for him.

"Do you remember the last morning? I met you at the Agency with coffee and breakfast. Danish pastries."

Slowly, she nodded.

"I told you goodbye then, with breakfast. Remember?"

Her eyes brightened as she recalled the very day he disappeared. "Oh, that's right. You never said goodbye except for that one morning after we ate. You made us dance slowly and sang a few lines of Frank Sinatra's Goodbye. You knew you were leaving?" Anya pulled herself away from his welcoming arms, no longer comforted. She'd hoped that he'd been coerced into betraying the Agency, his country, her. That couldn't be so if he had orchestrated their last moment. "Damn, you've always been a bastard!"

"Oh, honey." He grinned as she hastened out of the bed.

"Don't 'oh, honey,' me, Trent Winehouse! I am taking you in."

"No, you're not," Trent said.

"Yes, I am!"

The sound of choppers cut through the sky. Anya lunged away from the bed and away from the floor-to-ceiling windows. Bullets rippled through the glass windows and French doors. Shards of glass flew.

Trent calling her name was barely audible through the continuing shots fired. Anya scrambled toward a nightstand to shield herself from the line of fire.

***

"Mary Jane?"

Mary Jane's eyes popped open, yet again. The voice in her dreams, that voice was so familiar. It sounded like...

She looked at the doorknob as it slowly turned.

"Oh, my beautiful Mary Jane. It has been a while."

She gasped. "*Trent*?"

19

HE RUBBED A HAND THROUGH HIS WAVY, YET KINKY HAIR. THE biracial man had cool gray eyes. Although chilling, they complemented his steel-colored tailor-made suit. Handsome and lean, he had just enough muscle, indicating he implemented a flawless workout regimen.

"No, I'm not Trent."

Beasley walked in behind the man she knew as Trent Winehouse—who had just *denied* being Trent Winehouse.

"She doesn't know who I am?" Not-Trent questioned. He rubbed a hand against a neatly-cut beard then placed his hands on his lean hips.

"No, she doesn't." Beasley gazed at Not-Trent with worried eyes. It was clear that the hierarchy was topped with this new stranger. He was the boss of them all.

"That's good for you," he said. His shiny Armani shoes stopped right in front of her cage. He squatted, staring at her with squinted eyes, his mouth just slightly agape, a subconscious mannerism, as if he spent mounds of time ruminating. Then his head whipped around to Beasley.

"I retract my last statement. Her mild case of amnesia is

not good for you! Who the fuck does she think she is if I am *Trent*? And what's with that faint bruise around her neck, the scarring at her knees, the fucking blood on her calf leg? Beasley, speak!"

"I..." Beasley placed a hand over his heart, breathing slowly. "I'm not sure."

"Shall I mention—?" Not-Trent paused, his irritation blew away as he gave a reassuring smile to Mary Jane. Then his gray eyes darkened as he stared at Beasley. "I could murder you for slapping *her* face on every billboard from here to Texas. You better be glad I'm not selling her to any Russians or Japanese. The Arabs wouldn't even consider this crap! But what you better understand is that she's even more important than any bitch you've ever laid eyes on. She's mine."

"Bu—"

"My pet does not wear cheap makeup. Did you think I wouldn't see it? I've just about had it with your fuck-ups. Let this bullshit redirect into my court. I'm going to surgically remove your heart with no anesthetic!"

Beasley's fleshy cheeks jiggled as he nodded.

Not-Trent glanced at Mary Jane, his polite coolness returned. Somewhere within his spirit, a switch flipped and shut off emotion. His voice was soft and soothing. "What do you remember about me, honey?"

Mary Jane looked to the left then the right and folded her arms.

I'm not playing any games with you.

"C'mon, honey." Not-Trent's gray eyes liquefied into a warm metal. They pulled her in with every kind of lustful thought. He knelt, gazing eye-to-eye at her level. "Well, if you don't recall exactly who I am, we can always part ways with very fond memories of each other. You looked at me with desire when asking who I was. You love me?"

She frowned. Something wasn't right.

He stood up and his fine, tailored suit draped over every muscle of his body. "She was supposed to be in her cage, frightened beyond belief. Waiting for me! Waiting for me to save her. Waiting for me to tilt the fucking world and make it all better for her. Then I see her on a billboard and had to come running!"

Mary Jane glared at him, and he stared back like she was his sex kitten.

"We've had a lot of issues with this one." Beasley rummaged in the pocket of his own suit. "I wouldn't suggest—"

"Wow, this is pure comedy." Not-Trent gave a cocky smile, eyes on her. "I don't know how this fat fuck can even fathom that I require his opinion."

Tightlipped, Beasley walked to the cage with a key in his slightly-trembling fingers. The deadbolt snapped unlocked. He pushed the door open, undid the latch on her ankles, and waited for Mary Jane to come out. He nodded his head for her to exit. His eyes, finally, pled for her to comply. With a huff, he looked to Not-Trent. "I don't know what's wrong with MJ."

While he looked at Not-Trent for instruction, Mary Jane leapt up from her kneeling position and lunged at him. Beasley fell to the ground. His body flew back to the floor. The chains around her wrists clamped against Beasley's throat, and she squeezed tightly. Then Not-Trent grabbed the back of her neck, his manicured nails digging into her flesh as he pulled her up. Her legs dangled in the air before he tossed her against the wall.

"*Honey*, control yourself," he ordered in a calculating

tone, mouth pinched at the sides. "Sweetheart, nobody in this world but me can hit you. I guarantee I will patch your ass back up again too."

Beasley struggled to breathe, turning on his stomach and knees.

Mary Jane saw the rage and disgust in Not-Trent's eyes as he glared at Beasley. He stepped past Beasley over to her, gave a warm smile, and reached a hand out for her to stand up. *Shit, and I thought I was bipolar.* Ignoring the gesture, she turned over and got up, her chains clanking around her hands as she stood almost a foot beneath him.

Not-Trent did his best to hold in his aggravation as he ushered her back into the cage and swiftly locked the door behind her. "It appears you should stay in here until you recall a few manners."

"I – I'm g-g – gonna," Beasley grunted and got up, one leg after the other, his eyes brimming with fire. He stared at Mary Jane, who blinked a few times in return. "I'll kill the little whore!"

"Beasley, the only task at your disposal is breathing unless instructed not to. Do you comprehend?"

Beasley stepped back toward the door.

"Tr—" Mary Jane gulped and started over, "Could you tell me who I am?"

Still not breaking their connection, he took a seat, his eyes continuing to roam over her, lips slightly agape.

"Y – you loved me once." Mary Jane hated herself for attempting to appeal to any shred of humanity in the sociopath. Something told her in his sordid mind, he believed he'd once loved her. "Please?"

"Regardless of your temperament, I have *always* loved you. To the dismay of my heart, I always will," he replied wryly.

To another woman—who hadn't viewed Not-Trent lash out—his enduring glance would have had her swooning. Trying to hide her repulsion, Mary Jane smiled. At least they were making leeway with her identity. "I love you too."

"No, you don't." He shook his head. "*That's why you're here.* Tell me who you think I am."

She folded her arms, lips tensed.

"If you want to die knowing who you are, not as some Jane Doe, tell me! Who do you think you are? Who do you think I am?"

She sighed. "Anya Randolph."

He pointed to himself, his body tensed. "And me? Who am I to you?"

"Trent Winehouse."

At that, Not-Trent's athletic body shook with a laugh. "Oh, Mary Jane, you were always so naive. It's breathtakingly beautiful."

She looked at the playfulness in his eyes. The lust.

"Does the film—the hit blockbuster—*The Eradicator* ring a bell?"

She shook her head no.

"Charlene Shaw?" He waved a hand. Still, she shook her head.

"You and a friend had plans to see *The Eradicator II* when..." Not-Trent pulled at his silk tie in pure discomfort. "The A-list actress Charlene Shaw played Anya Randolph. Trent Winehouse was her hero in the movie...Charlene was one of your favorite actresses, so I couldn't forget her name if I wanted. You always said that action was your favorite genre. Those movies made you happy." His tense demeanor had faded as if the memories were welcome. "Anyhow, in *The Eradicator*, Charlene is working Trent who is ex-CIA or something. They're lovers in the summer blockbuster you've been imagining."

He abruptly stood up and walked toward her. His hand slipped through the bars and grabbed her chin. He pushed it upward to get a clear view into her eyes. Not-Trent snatched the prescription glasses from beneath the handkerchief in his front pocket. They went hastily over his eyes. "Hmmm, this is a breakthrough!"

Not-Trent went to the door as Beasley's head popped inside. He shoved a hand into the air, indicating that they needed more time, and Beasley slipped back out followed by Not-Trent.

"Damn it, Beasley. I could kill you! I *should* kill you."

Mary Jane listened intently as his voice rose in anger. Though the door was cracked open, their voices lowered. Not-Trent mentioned something about saving something from a cage, but Mary Jane couldn't distinguish much of the conversation. Then Not-Trent came back into the room. Walking slowly to his chair, he said, "I'll grant your wish. I hope you're prepared to know exactly who you are."

Trent pulled one arm after the other out of his suit jacket in a fluid, suave movement. He folded the jacket neatly, placed it on the back of the chair, and sat down with a wide grin.

This small act brought back a flood of memories into Mary Jane's mind. Every thought she'd ever had since she was a child came back. Growing up with a mother who spent most of her time looking for love rather than taking care of her two daughters. Sleeping on naked mattresses with bedbugs. Roaches scurrying everywhere. Washing her clothing in the bathroom sink with a bar of soap. Taking care of her younger sister. Magic tricks for the night's dinner. Moving at the drop of a dime because the current boyfriend was too demanding for Mother, hit Mother, or left Mother for another woman in town.

Now, the snippet of a memory that MJ was plunged into while driving that old Corolla was grounded in reality. The two girls walking home and bickering about going to the police meant the entire world to Mary Jane. Their mother had finally wrangled a rich man who was even more cruel than the others. Now, her memories of being a secret agent were displaced by another life.

***

"Megan!" Twenty-four-year-old Mallory threw the bottle of pain medication onto the living room floor of her lavish Beverly Hills mansion. The pills scattered around the Italian marble. Her stilettos stomped on a few of them as her younger twin sister, Megan, flew to the floor to save her beloved Norco, Vicodin, and Xanax.

"Stop it!" Megan's hair draped over her face as she cried. She pushed back a few clumped tendrils before shoving handfuls of pills in the pockets of her holey, soiled sweatpants. "These are mine. You can't control me!"

"I'm trying to save you." Mallory bent down into a fog of liquor and other toxic drugs that pumped through her younger twin's body. She placed a hand on the ragged USC sweater Megan had to have stolen while panhandling in the area. "Please, Megan, you have to stop. I can't support you anymore. You broke your arm. Do you know how ridiculous it was to hear that you had broken your arm to get more prescriptions? I'm taking you off my health coverage."

"Why, Mal? Is your spending money being cut? That's farfetched! You don't even have children to waste money on! Tell me if your loving, intelligent, chemist husband is cutting your allowance. How will you please Peter without designer clothes?" Megan snorted back tears and snot, obviously waiting for a rise

out of her sister. Not receiving any argument after her string of insults, Megan shrugged. "Awesome. You don't love me anyway!"

"You can't love yourself, with the way you treat your body. I love you enough to stop enabling you, Megan. No more money. No more doctor visits at my expense," Mallory said.

Megan stood up and kicked the side of the white leather couch. Smiling devilishly at her older twin, Megan stepped toward a landscape painting that dominated the span of the living room wall. She yanked and yanked at it until one half came crashing down, tilted, and cracked.

"Well, I hope you're done," Mallory said, folding her arms. "I've already found a good rehabilitation place for you. I'll visit you all the time."

Her sister tossed up her middle finger, stomping toward the stairs. She did not take offense, knowing her younger twin had once been her everything in the nightmare of the world their mother had created. She followed Megan upstairs saying, "While you're packing your things, don't ruin the guest room looking for the coke you stashed. In the bottom of the wall aquarium? Really? You've gotten good at hiding your drugs, but not that damn good. I spent half my life raising you and Mother!"

Megan sneered. "I'm leaving and not to a stupid rehab place, no matter how much money you spend on it. I hope this time when you feel guilty and look for me, you can't find me. I hope I die! I hope when you come lookin' I'm six feet under, and don't even think of burying me next to Mother! I hope I get cut into tiny pieces and..."

Mallory put her hands over her ears. She always hated this part of their arguing. This was the reason why she and Peter didn't have children yet. Well, one of the reasons.

But Megan was right. After listening to her go back and forth from being guilty to the victim, she'd tell Megan to leave. A month *or two later, either Megan would call, claiming to be clean, or she'd go looking for her twin.*

"You're my twin sister, but you don't fucking love me!"

Mallory wrapped her arms around her sister, hugging her tightly. It was in Megan's eyes that her bold statement was a lie. Mal loved her more than anything in the world. She'd endured torture for Megan to flourish when their mother finally settled down.

The man their mother loved only wanted one child. And the little sister had a good life. Mal had always had it the worst, until she met Doctor Peter Grienke.

Mary Jane gasped as tears flooded her cheeks. She recalled it all. Her stream of memories preceded and succeeded all others. It wasn't like the "Anya Randolph" premonition in which she'd only had just that one fragment of time spent with Trent Winehouse. No, this one was complete. As was the one where she and Megan had walked down the street in the nice neighborhood, where the ambulance was stopped in front of their home.

Growing up with a mother who followed her latest and greatest boyfriend, a redneck hillbilly who farmed marijuana, a drug dealer in Chicago, and more, she and her younger twin only had each other. They'd keep quiet around the men as they grew up, because a few of them had wandering eyes.

"I finally left them," Mary Jane whispered.

"Megan was turning into your mother," Peter agreed. "You barely finished high school with keeping her father off you."

"He was not her father—our father, Peter!" Mary Jane gritted out.

He held out a calming hand. "I know, honey. You called him...what was it?"

"The good uncle." She sank back against the bars and sobbed. It was a play on words. The man was vile, and 'uncle' well, that was another term she twisted because who didn't want a cool uncle when they were young?

"Because he treated Megan nicely. They went to dinner every weekend. You worked at Little Caesars Pizza after school. You weren't a part of the same crowd Megan was in while you both attended high school in Long Beach," Peter sighed. "You are very resilient, aren't you? A man who fucked your beautiful body after your mother and sister went to bed happy. And then I saved you, Mary Jane...I think I'd rather call you Mary Jane for now."

She held in her disgust for him as he smiled. Yes, he had saved her. Mary Jane recalled attending courses at Long Beach City College. She'd moved out with the little bit of financial aid she had, via purchasing a car and living in it. Then she'd gotten a job at Nordstrom's beauty counter. Peter had just bought a Rolex, and he'd seen her behind the counter. He'd stopped as if mesmerized. He'd been charming.

"What does my lovely wife recall last? You do recall defying me, don't you?"

With a reluctant nod, tears streamed down her face again. Peter had told her not to search for Megan. To let her be. He'd threatened her.

But there was nothing new about that. There was always this innate urge to keep her sister safe, no matter the consequences when she did.

"I did. I went looking for her, Peter."

"Keep talking, beautiful. Let it all out." His demeanor was dreamy, his tone soothing, but Mary Jane knew he was angry. There was a certain stiffness about him. It angered him immensely when she did not listen.

"I'm sorry, Peter, but I had to search for my blood. I did everything you asked. Everything else. 'Sit there. Look pretty,' I did it. 'Research my new investors and be prepared for conversation at the gala this evening,' I did that, Peter, because I love you. But just thinking about my sister somewhere lying dead in a ditch due to the company she kept, well I couldn't—"

"So you defied me. You always defied me!"

Her shoulders shook as she cried. She recalled the charming Peter she'd met and how brilliant he was. Too intelligent for his own good. Mary Jane now remembered that she'd taken self-defense lessons from a judo master in Hollywood to keep slim for Peter and to also release some of the aggression from having the life she sought-after as a child. She had the perfect life with Peter. The life of a trophy wife. It was ironic, the crazy saying that 'grass isn't always greener' never penetrated until she stopped coveting and truly had the 'perfect' life.

She recalled being in high school and seeing her sister finally survive and thrive when their mother married a man who was outwardly kind and good, but the bastard was disgusting.

Megan internalized the guilt, later turning toward drugs.

Mallory, well, she became numb to it, and Peter had given her a dream come true only to snatch it away.

"Your last memory, Mary Jane," he cut through her thoughts. "Tell me?"

"Okay," she murmured. "It was three months later."

"As usual," he sneered. "You were ever so predictable."

She rolled her gaze away from him and continued. "I went searching for Megan. She'd always been so outgoing, even as a drug addict. Friends at Venice Beach who worshiped her like the sun and the moon, or a motorcycle bar she frequented in L.A."

"She wasn't at any of those places, was she?" Peter probed. "You know where she was, don't you?"

His face was calm, yet his tone was filled with venom. Vile thoughts licked at Mary Jane as she concentrated on the best neighborhood they'd lived in as adolescents. The premonition she had before driving into Santo Cruces Police Station had been a dream. "The cops will help," she mumbled to herself.

"What's that?" He began to chuckle as it dawned on him. "I remember. You, Megan, and the Bitch," he referred to her mother, "had finally moved into a nice neighborhood. You'd have those dreams that the cops would help, didn't you?"

Though Peter made fun of her, she gave a subtle nod. "I did. I would dream of the nice house that we lived in and that the cops were coming to take away the man who lived there..." She paused to shake her head, still unable to say it. Mary Jane shoved a hand through her hair and sighed. "I can't believe it. I'd always search for Megan every few months. Most of the time, I'd catch up with her in Venice or the next stop. But that place was my very last stop."

"Did you go in?" Peter's lips curved into a sinister smile. He held up an iPad. "This program helps me. It's like a novel of your current memories. Usually there are prods attached to your skull, but I'm assuming Lyle did a good job the first week you were here, reconfiguring and connecting your psyche to my computer system. I know your memories. When they're all erased, I'll write a new set. Cognition and computer coding. It's fun."

She glared at him through tearstained eyes.

"But did you go in, Mary Jane? Bat those pretty eyelashes

at 'the good uncle' and save your sister for the umpteenth time?"

Entire body tensing, she held still. A while ago, Mary Jane was certain. Anya Randolph was just a movie. She'd somehow dreamt the movie Peter told her about earlier. But, now she had to analyze the mind of Mallory Portman-Grienke.

Her memories end abruptly. The only adult memories she had were of an actress in a movie and those with Megan. The memories end at...the Chevron gas station around the corner from the good uncle's house. She'd punched at the steering wheel with rivers of tears falling down her cheeks. Mary Jane bit her lip, pulling the puzzle pieces together. That fucking creep wanted her in a cage, and Beasley was supposed to keep her there.

"Did you knock on the door, say 'hello daddy,' because, honey, the man was not your uncle or just your mother's next piece of shit boyfriend. He was her husband, your *step-father*—just as taboo, right?"

He chuckled while waiting for a response. "It's okay that you don't recall. The memories at the forefront of your mind —the newest ones—are the easiest to erase for good. It appears they've been effectively erased." He nodded to the iPad again. "However, it takes four entire weeks to cleanse the brain. You should be operating on middle school memories at best. Apparently, Lyle and Beasley aren't doing their jobs."

Instead of placing all her cards on the table, Mary Jane kept quiet. She needed Hurricane to return. This asshole was screwing with her mental stability. And out of all the thoughts swarming through her mind, Mary Jane knew one thing.

Hurricane could save her.

20

TWO HOURS EARLIER

A BRAIN-SQUEEZING THROB PULSATED THROUGHOUT WULF'S skull. He lay on his left side against the broken window, fragments of dirt and glass embedded in his temple. Still in a semi-coherent state, he contemplated his last nightmare. *What the fuck was that?* He had to have dreamt it all. Some type of beast with a gnarled face leaned in the car.

Then there'd been shots fired. The sound was real, not dreamlike at all, but the bullets had buzzed past his face. Until a bullet pierced and exited his bicep. Then all the shooting stopped.

His eyes flickered open at the sound of footsteps echoing nearby. He wasn't on the box mattress in his trailer. He tried to unlatch the seat belt to no avail. Unable to brace himself, he turned his head toward the passenger window and assessed that he was in a wrecked car. He looked out the window in the same position that he'd stared at the nightmarish monster. That hadn't been a hallucination. It had been real.

With the Honda positioned onto the driver's side, stars dotted the sky as he looked up. He wondered how long he'd been out. And since they were on a back road, how much longer he had before the authorities came. He didn't have time to be stopped, because he needed to get to Mary Jane.

In the tight confines of the car, Wulf grabbed his knife from the holster and ripped the belt to shreds. Grimacing, he pushed with his legs until he had room enough to move away from the crushed dashboard.

After struggling out of the car, he took a deep breath, but kept his eyes peeled. There was no time to rest. He assessed that a truck had pulled up near the crash, and whoever was in it had taken Mary Jane. Wulf took off in a jog toward the bend in the road that linked up with the main highway was about two miles down. As he started jogging toward the main road, he dialed his own voicemail and found ten messages waiting. Quincy had called right back earlier this morning, around the time Mary Jane had him held hostage. The messages from Quincy became angrier and angrier.

"Damn, Wulf. You better be hurt—mildly hurt. Got your sister worrying." Quincy sounded as if he had worried too. "If you aren't here by this afternoon, I'm coming to Arizona to beat your ass."

In the last message Quincy just gritted out that he was boarding a plane and would be at his crappy trailer house by eight. Wulf looked at the time. It was well after ten p.m. Hopefully, Quincy hadn't left.

His trailer was on the way to Beasley's. So he had time to stop and get Quincy's help – but what about Mary Jane? Did she have time left?

21

Doctor Peter Grienke was world-renowned, though not as someone who fucked with people's brains. He was a self-made billionaire in pharmaceutical-grade facial care. Not just cosmetics—he had created a revolutionary facial line that works with a person's dormant 'good' genes. Peter had made a killing in the industry with miraculous skincare products treating wrinkles and age spots. Now the genius had other ventures, and Mary Jane knew she was one of them.

He said he loved her. She must've fallen out of love. With a damn *genius*. How could she forget what should've been the best day of her life? Sharing wedding vows with her husband. The memory she had was so tangible, so much more than being Anya Randolph. But where were the rest of the memories?

She'd been brainwashed.

"You're done with me, aren't you, Peter? I've done something unforgivable." It was almost laughable to put his needs and desires before her sister's safety and her own freedom. But she looked empathetic.

He gave a slight smile but shrugged.

Mary Jane continued with, "I've gone against your wishes one too many times, haven't I?"

Peter rose from his chair. "Are you thirsty?"

She shook her head. "I want to talk about us."

"There *is* no *us*." His eyes misted as he continued to stare at her with a sense of longing.

"Please."

"I've already unlocked as much of your memory as I'm willing to. Understand that all of them can be unlocked, with a little thought on my part. All until they're fully expunged. For now, you know enough about who you are." Peter pulled at his tie again, a sure sign that she'd gotten under his skin. "Enough to torment you."

"Didn't I make you happy?"

"For a time." He took a sip before crossing his leg at the knee.

"What happened?"

"Your sister."

Breathing slowly, holding onto the pretense of calmness, Mary Jane tried not to give into rage. He was angry about her sister? Oh well, her life had been awful, and it wasn't much better these days. She had a lifetime of memories now. Yet, she did not know everything. There wasn't a smooth chronological progression. Just bits and pieces of Peter playing the hero after her dysfunctional childhood.

"So, what did Megan have to do with us? I made a vow as your wife!"

"Megan," Peter breathed out, and then clasped his hands behind his head and leaned back, indicating that the conversation was complete. He absentmindedly closed his eyes.

Not a sound permeated the air between them until

someone knocked at the door. Beasley entered in a running suit. Hurricane stepped inside after him in overalls and no shirt, as if his disfigured face wasn't intimidating enough. Jagged welts and burns, at various stages of the healing process, defined his body.

"Mary Jane, are you ready to die?" Beasley sneered, taking a seat next to Peter. At the snap of his fingers, a maid came into the room, pushing in a cart with every kind of torture weapon imaginable.

Hurricane's hand grazed over a handsaw. Yellow, pointy teeth appeared as he grinned in delight. He flicked on the power tool, and it whipped to life. Slowly, he neared the cage.

Mary Jane's eyes bore into Peter's with a manipulative longing, oblivious to Hurricane's crazed desire for blood.

"Stop!" Peter's voice boomed over the sound of the saw.

Hurricane didn't stop. The lock cracked and broke as he yanked the bar door away from its hinges as Peter repeated the command.

It took Beasley's command for Hurricane to flick off the power tool and place it back on the table. His hellfire eyes turned toward Beasley, and Beasley shocked him with illegal high-powered animal Taser.

"You've been told to be patient, Hurricane!" Beasley warned.

She had anticipated that Hurricane was only loyal to Beasley. Mary Jane's lips twitched then turned into a full-blown smile. She suspected that Beasley must've told Hurricane that Mary Jane belonged to him now. Which was a bit premature due to Peter's ever-changing emotions.

"I would like a word with Mary Jane first," Peter said. He smiled back at her, as if in the assumption that her cordial appearance was for his benefit. Again, his eyes glazed over with lust as she licked her lips, enticing him to come closer.

Peter beckoned her out of the cage. She stepped out of it but leaned against the bars, casually glancing at Hurricane.

"Some dogs run wild with no masters," she whispered to him, hoping that he could hear.

The large freak didn't even look in her direction. He stood at the door, doused in jealousy, not too happy about the delay in carving her to shreds.

Beasley spoke in an annoyed, hushed voice to Peter. "You wanted to keep her in the cage and come save her," Beasley said. "Then you wanted to kill her. Now, you want another conversation. Which is it?"

She didn't have enough time to put together what Beasley meant about saving her from a cage, because she needed to persuade the animal.

"An owner loves his pet," Mary Jane whispered to Hurricane as her eyes never left Beasley and Peter. She needed the animal to break those loyal ties.

"Damn it, there are girls at The Petting Zoo if you want fun tonight! Let's get rid of MJ for good. I'll have a slew of girls at your disposal!" Beasley said through clenched teeth. "You can start over with one of my cunts or go home and find a new girl to play with."

Mary Jane stood, seemingly innocent, near Hurricane. "Dogs are a man's best friend."

Hurricane sniffled.

"Damn it, Hurricane, my skin is soft. Very soft. If you want to rip me to shreds, get rid of them. Peter wants to keep me for himself. Beasley listens to Peter. You listen to him. All you'll get is another blast with that Taser!"

At her yelling, they turned to look at her. Hurricane

leapt up. Hands balled together, he rammed them down on Peter's head.

Mary Jane ran out as Hurricane's wrath turned toward his master. She slid past the banister and took the stairs too hard. "Fuck." Mary Jane gritted her teeth to the pain in her calf muscle. But she couldn't fall, couldn't trip.

She had to survive. She chided herself, "Not so fast!"

Hands confined, Mary Jane shuffled down the last step and into the kitchen but stopped when a bullet whizzed past her shoulder. She placed her handcuffed wrists in the air and turned around slowly next to the refrigerator. "Peter?"

The sound of harsh screaming from behind him made the tiny hairs on her arms prick as Peter smirked at her halfway down the side stairs.

She asked, "Why don't you go save your friend?"

"Who? Beasley? He *worked* for me, beneath me. Now, he's dog food. So congratulations on advocating for that animal." Peter chuckled.

Mary Jane almost felt shame. Beneath the scars, Hurricane had to have been human before. But she concentrated on that sadness and spun it in her favor.

"Why would you hurt me?" She needed to keep him talking while looking for a knife, any kind of weapon. However, the immaculate kitchen didn't have one single item out of place. "I'm your wife."

"Are you?" Peter cocked an eyebrow. "We know who I am, obviously. But do you honestly know your own identity?"

"I'm Mallory Grienke. Your wife. You wanted to have me brainwashed, and you'd come to Beasley's home, to save me from some sort of cage. Be my knight in shining armor and take me home so we could start over, right? Why not kill me and just get a new wife?"

"You're right about something. I've had a few wives. One was brainwashed and returned to her perfect state. Then she pissed me off in a moment of passion, and I wasn't able to forgive her. But you, Mary Jane, were given to Beasley to clear out those memories in your brain. Despite whatever Beasley's done to you to make you believe you were an actress, I had intentions of bringing you home. I love your temperament. Everything but temperament is unchangeable, because it's a genetic predisposition. You'd be my amnesic wife. We'd start over. I'd train you in the ways I want you to be."

"So, I'm your wife. Your zombie wife."

"Don't be so barbaric. I prefer 'Stepford wife' to the term zombie. And no, I didn't put you through any trauma, albeit it's clear that these idiots have. I couldn't bring myself to brainwash you. You're beautiful."

Her eyes locked onto him. However, she didn't miss the hanging copper pots above him in her periphery. They were the only weapon. "Humph. Oh, I'm sorry you felt so guilty about adding Beasley into our marital issues. But, I guess you thought I wouldn't remember."

"Perhaps...or is it that I've always been one step ahead of you, as always?"

She offered a lost-kitten look because she had no doubt that he would shoot her before she could grab a pot. "I did the jacket gesture and Mallory's memories flooded into your mind. It's one of those nostalgic things. Usually a remote control, but certain actions are able to bring about memories when the mind is stuck in limbo. Mary Jane, you are in limbo at the moment because when I returned, we should've been redirecting your cognition toward making me the hero. You know, after such a horrible childhood, I'd be your hero again."

"Okay." She nodded slowly.

"But let me ask, Mary Jane. Do you remember how you got here? How Beasley came to chase you?" He stepped closer to her with each question. "When did you arrive at The Petting Zoo? No, I didn't think you remembered. Tell me, what's your last memory?" he asked, placing the gun at her forehead. "I asked you earlier, but you kept quiet. Now's your time to speak!"

Mary Jane huffed. Her last memory was from searching for Megan, sitting at the gas station near Vin's home. She'd felt so much hatred for the rapist.

"What if you're Megan?"

"I'm not!" Mary Jane's body prickled with hatred. "You just said I'm your amnesic wife! We had an entire discussion of how you saved me."

"True. You have Mallory's memories so obviously a discussion about said memories would be a logical progression," he replied softly, slipping the barrel of the gun across the angle of her chin. "You bawled your beautiful little eyes out, wondering if your little sister would come home. Wondering why she abhorred you so much to leave you. *After all you've done for Megan.* You drove to the good uncle's house. What all did he teach you again?" He sneered, eyes filled with lust.

Her mouth tensed. At every word he spoke, she remembered it.

"*Fuck you, asshole.* You're just trying to screw with me. I don't have Megan's memories."

He gave an obnoxious grin. "I'm sure you don't want to be the bad sister. The selfish one who had the perfect boyfriend in high school, who had the perfect father. But alas, remember I said, I had the perfect wife and she ruined it. She ruined it so much so that I was unable to redirect her."

"You killed—"

"I killed Mal, and you're Megan."

"It's a lie," Mary Jane gasped. "I won't believe you."

He held the gun toward her, and with another hand, placed the iPad onto the counter. Keeping his eye on her, he toggled with the touchscreen. "Maybe I killed Mal in a moment of passion. Found you. Redirected your memories, Megan. Redirected your thought process so that you'd be my doting wife. You look just like her."

Mary Jane gasped as her head began to hurt. She was plunged into another memory. This time, it was like being on the opposite side of the film. Recording it instead of acting. She was Megan, and she was watching the pain she caused her older sister. Receiving love from her new stepfather, being popular and having friends.

Then she was angry, so angry with Mal. Hating her luck, and her husband. Then Peter pulled her out of the torturous and disgusting memories.

"That's enough brain activity today. Anymore and you might suffer an aneurism," he said. His lips thinned into a worried line as he touched her clammy forehead. "Now you've acquired every memory of Megan's, right? Both sets end at pivotal points."

Tears streamed down her cheeks at Megan's ultimate betrayal.

"I'm not Megan. You are on a fucking power trip, asshole. I'm sure you get a kick out of the mind fuck. Well, I am not her!"

"No?" Peter asked. "Let's consider the past couple of days. Have you been the mother hen—like the woman I loved—Mallory? Or have you been the selfish sister that I considered redirecting?"

I was going to let Glenn be killed by the larger twin at the motel when he came into the lobby looking for me. I left Wulf. I've been selfish.

"Stop it!"

"But you want to know, right?" Peter cocked the gun toward the side door and motioned for her to walk. "The brain works similar to a computer. We all have an organized set of *schemas*. A word, a scent, a phrase can bring about an entire array of feelings or emotions or past experiences. In a sense, your cognition was filed away only to be fully destroyed, I believe, in another week or two. I have a cognition-erasing system that wipes out everything. Let's just call it your amnesia. It's only safe after a standard month of hiding your memories and setting them aside in another *schema*—see my reference to computer and brain. Your brain is organizing and filing away new information into your memory. I'm extracting all of it. Then I turn you into a tabula rasa, just like that. Any time before it, you'd have made a good robot, nothing more. Trust me, I'm working on cutting down the memory filing system. But you just fucking piss me off too much to save you!"

She lurched slightly when Peter shoved the gun further in her back. "Your promptness is much appreciated. I can hear Hurricane above. I'd rather not be in his line of vision when he's completed with Beasley."

Mary Jane continued through a hallway with statues and past a dark living room. "You seem to love me so much. Why not a Romeo and Juliet ending? You sick fuck."

"Adorable," he replied sarcastically. "Since we've decided to forego the entire brain-cleansing process, I could only

oblige and provide you with all the memories for my amusement and for Mallory's sake."

"I am Mallory." Mary Jane grabbed the door handle.

"Doubt is clear in those beautiful brown eyes. However,
the gentleman in me is leaning toward a family reunion."

"How so?" Mary Jane murmured as she gawked at two
large Rottweilers in a two-story cage before her. Their
massive kennel gave them ample room to run, but they
snarled, nipping at the fencing surrounding them as she
and Peter passed by a lap pool.

"Your sister is here. I couldn't dump her anywhere else
after lovingly squeezing that neck of hers." Peter chuckled,
pointing to the large dogs' cage. He pulled at the lock on the
door but it wouldn't give. "Hmmm, I did notice a maid
feeding the dogs through the top one day while Beasley was
out of town. Let's go." He gestured for the patio stairs that
had been built to wrap around the kennel.

"Fuck you," Mary Jane spat. "You couldn't get me to
follow you without that gun in your hand."

Peter nudged the barrel toward her back.

"Allow me to disregard that last comment. Back to the
family reunion. I'm not sure of your level of understanding,
so I shall elaborate. After my lovely Mal's unfortunate death,
she met King and Knight. And I dropped your ass off here to
be switched up. The cops wouldn't look for a crackhead, but
a replacement for my lovely wife was necessary. But now,
I've changed my mind."

She looked down to see the two Rottweilers' snapping
teeth, just as ghastly as Hurricane's. The muscles in their
limbs constricted as they jumped repeatedly. Mary Jane,
their dangling prime meat, was just out of reach.

Mary Jane's lips parted slowly. She tried to figure out
how easily it would be to steal the gun. She'd once been

untouchable, believing herself to be a secret agent. Now, her confidence had diminished, pulling her back to reality. *I could have gotten myself killed fighting those dumbass twins! And Wulf...*

Even though her resolve was crumbling, she couldn't allow her mind to think about Wulf right now. Just the thought of him crushed her heart.

"Stop it!" Mary Jane snapped. Deep inside her bones she had a feeling she was Megan. There was no need to continue this madness. "Shoot me and feed me to the dogs!"

"Who said anything about shooting you?" Peter's eyes glinted with hatred. "The dogs like to tear a body into pieces pre-mortem."

22

UNDER A FULL MOON, A BURLY BLACK MAN SAT ON A WICKER chair on a trailer porch with his feet propped up. Head dipped back, he snored softly. At the sound of a horn, he pulled a Beretta from under the Lakers cap nestled on his lap. He knocked back the safety in less than a second and aimed it, alert as ever. His eyes peeled to the darkness as a sixteen wheeler pulled over to the side of the road.

Swiftly, the Beretta went to his side, and he stood. Half swagger, half limp from a firefight on the job, he ambled down the steps. Then he noticed a familiar figure getting out, saying something and closing the door of the semi-truck. The man he knew for over a decade as a good friend moved on lead legs into the lot.

"Hey," Wulf gave half a greeting as he opened the driver's door to Quincy's rental.

Quincy's eyebrows furrowed. "Damn, Dylan, what the fuck happened to you?"

"This is your rental, right?"

"Yeah."

"Get in. I don't have time to explain," Wulf ordered.

Quincy tossed the keys over the roof of the sedan. "Well, hello, Quincy. How are you? Yes, I'm fine. No, really, my wife didn't get all up in my ass telling me I had to come see about you nor did she argue about you fucking up our vacation in order to check on you, which—mind you—had me confused," Quincy muttered as he got in the car.

"You only have one piece?" Wulf asked as he drove off.

"Nah." Quincy turned in his seat and added, "two nines were all LAX would allow. And that's only because my ex works there. Don't tell your sis. Anyway, you sound like I should've come strapped with tactical defense. Dylan, what the hell is going on? You never mess with the crazy chicks. What's up with the amnesia girl from your voicemail?"

The car climbed up a lone hill. "She's not safe. We have to save her."

Quincy scoffed. "You said the SCPD was corrupt. I assumed you messed with some chick, and she was family. Hell, in these small towns every-damn-body is some-damn-body's cousin."

Wulf swooped off the road at the edge of Beasley's property. He turned off the engine and cut the lights. It instantly went pitch black.

As they sat parked in the car, Quincy asked, "How many people?"

"I don't know."

"Are they armed?" Quincy asked as he got out of the car.

Wulf quietly shut his door. "Most likely. If they have a gun, shoot them. Except for Mary Jane. You'll know her when you see her."

Adjusting to the darkness, Wulf's eyes scaled the brick wall. After finding a groove in the blocks, he climbed over. Quincy was right behind him. They pulled out their guns, cocked back, and headed in the direction of a U-shaped carport.

Quincy gave a low 'click' sound with his tongue and pointed to the roof. Light sensors, possible cameras. They headed around the mansion toward the side that was dark, presumably with no one home. Finding an open window on the second floor above a trellis against the wall, Wulf began to climb. When his hands touched the windowsill, he hoisted himself up and into the room.

The bedroom had a frilly canopy and a bunch of pillows silhouetted by the moon. Teddy bears sat in a bookcase against the wall. For the lifestyle that Beasley led, the room was bizarre. Wulf did not recall the criminal having a family, and this appeared to be a little girl's room. He turned around and gave Quincy the go-ahead. Seconds later, he heard a sneeze. Wulf froze as Quincy climbed in.

A night light flicked on, and he knew the sound from the first time he'd heard it in the field. Someone had cocked a pump-action shotgun.

Pow! Pellets sprayed the wall above their heads.

"Hello, boys!" A blonde got up from the bed, holding the shotgun in both hands. She was skinny—sickly skinny—in a silk camisole and shorts. "They call me Sugarland, but I ain't hardly sweet. What are you doin' in my room?"

"Ma'am, we're looking for Mary Jane, that's all." Wulf spoke calmly from a hiding spot kneeling behind a treasure chest.

"Well, if Beasley's got her then she's his property now!"

Another shot went off, blasting through the stucco near Quincy's head. Sugarland shook her head. "No one move. See, that first shot was for Hurricane. If he's here, he's hungry. Who wants to die and who wants to be eaten?"

Her hand lifted for another pump. Wulf lunged at her.

They went sprawling onto the floor. Her thin body crunched beneath his girth. The gun clattered away from them. Her long fingernails dug into his face. No amount of restraining on his part slowed her down. Sugarland was clearly under the influence of some type of narcotic. He punched her in the eye, all in an attempt for self-preservation. But she continued to scratch.

"*You don't mess with Beasley! You don't mess with Beasley!*" Sugarland screamed on repeat as he caught her wrists above her head.

"Lady, just *stop!*" he screamed, fed up, as Quincy grabbed her shotgun. When she finally started to slow her struggling, he asked, "If I let you go, will you just sit there?"

She nodded.

As soon as he clambered off her, Sugarland began to claw again. In a swift, precise movement, Quincy hit her on the head with the butt of the shotgun. It was just enough force to render her unconscious.

"This is the twilight zone," Quincy hissed under his breath as they slowly made their way to the door. "Did you see the crazed look in her eye?"

"Expect the unexpected." Wulf rubbed the bloody scratches along his jaw and peeked through the cracked door. No one had come. They hurried down the right side of the stairs, all the while hearing commotion toward the back of the house. The voices. One of them belonged to Mary Jane. Relief slammed through him.

They slowly crept down the hall, stopping and hiding behind Greek goddess statues. They passed a large living room and looked around past a piano and couches. No one was hidden in the shadows. Then they entered toward the dining room.

They moved through the house and into the kitchen.

While their gaze quickly swept through the room on their quest to get closer to Mary Jane, Hurricane burrowed down the stairs.

"What the fuck!" Quincy shouted, attempting to aim his gun while Hurricane lunged off the last step.

Wulf shot between the eyes of his bumpy face, but the disfigured man moved too quickly. The shot pierced off the upper portion of Hurricane's ear. His punch dislocated Wulf's jaw before he slammed down to the floor.

With his fists clenched, Hurricane was about to hammer down on Quincy, but he stopped. Wulf fired off a shot that landed in his bicep, but it didn't seem to faze the beast. He took off running in the direction that Mary Jane and her abductor had gone. Quincy fired off a few shots.

"Shit, I don't think I got him," Quincy said.

Wulf gripped the bottom of his chin and reset his jaw with a quick jerk of the hand. "Next time, shoot something!"

They exited the sliding glass door to see Hurricane had climbed up the side of a massive fencing structure. There were stairs along the side of the Rottweilers' two-story high kennel where food could be dropped inside. Wulf could hear Mary Jane begging a man named Peter to stop. His eyes tracked her fearful voice, and then blood burned through his veins. Peter held Mary Jane by the neck, dangling her over the opening as the massive dogs growled and perched on their powerful hind legs, lunging as high as they could.

"G – get back!" Peter screeched as Hurricane pulled himself up on top of the kennel. "I swear! I'll drop her. Get back, you disgusting freak!"

"Mine!" Hurricane bellowed.

"Stop!" Peter yelled at Mary Jane as she scratched at his fingers and kicked in the air. With her taking all his attention, Hurricane lunged at him. At that same instant, Wulf rushed in a full sprint toward the stairs. Hurricane bumped into Mary Jane as he went for Peter's throat.

"Ahhh!" Down Mary Jane went, falling inside of the cage.

She clung to the wire roofing and pulled her lower body up. The tips of her boots locked onto the roofing fence as the barking dogs scrabbled for a bite, growling and snapping.

Peter shot at Hurricane and was clawed in the chest. He dropped to his knees. Hurricane lunged for the kill, falling over the side. The spikes of the wrought iron fence pierced Hurricane's spine.

"Stop!" Wulf shouted from the top of the stairs. He pointed at Peter as he lifted a foot to stomp down and crunch Mary Jane's fingers.

"Don't shoot him!" Mary Jane screamed.

Peter's lips curved into a sinister grin as he started to slam his foot down. Only he miscalculated, and his foot soared into the cage instead.

Wulf put the gun down and quickly grabbed Mary Jane's forearm and pulled up. She watched in horror as Peter fell past her. His fingertips barely grazed her boots as he tried to pull her down into the dog cage with him.

"I'm here." Wulf yanked her out. His back slammed into the roof, wrapping Mary Jane into his arms. She was positioned on top of him. Finally, safe, but she screamed for Peter.

"We have to save him!" she shouted.

"Mary Jane, it's okay. You're safe."

His abdomen hurt where Hurricane had hit him less than a few minutes ago. Gritting in pain, Wulf focused all of his energy on Mary Jane. The sound of gnawing, biting, and shrill screaming met their ears as he helped her to her feet, and they went down the stairs.

"No." Mary Jane pulled away from him at the last step. She looked back.

Peter's crying faded to nothing. His arms, face, and skin were ripped to shreds. The dogs continued to bite and gnaw at him.

Quincy put a bullet in each of the dogs' heads, silencing the night.

23

MARY JANE SAT QUIETLY IN THE STATE TROOPER'S VEHICLE. After the long night, she was mute. Wulf dreaded that the last couple of days had been wiped from her memory, because she was shrouded in the same hopeless demeanor from when they first meet. He sat in the back of an ambulance as a medic applied a dressing to his lower abdomen. When he refused a hospital visit, the EMT ended by compressing his abdomen. His eyes were glued onto Mary Jane.

The entire area of Beasley's home had been rushed by the troopers and SWAT. He'd been told that the same was happening at The Petting Zoo. Then the FBI entered the scene as the morning sun came over the horizon.

"All right." Wulf flashed at the EMT to stop the poking and prodding. The last of the binding was done and his eyes had never left Mary Jane's. She'd been the first one to be looked over by the medical team, but after a few bandages around her calf and a few Band-Aids to her forehead, she'd gone to sit in the car.

He slowly stood up, his heart heavy and sullen with

thoughts of Gracie—the young girl so in love she didn't rationalize that her life meant more. Peter had been literally preparing to feed Mary Jane to the dogs. Why would she be so concerned about his welfare? While medics assessed her, Quincy had mentioned that she was Peter's wife. In the field, he'd seen women take back husbands who'd beat them black and blue, some refusing to press charges. But this takes domestic abuse to another level.

He was thrust back into a world of caring for a woman who loved too hard—the wrong man, that is. Only Gracie had reminded him of a wayward foster sister. Her situation should have been recompense for not helping the only family he'd known as a child. And Mary Jane, their complicated relationship? Well, it all still pulled at his emotions. When the FBI came to take her statement, she kept staring at the road. The very same spot the ambulance had sped away from with Peter Grienke's chewed on body.

Wulf nodded to Robertson and Juarez, the male and female FBI agents on the scene, who'd thanked him and Jones for their rundown of the crime scene a while ago.

"They want me to stick around, but forget that." Jones patted his shoulder, stepping away from a dark-blue SUV. "I've been, at the very least, requested to keep my phone on for further contact."

"Yeah." Wulf nodded, knowing where the conversation was headed.

"Shelly wants me home asap. She chewed me out, and I have orders to bring you back with me."

"Yeah, I'm sure." The left side of Wulf's mouth turned upward, while he continued to stare at Mary Jane.

Quincy's gaze went toward Mary Jane too. "She's hot as hell, Dylan, but you know what I'm thinking, right?"

Wulf gave a slight nod.

"All right, I've given my two cents," he replied. "One of the squad cars is going to drop me off at your place on their way to The Petting Zoo, then I'm taking a quick nap. The next plane leaves this afternoon if you want to come back to reality, too. So far, Shelly has kept your mom from knowing what's going on but they're women. They worry. And shit, apparently, they have reason to."

Wulf handed Quincy the keys to his trailer. His mind was already back on Mary Jane, once again. He walked around the red sports car and the swarm of cruisers to the one that she sat in after giving her statement. Her eyes slowly lit up at the sight of him. His tension eased, even though he felt like crap.

"Wow," she cracked a smile, "I should've known it'd take a lot to get the big guy down."

"You've surprised me today too." He tried to kneel between the car and door, but his body screamed. He leaned against the fender instead.

"How so? I brought down an animal, a mad scientist, and a fat psycho all by myself." She jokingly grinned.

"Yes, all the credit belongs to you, Mrs. Mallory Grienke," he said, peering into her eyes.

Mary Jane bit her lip for a second. "I might not be her."

***

She recalled learning more about Peter Grienke and that he'd had a scientific discovery on facial products. The twin's only distinguishing characteristic had been Megan's scarred face. Ironically, drugs had done nothing to rot her teeth, but her face had become haggard from drug use. After using Grienke's products, Megan had returned to her youthful look, except for the anger that lay dormant in her heart and soul. Now, nothing separated Mary Jane from being either twin.

"But Quincy told me you're married to Peter Grienke."

Mary Jane stared at Wulf. There was something just behind his eyes or maybe it was the reflection of the sun rising in his pupils. "Let's keep this between us. The FBI and state police have verified me as Mallory Portman-Grienke. So we'll just keep it as that for all intents and purposes. But I might be Mallory Portman-Grienke, or I might be Megan Portman, Mallory's *identical* twin."

"That's why you didn't want me to extinguish Peter while he was a deadly threat to you?" He refused to give her a pass.

"Yeah." Mary Jane cocked her head, wondering where the animosity came from. No, wait, she wasn't the meek type. "Peter was about to tell me the entire truth. Now he's fighting for his life. Guess it doesn't matter now." Mary Jane shook her head and huffed. "I'm taking the Benz convertible that belonged to me or my sister, and I'm hitting the road. Stop looking at me like that. I'm driving 'til the gas runs out."

"How will you support yourself?"

"I knew you'd ask." She laughed wickedly, and then she silently mouthed, "Are there cameras or recorders in this car?"

He shrugged then held out a hand.

She grabbed it, got out, and they walked toward the perimeter of the war zone. When a cop gave him the eye—indicating that it wasn't safe for them to leave yet—he put his hand up, signaling that they just needed a little room. They leaned against the wrought iron gate.

"While I sat in that car, Jake passed me this." She dug her hand into her bra and handed him an envelope.

"Jake?" He cocked an eyebrow.

"Yup, Jake knows how to look out for a girl. He gets around well too." She shrugged. "He had on a State Police windbreaker."

Wulf opened the envelope. Out slid a set of keys and a note. His gaze couldn't take in the words fast enough.

It's beyond me why I love you. But I know keeping you around won't end well. Stay as far away from me as possible.

Take these keys to the train station at the edge of town.

–Jake

At the bottom of the note there was an address for a train station and a number to a locker for her to check. "See." Mary Jane grinned.

"Yes, the undertones imply obsession bordering on murder if you don't take heed."

"Oh, shut up, Wulf. Don't be jealous because Jake is dangerously hot," she said. He elbowed her softly and she chuckled.

"What are you going to do with this key, Ma—?" He stopped abruptly, not sure what to call her.

"I prefer Mary Jane. And I'm going to get my money."

"Of all the conclusions, how did you determine there's money in the locker?"

"Oh, so technical, Wulf. I don't know. Only money can pacify how I'm feeling now. If it's money, I can roam around doing nothing." She enjoyed his cringing as she spoke. "If it's not, I think I'll steal a few wallets on my way down to Mexico. Don't get your panties in a bunch."

"I don't fucking wear panties. What's your plan, MJ?" He was serious. Mary Jane could be delusional if she wanted, redirecting the craziness of these past few days, but he needed to know everything.

"If Jake left me money, I'm set. On the chance that he didn't, then call me Sticky Fingers. I'll nab just enough money to buy a small villa on the beach. Damn it, Wulf, you're still looking at me with those cop-eyes—extra *judgy.*"

"Judgy, really? So your plan ends with a small villa on the beach," he retorted.

"I'll grow my own fruit and vegetables and live off the land. It's a simple plan, a simple life."

"That's not a plan." He gave a soft chuckle to her joke, trying to keep it light for the sake of his abdomen.

"It is. Although I don't know how I'm going to steal a cow when I decide I'm done being a vegetarian." He followed as she started walking back toward Beasley's mansion. Her index finger to her lip, she really considered her options. "Wulf, I don't have a life to return to. I'm sure just improvising will outshine this current crappy life of mine."

"MJ, you've transitioned a good amount in the past seventy-two hours. You went from arguing and talking too much about shooting me and now, we're discussing cows and chickens. How is it that you talk so much, but you never really say anything?"

She laughed. "How is it that I know your anal ass didn't mean to joke, only offer an assessment, but I'm dying right now?"

His lips never cracked a smile. "Joking under the current circumstances?"

"Yes. Go ahead, keep looking at me like I'm crazy. You can go crazy with me. Come with me."

"I am," he ordered, grabbing her arm and pulling her toward him. His eyes held a note of pain from the movement, but Wulf didn't complain.

She gazed into those eyes. He'd travel the world with her. They'd have hot sex on the beach, and in the jungle, and in the sea. If Jake didn't leave any money, she'd steal and survive like she did as a kid, but that didn't matter. Wulf would be with her.

"Stop looking at me like that, Mary Jane. You can't talk

me out of going with you to the train station. I'm going, and there's nothing you can do to stop me." When she pulled away, eyes narrowed, he added, "Why are you so hard-headed? This might be a trick. Agent Juarez indicated that Jake's the only henchman unaccounted for that Beasley employed from The Petting Zoo."

She grumbled, trying to hide her disappointment of her assumption that he was going with her for the long haul. No, Wulf had only promised that their last stop together was the train station.

24

FBI PHOENIX HEADQUARTERS

AGENT ARIEL JUAREZ TACKED THE LAST DMV PHOTO ONTO the board. She stood back in her loafers and looked at all the evidence. Over thirty photos. Some were living victims, others newly deceased, then there were the bones—almost gift wrapped. *The ease of it.*

Her mind instantly went back to the dumping ground. Luckily, Beasley's men hadn't dug a mass grave. Though the area had teemed with forensic anthropologists who'd spent all night collecting skeletal pieces and decaying matter to fit almost ready-made puzzles, this was the extent of the now deceased Beasley's offerings. The remainder of her job would be difficult.

Ariel's eyes stopped on a profile photo of the affluent Whitley Rodgers—post mortem. The picture was taken less than a year ago. Whitley's pearly-white teeth were set in a captivating smile. The whites in her pale-blue eyes was so vastly different from the deceased woman—Sugarland.

Sugarland was plagued with infections. Her body hadn't accepted the change in lifestyle. Officer Wulf and Jones' story of Sugarland didn't fit with Whitley's profile. The twang in her tone, the manner in which she'd fought for Beasley—all of it was foreign. If DNA hadn't determined Whitley Rodgers and Sugarland were indeed the same, Ariel wouldn't have believed it.

But facts were facts.

Whitley Rodgers was an alumna of Harvard Law, attending with her then husband. Whitley had been the brains of Senator Rodgers taking office. Yet, Whitley *had become* Sugarland. They said she'd been plagued by rage, delirium, and aggression for Beasley. Whitley had technically *died* in a house fire just shy of a year ago. Her husband had escaped with second-degree burns. Senator Rodgers' popularity had increased after his heroic speech about attempting to save his wife during the fire. *Hmmm.*

Ariel looked at African American Tiana Clement, who was known in these parts as a new stripper named Diamond. Tiana's abduction was the reason for FBI interference with the state police's investigation. Ariel had been head-agent-in-charge of Tiana's ransom a few months ago. She'd disappeared at her extravagant "sweet *eighteen*"—for the well-to-do, every year was marked by an extravagant party. The autopsy placed Tiana's death at about thirty-six hours ago. The ballistics report indicated a forty-five gun with a hydro-shock bullet was the cause.

Though she didn't have as rough a transition as Whitley, Tiana had also been reared in an affluent family. Tiana Clement was "princess" of the bayou. Her Creole family had clout. That didn't help them get their daughter back when she had been kidnapped for millions. Juarez had turned the investigation toward the father's direction after receiving the call from the Arizona police.

During the ransom, Juarez had a gut feeling that Tiana's father was involved. It was revealed that Clement had opened a new life insurance policy just months before his child's abduction. Ariel reviewed the notes of accusations of child sexual abuse. The newspapers and townspeople were divided in their hatred or pity for Mr. Clement and his family.

"It's creepy, isn't it?" Agent Robertson asked as he sipped a mug of coffee. Their initial visit to retrieve Tiana Clement had erupted with more signs of kidnappings. Juarez and Robertson were given ultimate lead, with a force of agents under their wings. It had been a long week. He sat the mug on the tabletop and stuffed his hands in his suit pants pockets. She knew where his eyes were before he even plucked the five-by-seven DMV photo of Julio Perez from the board.

"I'm still wrapping my head around Perez's situation."

"By the way, our local authority liaison, who's on his way to provide the news of the death to Perez's wife, remembers Mrs. Perez. She came into the police station years ago. The cop said she was so young—a child herself, pregnant and married—when Julio started working for the Overtime Trucking Company. The officer who filed the missing persons report just *knew* the big guy had run off with another woman."

Robertson compared Julio Perez's photo to Hurricane's photo. The same height and brown complexion, but Julio had a slightly thinner build. The autopsy report indicated that the scars and wounds on his body spanned from fourteen years to present. His brain was abnormally smaller.

This is where Ariel's religious views parted with the law. She'd never been one to allow her personal beliefs to control her intuition or how she proceeded with an assignment. *Brainwashing? This is just out of my realm of understanding, but these women wouldn't give up their lives for Beasley. Not without coercion.*

She yawned. After Mary Jane, Wulf, and Jones' perspectives and comparable stories, they'd interviewed countless numbers of Beasley's employees. Half indicated brainwashing, and the other half weren't all there mentally. Julio Perez didn't have a rap sheet. His DMV record was spotless, a clean background entirely. Sometime within the fourteen years, he'd disappeared only to return as an animal—Hurricane. Mallory Portman-Grienke, aka Mary Jane, said he had a canine mentality.

She looked away from Robertson and toward the board. The remainder of the strippers at The Petting Zoo, those alive and those whose bodies hadn't been fully decomposed, had all been linked to important and/or affluent persons, either abducted or missing. There were more skeletal remains to assess. Ariel banked on her intuition. The people closest to these women had sentenced them to life in another mindset and in the hands of a monster. Instead of the usual statistic of the murderer being related to the victim, these women had been brainwashed.

Juarez could only assume this was a case of moral sins. A wife of the only doctor in a small town, who'd long ago remarried. A daughter of another rich man had been kidnapped.

But Ariel knew that this was just the tip of the iceberg. An intelligent, money-hungry man like Grienke had an entire organization that she had yet to unearth.

Through all her relationship-mapping of each dead woman, she'd found one woman who didn't fit in the neat puzzle piece. The forensic pathologist determined the woman's death was around five months ago. DNA records indicated a female Ukranian woman. A quick background search showed she had come to America to attend a prestigious university and was on her last year in the engineering program.

With a deep sigh and no leads on how the Ukranian had ended up in Arizona, Juarez turned her sights to Bonnie Timms. With dirty-blond hair and innocent eyes, hers was the only other body who had been identified but had yet to be associated with Beasley. Bonnie's age further separated her from the rest of the deceased victims—a death of approximately a month ago, give or take a few days based on the climate of her grave.

Ariel's own mother had given money—hand-over-fist—to the thirteen-year-old Bonnie's evangelistic father over the years. Her mom had asked repeatedly about the kidnapping on many occasions, even though it hadn't been assigned to Juarez. Bonnie's abduction had stayed within the state of Texas. Ariel just thought the young girl's father was a sham. He put to shame real Christians.

"We have a job to do," Juarez sighed, looking at a sea of faces.

"Once I let my brain wrap around the fact that serial killer Jakob Woods, aka 'Jake,' has a heart, I'll be sure to help you." Robertson gave a soft chuckle.

"I'm not sure that I follow." Juarez's face tilted slightly. She stared intently as he plucked the eight-by-ten of Jake, seemingly lost in the photo.

"I saw him." Robertson was unable to break eye contact with the photo.

"You *saw* Jakob Woods—excuse me, *Jake*, as our Mrs. Mallory Grienke, aka Mary Jane Doe, likes to call him—and you didn't try to take him down?" she scoffed, finding it rather ridiculous. "This man killed forty-five men, women, and children, and you laid eyes on him?"

"Fifty-four," Robertson said, still staring at the photo.

"His file indicates that he killed fifty-four people. Jakob Woods grew up in a militia household, half Afghan and Somali. His Muslim father smuggled their family into the country when he was still an infant, but that didn't stop the psychopath from developing a taste for blood, as did his parents. Though, unlike his family, he didn't have an interest in religious radicalism. Trust me, I read the 'Jakob Woods' manual as a rookie. His file was as large as a college text-book. I was young, ambitious, and disgusted, seeing what he'd done to one family. Well, he hasn't been active in the last seven or eight years."

"C'mon, Robertson." Ariel Juarez perched herself on the tabletop and retied her hair into a severe bun. "You couldn't have seen him."

"The moment we arrived on the scene, I noticed him." Robertson grabbed a tuft of his hair in shock. "Woods hasn't been active in years and-and the man I saw, well, he looked different. He had on a uniform like the rest of the state police. His eyes weren't so empty. Not in the way Jakob Woods would be, that's for sure."

Ariel's bottom lip dropped. "You've got to be kidding me?"

"I wish I was kidding you. I can't fathom how much of a rookie mistake I just made, it's like fucking partying with Bundy, Dahmer, and Wuornos and not being aware." He gasped. Robertson leaned against the table, finally setting the photo down. "Woods went to a cruiser, the one Mary Jane was in, and gave her a blanket."

The look in both of their eyes indicated that they needed to speak with Mary Jane STAT.

"Robertson, Juarez," Officer Samuel stated as his head popped into the room. He was a new black guy to the team, but had a wealth of accolades. "Lemuel Fetters, Lyle's brother, came in. He just told me something that I think you both are gonna want to hear."

Robertson and Juarez looked at each other. "Which room is he in?"

"Three. The cameras are a go."

"All right," Robertson said. "Get ahold of Mrs. Grienke and Officer Wulf. We need them here for more questioning."

Samuel nodded.

"And can one of you, for the love of God, get into Grienke's computer system?" she sighed, glancing at the computer team, all MIT grads and fresh-faced. Ariel gritted her teeth, she needed the bastard to survive. Grienke was in a coma after all his surgeries.

Robertson added, "Juarez, once we crack his firewalls, we'll have concrete evidence instead of hearsay."

"Yeah, well the 'hearsay,' in this instance, is very cohesive." Ariel huffed at how statistically impossible it was. As the two partners walked, she joked, "Robertson, you're the good guy today, or I will tell everybody that you laid eyes on one of the world's most-wanted men and let him walk."

Robertson released a deep sigh and opened the door to the room. He stepped in after she did. Ariel took the lead and made introductions.

"Lemuel Fetters, we've been told that you have a story for us."

"Do I? That's the understatement of the century. I'ma tell you a story my brother told me. I thought Lyle was crazy, but seems he can't be if Hurricane could go and rip Beasley up like I heard he'd done."

"And what story is that?" Juarez asked.

"Beasley and some guy named Peter–whatever, they brainwashed women. I was gon' buy my mom some of

Peter's face cream one Christmas on account that Lyle said it had to work, since these broads had gone all loyal to Beasley and all, but the shit was too damn expensive."

"Tell me more about the brainwashing." Robertson steered the conversation back.

"Started about fifteen years ago. Lyle would tell me every time some chick went missing. Not just any runaway or good-for-nothing women, but these were powerhouses. A woman from one of those cold countries, who'd invented this gadget about a half year ago, she went missing a month before the gadget started showin' up on commercials. Guess what? Her college roommate patented the idea. I thought Lyle was lying, but after I seen a commercial for the doohickey, I'm like maybe Lyle is on to something."

"Do you know the woman's name?" Juarez asked. *Could he be referring to the Ukranian grad student that was found at the dumping site? She was still wearing a sweater from a prestigious university.*

"She had a hard name to pronounce. Ya—Yoolo . . ."

Yoloslav? Juarez crossed her fingers and kept quiet. She didn't want to make Lemuel susceptible to interviewing biases by stating the name.

"Yoslo somethin'! I don't know. Anyway, every time Lyle tells me stories, he comes home with cash for days, while he brags about other important women and daughters of sick fucks who owned this, that, and the other shit. The last girl they got, Mary Jane . . . he didn't know how, but she was related to Peter. That brainiac who grew up here and hit the ground running after high school often came home, ever so often. Peter and Beasley were never friends growing up, but let Beasley tell you, the man made him richer than all his females. Lyle says Peter rarely dropped in, just to teach Lyle how to use some doohickey and boss Beasley around. But a while ago, Peter came around crying like a bitch."

Robertson interjected, "Tell us more about this return."

"Lyle said, Peter wasn't his usual flashy self. Just cryin', saying he just couldn't kill this girl. Peter wanted to save her from some sort of cage, then take her home as his wife."

"Was it his wife, Mallory Grienke?"

"I don't know, but he said he loved her. He just wanted them to start fresh. Lyle said, he wanted her to stop cuttin' up."

"Can you give us an estimate of when this happened? A week, a couple of months?"

"I don't know." Lemuel paused to drink down his glass of water. "Maybe he brought her about a month ago. The girls stay in a room for a while, Lyle said, before they change."

"Do you know how Lyle changed them?"

"No, well, some little pill then a computer thingamajig finishes them off. Clears their system, he says. Beta brain blockers and some other big words. Anyhow, this is the story. A few weeks ago, he was making his rounds, giving them their pills. Mary Jane was in one room and a young girl in the other, a *young* one. I mean, too young."

"Do you know her name?" Ariel held in her concern. *Thirteen-year-old Bonnie?* "Age? What did she look like?"

"Don't know. But when I say young, she was too damn young to be sent to The Petting Zoo. Lyle went to see the girl first. He said somehow the young'n was loose from her chains when he opened the door. She ran past him. Jake had just come by—oh, funny story."

Lemuel clapped his thighs.

"Lyle said Jake used to be some type of badass. Beasley and everyone but him knows his head has been screwed with. Lyle said when they got Jake, he was meaner than a rattlesnake! Lyle wet his pants a couple times he went to give Jake the medicine. Now, they say Jake's still crazy, but the computer thingy got him straightened out. So he just ain't crazy enough to cross anyone. And when I tell you crazy, I mean, Beasley bragged about being worshiped by a criminal —and I mean a fucking *war criminal*."

Ariel Juarez gulped softly, so Jake really was Jakob Woods.

"So, anyhow, the little girl...oh, I remember more about her. She was some big-time minister's kid. They said she'd pray all the time. That's all I know. When Lyle told me the pastor could afford to drop the little filly off with no remorse, it was beyond me. And I just wouldn't believe no church folk got *dinero* like that!"

Bingo! This must be Bonnie Timms' story. Ariel gulped. She just needed evidence to back-up Lemuel's statement. "Tell me more."

"So, Jake saw the kid but he didn't know 'bout the brain-washing. He doesn't usually see the girls until they go to The Petting Zoo. He has this one-track mind. When they get there, somehow he knows not to kill 'em. And he hadn't seen her 'round town either." Lemuel shrugged.

Ariel Juarez held in her emotions. Bonnie Timms' body wasn't as old as many of the other skeletal remains. The body had begun to decompose and with the heat of each day, the putrefaction process had sped up. However, the coroner's report indicated that she had a fractured skull, bleeding in the ears and eye sockets. She silently listened, waiting for his story to either match with the coroner's report or not.

"That child ran for her life, leaving Lyle in the dust. She was running down the stairs of Beasley's mansion. Jake had just come in, and he heard a bunch of commotion—"

"From the girl?"

"No, the movie."

"What movie?"

"Lyle was watching *The Eradicator II*. He'd said the movie just became clear enough to see on his Kodi Firestick. When Beasley was gone all day and the maids weren't there, my brother would go for a swim and eat like a hog. Heck, one time he tried to have a house party, but people were too scared to come. Anyway, Lyle had on the entertainment system and it was loud as shit. He said it helped pump him up, making him not feel sorry before he went to give the girls their pills."

On the TV screen, Special Agent Anya Randolph followed rogue agent Trent Winehouse onto the balcony of the beachfront hotel. Lyle rolled his eyes and took a swig of his beer. The romance parts were boring, but the remote control was on the coffee table next to his feet. Lyle glanced at his watch as Anya entered the hotel bedroom to ask Trent why he'd left her. Lyle had streamed the movie back to back. It was just that good. He thought about fast-forwarding it up to the next morning when the agents were blindsided by Trent's crew, but he needed to give Bonnie her shot and that sexy new chick too. He smiled, getting up to the sound of Anya and Trent rolling on the bed.

He grabbed the medicine case next to the remote and went into the new girl's room first. The room was quiet, aside from the loud surround sound of the television below.

He smiled at her. Her name was to be Mary Jane. She didn't look like one. She lay on her bed, the only piece of furniture in the room. He shrugged. He couldn't get a good look at her ample shape as she slept in a ball, meek and scared. When he grabbed her arm, she awoke. The chain on her left ankle chinked against the metal bedpost. Grienke's girl didn't put up much of a fight, just whimpered and cried and asked for Peter, over and over again.

He gave Mary Jane the cup and the pill. "You haven't started forgetting yet, girl, so keep in mind I have a gun and take your medication." He spoke harshly, although he wouldn't dream of touching her. It would be the death of him.

When finished, Lyle closed and locked the door. Cracking his knuckles, he headed to the next room. Little Bonnie always put up a fight. If only she'd fought her father off a few more times. If only she would have told on the pastor.

Just outside the door, he grabbed another pill. Bonnie had a few more days before her brain could be safely erased. Beasley planned to sell her for a ridiculous amount of money to a foreigner who wanted a child bride. With the syringe in one hand, he smiled at the sound of bullets blazing in the background. Yes, Anya had to be scampering off the bed and behind the side stand. He opened the door and fell back on his ass.

The chain and lock were on the bed. The blur that just rushed past him had to be little Bonnie.

"Fuck!" he screamed, knowing Jake should be here any moment to get Sugarland for her doctor's appointment. She wasn't transitioning well, although she'd been here for a long time.

"Bonnie, wait!" Lyle scrambled to his feet and ran the length of the mansion toward the stairs. Beasley would be pissed. If Jake was here, then any unknown person's life would be in jeopardy. He hastened down the left side. "Jake!" he screamed, noticing Beasley's reaper standing near the front door.

Jake's eyes narrowed as Bonnie ran toward him, making a beeline for the door. Bonnie stopped in her tracks and was getting ready to turn around when Jake grabbed her about the waist.

"Leave me alone!" she screamed, chomping her teeth into his taut forearm.

Jake grabbed her head with one hand and slammed it against the Greek goddess statue. The sound of her skull cracking was *deafening, even louder than the shots fired on* The Eradicator II *in the background.*

"Lyle even had a few tears in his eyes when he told me about the lil' girl."

Robertson and Juarez gave a quick glance at each other. Lemuel's story matched the coroner's report for Bonnie Timms' death due to blunt force trauma to the head.

"All right, you were saying there was something important that occurred on that day. Something happened to Jake?" Robertson asked. They still didn't have much of a reason to connect the national terrorist, Jakob Woods, to Beasley and Grienke's side business. Jake had been a mercenary until the cause that he fought for turned out to be a sham. Then he'd gone off, pillaging the countryside, killing all in his way. One day, he'd just stopped. The FBI agents on the case were stumped by the cold trail. With that erratic criminal profile in mind, Robertson mentioned the only possibility that would tie together all three men. "You said Jake had been previously brainwashed to do Beasley's bidding?"

"Yes, he was." Lemuel cracked a smile. "Like I said, Lyle had *The Eradicator* on, that action-love story. He said before Jake left for the evening, he seemed weird. Lyle heard him in the room with Sugarland. They were talking. Lyle said Sugarland had become childlike when they tried to brainwash her. That's why they always kept her in such a nice little room. Jake was in the room with her, having tea, and chatting." He laughed.

They stared.

"Y'all still don't get it?" Lemuel asked.

"Explain please," Robertson requested.

"All right. For the first time in his life, Jake didn't do as Beasley had told him. After Jake got all *Doctor Phil* with

Sugarland, Jake went back downstairs. He noticed the little girl and he cried—as if she was his own child—as if that crazy mofo hadn't killed her. Jake picked up her lifeless body, took her outside, and dug a grave for her; even put a little stone at the head of it."

"All right." Juarez waved a hand. Yes, Lemuel's story added up with the forensic pathologist's report. Bonnie Timms' body was the only one that hadn't been buried in the graveyard behind The Petting Zoo.

"You guys are really missing the big picture here!" Lemuel exclaimed. "Lyle also said, a few days later when Jake went to The Petting Zoo, he met Mary Jane for the first time. MJ was there so Beasley could taunt the guys with a quick look before she made her stay at the home while she learned to be a good girl. As I said, she had a few weeks before her brain was finished changing. Oh, the two of you are no fun! Listen, I think she turned into that super-agent on *The Eradicator*. Bad bitch or not, I didn't expect to see her ever again after disrespecting Beasley. Anyhow, Lyle told me that Beasley let Jake have her for the night. Jake fell in love! And Mary Jane turned into an *action* type chick like in the movie, and he was the costar."

Juarez and Robertson exchanged looks. She folded her hands thinking about how Robertson had said that Jake risked being identified to bring Mary Jane a blanket at the crime scene. However, he was previously brainwashed to do everything Beasley told him.

She remembered Mary Jane's story. Peter Grienke's wife didn't fit the profile for tactical abilities. How had she apprehended Officer Wulf's gun? Lemuel's farfetched story correlated with this.

If Jake heard the movie and the sociopath fell in love, and Mary Jane heard the movie and subconsciously learned defense skills—*Juarez, really?* She couldn't believe this outlandish story, she thought, while kneading the tension in her shoulders. Everyone who'd mentioned Mary Jane's fighting affirmed to her having no fear. She was a crack-shot with a gun. Had her brain internalized the female character in *The Eradicator*? Juarez hadn't seen the movie, but she could pretty much guess the farfetched action.

"Okay, Mr. Fetters, did your brother ever seem brainwashed?" Juarez asked. "If Jake was brainwashed previously to become Beasley's 'human weapon' and he was so susceptible to becoming brainwashed again, due to *The Eradicator*, like you indicated, did it ever appear that Lyle was brainwashed as well?"

"Hell, no."

She had lower level agents working with the strippers at the club to identify any information, because although the FBI needed to keep this case under wraps there had to be a million bones in Beasley's dumping ground. Bones belonging to dozens of women.

So far it was reported that all the women were highly loyal. Each one had a special agent assigned to her while undergoing medical examinations. In addition, the lower level henchmen Beasley hired didn't seem to know anything. So right now, Ariel knew she and Robertson were grasping for straws.

"Okay, so you're saying that Jake and Mary Jane were sustainable due to their brainwashing. Sugarland internalized the brainwashing and...Hurricane? Can you tell us his role in being brainwashed? I assume he stayed at Beasley's mansion."

"He spends most of his time locked up like Knight and King." Lemuel chuckled. "Hurricane was Beasley's favorite dog to torture. So, I reckon he was tortured while he was being brainwashed."

Ariel nodded and allowed him to continue with his story. A lot of the stories he'd heard secondhand from his brother, Lyle, corroborated with the missing women found in the dumping ground. Once completed, she and Robertson stepped out of the interrogation room.

"Learn something new every time we walk into work, huh?" Juarez shook her head as they walked down the hall.

"Some days more than others."

"So Beasley received some sort of kickback from Grienke for altering the minds of women, and I'm assuming Grienke was paid out the nose to get rid of certain people."

"We're in a shit storm," Juarez said. "For now, we've placed Mrs. Portman-Grienke at the scene because her husband was too much of a pussy to clear her own brain with his own system. He just wanted to come and save the day."

Robertson chuckled. "Yeah, I could see an asshole like him. Those grandiose delusions offer him a role as her savior. You'd think he'd lock her into a palace tower, a more romantic scene than Beasley's cage. That warrant we had for his cell phone provided us with enough clues to add a shoddy fairytale ending to their story. He was on his way here to bring his confused, little wife home."

Her steps faltered for a moment as she considered, "But he did try to feed her to the wolves—*ahem*, dogs."

"C'mon, she probably pissed him off again. And the poor man snapped."

The two agents stepped into a conference room next door to the interrogation room. Officer Samuel sat at a table, looking through the two-way mirror at a lone Lemuel. His dark eyes slowly turned away as if he was still attempting to absorb the man's story.

Juarez said, "Samuel, what's the ETA on Officer Wulf and Mallory Portman-Grienke's arrival? I want them in different interrogation rooms like yesterday."

Samuel stood up. "They haven't answered their cell phones. I've already sent a team to Wulf's address."

Ariel Juarez huffed. She needed them to tell their stories again. After Lemuel Fetters' statement, everything was beginning to add up. Yet more puzzle pieces were appearing.

Robertson rubbed his goatee. "Okay, so Lemuel Fetters has put the puzzle together in ways we haven't even begun to."

"Yes, he has."

"We have a team devoted to searching for double-brain-scrambled Jake. I almost wish Fetters' story was one hundred percent concrete, and we could turn Jake into the Pope. Seems like a more noble way to fuck with people's heads, right?"

"That would be nice." She nodded.

25

AFTER THEY'D ALL TAKEN TURNS SHOWERING AT HIS TRAILER, Wulf rented a Malibu. They dropped off Quincy at the airport. Now, they were headed to the train station. He checked the magazine clip in his Beretta as she drove.

"Wulf," she began, glancing at him. Though she'd stood in the background while he parted ways with his friend, she'd listened in. Jones had good reason for Wulf to return to L.A. Wulf had been selective of his words. She wasn't sure if he knew she'd eavesdropped, but he was putting her needs before his very own life.

Now they were headed to the train station. "I know you're returning to Los Angeles," Mary Jane began.

"I might as well go home, maybe at the end of the week when Juarez says I can leave town. I've come to realize that disappearing is not an effective way to escape the past."

"About Gracie?" she asked sincerely.

He nodded.

"I'm sorry for how things transpired with her. But, before you go, can I tell you my story? Well, two stories. I have Megan and Mallory's memories in my head. Their shortcomings, their trials and tribulations—I don't want to travel the world and have them stuck inside. You know, it's hard keeping a secret." She paused from all the rambling, while pulling into the train station parking lot. "Never mind, you're right. I have been hit in the head too much."

"You can tell me." He put away the gun and gave her all his attention as Mary Jane found a spot in the second row.

"Nah," she said, unhooking the seat belt to get out. "I have two lifetimes worth of stories. It would take too long. Just stay on the lookout. If there are any signs of Jake, and you're right about him wanting to love and kill me, please shoot his ass. To be completely transparent, if there's nothing in this box, I might hunt him down and shoot him myself."

He chuckled softly at her attempt at a joke. They both knew this was almost the end of the line for them. Wulf was a short chapter in her epic, crummy, never-ending tragedy of a life.

Inside the one-room train station, Mary Jane smiled at the clerk and turned in the direction of the lockers against the left wall with Wulf close behind her. She passed by two wood benches and pulled out the letter from Jake, which had the exact locker number. For some reason when he first gave her the six-digit locker code—she assumed it was a phone number. He had said the rest of the clue about getting to the train station was in the trunk of the Corolla. He'd said if she was found, he didn't want one of Beasley's men taking the code and the locker number. After a shaky breath, she put in the code and opened the door to see a large duffel bag.

"Let me open it," said Wulf.

"No way!" Mary Jane snatched it out.

"What if there's something dangerous inside?"

"What if it's *my* money?"

And don't be so good to me, Wulf, you haven't even promised to come with me.

She pulled at the zipper. It stuck and she yanked, but it wouldn't give. Wulf grabbed the bag. He pulled at the zipper, and stacks of money flew out. They quickly grabbed the bills and stuffed them back inside, though nobody was around.

"It might be drug money," Wulf advised.

"*It just might, Wulf,*" she said, exasperated. "Don't you understand that I don't give a damn? A naive conscience isn't the same as a guilty conscience. While the SCPD is a wash, I'm sure you aren't going to rat me out."

She snatched the bag, and they hurried out the door. She went to the trunk of the car, pressed the remote, and it popped open. She placed the duffel inside and closed it. She laughed giddily.

"Do you think Glenn will sell me his Grand National? Never mind, just drop me off at the first used-car dealership you see, Dylan. I'm getting a badass bungalow on the ocean!" She rubbed her hands together.

He stopped at the door. "Why'd you call me that?"

"Huh?"

"You just called me by my first name. We've already established the reasons you call me *Wulf.*"

She stroked a hand over his broad chest saying, "I can call you whatever I want." *C'mon, Wulf, don't make me ask you to come with me.* She sighed. Sex as manipulation might work, but she didn't want the guilt of making Wulf leave behind some shitty town for a life with her, to only find out her crazy ass wasn't worth it. But the part of her that was Megan didn't care. That very part of her craved happiness and didn't consider remorse or regret. It craved Dylan Wulf.

He took hold of her shoulders and looked down at her. "Not Dylan. You only use my given name when attempting to manipulate me. You're highly aware that I don't take kindly to deception."

She pressed her mouth to his in a searing hot kiss, one that left her as breathless as she hoped he was at the moment. "Even if sex is involved? There's a lot of road between here and L.A. I don't mind dropping you off on my way to Mexico, but you can't whine when I grab a wallet or two along the way."

"Let's not disregard the fact that this is my rental. But you have a bag full of money!"

"Old habits die hard."

"Whose habit was that? Mallory's or Megan's?"

The happy banter died down. It took her a second, but she mustered up the courage to speak. "Mallory's. Then again Megan liked to use sex to get what she wanted." Her fingers nestled in between his belt buckle. "I know exactly what I want, Officer *Dylan* Wulf."

She crushed her mouth to his, demanding a fierce kiss. She feasted on his mouth, his tongue, his sexy lips. *Could I blow your mind enough to come with me?*

Her hands worked their way to the back of his neck. Mary Jane pulled up on her tippy toes as he moaned into her mouth. Lust pulsated between the depths of her thick thighs, but she thought better of jumping up and wrapping her legs around him as she'd done during one of their trysts on their first night together. Wulf's abdomen needed to rest a while. As her tongue wiggled into his ear, she ordered, "Open the door and get in."

"It's daytime."

"Oh, let's not make that a problem." She winked.

She got into the passenger seat as he adjusted the

driver's side and closed the door. She unzipped his pants and pulled out his erect dick. Her mouth watered as she stared at the sex in his eyes. Licking her lips, she leaned toward his length and opened wide with a warm laugh.

Slowly his muscular frame began to relax. Mary Jane marveled in how much power she had over him in this instant. Her breath caressed the tautness of his cock. Her tongue slipped out and twirled around the magnificent king's crown. Flicking, teasing, and pleasing were part of her plans as her throat expanded to receive him. Arousal pooled into her mouth and she gulped it down along with half of his cock as she sucked.

His erection banged against her tonsils with each thrust.

"Fuck me," Wulf groaned, twining his hand around her ponytail. He pumped her up and down. Her mouth fucked him sloppy, leaving a wet gloss along the hard, never-ending ridges of his cock.

She moaned and groaned as his cock beat against the back of her throat with each thrust.

"MJ," he sighed, hardly able to speak. "Fuck, beautiful, I'm about to come."

Every inch of her body tensed, the warmness inside her gone. The anticipation of pleasing him frozen in time.

"MJ, don't tease me," Wulf begged, his eyes opening. The warm, wet, tight funnel was no longer over his cock. When he noticed the tears in her eyes, Wulf caressed her cheek with his callused palm. "Beautiful, what's wrong?"

She sat back in the seat. *Oh, God, this is exactly why I can't ruin Wulf's life with my story.*

"Tell me." His voice was woven with authority and serenity.

She dabbed at her eyes with her palm. "Mallory was bitten by a dog."

"What?"

She gagged, having a vivid image of Vin.

"MJ, talk to me, what's wrong?"

His concern was tangible, wrapping around her shoulders. But Mary Jane couldn't get the disgusting taste out of her mouth. Nor the thoughts from her head. Mallory looked to be about fifteen years old. The first time Vin had tried to get her to go down on him, she'd bitten his penis. His pit bull had retaliated at his master's screech and bit her in the back of her calf muscle.

He cautiously moved into a seated position with her next to him. "Why are you crying?"

"I can't tell you." She turned away in embarrassment. His tender eyes were too much. She drowned in his sincerity.

He maneuvered around, grimacing slightly in pain. His callused thumb took hold of her chin, gently pulling her gaze back to his. "MJ, you can tell me anything in the world. We've been through so much shit."

"We are tied together," she murmured in agreement, still stuck in another world. Damn it, but his beautiful deep voice and the promises he began to make couldn't bring her back. Vin and his foul taste clung to her.

"MJ, I'll always be there for you. If you want to run around Mexico for a while, I'll go. Shit, I will not let anything happen to you in this world, so I *am* going."

"Wulf, we've connected in ways I've never thought possible in just a few token days. But no matter what crap you and I went through, I'd still feel guilty. I haven't even told you their stories. You'll want to get rid of me," she sighed. "I don't want to know."

She couldn't get the image out of her head. Vin had popped the dog on the head after the pit bull had gotten good and locked onto her calf muscle.

"I gotta get out." She tried to open the door, but her finger slipped on the handle and pain instantly shot through her nails. "I can't even be Mary Jane with you. I wish I could, but I can't." She continued to struggle with the door, tears blurring her gaze.

Wulf took her arm. "Wait, what's wrong?"

She couldn't tell him. She'd be so ashamed and disappointed if she was Megan.

"I know how to figure out who I am. Regardless of matching DNA, I could tell you who I am, Wulf. I know how to tell now."

"Fuck, Mary Jane. Just tell me how you know?"

"I can check the back of my leg. As a teen, Mallory was bit by a dog. Peter always said it was her only imperfection when he was angry." She lifted her foot onto the seat and began to shove up the tight jeans.

"Wait." Wulf placed his hand over hers. Their eyes met again. This show of emotion made her uncomfortable, but she couldn't break their connection. She'd spent days wracking her brain, wondering just who she was. Mary Jane was now plagued with two identities. Of all the questions she'd had, Wulf proceeded to ask the most important one, "Who do you want to be?"

Her lips curved slowly. "Mary Jane." *No connection to Grienke or Portman.*

His hand went to her cheek. Wulf reached over, fighting through the pain at his side, to kiss away all of her worries. "Then be Mary Jane."

VOLUME II

ONE YEAR LATER

When love is not madness it is not love...
Pedro Calderon de la Barca.

26

EL PASO

Mary Jane Aguayo sang along with the Spanish music as she swayed in the upstairs bathroom of her small home. In a red lace lingerie set, she puckered her crimson glossed lips with an hour left to prepare for her *papi*—sugar daddy. The light on the curling iron beeped. She pulled down a section of her thick, black hair and began to twirl it around the rod so it would be perfect for him.

A faint ringing sound reached the bathroom door. Mary Jane pursed her lips. She had an hour to go, and Papi was never on time. The doorbell rang again. Mary Jane unclamped her hair, leaving the one perfect spiral underneath.

"If I'm not presentable, then you came too early," she mumbled to herself. Her ample hips caught the rhythm of the quick mariachi music while she ambled down the wooden stairway. At the front door, Mary Jane plastered a fake smile across her face, then a genuine curl ticked up the edges of her thick lips as she thought about his money. He had a big mouth that he used for all the wrong reasons—

like complaining—but his pockets were bigger. She opened the door.

"Papi..." Mary Jane pressed back on the heels of her stilettos, so as not to fall into the stranger. The man before her had taken up the entire space of the doorframe. Though she was confused by his sudden close proximity, she eyed his muscular build.

"Uh..." She attempted to speak English, knowing that the stranger wasn't Mexican. An unsettling feeling churned low in her abdomen. Mary Jane glanced around. With the rose bushes that pushed all the way up to the stairs, her neighbors would have to be right in front of her house to notice what was going on. In addition, she had no neighbors across from her, just an empty field.

"Mary Jane?" The unexpected visitor uttered her name as if he'd known her for a lifetime and loved her even longer. His tone set her at ease. Too bad he didn't look rich enough in jeans, a white undershirt, and scuffed steel-toe shoes. If one could drink in looks then she'd be drunk already.

"Me no speak, eh...English." With a friendly smile, she tried to shut the door on the stranger. His steel-toe boot wedged between the space.

Mary Jane's deep browns burned with rage. She spouted off in a mix of English and Spanish, "You loco—"

Searing pain, as hot as lava, pierced her chest. It took an eternity to realize she'd been stabbed. The pointed object jabbed into her chest, her abdomen, and shoulder blade in quick succession. Her knees crumbled. The stranger tried to hold her by the shoulders to let her fall gracefully to the floor.

Tears burned her eyes as the pain subsided and total

shock took over. And then her scalp stung sharply as she was dragged.

Blood smeared across the wooden floor, leaving a trail of pain, sadness, and confusion as her murderer pulled her along the living room floor and behind the couch.

***

Jake watched Mary Jane intently. The rage boiling within his veins felt awkward. This was not enjoyable, not a single bit. Setting aside his feelings, Jake took in her peaceful face. Her breath was shallow; the screwdriver hadn't finished her off.

More time would help. He needed more time with her. *Every* single time *she died*...he stopped his rushing thoughts with a quick shake of his head, as if the mere act eased the mental torment.

His obsession was with killing Mary Jane.

He always told himself to be patient, take his time before murdering her. Patience was a necessity he'd all but forget the moment his eyes landed on hers.

"We never have enough time, do we?" Jake sighed.

Her pretty little mouth opened. He reached over and swiped a hand across her lips. He preferred the natural color not the painted red stuff.

Mary Jane began to pant. The shock, so vivid in her eyes, caused him to smile.

"See how I save you, MJ," he told her. "This isn't the life for you. They won't bother you anymore."

"I spent a lotta money on you. Dolled you up! Let you take pretty pictures. This is the thanks I get?" Beasley's fleshy fingers coiled through Mary Jane's hair. They were at the mansion in his master suite. There were professional photography cameras and lights all around. They'd just finished the photo segment that he

planned on having flyers made from, for posting on billboards around the state.

Jake stood at the door. His teeth gritted as Beasley pushed Mary Jane back on his bed. Her arms flew, hitting him wherever she could. Somehow, he turned her around and slammed her face into the mattress.

Hands balled into fists, Jake shouted, "Beasley! You, just spent a fortune on the girl."

Beasley let go. She gagged and swallowed air, then grabbed the silk sheets from the bed and wrapped them around her body. Jake waited for her to look his way, meet his gaze. The sweet look in her eye was what he survived on; he thrived by saving her. : He watched as the girl stumbled from the bed. She wasnot the strong woman his mind had conjured up.

Mary Jane should've been stronger. Albeit, he'd always save her if necessary, but she was badass. They were assassins. This was their mission. Like a fucking movie, they had to work Beasley, and then he'd ultimately save her from Beasley—

But there are greater threats, *another voice whispered in his mind.*

Jake disregarded that thought. Beasley gave her one last look before storming out of the room.

"Come with me, MJ. Let's get you cleaned up. I'm Jake." He held out his hand. This moment filled him with elation. Saving her. It hurt his heart that she always forgot about it, but he'd saved her a million times.

Her gaze met his. Not with those sweet, confident eyes, but with a dark rage. She gritted her teeth. "I will—"

"Kill me," he finished her sentence. "Shit, I deserve to die a hundred deaths." He placed a finger to his temple. "But bad people don't go down easily, sweetheart. And you, darling, are the luckiest broad to step foot into The Petting Zoo. From today on, you have me."

Jake blinked as the memory began to fade away. He was sitting beside her, on the floor, leaning against the back of the couch. This was all the comfort he was able to provide, his closeness.

Blood began to pool at her abdomen.

There it was, the slight tremor. She still lived.

"I'll always save you from them, Mary Jane." He stood.

Jake rubbed his hand onto a crocheted blanket draped over the back of the couch. Red tarnished the vibrant blues, oranges, and purples of the soft material. He turned away from her as she slowly faded away and looked at the photos on the side table. One, in particular, caught his eyes as Mary Jane lay dying on the floor. It was the reason he'd dragged her body over, to get a closer look. He picked it up. An eight by eleven of the beautiful Latina, her lips puckered in a kiss that had to be for the photographer. His thumb smeared Mary Jane's blood over her face in the frame, obstructing her view. He placed the photo down and picked up the phone.

He dialed nine-one-one.

The dispatch replied promptly. "What's your emergency?"

"The name is Jake. And I'm killing Mary Jane...again."

"Sir–"

Jake pressed END.

A small vibration came from the pocket of Jake's pants. He grumbled, not really wanting to answer the phone, but unbeknownst to him, his brain was prewired to cooperate.

UNKNOWN: Did you kill her?

JAKE: Working on it. Can I?

JAKE: Or do you want something else?

This should've been a peaceful time for him. This ritual of allowing Mary Jane to rest in peace for all time, but the new boss had started the micromanagement bullshit when Peter went to jail.

UNKNOWN: Get it done.

Jake's eyelid twitched. He shoved the phone back into his jeans pocket, picked up the ceramic clay sun from the end table and weighed its heaviness in his hand. With both hands, he raised it high. Swiftly, he brought it down on Mary Jane's face with a loud crunch. He did it again and again. The slushing sound of her brain and skull being crushed helped his heart rate slow.

The breathing stopped.

The innocent could finally rest in peace.

For now.

27

GENEROSA, MEXICO

CRISP WHITE SHEETS COVERED HER CURVES. MARY JANE grinned as Wulf reached beneath the linen to grab the meat of her thigh. Their bodies were warm, naked, and couldn't be any closer.

"Someone's awake," she said, locking her calf around his leg to hoist herself up onto his thick waist. Her finger dawdled over taut, flawless skin.

"What are you doing, MJ?"

"Wondering how hot you'd look with my name tattooed on your chest."

His growl was sexy. "I meant, what are you doing awake? You woke before me."

"Did I? Maybe I sleep-walked—*ahem*—sleep-crawled down the bed while dreaming of tasting you." She arched an eyebrow and glanced down at his thick shaft. "Then Detective Wulf woke."

"Nope, not going to happen."

"What?"

"You referring to my dick as Detective Wulf. I hate that shit."

"All right, officer. As I said, I dreamt of tasting you. Obviously, I was asleep. Then I was stabbed in the eye by 'you know what.' So 'you know what' woke me up."

A hard laugh rolled through him.

"You are beautiful. Crazy beautiful," Wulf said, cupping her face before he tasted her mouth.

"What does that make you?"

He shook his head. She always had the last word. Her almond-shaped eyes brightened when Wulf flipped her above his steel girth, pressing their bodies together chest to chest. Her hair draped over them, tickling at his biceps. "That makes me a lucky man."

"No. Not lucky; it makes you crazy for rolling with me."

This time his mouth dominated hers and the silly grin on her lips disappeared. A hunger took over as her strong limbs tangled with his. Wulf growled and clasped her neck, holding her steady enough to be able to give her a hard kiss, just as Mary Jane began to pull away. Her tongue coiled with his once more and her lips pressed a bruising kiss against his; then she made her way down his thick frame.

A sigh of pleasure hummed from her throat as she wrapped her lips around his manhood. Mary Jane started off slowly, savoring the taste of him, loving the feel of the rippled veins in his powerful flesh, each one of which she took great pleasure in and knew from memory.

"MJ," His deep voice coaxed her movements to quicken. He gripped her ponytail and pulled.

Mary Jane grinned, lips flush against the head of his cock. She climbed back up and positioned herself just above his groin. As wet as she was, Mary Jane arched her hips and easily slid down onto his length. With the taste of his cock still on her lips, Mary Jane grinded down onto him.

Swoosh. Her ponytail slapped against her cheek as Wulf

dominated the bed. Now, his heavy muscles were above her. In one fluid motion, her thighs were around his waist. His mouth slammed a moan back into her throat as he kissed and made love to her.

Her hands glided across his warm skin to rest at his butt cheeks in an attempt to speed him up, but Wulf was meticulous at cherishing her.

"Wulf," she repeated until her throat was too tired. Her lungs were about to cave in. Each stroke of his cock caressed her swollen, sensitive sweetness until they climaxed into each other's arms.

They lay there—her holding him in position, him bearing his weight on his forearms so he wouldn't suffocate her. Mary Jane wouldn't let him go. This was her habit. Wulf could be nurturing and concerned for her in or out of the bed, but it was only at this point that Mary Jane was at her most vulnerable. Her lungs couldn't catch a steady rhythm with his body crushing her. Wulf planted most of his weight on his forearms, but she still refused to let go.

Her eyes closed. Their hearts slammed against each other, chest to chest. And then Mary Jane let go.

Wulf sighed heavily and rested his body next to hers.

A lazy grin tugged at the edges of her mouth. "So, are you going to read the newspaper this morning?"

"Did that kid come by already?"

"Oh, I hear a slight intonation when you say 'kid.' Are you jealous of my little boyfriend?" She grinned. Mary Jane paid ten-year-old Tito to bring newspapers in the morning.

"I'm the one who says 'slight intonation,' not you," Wulf corrected. "When I offer to take you deep sea snorkeling, for example."

She giggled. When it came to adventure, Mary Jane had

thought she'd be the outrageously fun one, but Wulf wanted to do all the barbaric slap-your-fists-against-your-chest stuff. She wanted simplicity. And they truly had it. Except for when it came to the news. Every morning, Tito came by with papers from the *New York* and *Los Angeles Times* and Wulf searched through each one religiously. He expected the Feds to drop some sort of information on Beasley and Peter's dealings while Mary Jane had always been a skeptic. If those psychos were featured in an article, they'd make headlines even on the local news in a different country.

Wulf kissed the top of her head. "I'll read the paper later. But my offer to go deep sea snorkeling still stands."

She chortled, "You'll have better luck reading the paper and seeing the media outcry about brainwashing. Oh, but those Fed-fucks are covering up everything."

"Juarez and Robertson are probably not on the case anymore. North Korea would nuke us if they knew the States was aware of a program that frazzled people's brains," he said, giving her another forehead kiss.

"Well, it's a good reason we didn't stick around."

"Something tells me that even if the Feds were transparent, you'd still prefer the incognito lifestyle. Remember what you did to my socks and cell phone over one measly call?"

"I'm very sorry about your socks. Clean socks are near and dear to my heart, but you cut me deep." She chuckled. Somewhere, in the back of her mind, she felt sad for Hurricane, Sugarland, Diamond, and all of the women who'd died. They were just victims of a psychotic scientific experiment meant to exploit humans for money. She even thought about how the other survivors had meshed back into society. Mary Jane wondered if that was a trait from Mallory or just residuals of her wonky brain believing she was secret agent, Anya Randolph. *You can't save everyone, MJ. Not with this scenario.* She took a deep breath and counted on the perfect life she'd made with Dylan Wulf.

28

ONE WEEK LATER, THE JUNE SUN BATHED HER CARAMEL SKIN with warm kisses as Mary Jane sat back on a beach cot in a white bikini. She sipped on a mango margarita rimmed with salt, a tiny colorful umbrella poking out the top and looked over at Wulf. The sun glowed on every inch of his exposed, muscular body.

She felt like pulling off his trunks to straddle him, but people were around. Generosa wasn't a vacation spot like the surrounding areas, but it had the best beaches gringos never visited.

Instead of tantalizing Wulf, Mary Jane decided to screw with him. She plucked the umbrella from her drink and tossed it in the sand.

On cue, Wulf spoke in that commanding voice she enjoyed, "Pick it up."

"Not gonna happen," she retorted with a half grin. Even though he no longer worked, Wulf was the epitome of a Super Cop. "I'd like to think we were stranded on a secluded island. And being that it's *my* island, I'd have to kick you off, if you don't stop harassing me."

"You must love when I harass you," he assured.

Hiding a grin, she tossed back the rest of the drink. The slushy bits of liquid weren't strong at all. With an unsatisfied smirk, she picked up the umbrella and placed it back into the glass before nudging the bottom of the glass into the sand.

Mary Jane lay back and closed her eyes. Bright orange orbs highlighted against her eyelids due to the sunny day until, as if a cloud passed over, her skin didn't feel as warm and the brightness from over her eyelids faded. She opened her eyes. Ripples of tanned muscles were her first line of vision. Wulf stood there. "*Dylan*, you're in my sun."

"Yeah, I am."

"Okay, how does this sound? If you don't move, I won't help you get 'em down." She grinned, zeroing in on his swim trunks. He was rock hard.

Wulf scooped her up caveman style, draped her body over his massive shoulder, and took her toward the shore.

"Stop!" she squealed as splashes of cool water prickled her face and he moved further into the sea.

"Wulf, stop!"

In one fluid motion, Wulf pulled her from over his shoulder until she was back in his arms again. He gave her bottom lip a little nibble. "Bad girls have to pay."

Laughing, Mary Jane licked at her lip, staving off the sting and Wulf tossed her into the crystal-clear water.

She went under. Bubbles of air tickled her body, the current plunging her even lower. Mary Jane's eyes opened slightly beneath the clear blue sea. Beneath the water was a man with reddish hair, a spray of matching freckles, and kind eyes. Mirroring the stranger's smile came naturally.

His next move came out of nowhere. He kissed her!

Alarmed, she pushed swiftly away, grateful he hadn't held onto her arms or shoulders.

Her feet touched the ocean floor, prickling on shells as little fish flitted by. She soared back up to the surface, her body popping out of the water just as another wave came crashing down. The current overtook her, making her panic enough to take in a gulp full of salt water. She flipped over. Water burned up her nostrils, and her lean arms and legs went to work. She swam towards the shore. When Mary Jane emerged from the shallow water, she shoved her hair back.

Wulf stood at the edge. His left eyebrow lifted when she didn't try to slug him for tossing her in, but the stranger consumed her mind. She turned around and waited for the redheaded guy to come out of the water. They would exchange words. She might even conjure up some of Mallory's Hollywood kickboxing skills or Agent Anya Randolph's even more outlandish combat coordination. When the freckled guy didn't show himself, she ran back into the water, leaping over shallow waves and soaring into the water. Beneath the deep blue, her eyes opened wide as she took in the clear turquoise sea. A little boy was swimming toward the lagoon a few meters out. A Mexican couple was making out in the water.

No gingers in sight. She swam back to shore.

"What are you doing?" Wulf asked.

"Nothing," she mumbled. Eyes narrowed, she walked toward the lounger, plopped down, and tried not to think. After discovering that Peter Grienke had taken away her memories, she'd learned that her identity was either Mallory Portman-Grienke, his wife, or Megan Portman—Mallory's twin sister. That was the problem. Mallory had married Peter, but he'd bestowed Mary Jane with both sets of memories as a form of vengeance.

Now she had two sets of memories and no clue as to which was real. The good life with Peter, until the scientist got tired of her trying to save Megan from a life of drugs? After finding her in New Mexico when she'd been on the run from Beasley, Peter had originally led her to believe she was his wife, but at the end he'd twisted those memories and implanted Megan's. It was hard to swallow, not knowing which was real.

MARY JANE GAZED out to sea. Sunshine sprinkled like diamonds over the turquoise waves. The sea was so expansive. Could a guy with cute red hair and freckles be a trick of the mind? Or was he a familiar ghost from the past?

"MJ, you're too quiet." Wulf wasn't staring at her like the object of his affection. Her beauty had become second to his concern. He came over and kneeled down beside her, rubbing a hand in her hair. "Talk to me."

Shit, I am gonna go crazy. I can't have Wulf see me like this. After a moment, she pulled her gaze away from the ocean. "This place is so beautiful. Let's go home. I want to get you alone for that stunt you just pulled." She licked her lips, a sign that his punishment would satisfy both their desires.

"Mary Jane." Wulf stressed her name, not convinced that she wasn't fighting her demons alone like usual. "Ever since you found out who you are, you've stared off into space. Talk to me. I'm not going to continue to ask. When we took this road trip here, last year, you told me everything. Now...you know who you are and you're—"

"Wulf, really it's nothing." She thought about trying a reassuring smile but knew her lips would tremble.

Peter now rotted in jail—massive mauling scars and all. Grienke Pharmaceuticals had been conquered and divided by his board members. Everything else was under the radar. Nobody in the world—besides the Feds—knew about the other women. There was not a single clue of where these confused women had gone afterward. Now she was about to hyperventilate.

I'm aware of who I am, and I fucking hate it!

"Okay, you're right." Mary Jane's mouth tensed. She stood and gazed up at him. "I don't like who I am."

"Who you *were*," he corrected, caressing her cheek. "Okay, okay. Just talk to me about those feelings, because ultimately, you've chosen your destiny, Mary Jane."

The longing in his eyes compelled her to speak. A part of her wanted to keep some of the horror at bay; Wulf knew the greater scheme of things, but he didn't know it all—he couldn't begin to fathom it all. No matter how much Mary Jane tried to change the facts—her reality—she knew that Peter had ruined her.

"Talk to me," Wulf barked.

"I'm good." She placed her hands on his thick biceps, rose to her tippy toes, and gave him a reassuring kiss.

She couldn't give him what he wanted, let alone what he needed. He'd ultimately asked her to return to reality. Mary Jane was incapable of such a thing, but she couldn't leave Wulf alone. She hoped the taste of her lips was enough to keep him captivated. The rest of the world could work nine to five. Jake had given her enough money for them both to stay in paradise. It would break her if Wulf ever decided to return to L.A.

It was inevitable that he'd return one day for his family and work.

Mary Jane refused to go.

29

SPECIAL AGENT ARIEL JUÁREZ RAN HER HAND THROUGH HER shoulder-length hair and tied it into a hasty ponytail. She took the keys out of the ignition and got out of the unmarked SUV. Wearing a stiff, navy-blue suit and a void expression, she put on her game face and stepped onto the cracked curb of a small community in the lowest parts of California. A few hours ago, Fed dispatch had picked up on a call about the homicide of one "Mary Jane."

She and her partner, Robertson, were on cleanup duty. The women who had been strippers and prostitutes for Beasley had all been given reparations straight from the honey pot, and Grienke had just about a never-ending pot. The selected tech team at the Federal Bureau of Investigations knew how to work Grienke's brainwasher system, so they'd given each woman a clean slate and cleared their minds of their innate alliance to Beasley, not knowing that the reworking of Grienke's deception had just begun.

Ariel pinched the bridge of her nose and sighed.

"Let's see if the dynamics fit," Robertson said glumly, rubbing a hand over his buzz cut and closing the passenger door. They'd already tied Jakob Woods to five deceased Mary Janes in the past four months.

It took them ten days to learn more about Grienke's dealings. After the computer forensics investigators bypassed Peter Grienke's firewalls, they had concrete evidence regarding a billion-dollar a year industry. Rich people were selling their family members to Grienke because they didn't want to have their wives, daughters, or friends murdered. Beasley was not provided with all of the women. There were others all over the world.

Ariel's mother would douse holy water on her if she knew Ariel and the Feds were doing nothing about the women and young girls who were successfully sold into the international sex slave industry. Some less attractive women and children had become indentured servants to wealthy homes. Their "employers" had given Grienke a *nominal fee* instead of paying them monthly.

They just couldn't be saved.

And domestically? Well, fathers of women like Bonnie Timms and Tiana Clement lived scot-free at this very instance because Grienke's dubious dealings were not being brought out in front of the media.

This was by presidential order.

Everything that the Feds actually had a hand in, such as reparations to Beasley's freshly brainwashed girls, seemed to be tied up in a nice, little bow. Well, that's how the president saw it after being debriefed. He'd given the ultimate order not to pursue those trafficked internationally.

Yellow tape clashed with the paler shade of yellow roses around the scene, leading to a tiny entry way, made even tinier by more rose bushes. Ariel and Robertson flashed their badge to a uniformed cop standing at the front of the yard. His pupils widened, but then he nodded. Ariel stepped onto the porch of a very tiny house. Clay pottery lined the narrow porch, outlining an artistic clay sun at the top of the door. The all-too-familiar smell of death greeted them first.

They entered the perimeter that the local police Crime Scene Unit had constructed. The lab boys, the department's Science Investigation Division, cased the tiny entry way. One, a latent-print expert, worked at the handrail of the tiny stairs.

In the quaint living room the team surrounded a spot right behind a lumpy loveseat. There had to be a coroner, most likely kneeling next to the body on the floor. And right on cue, a male voice mumbled about the time of death, which Ariel already knew. The instant dispatch recorded a call about a homicide linked to the name Mary Jane, the agents were on their way.

A short black woman wearing a black suit and with braided hair glanced over. In a voice of authority, she snapped, "What are the Feds doing here?"

Ariel flashed a respectful smile, knowing the obstacles this woman had had to surmount to become a detective. She wanted to tell her she empathized with her, knowing full well how hard it was as a female minority in a male-dominated workplace. "Special Agent Ariel Juarez, and this is my partner Robertson. We'd like to offer our–"

"Correct me if I'm wrong," the head detective placed a hand on hips that seemed to encompass the living room, "but isn't a homicide a local affair?"

Robertson and Ariel glanced at each other. The fleeting look spoke volumes. He told her not to chew out this head detective and she responded with a glimmer of a smile that indicated she'd try her best to play nice.

"We believe your Mary Jane Aguayo may be the next victim of a serial killer."

The detective's eyes glittered with interest. "How so?"

The rest of the team gave their attention as well, and an Indian man stood up. Ariel figured he had to be the coroner who was just interrupted.

"We've collected a few bodies, all of which had the given name, Mary Jane," Robertson said. "If you would be so kind as to allow us a moment to view your MJ and the scene, we'd be glad to provide our expertise if this is *Jakob Woods'* handiwork."

"Dispatch stated that the perp identified himself as *Jake*," one of the detectives mumbled in disbelief. Apparently, he hadn't heard the bomb drop.

"The *terrorist* Jakob Woods?" The head detective arched her eyebrow. Even the photographer stopped taking photos. "He's got a new skill?"

"Yes," Ariel confirmed.

"Well," the coroner took over. "I'll have more later, naturally. For now, I can say that your—*our* victim has been dead for about ten to twelve hours. From the type of stab wounds, the weapon was not a knife, but indicative of an ice pick or maybe even a power tool, screwdriver or the likes. And then we have the repeated, blunt force trauma to the skull."

The coroner consulted with a small notebook as they stepped around the couch to see *this* Mary Jane.

The woman's long black hair was matted with blood. Her face was indistinguishable due to the brutal disfigurement of her face and exposed brain matter and skull fragments.

"Given the amount of wounds, you'd expect more erratic movement, but no. The stab wounds are meticulous. None appear near vital organs or major arteries. The perp didn't want her to die until he was ready."

As the coroner gave his expertise, Ariel took in the

remainder of the scene. Her eyes stopped on a photo at the end table and her heart sank.

She pulled on her gloves, grabbed the picture frame at the edge and looked at the photo. As with all of the other Mary Janes, Jake had smeared blood over her eyes as if the act blinded them from his sin.

Jakob Woods had added another notch to his resume. He was a serial killer.

She and Robertson took a step outside. He made the call as she took down her ponytail, forked a hand through her hair, and then redid it in a severe bun.

Robertson ended the call. "Our team will be here stat."

"We can keep the lead detective on as liaison," she said. "But ultimately, Robertson, this shit is going too far. The crew finding Mary Jane—Portman-Grienke, or whatever the fuck she wants to be called these days, needs to move it!"

"They're on it, Ariel. Breathe."

She wanted to smile. Her partner always kept her grounded, but this situation was spiraling out of control. "I'll try, but when we get her in our grasps, she's not to be out of our sights—and I mean, you or me, not the team, but us. We keep an eye on her, and we will force her to fix this mess Jake has caused."

He sighed. "We'll feed her to the wolf?"

Her eyes trained onto his. This was not the time for religion or morals to clash with the truth. "It must be done."

30

Wulf, seated at the edge of the bar, tossed back a few salted peanuts. He fisted his cell phone in one hand and chased the nuts with a double-shot of tequila.

"Crazy broad?" he mumbled through tense lips.

"Yeah," Jones repeated. "Dylan, are you still with that crazy broad?"

"Man, don't fucking do that."

"Do what? D, you've always been the one with a good head on your shoulders. Despite your childhood, you were a big brother to thugs and gangbangers, even in our department. Remember Hesler?"

Wulf recalled Hesler who had attended the academy with them. He'd chosen the narcotics unit when it was time to get off the road and move up the ranks. The bottom of the totem pole in that regard involved an undercover role, which left his friend Hesler hooked on the very thing he was ridding the streets of—heroin. "I did nothing for Hesler."

"Yeah, I'm sure you love pushing that self-deprecating crap. Regardless of it being his ultimate choice, you encouraged that fool to go into rehab when Cap was threatening his pension. Wulf, did you forget about that half a million-dollar home you own in Claremont? It's just sitting there."

How could he forget? When Gracie's social worker had offered him a chance at placement, Wulf had been too busy. A few months prior, he'd purchased a house on a whim in a new housing tract. The homes didn't seem so cookie cutter and he'd had the good intention of commuting to work once he'd settled down with a family. "How about you bring the kids down. We'll barbecue."

Quincy changed the subject. "Look, your father may have had you stealing shit as a kid, but that became your motivation to become a better man. You save people, Dylan. Man, I commend you for this one. Your *friend* is just a beautiful face. Let her ass roam around Mexico. Come home."

Wulf glanced at a man and woman a few barstools down. Their arms were all over each other. They were whispering and smiling their asses off. Though Wulf hadn't said the words to Mary Jane and doubted she'd utter them back, he loved her. There was no way in hell he'd let her out of his sight for too long. She was his. Muddled mind and all, he loved her.

A foster kid like him knew you didn't abandon someone you love. Shit, you could be treated the worst, but love kept you from leaving. He believed Mary Jane had feelings for him. "Is this you talking or Shelly?"

"Hell, it's me talking. It's also Shelly and your mother, Brenda, who, mind you, has had so many foster kids in the past—she's had enough worrying about you, Shelly and the others. So take that into consideration. Everybody is looking out for you, but you."

Wulf scoffed. "Bro, you're getting on my case. We'll come

back soon. Besides, I'm sure Juárez and Robertson have come searching for us. It's only a matter of time before they find us. Better us to go to them first, right?"

"That's right, D. And you're damn right they came by. They sent an L.A. based Fed. He left his number and everything."

"Well, thanks for calling me on a burner phone."

Quincy's deep chuckle rasped through the phone. "Speaking of thanking me, while that selfish girl has you running around doing nothing, I found her sister."

"You found Megan?" Wulf eyed the bartender and gestured toward his empty shot glass.

"Yup, you're welcome. You asked, and I found her. You'll be surprised just how *crazy* she is compared to Mallory. You want a breakdown on Ms. Megan Portman?"

"Not yet." Wulf's teeth gritted; his so-called best friend was overstepping. A year ago, Grienke had manipulated Mary Jane into believing that he'd killed one of the twins. Wulf's intuition rang out like fireworks; it wasn't quite the best time to meet Megan Portman.

"Thought you'd say that," Quincy scoffed. "There's more."

"What?"

"I'll hold off on that for now. You take baby steps; I take baby steps."

"Quincy, dude, last year I was a fucking mess. I asked you to keep my mom and kid sister safe, right?"

"You did."

"I thank you for that. That's all the fuck I'm going to thank you for, Quincy. Aside from always keeping bullets out of my ass. Mary Jane is going through some shit right now, and I'm not leaving her."

"I'm just trying to get you to see the light."

"Oh, I see the fucking light. Nevertheless, I had a hunch when you just said, 'there's more.' Whatever you set in motion, kill it." Wulf ended the call.

***

WHEN WULF RETURNED home in the evening, he had a letter in his back pocket from Glenn Tsoosie. Glenn had placed his life in jeopardy to save Mary Jane's a year back, and the two still exchanged letters like they were bonded by blood in a different era.

He held a brown paper bag of street tacos in his hand for dinner. They weren't fans of cooking but once a week they'd built a tradition around making a new dish. Their tiny home would be filled with laughter and the story always ended with food in their hair—purposefully or otherwise. Food, sex, happiness.

The bedroom door was open as he entered the living room, and Wulf's gaze went straight to Mary Jane's ass. She was donning a black dress that clung to her curves, leaning down to pick up a pair of stilettos. Without taking his eyes off the stunning vision, Wulf whistled and set down the bag on the end table of the couch.

She turned around, contentment twinkling in her brown eyes.

Thank God, she's happy. Somewhere deep down, Wulf knew that Mary Jane hadn't come to terms with her past yet, but with her, living in the moment was always perfect.

He went to her, pulling her body into him, and pressed his mouth against hers. "You look beautiful."

"I know." She took the letter from Glenn that he handed

over and cradled it to her heart for a second. "Don't be jealous. I'm Glenn's *shero*. She-hero, you get—"

"I get it. Please don't tell me he still thinks you're a super hero."

"He does." She rose to her tippy toes. Their mouths met and instead of kissing, they chuckled softly. "You're my hero, Dylan."

His hand pawed her ass.

"Get ready," she said, the resolve in her voice beginning to break again. She was damn good at pretending, but this evening the sadness just seemed to wash over her as she elaborated, "I have to get out of this house. I had the dream again...so I have to get out of the house."

At that, Wulf placed his hand at the center of her shoulders, rubbed his thumb along the nape of her neck, and kissed the top of her head. She was like a caged animal. Like a glorious firecracker, sparks flying though not quite exploding yet. Because of his own childhood, he didn't know the first thing about how to mend her heart. His father had only voiced his love when a young Dylan manipulated his way into the extravagant homes of their planned invasions and he didn't even have a fraction of a memory of his real mom. Sure, his adoptive mother, Brenda, taught him that he could be loved, but he didn't have the strong foundation for helping Mary Jane.

Wulf pinched the bridge of his nose in thought. *Shit, how do I help you become comfortable knowing that you're Mallory?*

"Wulf, stop pawing at me. Get dressed." She pushed him away, smiling weakly.

"Just tell me about the dream, already," he tried.

"I can't."

After a few beats, Wulf asked, "Is it because you're Mallory or the dreams?"

"Which is worse?" She gave a wry chuckle, yet the longing in her eyes spoke volumes.

Wulf bit his bottom lip in contemplation. Much of the time, all he had to go on to understand Mary Jane was her body language. She could live with being Mallory; she had to. But those damn dreams made him want to break into the supermax facility Grienke currently resided in and finish him off.

It was the dreams again. These days, shit piled on top of more shit. Peter controlling her through night terrors was just the cherry on the top. The dreams had started a few months ago and each one ended with her crying in the middle of the night. He'd hold her as tightly as he could without crushing her but he'd have to grip her shoulders and rattle her like a rag doll to wake her from her night-marish stupor, and then he'd have to remind her that Peter had made threats to their *happily ever after* only in her dreams.

His thumb skimmed along her jaw. "Peter's not taking you from me, I promise you that."

Mary Jane's eyes connected with his. "Ha! Wulf, you'd have to get rid of me instead."

He cracked a half smile.

Though worry clouded her gaze, Mary Jane winked. "I'm too selfish to let you go. Get dressed, Wulf. I need to get out of this house for a while."

As she headed toward the living room, Wulf gripped her wrist. The movement was fluid, perfect. She spun around on her heels. His mouth went to her earlobe, lips brushing ever so softly against her skin as he said, "Or we could stay in and I'll have you screaming my name until that crazy brain of yours replaces you and your worries with all of me."

"Oh, Dylan," she sighed.

He nibbled at the pulse of her neck, pressing his hardness against her body.

"So, I'm consulting with the bad you. *Dylan*, stop it. Now! You need to shower." Though she reprimanded him, her eyes glittered with laughter.

"I thought you liked me dirty?" he said, peppering her cheeks and throat with kisses. Before she could argue, his mouth descended on hers. Recently, she'd been even hornier than usual, which was saying a lot because their sex life was still so fresh, new, and crazy. Wulf's fingers gripped her collar. He tugged until the material tore against her skin. He wanted to purge every last seed of hopelessness that she felt Peter instilled in her during dreams.

A gasp squeezed through her lips. "I'm going to kill—"

He spun her once more. His heavy cock slammed against her ass as he held her close and nuzzled the back of her neck.

"Oh, you're really playing dirty," she groaned as her palms pressed against the wall. He dropped to his knees and sank his teeth into the flesh of her ass as he tugged down her thong.

"You smell so good." He bit her once more for good measure.

"Still gonna kill you." Her voice was light and airy.

He stood, his toe swiping at the inside of her heels. Although grinning, Mary Jane glared at him over her shoulders, keeping her stance wide. Wulf unzipped his pants and pushed both them and his boxers down. His swollen manhood sprung free.

She arched her back, pressing her hips towards him.

Wulf glided into her from behind. "You want it soft or rough?"

"Rough." She bit her bottom lip. Like a lioness, she clawed at the wall as his cock slammed in and out of her.

Wulf skimmed his hand over her hips, up and over her flat abdomen then began to gently knead her breasts. He could feel the tension fusing within her body.

"Oh, Wulf," Mary Jane purred, relinquishing her animalistic rage. No longer attempting to clasp and claw the wall, she leaned back against his hard chest. Rising onto the balls of her feet, she moaned as the position offered a deeper penetration. With her head on his shoulder, she reached up to caress his neck while Wulf nibbled at her earlobe.

His tongue twined into her ear. Sweet words of adoration were at the tip of his lips, but Wulf stopped himself as Mary Jane always held a bit of herself at bay. The way her body molded to his, he knew that this was just enough. Instead of telling her he loved her, he decided to drive her to madness. Shit, she seemed to prefer it.

Maintaining a cocky grin, he clasped her wrists.

"Wulf." Her ragged voice was hesitant with curiosity until Wulf pressed a hand against the small of her back. Her upper body folded until her hair draped over her toes. The force of his cock drove away her tension with each thrust. Knowing her body so well, Wulf released just as she shattered into ecstasy.

***

An hour later, they both showered, ridding themselves of the sweet fragrance of sex and sweat. Mary Jane put on a gorgeous dress he didn't recall seeing before, so to keep things even He donned his nicest pair of slacks and a short-sleeved coal button up that strained against his biceps. After a quiet drive to the neighboring tourist city of Puerto Vallarta, they ended up at one of the most expensive hotels along the shore. Wulf couldn't take his eyes off her alluring gaze as he helped her out of the car. He also noted how beautiful and soft her skin was, and how her thick, wavy hair gracefully kissed the side of her neck in the wind. *Shit, I've got it bad for her.*

He placed the keys to their '87 Honda in his linen pants and swept a hand around her waist, pulling her closer and breathing in her flowery scent as they walked up the veranda.

The other day, she'd stood in a new bikini at a beach shop, trying it on for him. He'd picked out more. She'd handed the inexpensive, sexy little numbers to the clerk until he'd found an olive green bikini that he knew would look perfect on her. He'd swallowed, wanting her all the more when she stepped out of the changing room and twirled around in it—and then her breath caught as she snagged on her own reflection.

Damn, how could he have forgotten? On their last day in Santo Cruces City, Mary Jane told the story of how Mallory had been bitten by Vin's dog when she'd disobeyed his advances. Wulf had already known who she was the first time she'd told him about that motherfucker, Vin. Something compelled Wulf to ask Mary Jane which twin she'd rather be. The light that died in her eyes while talking of Vin blossomed the instant she murmured her desire to 'just be Mary Jane.' And for a year, their lives had been perfect.

Dylan Wulf and *his* Mary Jane.

Until the day she'd viewed the gash on the back of her calf. One minute, Mary Jane was beautiful as ever, twirling around in a tourist shop, the next, she was running out of the store in his favorite bikini. She'd finally noticed the gash on the back of her calf leg. Wulf hastily paid the attendant and ran after her. He eventually found her crying at home.

Why wouldn't she want to be Mallory instead of the drug addicted twin?

He held the gold-framed door of the five-star hotel open, still raving at her beauty. "Nobody can keep their eyes off of you," he whispered in her ear as she passed by.

"Aww." She welcomed his kiss as he took her hand and strolled alongside her.

Wulf breathed a little easier. Mary Jane had this ability to alienate herself. She'd withdraw for a while after telling him the stories of Mallory and Megan by taking long strolls on the shore. Last winter, he'd found her sitting in wet sand, rain soaking her to the core, and held her until she'd stop shaking from the chill.

It took everything in him not to have his old contact at the LAPD find her stepfather, Vin.

"Wulf, for two," he told the maître d' as Mary Jane stood just inside the entrance and viewed a three-story high aquarium stocked with bright-colored exotic fish.

The man skimmed the list then looked back up at him. "You don't have reservations?"

"No," Wulf started with a sigh. "Please, my woman is having a bad day. I wanted to make it up to her." He pulled out his wallet.

The attendant rolled his eyes, thoroughly insulted.

"Hey, you can share a table with us," a woman with a short blonde bob told Wulf, and then quickly mentioned her last name to the maître d'. She had a bubbly aura, which was enhanced by a pink polka dot pantsuit.

"Ah...no, thanks." Happy-go-lucky tourists were the brunt of many of Mary Jane's jokes these days.

"Just a few moments, Miss Blackwood." The maître d' gave her a curt smile.

"Thank you," the blonde replied.

"What's going on?" Mary Jane walked up.

"I think my wife is inviting you all to our table," muttered a man who'd also been viewing the fish. He carried a glass and had neatly cut, dark blond hair. "C'mon, buddy, this place is *never not* booked, so excuse me for the double negative. Ha! We reserved a table when planning for the trip."

"All right." Mary Jane nodded.

Wulf's eyebrows rose. From what he'd observed, they embodied all that Mary Jane didn't believe in. People could *not* be genuinely happy this way. Before he could ask if she was sure, they were escorted through the packed restaurant which was draped in white linen from the table tops to the windows. A single candle decorated each table, adding to the ridiculousness of the place. He knew upscale, and this shit wasn't it.

The man shook Wulf's hand, stating, "They call me Tom. This is my lovely wife, Amy. Amy Blackwood. How nice is it to say that? My wife, Amy Blackwood."

Amy's smile held the same pride as her husband's.

"How long have you been married?" Mary Jane asked.

"Two weeks, one day and five hours," Amy replied.

They finished the introductions and soon were chatting and laughing the night away as gourmet plates of artistic cuisine was put before them. Wulf knew he should've eaten those tacos first, but he was content watching Mary Jane acclimate to society.

"Oh, no, Tom, enough with the jokes already," Amy chided her husband as she and Mary Jane giggled.

"No, he's right," Mary Jane said. "This food was cooked in real butter, oodles of it."

Wulf watched the way her eyelids slightly kissed and heard the moan she made as she ate black tiger shrimp. The women he'd dated in the past hardly ate around him, but he could watch this woman eat all day as she devoured every bit of the food.

"You love it?" His lips kissed her ear.

"The best thing I've ever had," she replied. "Almost."

31

THE AIR IN MARY JANE'S LUNGS EVAPORATED. HER THROAT clamped tight. She glared into the eyes of her tormentor—Peter wanted her to submit to him but she'd rather die than submit. Aside from his eyes, nothing was the same. The Rottweilers—Kane and Knight—had mauled him so severely that the skin grafting he'd received had not been enough. His face was a nightmare, folds of grayish, plastic-like skin. His usual Tom Ford suit, which always draped over a perfectly toned body, was loose and fit like cheap drapes. In the darkness, she saw a glint of the knife as the smooth steel grazed her chest. Her wrists were bound above her head.

They'd returned to the black-walled torture room in Beasley's mansion.

"I own you, Mallory."

Though her throat was dry, she hawked out a weak spray of spittle. A swift backhand to her face sent Mary Jane's body swaying but still her knees didn't buckle.

"You know who you are now, Mallory?" He chuckled softly as he pulled the stool from next to the examination table and sat down. "My little trick...I'll keep screwing with you."

Mary Jane endeavored to retreat within her mind. Sure, he could trick her past memories, but he didn't have control over the here and now. Tune him out, *she told herself.*

"I've had wives before you. But you?" He shook his head. "I loved you. I couldn't allow you to die. What a mistake that was, right, since you ruined our lives. We were supposed to be happily married, but you allowed your sister to defile what we had. That fucking unchangeable temperament of yours kept you longing for family. I WAS YOUR FAMILY!"

"Kill me," Mary Jane gasped. She knew it was a dream. She didn't believe dying in dreams meant death in real life, yet it scared her all the same.

"No," Peter replied selfishly. "You've been the adulterer. I have something for you and that asshole. Wulf stole you away from me. But I'll separate the two of you if it's the last thing I do!"

***

Mary Jane's eyes popped open. It was midday; she had a hard time sleeping at night and hated herself for being so groggy recently. Sleep never recharged or invigorated her anyway—it just left her with more questions.

Peter knew about Dylan Wulf?

How?

Wulf and Peter's lives had hardly intersected when Peter attempted to feed her to those blood-hungry dogs. They hadn't even spoken to each other, had they?

"Your mind is playing tricks on you, MJ," she mumbled to herself. Yet, even in her sleep, there was no getting away from her ex-husband – Peter meant to torment her all her life. She concentrated on the fact that the nightmare was just a residual from the horrible time in her past. *My future will be much better.* She snuggled closer to Wulf, pulling his heavy, muscular arm around her waist.

"No waking up early in paradise," Wulf murmured.

"Tell me about a happy memory with your dad?" she asked. The words seemed foreign to her ears. Though they'd both shared their stories, Wulf's had been told in broken bits, like he hadn't been a part of it.

He grumbled inaudibly.

"I know you said the only thing he bought you was a fake-ass boy scouts uniform so that you could survey rich homes. But did you guys ever have any good days before Child Protective Services caught up with you?"

His strong, heavy body turned over. Wulf rubbed a hand over his eyes and scratched along his bristled jaw. "I guess we had a few good times. My dad taught me how to play dice and dominos. Oh, and we went fishing sometimes. We'd catch fish with our bare hands." He pawed at her ass at that tidbit.

"Fishing?" She giggled. "With the ocean in our backyard, that would have been nice for you to teach me."

He chuckled. "Not sure if I remember how. But we can try."

***

On the Blackwoods last night in town, Mary Jane and Wulf agreed to meet them for dinner at the resort where they were staying. Mary Jane noticed that Wulf seemed surprised about her willingness to meet with the newlywed couple again.

They both knew she was a pessimist but for that one night, during their first encounter, Mary Jane felt a connection to the human race—aside from this innate trust she had for Wulf. And she had a question to ask Amy Blackwood.

When they arrived, Mary Jane rang the doorbell. Wulf had a plastic bag filled with ice, surrounding the bass he'd caught.

"Hey, guys," Tom said, opening the door.

"We brought bass," Wulf said.

"Oh, great. The grill is fired up. You two went fishing? I didn't take you guys for the outdoorsy type after you declined a trip in our RV down the coast."

Wulf laughed. "Well, technically I went fishing."

"I was bitch-slapped by the fish's tail," Mary Jane stated, dropping her bottom lip, pretending to be in shock. She pushed her hip against Wulf before walking into the house. "It was rather traumatizing."

"Yeah, MJ has finished that chapter in her life," Wulf said behind her. "Besides, my woman has had quite the appetite these days."

"Hey, I work out to eat, and I eat to work out," she scoffed before entering the living room. The traditional couch, table and chairs, and sporadically placed paintings in bland brown hues were common for the resort. A melody from a Spanish acoustic guitar floated from the surround system. There were bottles of Corona on the patio table, while hotdogs and hamburgers roasted on the grill. Tom added the fish to it.

A short while later, Amy came out of the bedroom door dressed in a wrap and a sombrero, which made her look even more like a gringo. "Hola, mis amigos," she said in a fake Spanish accent.

"Hola," Mary Jane replied. In full Spanish, she added, "You look lovely. How was your trip to the Yucatan Peninsula?"

"Uh...uh..." Amy's cheeks turned red. Tom called her a goofball and took off another hamburger patty from the grill in order to give the fish more space.

"You know Spanish?" Wulf whispered to Mary Jane as they added lettuce and tomato to their burgers.

Mary Jane chewed her bottom lip. The words had been an automatic response yet, even with two lifetimes worth of memories, she didn't recall ever learning Spanish.

"That's just high school stuff." She waved it away and took a seat at the patio table next to Amy. With her own astonishment of being bilingual in the back of her mind, Mary Jane restarted the conversation about the Blackwoods recent sight-seeing trip, this time in English. Tom went on and on about every detail of their lives. He didn't miss a single thing, from the time they awoke, to recounting some of the jokes the tourist guide gave while a tour bus traveled along the coast of Mexico.

Leter, while the guys sat in the living room watching baseball, Mary Jane and Amy stepped off the patio at the oceanfront resort. They stopped a few yards away from where the water had receded into the ocean and sat on the damp sand. Off in the distance, clouds cluttered around a blood moon. For a while, the women were comfortable in the silence. Mary Jane shifted sand through her fingers. A year had come and gone since she had formed any new friendships; that had begun and ended with Glenn, the only loyal friend she'd made besides Wulf.

The Blackwoods could teach her a thing or two about returning to society and life...for Wulf's sake. In her mind's eye, speaking with Amy was the equivalent to a therapy session.

She expected Amy to carry on where Tom left off hoping she'd then have the opportunity to squeeze in and mention how happy Amy was. *Now, where the hell is the happy juice? I would like some too.* Yeah, Mary Jane assumed that would be how she ushered herself into the conversation. But Amy was quiet. During both of their dinner encounters, the Blackwoods carried the conversation, jokes, everything. And now, when Mary Jane most needed to learn how to be content with just herself and not due to Wulf—but for Wulf's sake—she couldn't.

"It's not every day that I see love, true love," Amy eventually said, turning to look at her. "The way I see it in you and Dylan. May I ask, why do you call him Wulf? It seems so formal."

Mary Jane smiled. "I... guess it all has to do with how we met. Wulf thought I was a drugged-out stripper when I drove into the back of his police cruiser. Being the straight-and-narrow cop that he is, he was angry that my *owner*, a man named Beasley, was coming to bail me out of jail. So, our relationship started quite unconventional."

Amy laughed so hard Mary Jane decided not to tell her that it wasn't a joke. Her head cocked to the side. "Wait, Amy, you said love. Me and Wulf...you think he loves me?"

The tears of laughter disappeared from Amy's cheeks with a rub from the back of her hand. "Yes, it's obvious."

A voice with a thick Mexican accent broke through the darkness, "Lalina?"

A wave of alcohol met them as a man in shredded jeans and a holey shirt walked along the shore. He was muttering in Spanish.

"You are La Luna?" he asked, his dirty nails pointed toward Mary Jane.

"Wh-hat?" Amy scooted closer to Mary Jane, visibly shaken by his intoxicated speech.

Mary Jane stared into his eyes and couldn't speak, although she understood him clearly. Silently, she came to her feet.

"We–yes... oh... *la luna* is the moon." Amy struggled to understand, pointing at the rust-red orb behind the transient. "Yes, it's a blood moon." Visibly shaken, she stood up with Mary Jane's help.

They backed away from him as the reek of alcohol assaulted them.

Again, he murmured, "Lalina . . ."

32

CANELO RUBBED A HAND THROUGH HIS THICK BLACK HAIR, staring at his nemesis. His terrorizer sat in a wingback chair next to the hotel room door, her beautiful, listless eyes gazing at his muscular body.

Soledad licked her red-painted lips and crossed a shapely, toned leg. Though Canelo looked ominous with his greasy long ponytail, bulldog face, colorful vicious tiger tattoo on his chest, and seven-foot-seven height, he trembled at the sight of Soledad. A mixture of pure hatred and disgust made him glare at her. If looks could kill, she'd be riddled with gaping holes all over her body.

Canelo turned away from the devil.

He picked up the bottle of Jose Cuervo next to his brass knuckles and tossed it back. He gulped and gulped, and then wiped the alcohol dribbling down his chin with the back of his hand.

"You better not be getting drunk!"

"I know," he replied with bite. If she said something about his tone, he'd blame it on the alcohol.

"Your time is running out," her soft voice almost teased.

"*I know*," his boomed as he placed the bottle back on the expensive marble mantel. He turned away from the empty fireplace, only to catch the gleam of hatred in her eye.

Canelo's cell phone vibrated in his shiny, gray suit pocket. He pulled it out. "Si, si...*Idiota!*"

He hung up quickly.

He turned around. Soledad was pretending to watch the fashion event on the large flat screen, but her eyes slid back to his, boring through his soul again.

"I've found *her*," he replied.

"Humph." Her slender nose turned up. "So one of those drunken transients you had keeping eyes on the streets came through? I was rather anticipating how you'd serve me instead."

"Take me out if it makes you feel better, Soledad! But if he asks who found her, I *did*," Canelo replied. He grabbed the keys to his Benz, looked back, and glared. She was coming. She stopped to pick up a high-end designer leather jacket with fur trim.

Canelo restrained his frown as her arm wriggled into his. From appearances, they were a couple. The beauty and the beast. The devil and the lamb.

They entered the elevator and rode down to the lobby of the five-star hotel, mixing and mingling with the wealthy as they passed through. The Mercedes AMG was curbside as soon as they made it out the sliding glass door.

All eyes were on the beauty on his left flank. All thinking him a lucky, ugly bastard when his deepest desire was to slide his curved-knife across her slender neck.

The valet watched her every movement as she swiftly got into the passenger side. Canelo slid into the driver's side and slammed the door in the valet's face. No tip.

The ride was long and quiet as they drove toward the

resort. A second-rate location, although too nice for the bum to have been strolling around. Still, he'd found *her*.

Canelo kissed the diamond-crusted rosary around his neck. Soledad rolled her eyes.

A few blocks from the resort, they got out of the car and walked toward an alley. Soledad's stiletto boots clopped against the cracked cement as she went, head high, narrow shoulders square.

Canelo smelled the man before laying eyes on him. In Spanish, he asked him where he'd seen Lalina.

"Over there," the guy rapidly replied, pointing towards the ocean. He scratched the palms of his hands, and then held a palm out for payment.

Soledad's top lip curled.

"Mi dinero, mi dinero." The guy clapped his hand into his other palm.

"Si, si," Canelo replied. "Is she still there? Did you see which way she went?"

He quickly replied, "Lalina went back to the resort with a wetback, and then left minutes ago. She walked with another man toward Bogota Lane."

A man? Canelo rubbed his chin in thought.

"Mi dinero," the guy again ticked with anxiety.

"Si, mi amigo," Canelo answered in a calming voice, smooth as amber liquid.

Canelo stepped closer to the homeless man. The curved, hook knife from his utility belt was off in seconds. The soft clean slice across from ear to ear was precise. Blood squirted out. The next rip went from his forehead, split his left eye, and down his chin. The transient's mouth opened in a shrill cry, yet blood curdled out instead.

Canelo yanked at the bone until it broke. He gutted his knife up the man's lower abdomen, while gracefully holding his back. In a voice of sheer sympathy, Canelo murmured in his ear, "I'm sorry, mi amigo."

It was true, the apology. The devil beside Canelo didn't allow anyone to live. And their calling card was to leave a body fully mutilated. This man was now marked as Devil's Blood. And Canelo was just the minion to oblige.

Soledad cleared her throat as Canelo gently laid the man on the ground and said a quick Hail Mary.

"Must you get in my car so dirty?"

"No," Canelo replied, tugging one arm and then the other out of his button-up. More of his tiger tattoo was exposed. His well-defined biceps rippled as he rubbed his A-shirt on his hands then gingerly wiped off his favorite knife and placed it back inside his belt.

"The *have nots* sure know how to continue the trend," Soledad argued as he tossed the clothing in the trash on the corner. They started for the car, and she continued to reprimand him for throwing away his clothing. "I bought that suit, Canelo."

"And you'll buy the next suit," he said, glare locked onto hers.

She stood in front of him. Six feet tall, they were almost the same height due to her mile-high stilettos. "Obviously, if Lalina is delivered on time."

When he didn't reply, she continued to goad him. "If she's not delivered, your death will be worse than those nightmares you have, Canelo. Mark my word." Her slender fingers took hold of his testicles. "I'll be the owner of these."

He wanted to say, *you already own them*, but instead, Canelo brushed her hand away and declared, "You will have your Lalina soon."

33

CANELO RUBBED A HAND THROUGH HIS THICK BLACK HAIR, staring at his nemesis. His terrorizer sat in a wingback chair next to the hotel room door. Her beautiful, listless eyes gazed at his muscular body.

Soledad licked her red-painted lips and crossed a shapely, toned leg. Though he looked ominous with a greasy long ponytail, bulldog face, colorful vicious tiger tattoo on his chest, and seven-foot-seven height, he trembled at the sight of Soledad. A mixture of pure hatred and disgust made him glare at her. If looks could kill, she'd be riddled with gaping holes all over her body.

Canelo turned away from the devil.

He picked up the bottle of Jose Cuervo next to his brass knuckles and tossed it back. He gulped and gulped, and then wiped the alcohol dribbling down his chin with the back of his hand.

"You better not be getting drunk!"

"I know," he replied with bite. If she said something about his tone, he'd blame it on the alcohol.

"Your time is running out," her soft voice almost teased.

"*I know*," his voice boomed as he placed the bottle back on the expensive marble mantel. He turned away from the empty fireplace, only to catch the gleam of hatred in her eye.

Canelo's cell phone vibrated in his shiny, gray suit pocket. He pulled it out. "Si, si...*Idiota!*"

He hung up quickly.

He turned around. Soledad was pretending to watch the fashion event on the large flat screen, but her eyes slid back to his, boring through his soul again.

"I've found *her*," he replied.

"Humph." Her slender nose turned up. "So one of those drunken transients you had keeping eyes on the streets came through? I was rather anticipating how you'd serve me instead."

"Take me out if it makes you feel better, Soledad! But if he asked who found her, I *did*," Canelo replied. He grabbed the keys to his Benz, looked back, and glared. She was coming. She stopped to pick up a high-end designer leather jacket with fur trim.

Canelo restrained his frown as her arm wriggled into his. From appearances, they were a couple. The beauty and the beast. The devil and the lamb.

They entered the elevator and rode down to the lobby of the five-star hotel. They mixed and mingled with the wealthy as they passed through. The Mercedes AMG was curbside as soon as they made it out the sliding glass door.

All eyes were on the beauty on his left flank. All thinking him a lucky, ugly bastard when his deepest desire was to slide his curved-knife across her slender neck.

The valet watched her every movement as she swiftly got into the passenger side. Canelo slid into the driver's side and slammed the door in the valet's face. No tip.

The ride was long and quiet as they drove toward the

resort. A second-rate location, although too nice for the bum to have been strolling there. Still, he had concern that the amenities weren't choice enough for Lalina... oh, well, he found *her*.

Canelo kissed the diamond-crusted rosary around his neck. Soledad rolled her eyes.

A few blocks from the resort, they got out of the car and walked toward an alley. Soledad's stiletto boots clopped against the cracked cement as she went, head high, narrow shoulders square.

Canelo smelled the man before laying eyes on him. In Spanish, he asked where the man had seen Lalina.

"Over there," the guy replied back rapidly. He pointed toward the ocean. He scratched the palms of his hands, and then held a palm out for payment.

Soledad's top lip curled.

"Mi dinero, mi dinero." The guy clapped his hand into his other palm.

"Si, si," Canelo replied. "Is she still there? Did you see which way she went?"

He quickly replied, "Lalina went back to the resort with a wetback, and then left minutes ago. She walked with another man toward Bogota Lane."

A man? Canelo rubbed his chin in thought.

"Mi dinero," the guy again ticked with anxiety.

"Si, mi amigo," Canelo answered in a calming voice, smooth as amber liquid.

Canelo stepped closer to the homeless man. The curved, hook knife from his utility belt was off in seconds. The soft clean slice across from ear to ear was precise. Blood squirted out. The next rip went from his forehead, split his left eye, and down his chin. The transient's mouth opened in a shrill cry, yet blood curdled out instead.

Canelo yanked at the bone until it broke. He gutted his knife up the man's lower abdomen, while gracefully holding his back. In a voice of sheer sympathy, Canelo murmured in his ear, "I'm sorry, mi amigo."

It was true, the apology. The devil beside Canelo didn't allow anyone to live. And their calling card was to leave a body fully mutilated. This man was now marked as Devil's Blood. And Canelo was just the minion to oblige.

Soledad cleared her throat as Canelo gently laid the man on the ground and said a quick Hail Mary.

"Must you get in my car so dirty?"

"No," Canelo replied, tugging one arm and then the other out of his button-up. More of his tiger tattoo was exposed. His well-defined biceps rippled as he rubbed his A-shirt on his hands. Canelo gingerly wiped off his favorite knife to place back inside of his belt.

"The *have nots* sure know how to continue the trend," Soledad argued as he tossed the clothing in the trash on the corner. They started for the car, and she continued to reprimand him for throwing away his clothing. "I bought that suit, Canelo."

"And you'll buy the next suit," he said, glare locked onto hers.

She stood in front of him. Six feet tall, they were almost the same height due to her mile-high stilettos. "Obviously, if Lalina is delivered on time."

When he didn't reply, she continued to goad him. "If she's not delivered, your death will be worse than those nightmares you have, Canelo. Mark my word." Her slender fingers took hold of his testicles. "I'll be the owner of these."

He wanted to say, *you already own them*. Instead, Canelo brushed her hand away and declared, "You will have your Lalina soon."

34

THE EARLY SUN WARMED WULF'S BARE BACK AS HE JOGGED along the coastline with Mary Jane at his side. He slowed down when his phone vibrated in the pocket of his khaki shorts. He watched the contours of the muscles in her neck and back, and then her ass as she continued ahead. Mary Jane turned around, running backwards, and gave him a teasing look like he couldn't keep up.

"Okay, super-agent, you've got me beat." He held out his phone. "It's Quincy. I have to take it." *Because this asshole is overstepping his boundaries recently.*

She gave a quick salute and kept running.

Wulf answered at the last second. "Q, what's up?"

"D, you're mad at me, I get it. And, shit, I'm angry with you too. And I know how good you've become at alienating yourself, so I might as well come clean. I told Megan *why* I found her. I told her was searching for her on the behalf of Mallory Portman-Grienke."

"What?" A heavy weight slammed against Wulf's chest. He'd initially asked Quincy to find Megan just to ensure she was safe for Mary Jane's sake. Mary Jane didn't need to be bothered with her sister, she had enough baggage of her own. He'd planned on subtly mentioning that he knew of her sister's whereabouts during a conversation about her past, whenever Mary Jane was ready to talk about it.

"I'm saying your friend's sister is in town. She filed a missing person for Mallory Grienke a while back. They're in Generosa, Mexico."

"*They?*" he growled.

"Megan and . . . a friend of the family."

"Exactly how do they know Mary Jane is here?" Wulf asked the obvious.

"They know *Mallory Portman-Grienke* is in Generosa, because I told them. Dylan, we've been friends too long. Mallory needs to see her family. She needs to mesh back into society."

"Quincy, you do not know Mary Jane. Don't speak for her."

"All right then, you! *You've* spent enough time out of touch after dealing with the Gunner gang. Nobody can bring back that kid, Gracie. She was born in the gutter and died in the gutter. We got out, D. You moved to New Mexico to take some time after getting the Gunners. *Time taken.* Remember, we got out of the gutter. *Stay out.*"

Wulf glanced off in the distance as seagulls squawked, fighting over something in the sand. "So, you're saying Mary Jane is from the gutter?"

"I'm saying she has no objective, no aspirations. Look, I was in Santo Cruces with you guys for all of twenty-four hours. Shit, I'd go mad if I were her. She's got issues. No matter how fine she is, the girl has baggage. This is not you, Dylan—you've always had a plan, stuck to it like clockwork. That is, since you finally grew up. No beautiful girl has ever made you change."

Wulf snorted. "Are you done, Quincy?"

"One last question: did Beasley and Peter Grienke brainwash you too?"

"Fuck you, Dr. Q." Wulf hung up. His phone vibrated again. A quick glance told him Quincy had left Megan's contact information and implored him to tell Mallory.

Knowing he couldn't catch up with Mary Jane, he headed the mile back home.

On Bogota Lane, he entered their beachside villa and sat at the two-seater table in the kitchen that offered a picturesque view of outside. He couldn't fathom why Quincy would push Mary Jane's mess of a sister on her when she had her own problems to handle. No way was Wulf allowing anyone else to hurt Mary Jane, emotionally or otherwise.

35

THEY'D ARGUED ABOUT WHOSE TURN IT WAS TO COOK LUNCH until settling on a street vendor and getting a plate of tamales to bring back to their tiny home. Mary Jane frowned as she stared at Wulf, who was lying on the bed eating. She'd almost said she'd loved him during sex. Fear of Wulf awakening one day and mentioning returning to Los Angeles kept her from uttering the truth. Mary Jane knew she couldn't keep him forever, no matter how hard she tried to make their reality into paradise.

She mulled over some of the times that they'd slept together. Often, it felt like making love. Well, compared to being married to Peter Grienke who had a lot of demands in bed–specific, strict requirements, Wulf's spontaneity felt a lot like love. She snuggled closer to him as they enjoyed their evening fix of Telenovela, which meant interpreting the actors' words based on their overly dramatic mannerisms. Except Mary Jane didn't tell him that she understood the words now—it was like a light switch had gone off in her brain.

The language was coming back to her. *How, MJ, how is the language returning to you? You've never learned it.*

As they lay in bed, Mary Jane joked about the actress on the screen.

"What do you think about adopting?" Wulf asked as he rubbed her hair.

She pushed herself off his chest and sat up, staring dumbfounded. She squinted in an attempt not to cry. Being Mallory meant she couldn't have his kids and she knew Wulf badly wanted a family. He'd make a good father, and he deserved to have his own kids. She tore her gaze away from his as it was on the tip of her tongue to declare that she wouldn't make him settle, but she chickened out. She was too greedy a woman to let a good man like him go.

"Maybe in another year or two. When we get back to Los Angeles," Wulf continued. "So what do you think?"

It hurt that she couldn't give him children. Making Wulf happy was what she craved most in the world. For all Megan's faults, not being able to bear Wulf's kids was the sole reason why she did not want to be *the good twin.*

He spoke for her. "I take that as a no?"

"I don't...know, Dylan," she mumbled, arising from the bed. Something in her abdomen churned. Their life was too good. Good shit didn't last. Why not break his heart before she loved him beyond repair?

I already do.

Mary Jane went into the bathroom and closed the door. Wulf understood her – at least she'd thought he did until he made that comment. Her hands went to her belly and her body trembled with rage. It was at these moments that she wished she were Megan...even a drugged-out whore could have a child.

Turning on the water spouts in the shower, she undressed and stepped inside.

While the hot water stung her skin and steam curled around her, Mary Jane cried.

"MJ, let's go dancing," Wulf said, head just inside the door.

She rubbed the fog from the glass and looked at him. Why wasn't he angry with her? He'd set aside his life for an entire year for her own selfish needs. She nodded slowly. "Uh, all right."

When she got out she wrapped herself in a towel and made her way into their bedroom. Walking around the full-sized bed that engulfed the entire area, Mary Jane headed for the closet. She rummaged through her clothes for the most provocative dress she owned; the red number made of stretchy material would surely keep Wulf in her world longer.

***

An hour later salsa music sent thrills up and down Mary Jane's spine. The slight buzz from a few cheap margaritas made her dance nonstop. Wulf said he had a surprise for her. It had better come with a few more months in Mexico, or maybe they'd travel down to South America and visit Peru or...or blaze over to Europe and salsa in Spain. Anywhere but reality. They didn't spend much, but Jake had given her enough money for the wonder never to end.

She switched partners with each song. Though her ass was enough to tempt each of them, she kept smiling at Wulf who didn't dance. Every time she turned to look at the bar, he was there, not taking his eyes off her. He held a shot glass–probably the same shot from a few songs ago. She assumed he wanted to continue their talk about leaving Mexico later on.

With that thought in her head, she gave the current man her full attention. He was short, bathed in cologne, and had a winning smile but the guy had her spinning like a vinyl record.

If it weren't for his suffocating cologne, she would've kept him as her salsa partner. She decided that one more tango wouldn't hurt, right as a gorgeous woman took a seat next to Wulf. Her eyes cut to him, but he was no longer watching her dance. He was conversing with the Latina, whose hair spilled over the side of the barstool and down her back.

Mary Jane stopped dancing. Her partner rubbed her forearm, asking for her to please continue but she stepped around other couples and away from Mr. Cologne.

"What happened?" A man in a shiny gray suit stood in her way.

Her gaze shifted up toward the ceiling. He was up there in the clouds as far as she was concerned. He had big ugly lips and a fleshy face. She noticed the cross at his neck and responded with, "Excuse me?"

"Your smile has disappeared," he said, as she kept one eye on the current conversation and another on Wulf, who smiled at the Penelope Cruz wannabe.

"I'm sorry." She rushed past the giant, but Wulf wasn't talking to the woman anymore. He'd gotten up from his chair. She assumed Wulf was heading to the restroom until he passed by the door and continued toward the entrance of the bar. Eyes narrowed, Mary Jane hurried along through the crowd. No, the Latina wasn't with him but someone else was...the ghost!

The redheaded man from the sea.

"KEEGAN?" THE GHOST OF HER DREAMS WAS ALIVE...REAL. A rush of memories of *him* flooded into her mind. Touchable reddish-brown curly hair, freckles that gave him a demeanor of contentment even when angry. Keegan rarely became angry and he'd captivated Mary Jane as he stood next to her sister at the entrance to the club.

He'd worn a simple pair of jeans and a checkered button-up. The ease of inserting herself into his world had been sweet, like the memories of love now very evident in his eyes along with the simple smile he gave. Mallory had once worn distressed or frayed jeans and frumpy t-shirts, or if given the chance, tights, a top, and ballet flats, and she used to be at Keegan's side. They had been great debaters and chess players, and they'd had the perfect all-American childhood. They'd always been together.

Keegan belonged to a world her mind had purged. And standing beside him was her sister, Megan . . .

Peter Grienke hadn't just brainwashed his wife into leaving her sister and the plagued memories of her mother and stepfather, Vin.

No, Peter had brainwashed her long before that. Her entire world, Mallory and Megan's past, was always meant as a ruse to keep her away from a family that loved her. She could only assume that the second brainwashing she'd endured at the hands of Lyle and Beasley overrode the original one.

The one that made her his docile wife.

"And you are?" Wulf questioned. As he was standing with his back to Mary Jane, he didn't notice her as he began to shake Keegan's hand.

"Keegan Little," Keegan said, his eyes drinking May Jane in with pure fascination and adoration. "I was Mallory's fiancé a few years ago."

"Oh." Wulf turned around as his line of vision met up with Keegan's. They both stared at MJ, each with his own set of memories connected to the same woman. But Mary Jane had been another girl when she'd loved Keegan. Now she was a woman, and she loved Wulf with every bit of her.

The true memories had been slowly coming back to her since she'd seen Keegan in the ocean, but she hadn't gotten around to telling Wulf. There was no need. They had built a life, and that life was perfect.

Mary Jane hugged her sister. Yes, Megan had fit into the scheme of things. Unchangeable, because Peter had given her a false world that revolved around Megan, but he hadn't given Mary Jane a fictitious scenario for Keegan. Her fiancé hadn't fit into the diagram of lies that Peter had cultivated within her brain. Keegan had been—erased. Peter had just transformed Megan into the worst type of sister anyone could have, and Mary Jane still couldn't wrap her mind around that. He'd said that temperament wouldn't change.

Technically, that was true, because Mary Jane still sought out her sister even after all the *vile* things her sister had allegedly done, but now she did not want to know her. The twins had once been attuned to each other, closer than anyone could be.

The memories of searching high and low for a strung-out panhandler every few months were incorrect. There had been no fights between the twins about rehab. No traveling the worst parts of L.A. to Long Beach and back again when Megan ran off. All of it was a lie.

Guess I've gotta hand it to him. Peter was very self-centered in his tastes. From the beginning, he made himself my savior, with his story of rescuing me out of a hard life.

After hugging her sister, who held onto her tightly and for a long time, Mary Jane let go and looked at Megan for the first time in years. They were the spitting image of each other, except that Megan's short hair was in a ponytail and she wore khaki pants and a collared shirt.

"Thank you." Megan went to Wulf and hugged him. "Thank you so much for allowing me to see my sister."

She broke down crying as he let her go. "I'm not a drug... I'm not a drug addict." She lifted the sleeves of her blazer to show there were no tracks of drug use, as if proof was needed, and the words burst out of her in a streamlined-rush, as if she had to get it all out. Wulf nodded continuously as she spoke. Megan needed the others to believe her while the proof slapped them in the face. Her entire persona was too clean for the lies Peter had fed Mary Jane.

She continued, "Mal and I..., we got along all throughout our youth. We weren't the kind for sibling rivalry. We were friends. That's the way we were raised." Megan's tear-drenched eyes turned to her twin as she pleadingly said, "Remember, Mallory?"

There were no words for Mary Jane. She didn't even succumb to the polite nodding Wulf had done to agree with her sister. She silently listened as Megan tried to prove she was not a bad person—and Mary Jane also remembered.

She'd once been a good girl. She'd taken AP Spanish and Chemistry courses, and if Physical Education had an honor class, she'd have added that along with her other courses, too. She didn't have a mother who sold her to boyfriends as a child. That was all a story Peter had given her, and a story Mary Jane wasn't aware that she was feeding to Wulf until just recently. There had been no reason to divulge the truth, until it came to her door.

"Let's go sit inside of Umberto's," Wulf suggested as partygoers walked by them.

"Yes," Megan sniffled, pushing her sleeves back down. "Mal, I promise you, I'm going to show you everything we used to do. Mom and Dad loved us. Please just listen. Okay?"

"All right." Mary Jane glanced as Keegan gave her sister a shoulder rub. She'd stomach the woman's presence, though she didn't need a history lesson regarding her true identity.

She still hated it.

37

THEY SETTLED DOWN INSIDE UMBERTO'S.

Why did I bring them here? Wulf thought. He'd made memories here with Mary Jane. They'd eaten so much their first time. Wulf reminisced on how he'd held the door open for Mary Jane and instead of being able to enjoy the sight of her ass on the way out, she'd held a hand over her stomach and asked him to call an ambulance because they'd eaten too much food. He'd laughed when she'd said the only way she'd make it out alive was on a stretcher.

Umberto's had become a Tuesday night tradition. But now they were here with two people that Mary Jane was visibly uncomfortable with. Shit, he was holding in his own discomposure as he ordered a round of beers.

Mary Jane's hand found Wulf's under the table, but her eyes found Keegan's right across from hers. Wulf's hand tensed. *This is her fiancé.* The thought slammed into him. Peter had done something to Mary Jane prior to the crap that happened in Santo Cruces City. He glanced at the perfect people sitting across from them, perfectly good people.

Wulf's mouth tightened, yet Mary Jane leaned her head on him. While the round of beers was being dispersed, he contemplated punching the shit out of Quincy's face. No warning, just like he felt now. His friend should have given him a head's up.

Megan opened her turquoise and yellow paisley satchel and started placing photos on the table.

"We were five when I got my tonsils taken out. We tricked that nurse something good. She didn't want to give you ice cream because you weren't a patient, so we switched places and kept her going." Megan smiled through her tears as she hurriedly tried to prove her point.

She pulled out an old video-recorder. "Sorry, I wanted to make sure you viewed these and nobody has VHS these days. Mal, I have videos. Your ballet classes and chess matches, my first time helping mom with a soufflé. Oh, and there's one when you won first place for your chemical compound. Mr. Wulf, it was the entire school district. Mal received a scholarship for—"

"Fuck," Mary Jane said, "we don't have to do the videos, okay?"

Wulf stopped bashing Jones's nose in in his brain.

Megan flinched.

"I'm sorry," Mary Jane murmured. "I just had a little too much to drink tonight. My head is spinning. We should get together sometime later."

"Well, I have Tylenol in my purse." Megan started rummaging around and pulled out a bottle.

Her lips tightening into a line, Mary Jane snatched the two capsules from her sister's hand. She swallowed a couple with a bottle of water, pushed the bottle over, and reclaimed Wulf's hand again.

"Mal," Keegan began, "remember when we came out

here to plan for the wedding? We were going to get married in Cabo San Lucas, and then we were considering Puerto Vallarta. You do remember, don't you?"

"No," Mary Jane replied flatly.

As a body language analysis, Wulf knew she was lying. But Megan had photographic evidence of everything. His heart sank the moment she displayed a picture of the very painting Mary Jane bought from a vendor a few blocks away. It was odd for Megan to take a photo of a canvas on the wall, yet he understood her need to persuade Mallory and rouse her memory.

"How much did you buy it for?" Wulf asked, recalling that Mary Jane tried to pay the man too much for the canvas painting.

"Twenty bucks, why?" Keegan asked.

Wulf nodded. That was the exact amount Mary Jane had offered the vendor a few blocks away from their home, and the woman had laughed and said if they were in Puerto Vallarta, yes, but she gave them a deal anyway. Mary Jane had lied to him. She had to have recalled the amount she spent on the painting in the tourist area with Keegan. But Wulf was riddled with doubt: why would she purchase the same painting again?

Did Mary Jane purchase the painting while reminiscing about Keegan?

Or was it a subconscious effort and she did not recall?

Fuck! You're reaching and being ridiculous, Wulf told himself. He tracked his hard gaze over Mary Jane for a nonverbal evidence of a lie.

"I didn't know. Wulf, I did not know." Mary Jane's eyes searched his for a hint of softness. When his tensed jaw didn't relax, she turned to their company. "Look, Megan, Keegan, this has all been too much."

Wulf pulled his hand slowly from hers, and he took a sip of his beer. He tried to determine whether Mary Jane was telling the truth; maybe her mind had offered such a mundane part of her past but it was growing harder to believe by the minute.

Keegan continued, "We left the tourist site. Got a little place on Bogota Lane—I remember because that's the capital of Colombia—and we stayed an extra week because you were mad at your dad. I think it's around the corner from here."

Bogota Lane was the same street where they currently resided. Wulf's lips tensed slightly.

"I didn't know, Wulf," she whispered.

"But Dad wasn't bad. He just didn't think you two were ready for marriage," Megan interjected.

Keegan continued his attempt to jog her memory, pull her back to him. "Your mom finally talked you into returning, then..." His voice trailed off as he realized he'd hit the end of the road and needed to make a U-turn toward cheerful times. "The happiest day of your life, I'll never forget when you came home after..."

Wulf stood. "I'm going to let you all get reacquainted."

"Thanks," Megan said. "Maybe tomorrow we can all get together and watch the baby videos. Dad made them for every year of our lives. Every Christmas, Easter, our Christening, it's all there."

"That would be great." Wulf gave her a smile and walked toward the exit.

38

MARY JANE CRINGED. SHE WANTED TO TELL WULF THAT HER buried memory of being at Bogota Lane and the damn canvas painting hadn't come until this very moment. It was the honest truth that she'd just realized who Keegan was and how important he used to be to her.

She listened as the two continued to draw her back into them. Sucking the life out of her. They wanted so desperately for her to fit into an outdated model but all the while, in the back of her mind, she recalled her family's numerous attempts to visit her at the Grienke mansion.

After an hour of photos, with Keegan and Megan taking turns sharing the sappiest moments of her life, Mary Jane allowed them to walk her to her street corner.

"See you later," she mumbled and waved them away.

"We're staying at Aries Hotel," Megan tried in a chipper demeanor. "Wulf knows the room number if you forget. Oh, gosh, I'm sorry—"

"Yes, if I *forget*, I'll ask him, thanks." Mary Jane nodded. In her heart, she knew Megan meant no harm so, walking backwards, she gave her a weak smile then brusquely turned around and continued down the dimly-lit street. When she looked back, they were still standing next to the T in the road, watching to make sure she was safe. Or maybe they wanted to ensure she hadn't forgotten where she lived for the past year?

She continued down the street with a vivid image of Megan's nose crinkling as she'd cursed. Megan didn't like profanity from the looks of it, and if memory served her correctly, Keegan wasn't much for it either. Her memories of them hadn't fully returned. However, with Megan's probing by way of photos and videos, the truth was flooding back.

Flooding back so quickly that Mary Jane felt like sinking.

She bit her lip in anger, considering all the concern in their eyes. The pity. She hated the pity the most.

A rustling sounded behind her.

She turned quickly. Megan and Keegan were no longer standing under the streetlamp watching her. She peered into a dark alleyway slotted between two units and could see the black ocean and a figure.

An orange glow from the tip of a cigarette outlined the shape of a person leaning against the left house. The eeriness of it made the hair on the nape of her neck stand on end. *I'm not a super-agent.* She recalled the bravado she'd had when first meeting Wulf.

She was washed in illumination from the hood lights of a car navigating at a snail's pace toward her. Mary Jane glanced back over to the house she had to pass before getting home, but there was no shadowy figure holding a cigarette. With quick strides, Mary Jane rushed down the street as the car proceeded down the lane. She hurried into her yard and looked back at a luxury car. In the dark she couldn't see inside the shadowed interior. She glared hard, determined not to be afraid. Fear was reserved for nightmares.

There was a man and woman in the Mercedes, most likely coming home from a date or lost their way back to one of the swanky resorts a few miles away.

She zipped up the stairs and felt for her keys inside her purse. Pulling them out, she quickly unlocked the door.

Once inside, she kicked off the shoes that had long ago sent a throbbing pain through her arches. Not the most comfortable knock-offs.

A bluish TV glow came from the bedroom. Her hands on her hips, she glared at Wulf as he slept propped up, the TV remote cradled in his hand.

She picked up a pillow and whacked him across the face.

He jolted awake. "What did you do that for?" he asked in a groggy voice.

"Have you lost your mind?" She stood tall as he got up from the bed.

Wulf combed a hand through his hair and glared down at her. "I reunited you with your family, Mary Jane. I should be receiving a grade-A blowjob at the very least."

"I never wanted to see those people!" She pushed against his chest.

Unmovable as ever, Wulf cocked an eyebrow. "Why not?"

They...they want to change me. Her eyes slid away from him. She licked her lips and sighed. "I haven't seen them in ages, Dylan. I wasn't ready."

"All right, MJ, I'm sorry." Wulf tried to hug Mary Jane, but she sidestepped his touch.

"It's okay," she mumbled.

He stood just behind her as she prepared to undress for the night. Mary Jane held her head high, concentrating on the sound the zipper made as Wulf pulled it down for her.

Tell me you love me, Wulf. Please.

Her heart was weary. Of all the comfort he gave, all the friendship, and an open ear for her to vocalize her crazy life, he'd never given the thing she desired the most. Himself.

When she turned around, he sat on the bed and flipped channels.

I love you so much, Wulf. She picked up a pillow and the blanket from the bed.

"MJ, what are you doing?"

"Like you have to ask," she retorted, heading for the living room.

"Come to bed." He got up again and leaned against the doorframe as she made herself comfy on the entirely too short loveseat.

"I'm fine where I am." She fluffed the pillow with heavy punches, just waiting for him to say he loved her. Instead, he returned to their bed. The threat Peter made about coming between her and Wulf took root. She gave the pillow one last whack, much too stubborn to give in now, after all, this was a lover's quarrel and Peter could only torment her dreams.

***

The next morning, Mary Jane pulled herself up into a seated position. In their bed. She glanced around and smiled, shaking her head. Wulf must've picked her up while she was in a deep sleep and placed her back in bed.

Now, his side was empty. A glance at the digital clock on the nightstand read that it was just about 7 a.m. and almost thirty minutes into their usual work-out regimen.

After a quick bathroom routine, Mary Jane pulled out a bra and short set for running, but instead of getting dressed, she impulsively scooped out all of her undergarments and shirts and dumped everything onto the bed. She grabbed all the rest of the items from her side of the dresser and then yanked every item from her side of the closet rack, trying to rationalize the thought that had popped into her head.

She was going to move back to Los Angeles with Dylan Wulf. The ease of her sudden realization brought a smile to her face. Wulf had mentioned purchasing his first home in Claremont once. It had been during a walk home, with the evening sun warming their skin. They'd just left an ice cream shop and a little girl had chatted with them for almost an hour. Her mother had apologized and tried to get the girl to turn around in her seat, but Mary Jane was glued to the kid's infectious laughter. Maybe she couldn't give Wulf children, but he hadn't been talking about his abandoned, brand new home for no reason. He'd offered her a future.

"Wulf," she worked on how she was going to persuade him. "Those people belong to a world I no longer live in. I don't know them. I don't need to know them."

Although, she'd unknowingly divulged untrue horror stories, he had to understand that all the memories of herself and her sister, the good—the truth—meant nothing now. And the bad—Peter's invention—well, that meant nothing now as well.

We have us to consider.

Eyeing the pile of clothes on the bed, Mary Jane stalked to the closet and grabbed her luggage. The thought of her and Megan having lunch today, as her sister had requested, forced her to hurry and toss things into each case.

"Let's get an RV and travel like Amy and Tom," she told herself with a smile of contentment. "I love you, Wulf. Let's just go traveling a little while longer. Maybe just another week before settling in Los Angeles. I'll go home for you... because wherever you are, I am home."

Mary Jane stopped packing her bags. The thought was profound. *I don't mind going back to reality for Wulf. He's home to me.*

"Yes," she continued to work out her story for him. Listening to herself chatter on with no one around should've made Mary Jane feel bizarre and crazy but it just felt like purging Mary Jane's previous need to alienate herself from the world.

She stopped packing. "I love Wulf!"

Voicing it was new and the words felt like sunshine after the rain. Mary Jane slipped into a shirt and shimmied into her jeans before she rushed through the living room and to the front door.

The warm sun bathed Mary Jane and the bliss she felt grew exponentially as her bare feet padded along the cool sand toward the back of their home. Cupping her hands around her forehead, Mary Jane glanced around. There was a trio of surfers navigating the choppy, cold water off in the distance. A lone woman powerwalked near the edge of the water. It was too early for a swim. Biting her lip, she searched the miles of shoreline for Wulf.

They usually ran for about an hour and a half. Taking a few steps back, she meandered back toward the house. Determined to maximize her time, she headed for the closet to begin packing Wulf's luggage.

In the living room, she left the screen door open to let in more natural light. "False past or not, I'll have everything ready like Megan and Mal did when their mother was running away from another boyfriend," she sniggered to herself upon entering the bedroom. She stopped and shook her head, laughing at how she had just referred to herself in the third person. "I am no longer Mallory Portman-Grienke," she uttered her new motto.

A creaking from the front door made Mary Jane drop his rollaway bag in its spot in the closet.

"Wulf," she started for the living room. "Let's take a short road trip before heading to Los Angeles—"

"That sounds lovely," said a beautiful stranger. After a moment, Mary Jane recognized her as the gorgeous Penelope wannabe from the bar. She was now wearing riding pants and very expensive leather riding boots.

"Who are you?" Mary Jane's skin prickled.

The woman removed a light pink silk scarf from around her neck and began to twine it around her finger. "I much prefer the Glades during this time of year, Lalina. It's very beautiful, though you won't ever get a chance to venture there. That is, if you haven't already."

This is not happening, Mary Jane told herself as she kept her eyes trained on the woman who seemed at ease in her home. Danger burned hot goose bumps along her forearms as she stared at the frightening woman and, behind her, the humongous man from the bar last night. He'd been the one who'd stopped her when this woman standing before her now had taken a seat next to Wulf. The man was menacing; tall and huge—and he reminded her of Santo Cruces City.

"Who are you?" she murmured again, inching toward the bedroom door as they blocked the exit from her villa.

"My name is Soledad," the woman replied with a soft smile. "This is Canelo. He plays nice if you do."

Canelo leaned against the wall next to the kitchen door with his ankles crossed. There was something in his gaze that told her he'd rather be a thousand miles away. Had Soledad screwed with his mind? Was he just a vessel? A means for Soledad's safety or defense such as the role Hurricane once played for Beasley? Of all the times to choose fight or flight, Mary Jane's mind was her biggest threat again.

In two strides, he towered before her. His voice was a mask of sincerity which Mary Jane knew was a lie as he implored, "Come willingly, Lalina."

Of all the possible options at her disposal, Mary Jane closed her eyes. She willed some of Anya's defense skills to wash over her.

Nothing came.

Shit, shit, shit, she told herself. A slight trick of the mind would have left Mary Jane feeling more than competent at saving her own life, but now she knew Anya wasn't real, she no longer had the confidence to react.

"Lalina."

"What are you saying?" Her eyes snapped open.

"Lalina, you're—"

"I am Mary Jane." The inherent need to continue with the same identity urged Mary Jane to react. With right leg anchored back, Mary Jane tossed a forearm punch as if she were aiming to punch through her target. Not only did she want to break his nose, but to obliterate Canelo's entire face. Her knuckles slammed against his bridge.

When her leg flew up, knee ready to slam against his cock, Canelo pressed his hands against her chest with such force the air expelled from her lungs and fire burned down her spine as the base of her skull crunched against the wall. Losing all power in her legs, Mary Jane sank to the floor, her vision hazed with spots from the blow. Her enemies became shadows.

"Okay, Lalina. You've proven your point," Soledad said.

In a daze, Mary Jane's gaze followed the voice. Her blurred vision straightened as Soledad held a gold-plated nine-millimeter at her side. Eyebrows kneaded she glanced up at Canelo. With her vulnerable position on the floor, he could do virtually anything he wanted to her.

He pinched his nose and hardly looked in her direction.

"Canelo, do not get any blood on the floor. We don't want our little bad girl's friend to worry too soon. No struggles." Soledad   arose.   She   moved   toward   Mary Jane. "Hmm..."

Mary Jane looked upward and tried to stand but couldn't. Soledad was over her, but not paying her any attention. The woman was analyzing any signs that Mary Jane caused damage to the wall.

"No issues there, good. He won't know." Soledad headed for the bedroom. "Oh, great, she already packed her things. Were you going home, Lalina?"

Soledad's laughter was rich from the bedroom as Mary Jane placed her palms and knees on the floor and groaned. Canelo had walked away. She heard the sound of flushing. He was probably disposing of tissues.

When he returned, Mary Jane was willing herself not to cry. Placing one foot before the other, she mentally told herself to move toward the kitchen, but the man had knocked her lights out and half the spirit in her too.

Grab a knife, kill these motherfuckers. She forced one foot after the other but before her feet could pass the threshold for the kitchen, Canelo grabbed her around the waist.

His hot breath assaulted her ear as he whispered, "Better for you to just—"

"What the fuck is going on? Why am I carting her luggage while the two of you tango?" Soledad whined from the bedroom door.

"Just do nothing," Canelo finished with a low murmur. He grabbed Mary Jane's luggage from Soledad's hands.

Mary Jane glanced at the bitch and her lap dog, then back toward the kitchen. The knife was in the butcher block, about five yards away, but Canelo's legs were almost double the length of her own. And could she survive another one of his hits? As he hefted her luggage, Mary Jane felt something sticky and wet slide down the nape of her neck. She reached a hand back and touched the warm liquid. Blood.

Soledad shoved the scarf at her chest. "Take this. Keep it."

Their eyes connected, both women obviously full of rage. It shook Mary Jane to see that Soledad was regarding her the way Beasley and Peter had, as if she owned her.

Mary Jane knew that her enemy didn't want there to be any signs of a struggle. Besides, she'd just packed her own things to be taken. She applied the scarf to the nape of her neck, lips set in a sneer. Canelo pushed two pieces of luggage and had a third under his arm as he opened the door. Soledad stalked out first. Canelo cocked his head for Mary Jane so she gulped down trepidation and followed. She'd had an attitude with Wulf last night. He'd think she left. As flighty as Mary Jane was, it made sense for her to leave.

Her throat constricted, and she wanted to cry. This was worse than her nightmares with Peter.

Yet, even in her desire not to conform to societal norms, there was *Wulf*. He was always there for her, and she owed him a great deal. She glanced back into the house that they'd shared.

She reminisced on their first and only Thanksgiving together. The golden turkey that was rather bloody on the inside had been traded in for their favorite street tacos. She glanced at the very spot on the living room floor where they'd exchanged Christmas gifts. She had giggled as Wulf ate the popcorn he was supposed to be helping string for the tree. She remembered his chuckle when she'd handed him a perfectly wrapped box. He'd expected a gag gift.

The contents had been a police uniform—the kind strippers wore. His laughter roared in their little beachside home. Wulf had arched a sexy look her way and obliged her.

She'd received a seashell necklace—something that she'd cherish. Now, she started moving forward, hoping to God that Dylan Wulf knew she loved him and would never leave unless by force. With heavy legs, she went down the two porch steps and toward the couple's Mercedes.

"Mary Jane, is that you?" Amy called after her.

Mary Jane tensed, her spine went rigid.

"Don't start anything, Lalina," Soledad warned in Mary Jane's ear as she gestured for Canelo to get the door. "He'll murder your friends right in front of you."

"I have to say 'hi' or they're going to wonder what's going on," Mary Jane grumbled. Receiving a sharp nod as response, she turned around, ready to fall to her knees and cry.

All those times in the past where her life had been in jeopardy, it always seemed like she was alone. Even when Glenn and Wulf came to save her, Mary Jane had pushed them away, not accustomed to support. Yet here Tom and Amy were in the flesh.

"Hey, we told you and Dylan we'd try to do like the two of you," Tom said, hand holding his side, winded from his morning run. "Although, we stopped at every spot in between for a cool glass of lemonade."

There he was, droning on in a happy oblivious manner that Mary Jane never adopted herself. Though she didn't know for what purpose, she knew for a fact that Soledad and Canelo planned to use her. Still, her tongue cleaved to the roof of her mouth. What to say, how to address them without putting their lives in jeopardy too?

"You're embarrassing us," Amy confessed while patting his shoulder.

"Oh, no," Mary Jane searched for the right words while attempting to hide the tremble in her tone. "You guys are awesome."

"Looks like you and Dylan have made some new friends?" Tom's eyes lingered on Soledad before he said, "We're headed back to California. Just wanted a morning run and to say a quick farewell. You'll never forget the friends you make on vacation, ma'am."

Soledad glared at his hand as he attempted to shake hers.

"Where's Dylan?" Amy cut in. Tom kept glancing at Soledad.

Mary Jane removed her hand from the scarf, hoping it would fall and they'd notice it as they left. She shrugged. "He's running on the beach. I decided to stay behind to make lunch."

"Oh."

"If you see him around," Mary Jane said as Canelo's arm slipped over her shoulder like an old friend. He was holding her scarf in place. "Tell him I *caught* a few bass and lunch will be ready soon. He loved my bass."

"Yes," Soledad said with a smile, "ever the little home-maker. Well, La–Mary Jane, let's go shopping so you can return to your domestication."

"Wait," Amy said as they continued down the sidewalk. She hurried toward Mary Jane, Canelo's hand went into the pocket of his suit as the women hugged.

"I'll miss you, Mary Jane."

"Me too," Mary Jane sighed, wishing she'd been granted the time to cherish the moment of meeting true friends. Instead, all she felt was fear for what these two planned to do with her now.

Mary Jane watched them head along the side of the beach house. She placed all of her faith in the Blackwoods, hoping they'd cross paths with Wulf on his return from a run.

39

WULF PULLED HIS SHIRT OFF AS HE SLOWED TO A JOG. HE'D run hard, crushing his lungs to keep Mary Jane's fiancé from his mind. As soon as he'd left the trio at Umberto's to get acquainted, he'd called Quincy. They'd gotten into an argument about Keegan not being mentioned during Wulf's agreement for them to meet. Quincy quickly briefed Wulf. Keegan Little was a History teacher in Long Beach, California. Little's only run-in with the law were two parking tickets, each of which were paid within the allotted time.

Wulf trudged through the sand for Bogota Lane. He noticed Tom and Amy meandering down the stairs that led up to his villa.

"We wanted to say farewell before heading out," Tom said.

"Okay." Wulf wasn't one for goodbyes or the like. "Did you see Mary Jane?" *Is she still pissed?*

"Yeah, she was on her way out," Amy confirmed.

"Oh."

"She had luggage," Tom chimed in. "Her friends seemed a bit rushed."

"What friends?" Wulf's mouth subtly tensed.

"A guy and a *woman*." Tom gave a sheepish grin.

Amy elbowed him in the rib and snapped, "Really, Tom?"

Wulf cut into the jealous dispute. "Did she say where they—"

"I can't believe you!" Amy burst into tears. "We're still on our honeymoon! Don't think I didn't see you take a double-take at the girl with a G-string bikini on the way over here either."

Amy stalked off, leaving Tom to brew in the storm she left behind.

"Dylan, you have my number. I'd better catch up with the missus." Tom hustled down the last few steps and trudged through the sand.

"It was her sister, right?" he yelled out to Tom, the insecurity from last night still eating at him. Hearing the words aloud hit hard. But with Tom and Amy arguing about twenty yards away, Wulf didn't receive confirmation of what he knew was true.

His Mary Jane had left with Megan and Keegan.

How could she? Apparently, Mary Jane had been planning a wedding to Keegan when she ended up married to that rich fuck. He told himself not to be an asshole. Peter stole her entire life. She deserved to be happy.

She deserved happiness. But the only road to his own contentment led to Mary Jane. Wulf's mind dissected the past few months. They were like an explosion together. Loving her was a drug. But recently Mary Jane had grown agitated – she'd found out her *true* identity. Why wouldn't she prefer her family and the history she had with Keegan over the bullshit start Wulf had built with her?

Then she'd made that comment about adoption, which

Wulf hadn't believed. She liked children, he was sure of it. She always smiled and engaged with kids when they were out. She took pity on Tito who would be standing in the heat selling toys to tourists all day if she hadn't given him a task to bring a newspaper by in the morning. And she'd paid him generously.

The sound of children's laughter brought Wulf back to the present. Families were beginning to line the beach for a dose of mid-morning fun in the sun. There were blankets and ice chests and people sporadically placed all around Wulf when he realized he'd been standing in the same spot for almost an hour.

He grabbed his cell phone from his pocket and texted Quincy.

WULF: I'm coming home.

QUINCY: Good. I'll pick you up from LAX.

Without responding in kind or otherwise, Wulf powered off his phone. He didn't need it for now.

***

It took all night for Wulf to return to the home they once shared. The moment he stepped in the door, he visualized them arguing about who'd cook dinner, which ended with them making love on the kitchen counter. Every room held a memory.

He picked up a lamp, yanking the cord from the socket.

"Fuck!" he shouted, tossing it against the living room wall. The turquoise glass shattered. He wanted to let the anger brew in his gut as he thought about their good times together. His Mary Jane.

But she was never his to have.

Peter stole her happiness. Wulf told himself not to be angry with her. She had an entire life to return to; an ex-fiancé who was compelled enough to take a trip with Megan to retrieve her. To reinsert her into their happy lives together.

He ruminated on pulling her beautiful body into his arms and cuddling her close after a dream where Peter threatened to break them apart. After she'd told him about those dreams, Wulf always declared that he'd never leave her. That wasn't just truth in his mind—it was law.

"Good luck, Mary Jane," he whispered, wanting the best for her.

***

It took Wulf less than an hour to pack his bags. He sat at the airport all night long on standby for any cancelations to get an early morning flight and finally lucked out. As expected, a Federal Agent was waiting for him in the terminal when Wulf landed, since he'd used his debit card to pay for the flight. He and his luggage were transported to an FBI satellite location where he was met by an old associate since the LAPD and FBI have a liaison program in full effect.

Agent Luke Gaston had offered his services once Wulf's team made a connection to the Gunner gang and various FBI most wanted persons from a Mexican cartel. They sat with cups of coffee and for the most part talked about old times.

"So what, you're babysitting today?" Wulf asked.

"I'd like to say I'm catching up with an old friend. But for now, yes, I'm keeping an eye on you, Wulf." Gaston took a sip from his mug.

Wulf shrugged. "So tell me, how are Beasley's girls?"

Gaston shook his head. "I don't wanna know about it, don't need to. Agent Samuels should be here in the next thirty minutes."

"I get it. The less you know—"

"The better," Gaston ended, giving a gruff laugh. "Sounds like you've moved on to bigger and better things since ridding the street of the Gunner gang."

"Better," Wulf mumbled with a huff. He didn't recall Agent Samuels until about an hour later when the black man walked into the room. The Feds weren't even consulting with their own agents on the Grienke case. Gaston's thick eyebrows were less furrowed as he made his exit.

"The moment I used my credit card to book a flight home, they sent you?" Wulf asked as the man who was roughly the same age as him sat opposite.

"Where's Mallory Portman-Grienke?"

"So this is what we're doing." Wulf gestured between himself and Samuels. "Answering questions with questions? All right, my turn, where are the women who were *rescued* from Beasley?" He cocked an eyebrow. Every once in a while, Mary Jane would bring them up and her shoulders would slump in guilt. Now, his own shoulders fell as it sank in that he was thinking about her again.

"Safe. Mr. Wulf, if you would like for us not to bring up charges as you've clearly impeded an investigation—"

Wulf slammed his hand down on the steel table, the sound resonating against the wall. "She couldn't stay there!" He shook his head and gave a tight chuckle. "You expected Mary Jane to stay in a place where she was abducted, chased, and—"

"You're still calling Mrs. Grienke that name?" Samuels leaned forward. "She's gone, isn't she?"

Chewing on his bottom lip, Wulf tried to determine what motivated the agent. With the cover-ups going on, there was no way in hell he'd give him information about MJ.

With a cocky smile, Samuels reached into the inside of his suit pocket and pulled out a photo of Mary Jane and Grienke, pearly white teeth were on display as they held each other like two lovebirds. She wore a custom lace wedding dress that gave Mary Jane an ethereal aura that didn't quite ring true, but she was still gorgeous.

"You know, Mrs. Grienke was an intern at Grienke Pharmaceuticals, planning her wedding to another man, Keegan Little. And they had been friends throughout high school and college. I wondered if it was brainwashing myself while interviewing Little and the Portman family. I even went so far as to speak with the few police officers who were on the original case, when our little ditzy girl didn't come home from interning. Funny how she ended up married that weekend to the wrong man."

Wulf stopped himself from rubbing the bridge of his nose. His outward façade was emotionless. Internally, these very thoughts had roamed through his mind when Mary Jane decided to return home with her family. *If the idiot takes a ride to the Portman house, he'd know she is home with her family.*

"You know, Wulf. I initially thought, a smart young woman like her—excuse me, she *was* extremely intelligent —must've been working so many angles as an intern for Grienke. She used all that intelligence, all those lovely assets. She married Peter Grienke for his money, right? No brainwashing necessary to inherit a billion-dollar empire."

Now, Wulf scratched his temple. "Wait, since you're connecting motivation, I thought Grienke's company was sold off, shares given to his other board members? Out of all the news flying low under the radar, I'm assuming the money bit was the most important."

"This isn't about the money, Wulf, but you're right. *Mrs.*

Grienke has survived for over a year without using a single credit card. Grienke had other offshore accounts. So, what? She traded you in while in paradise, the same way she did with Little?"

Wulf's skin was on fire. Damn right, he wanted to bash in Keegan Little's face. He gave a listless stare and asked, "Are you holding me?"

"Not at all. I'm going to watch you instead. Maybe I'm wrong about Mrs. Grienke. Maybe she's here in Los Angeles. When you cross paths, I'll be there."

***

It was almost noon when Wulf was transported to his adoptive mother Brenda's home in West Los Angeles. The home had character written all over it. Light yellow paint, just enough to be cheerful without being too bright. Light hued roses were in the garden as well, and it was the only garden on the block. Wulf recalled raking leaves as a chore while he moved his rollaway up the sidewalk and to the door.

Today, the yard was cluttered with two blue bicycles and a pink Big Wheel. Quincy and Shelly, along with their three children had moved into the home with Brenda a few years ago after her hip replacement.

Wulf's hand was poised to knock on the door, and it flew open. Before him stood Brenda Miller in one of her shades of orange, rose-print cotton loungers. She was the reason Wulf hadn't reclaimed his unscrupulous ways as he grew up in her home—learning the difference between what did or did not belong to him.

Her brown eyes widened. "Dylan, my baby boy!"

Wulf's chin rested on the top of her puffy gray hair as they hugged. It was enough to settle him from the past twenty-four hours.

40

LUSH FORESTLAND SURROUNDED THE VILLA IN CENTRAL Mexico. Stucco walls, clay floors, and custom furniture spanned over seventeen-thousand square feet. A Hummer, Bentley, and a Mercedes SUV were in the U-shaped driveway with ample room for more. But the mansion was empty except for Soledad, Canelo, and their unwilling guest.

Mary Jane woke up in a cream-colored room on an intricate wrought iron twin-sized bed. She'd been drugged prior to the arrival and wasn't able to take in her surroundings. She didn't know what day it was, since she'd recalled waking up various times in the back of Soledad's car, only to be given another sedative.

The sun shone through the unshaded windows. Canelo's fleshy face was inches away from hers. He stared at her attentively. It didn't remind her of the creepy twins who'd worked for Beasley and tried to rape her, because firstly, his tongue wasn't lodged down her throat and secondly, his eyes held a spark of concern.

"You've had a nightmare." Canelo crouched down

beside her.

"Leave me alone." She sat up and folded her knees to her chest.

"Canelo!" Soledad's voice carried from down the hall.

He left.

Alone again, she contemplated on Tom and Amy. Had they crossed paths with Wulf?

What if they didn't tell him the code phrase?

What if he thought she left with the wrong man and woman?

Her mind ran rampant with reasons why two strangers had kidnapped her. Switching focus to the high fashion model, Soledad, and her giant watch dog. Watch dog... While Mary Jane attempted to concentrate on who they were, her thoughts slipped to Hurricane. After he'd captured her, Mary Jane had figured out that he'd been brainwashed into doing Beasley's bidding. There was too much of a correlation between Hurricane and Canelo.

Peter?

In her dreams, Peter began with the psychological mind-fuck. He warned her that she'd never see Wulf again. Canelo and Soledad ignored Mary Jane when she asked what they wanted, therefore, Peter must've sent then.

Don't sleep.

Don't sleep.

Don't sleep.

Don't dream.

Don't dream

Mary Jane lay back down and closed her eyes, willing herself to see Wulf's kind eyes, hear his laughter. Vivid images of herself in Wulf's arms after bad dreams pacified her instantly. The memories of love were tangible until hot tears rolled down her cheeks. He wasn't here. She was alone.

41

"LINDA CURBELO IS MISSING; MALLORY PORTMAN-GRIENKE IS missing," Ariel mumbled, sinking down into her seat at the hotel room she was renting in Los Angeles, California. Her boss had been shoved aside to cut down on the chain of command. She was the special agent in charge—for the moment. The Deputy Director had made that very clear.

The ice in her whiskey clinked against the glass as she tossed back the drink, savoring the hard burn, needing it like punishment.

The director had indicated that if the various facets of this case weren't wrapped up soon enough, they'd have to shove her back down to supervisor. "Because let's face it, Juarez, they kinda need you," she mumbled to herself. With the president breathing on everyone's neck, she couldn't determine if it was her saving grace or condemnation. The higher-ups wanted to keep this case as classified as possible, and there were already at least a hundred tied to the Grienke case with the FBI computer and psychological scientists aware of certain dynamics. The floor-to-ceiling windows showcased the sky with an indigo mask and faint stars. Nothing like back at home in Louisiana where the original case had begun for her surrounding the abduction of Tiana Clement. Had it not been for Clement's case, she wouldn't be assigned to this one and not for the obvious reason. She had to believe she was the best.

Her cell phone buzzed on the coffee table next to her. Ariel answered the phone without screening the call. "Juarez."

"It's Samuels. Wulf has been home for just about seventy-two hours now. Should I bring him back in, grill him more?"

It was on the tip of her tongue to tell him yes, to get the information about Mrs. Grienke out of him by any means. "No. He loves the girl too much. He won't break." *And you'll keep showing your hand, such as telling him we plan to smoke out Woods with her as sacrifice.* "We have agents working the Mexico angle. Either she's there or she'll return to Wulf."

42

LOUD, REALISTIC SHOOTING SOUNDS TRAVELED FROM THE DEN where Wulf's seven and eight-year-old nephews, Bryan and Ryan were playing. He sat at the kitchen table with his four-year-old niece, Bree, leaning against him and sucking her thumb. She was a weird one and not at all hypnotized to cooperate when it came to cartoons.

Wulf smiled at her big sparkling eyes and offered her a *keke pua'a*, a steamed bun made of pork. Brenda had learned about Wulf's culture the moment she took him in her home. And today, it seemed she planned on mending his broken heart with food.

Bree grinned, taking the bun from his hand.

He kissed her forehead. "Why don't you run around, play, terrorize your older brothers?"

The toddler just continued to sit there and eat.

Brenda laughed from her spot at the stove, content with cooking even more food. "I'm surprised the baby even recalls who you are as long as you've been gone. But she's stuck to you like glue."

"How about a book?"

Bree nodded.

"Go grab your favorite book on your bookshelf and when you come back down, I'll be ready to read."

With that, Bree took off. Shaking his head and smiling, Wulf pulled out Shelly's MacBook that she'd allowed him to borrow. Yesterday, he'd focused long enough to review his resume.

"Dylan," Brenda placed her hands in the pockets of her muumuu and took a seat in the breakfast nook. "Are you still thinking about that girl?"

"No."

"*Yes*," Shelly stressed as she came into the kitchen scooting into the breakfast nook next to him and started to grab a *keke pua'a* off his once discarded plate. Wulf swatted her hand.

"Shi—sheesh!" Shelly stopped herself from cursing and waved her hand around. "For all the snitching I did as a child about you sneaking out when you first moved in, Dylan, you always got my back."

"Yup. Your hand was always in my food." He laughed.

"That stings," she said, still flapping around her hand.

"I'll make you a plate," Brenda said with a smile as she rose. "I've got my court shows to watch. You two remember how old you are. No fights."

"Dylan is head-over-heels for little Miss Crazy. She left him." Shelly got the last word in as Brenda exited the kitchen.

"Thank you, Shelly," Wulf replied, clicking a hyperlink for a private security job with an amount of pay that would've made him leery if he hadn't received the lead from an old colleague.

"You're welcome. Now that the little zombie head is—"

"What?"

"Brainwashed woman. Does that sound better?" Shelly asked.

"Quincy told you," he grumbled.

"Hell, yes! Anyway, I think Quincy only told me about Grienke being her husband so I would stop applying Grienke facial products. That's what you get for introducing me to your cheap friends."

"You married my cheap friend."

Her eyes narrowed slightly in thought, as she grinned devilishly. "I ought to tell Brenda you're moving *in* for good. She'll be so hopeful."

Wulf chose not to react to the threat. He loved his sister, and she loved goading him.

"Look, Dylan, you're my brother. That woman owes you an explanation for leaving. I'm going to be as annoying as I was when we were teens, trying to get you not to go AWOL until you get closure."

"My life isn't some tragic love story, Shelly."

"I'd rather like a tragic love story after all you've been through for that girl. She needs to apologize; she owes you closure."

"She tried."

"When?"

Wulf grumbled. "I got a few texts and voicemails from Megan's phone. Mary Jane—"

"From her sister's phone? Why would she call you from her sister's phone?"

"Can I speak?" Wulf asked flatly. When she nodded, he added, "MJ and I shared a phone in Mexico. The person who would be out took it. We didn't have bill collectors calling in paradise," he finished, taking a deep breath. "So she called and texted. I deleted them without reviewing a single one."

"Why?" Shelly's head tilted.

"Because Mary Jane would've offered an apology and tried to rationalize it. She would've wanted to lighten the blow by telling me." His voice drowned out. In a tone devoid of emotion, he finished strong with, "She would've told me that no matter how much she cared for me, she loves Keegan."

Shelly's brown eyes brightened with tears. Her mouth opened and she hadn't quite gotten the right words to say when Wulf gestured toward Bree. The tot bounded back into the room with a humongous Disney princess book that filled up both of her arms. "No more shit talk," he whispered to his sister. "It's reading time."

Shelly scooted out of the nook and kissed Bree on her forehead before she claimed the spot.

"All right then, Dylan," she said as she started walking backwards toward the hallway. "But before I go. I know you mentioned searching for apartments, but I'll just tell Mom you're moving in. How are you liking the bottom bunk? The boys just love having you in their room."

He chuckled.

***

An hour later, Wulf had finished a book about a princess whose hair was so long it tangled all the way down to her feet and wrapped around the perimeter of the tower she lived in. He'd also put a sleeping Bree into her bed, and then caved in to Shelly's threats. They were almost locked out of the LAPD database but Shelly had figured out Quincy's password on the third and last try. Wulf held the address to Megan Portman's home in Lakewood, California. It read that she lived with her parents Lieutenant Colonel Vincent Portman and Elena Portman.

Forty-five minutes later, he sat in Quincy's off-duty

Charger and stared at the one-story house across the street. Even the home reminded Wulf of the *house of terrors*. The home was kept well, the yard neat, and the house with a fresh coat of paint. Symbolic of the perfect life Mary Jane was never allowed to have. It was like living in the perfect dollhouse, though people weren't aware that it was a haunted house in disguise. He then thought of Vincent Portman, Mallory Portman's biological father. The name was very familiar. *Vincent. Vin.*

The man Mary Jane knew as Vin had been abusive mentally, emotionally, and sexually. *This* man had been her biological father. He could only assume that Peter wanted to strike fear in Mary Jane's heart at just the mention of her father. Maybe if father and daughter crossed paths in real life, she'd react so adversely that there'd be no weeding through the lies.

43

CLINK, CLINK. THE DOOR WAS UNLOCKED. CANELO ENTERED and on cue Mary Jane's stomach rumbled with striking nausea. When she paid him no attention, he tossed the oily brown paper bag onto the bed beside her. She hardly glanced at it. While they were traveling, they'd gone through many drive-thru eateries. They couldn't poison her because she'd watched them grab the food.

"You vomited early this morning. Aren't you gonna eat?" he gritted out.

The growl of her stomach was just as loud as her whisper, "No."

"Why not, Lalina?"

"Fuck you! I am not Lalina!"

Canelo sat on the bed beside her. Internally, she recoiled from the strength in his physique. Outwardly, she glared at him, up and down.

He pulled a Snickers bar out of his jacket pocket and placed it into her lap.

She folded her arms. The "good guy, *bad* bitch" routine had almost reached its peak. He walked out.

***

In an orange bikini with gold designer emblems, Soledad sunbathed beside a salt-water infinity pool. She sipped a frosted glass of Pina Colada as Canelo stepped onto the pool deck. Canelo imagined her evil eyes boring holes through his brown complexion through the shade of her sunglasses.

He needed to tell her about the young woman. The girl they had taken could not be Lalina. Although, Lalina and Mary Jane were the spitting image of each other, Escobar's daughter was never allowed to be in the presence of a single man. Moreover, Lalina's life was sheltered, perfect even. The Puerto Rican drug cartel made sure his daughter lived a precious existence. She had a security team, but Canelo had learned this Lalina lived with a Polynesian man. The man's life would be marked for just looking at Lalina on the chance that Lalina might run away with him. And then there was the girl claiming that she wasn't Lalina. Which made sense. There were warnings to tourists not to wear jewels in Mexico. It was like Mary Jane was claiming not to be this rare, exquisite jewel to a world renown thief. So she was lying about her identity and had run away from her father. With a man. But her father's team should've found her, killed him, and escorted her home by now.

Escobar would start a drug war if Canelo's boss, Hector, had so much as sniffed in Lalina's direction.

Canelo's people wanted to wage war. So why wasn't Escobar adding fuel to the flame? They had a pawn. No, they had Escobar's pretty, little princess.

As he stepped closer, the sound of Soledad slurping up the last bits of chilled alcohol aggravated his eardrums. She held up the empty glass. He grabbed it and went into the house to refill it. When he stepped back out of the large villa, she'd turned over. He placed the drink on the end table next to her chair. As he'd been trained, Canelo picked up the tanning lotion to apply it to her pale skin.

"Soledad," he finally began. "I don't believe she's Lalina."

"Are you paid to think?" She sipped at the now slushy-like drink.

"Hector will flip when—"

She began to laugh. "Again, we are conversing about matters that do not concern you. Are you the boss?"

His hands itched to wrap around her slender neck.

"I didn't think so." She undid the straps of her string bikini bottoms. He rolled his eyes. What skin hadn't already been visible before became so as he pulled them off her. He began to massage the lotion over her bottom.

Her hand took hold of his and gently glided it into her wetness.

Contrary to his hatred of Soledad, his penis began to rise and strain against his jeans. Canelo opened his mouth to let Soledad know that he wasn't in the mood. But hell, the last time she made such a fit, she'd forced him to screw her longer, harder.

He was loyal to Hector, the king of the El Toro before Soledad arrived.

When Hector took Soledad as a mistress, Canelo's life changed for the worse. Although he'd already had sex with her in his mind after first being introduced to her, he never would have initiated a physical relationship with her. She was walking death. She belonged to *Hector*.

However, this mistress wanted more sex than the others were required to give the old bastard. Hector couldn't keep this one satisfied.

The beautiful demon turned over, signaling him for more.

44

WULF STARED AT THE HOUSE ACROSS THE STREET WITH ITS light blue shutters, pink rose beds, and well-kept grass. Vin had been given a bad rep like Megan. Like her mom, Elena. All to keep Peter's beautiful wife from coming home. But this was sick. Why make Mary Jane's real father out to be such a monster?

A disgusted feeling churned in the pit of his stomach. Scenario after scenario wrapped its claws into his mindset. He concentrated on Peter Grienke's current whereabouts at a super-max facility. Grienke had no means to hurt Mary Jane *ever again*.

This had to be her family. Regardless of the truth before his eyes and Quincy's confirmation, he'd tread cautiously.

He got out of the car, noticing a woman with very light skin and a silky, long silvery braid down her back who was clipping the flowers. He told himself that she reminded him of his mother, Brenda, needing the personal reference to humanize a woman he'd grown to loathe.

She appeared to be of Latin descent. From his side angle, Wulf knew she was none other than Elena Portman even though, strangely, she didn't have any recent DMV photos on file. Elena squatted down in a long white skirt, a look of serenity on her face as she pruned a rose bush near the base of the porch.

"Excuse me," Wulf called out.

At first, her shoulders tensed, then Elena stood up without warning. He had yet to glimpse her face before she scurried around the side of the house.

What the fuck is going on?

"Ma'am, I apologize if I've frightened you," Wulf stated. It was too late to turn back now. He had to know about Mary Jane. She owed him an explanation. He went to the short white fence and pulled at the latch; it sprung free. He opened it, calling to Elena.

"What the fuck are you doing on *my* property?" The booming voice came from a middle-aged man about five-foot-six with lean muscles for his age. This must be none other than Vincent Portman. He had dark skin from hours of an active, outdoor life. He wore a wife beater and jeans and wiped a cloth with his oily hands.

"I'm looking for–"

"You're Officer Dylan Wulf." The anger dissipated from Vincent's voice.

Elena peeked around the side of the house. Her profile was identical to Megan and Mallory's, full lips and nose. Only her eyes were melancholic instead of hypnotic.

"Get back, Elena!" Vincent ordered, and she immediately disappeared again.

Wulf opened his mouth to address the manner in which Vincent spoke to his wife. "Lieutenant Portman–"

"*Where is she*?" Though the man was tiny, his voice carried.

Wulf's eyebrows knitted together in confusion as

Vincent asked the question that should be coming out of his own mouth.

"Where is *my* child?" His record indicated he was pushing seventy but his mannerisms were that of a man in his prime, ready to pounce.

Wulf said, "She left...for home with Megan and Keegan."

"No, she did not!" Vincent stepped closer to him. His chest puffed out, solid muscle. "I've read about you in the paper. Super cop brings down Gunner gang! Blah! The Gunners haven't done nothing but kill themselves and innocent women and children so anybody could've done your job. And you can't even fucking tell me where my daughter is. How is it that you can go about defiling Mallory in Mexico for a year and *now* have no idea of her whereabouts?"

He sucked in a deep breath of oxygen, gulping a deep breath of air before he could respond. "I was told that Mary Jane left with a man and wom–"

"*Mary Jane*, that's bullshit! My child's name is Mallory Portman fuckin' Grienke and that's only because the bastard threatened her to marry him! Stop with all that Mary Jane crap."

"Vin," Elena called, her head appearing around the side of the house again.

Vincent turned around, his anger evaporating with a sigh. The only thing left was pure adoration for his wife. "Mal will be here later on. Go in the house, Elena, please."

She nodded and looked at Wulf in the eye for the first time. The faintest hint of a smile appeared within the depths of her dark eyes, and then she was gone.

Vincent turned around. "Find my daughter, or," his finger wagged in Wulf's face until a Chevy Spark pulled into the driveway.

Megan hopped out of the tiny car with a bag of groceries. "Dad, what are you doing?"

"This idiot let Mallory run off with some folks. He thought she came back with you and that faggot."

"Dad," she reprimanded.

"I can say what I want!"

"I know." Her voice smoothed over his snappiness. "Let's go inside and talk about it."

"He is not welcome in my house. Not without my daughter!"

"Okay, Dad." Megan put the groceries by the door. "Can you take these in the house? Mom's cooking lasagna, remember? Your favorite. I ran out to get the—"

"Don't talk to me like I'm a fool, Megan! I am from the..."

Megan repeated his army ranking under her breath, as he spoke. "Daddy, please."

Vincent turned back to Wulf. "Find her or I'll find you. I'm certain you are aware of my credentials."

He snatched up the bags and went around back.

Megan gave Wulf a half smile. "Our dad will tell you where he's from about twenty thousand times. I guess it sounds like a gang where you're from." Her chuckle fell flat. "Now that you met the family, I think the reunions will run more smoothly. So, what is it Dad says about you not having Mal–Mary Jane?"

He was surprised. Megan was night and day compared to Mary Jane's stories; she was even respectful enough to abide by her sister's wishes not to be called Mallory.

He cleared his throat of that innate desire to dislike her and said, "I was told she left with a man and a woman."

"Well, unfortunately it wasn't with me or Keegan. I'm sorry for Dad's tone. He sounds homophobic, but you would be surprised that even with the *don't ask don't tell* policy in the army, we don't discriminate. He just doesn't like Keegan. Nobody is good enough for his daughters. Even before Mal married."

"Oh, okay." Wulf started to back away, his brain working overtime with scenarios about what happened to *his* woman. He needed to wrap his mind around everything that had just occurred without staring at this beautiful creature. Even with short hair and style fit for teaching kindergarten, Megan reminded him of Mary Jane. *Where is she?*

"Do you have a moment to get a drink? There's an Irish Pub around here." She laughed when he looked her over. "Yeah, I know it doesn't look like I'd drink a beer but there are some good draughts at the pub. Besides, there are a few things you need to know before you leave."

"I..." His mind was already calculating how majorly he'd failed Mary Jane. Seventy-two hours. The first few days were most critical and he hadn't even started searching.

"Please," she implored. "With that look on your face as you spoke to Dad, I could just about bet you had no intentions of returning—with or without my sister. I know whatever is going on with you and Mal, you'll find her. So please, just one drink. I won't take too much of your time."

***

They ended up at a tiny restaurant across the street from the Lakewood mall with dark wood walls, low lighting, and a set of framed family photos. The beer was better than he expected.

"I stopped praying," Megan began after taking a few sips of her own root beer. "After Mallory married Peter, I just couldn't believe that she forgot her upbringing. She turned away from everything Mom taught us. So I stopped. But, Mom, she prayed harder. Anyway, that's not what I wanted to talk about, Mr. Wulf. My dad and Mal had an awful relationship."

And when I find her, she's not coming back here. He rubbed a hand over his jaw so as not to give away his feelings.

"Dad isn't a monster. He's very stern with outsiders. But he's no villain," Megan paused to take a sip of her drink. "Have you heard the saying that people who act the same clash?"

"No," he mumbled, ready to close himself off from the Portmans.

"All right. Well, they're just about the same darn person, too stubborn. They clashed when she was a kid. The first big fight was after he came home for good. You see, we were used to vacations and trips with Dad, and then he'd leave for overseas. With Mom, our house was a democracy. When we were sixteen, Dad came home for good. Mom went on vacation."

To Wulf, it sounded like Elena may have run from her husband, especially if the familial dynamics always called for him staying away. She probably loved him best a thousand miles apart, but a tinge of sadness was in Megan's voice.

"They called it a vacation... Then here's our stern father measuring how tightly our bedsheets were tucked in. He made life a living hell when Mom came home wearing braces. See, it wasn't a real vacation. It was to recover. She'd actually been assaulted one afternoon while taking tithes for the church to the bank."

"Wow," he sighed.

"Mal and I weren't aware that she'd spent her *vacation* time in the hospital and the braces she came home with were wires. Just that Dad came home unexpectedly, and he's the kind that wants to shelter his family—even though we were old enough to know. It probably tore Dad to shreds. You go away to keep the country safe and leave the home front unguarded." Megan pushed her drink away. "Dad started teaching us self-defense like a man possessed with our safety. Hardcore, three-hour regimen defense lessons that left just enough time for homework and sleep."

"That must be why MJ knows how to fight," Wulf thought aloud. He leaned back in his chair, not so angry with Vincent anymore. He now understood Elena's paranoia. Vincent didn't reprimand his wife. He'd just catered to her horrors.

"Mal's so smart." Megan smiled, far away in her thoughts. She crunched on a few pretzels. "Mal got good grades. She had a check mark for every requirement our dad had and even more. And to top it all off, she was queen of the chess team. Like Dad, life was a competition. She was missing the club meetings due to Dad's rigorous self-defense schedule. One day, she just snapped. She just stopped throwing combos and cussed him out."

As Megan talked, Wulf found himself madly in love with this Mallory Portman. There were parallels in the temperament with the woman he couldn't help but love. She was a witty, willful woman and he needed to find her.

"Jeesh, I don't even think Mal knows the entire truth about our dad's obsession with our self-defense lessons. But I hope you can see we are a family... We were once a *happy* family."

Megan had painted a picture of a family that cared for each other but were caught up in circumstances. He needed to be sure of Vincent's love for his daughter because he wouldn't rest until he found Mary Jane. "All right, thank you for chatting with me." Wulf grabbed his wallet from his back pocket, prepared for the long journey ahead of him, but Megan stopped him.

"Look, I know you'll find my sister, but honestly," she shoved a hand through her hair, "I need you to bring her back here when you do."

"I will find her," he assured.

"I understand that time is of the essence and Mal is tangled into a bizarre story, but you've gotta understand that we're a family. One more story, if you don't mind."

"You're right, Ms. Portman, I don't have time." There was a softness in his gaze, but he attempted to be polite.

"Mal was studying for a PhD at USC. Only twenty-two years old and half way there." Megan smiled though her face was marred with sadness.

Wulf placed money on the table and leaned back.

"My sister just started an awesome paid internship at Peter Grienke Laboratories. She stayed with Keegan, her high school boyfriend, through it all. Anyhow, Mal and Keegan were getting married. They went to Mexico. Come to think of it, they stayed right near where you two lived. Mal often felt weird at Grienke Pharmaceuticals. However, Peter was one of the only employers that paid for internships, and just his name on a resume was career gold. Just so you have a visual, the internship actually *paid* for flowers and other wedding vendors."

Wulf nodded.

"Then Dad found out about the wedding. She'd wanted to tell him at the last minute, more of a silent 'you'll get the invite in the mail' type of request. Dad flipped and forbade her to marry the *boy*. Mal was at work, and we were speaking about a dinner to calm the waters at her lunch break. Mal became eerily silent and then she said she'd found something on Peter's computer. She never came home that night.

"Dad was at our apartment, angry but quietly waiting for Mal to come home. I'd decorated and cooked, and Keegan just sat there embarrassed as we all waited for her in silence. The next thing I knew; she was married to Peter. She never came home. *He* wouldn't let me see her." Her voice broke.

"Peter wouldn't let you come around?" Wulf started to connect the dots. It was easier for Peter Grienke to make Elena and Megan out as the bad people and to totally send Mary Jane into repulsion over Vincent. So, keeping Mary Jane away from her family worked.

"Yeah. The one time I visited my sis, it was by accident. The gate of their mansion had malfunctioned and she answered the front door." Tears welled into Megan's eyes. Her voice broke with emotion. "My sister hugged me tightly after almost a year of not one single word. She told me she would put me in rehab and do whatever I needed if I'd stop doing drugs. Drugs!" Megan gasped. "So you have to understand. Our family has fought for Mal to return home. You're our only hope."

45

BEFORE WULF MERGED ONTO THE FREEWAY HE CONNECTED A call with his sister, Shelly, and gave her a short rundown of what had occurred. Wanting to help, she logged back into the LAPD database using Quincy's credentials to provide Wulf with the address of the Blackwoods. As the last people to see her, the detective in him decided to begin there.

The Blackwoods lived about thirty minutes away in a luxurious condominium characterized by tennis courts, day spas, and ample room for joggers. Wulf found an empty spot in the parking lot across from their home just as a middle-aged man and woman went running along the trail before him, their smiles and chatter fit for a commercial. This was the type of place Mary Jane would be leery of. *Don't fucking get caught up in emotion, Dylan. Focus on finding her instead.*

Wulf walked past the trail that surrounded each home and opened the gate to the Blackwoods' lot. As he knocked on the door, a savory smell of meat and spices wafted to him.

"I'll be," Tom said, opening it. "Dylan, to what do we owe the pleasure?"

Before Wulf spoke, Amy appeared and wrapped herself in his arms. They weren't the type to question his unexpected arrival, she just smiled. "I've just finished the beef stroganoff. Come in, come in. Where's Mary Jane?"

"That's why I'm here." Wulf stood rooted at the welcome mat. He quickly explained that he hadn't seen Mary Jane since the morning they left for home. "When you said goodbye to her, who was she with?"

"I dunno." Amy began to fret. "They were rude. Hardly even spoke to us."

"Real tall guy," Tom said. "And...a woman."

"What did they look like?" Wulf asked.

"Mexican," Amy chimed in, shrugging as if that sole fact was description enough. As Wulf waited, she sighed and continued, "Well, the female, she had a little Spanish flair about her. Lighter skinned. Penelope Cruz with a snotty attitude. Her hair was very long, past her waist. But the guy was dark skinned, really tall, and real uhhh...ugly with a puffy, fat face—"

"Yes, he had a boxer face," Tom finally got a word in.

Amy nodded. "He had on one of those shiny gangster suits. Not as tailored as the woman's. Her clothes were very expensive looking."

Wulf probed, "Anything else? Ages? Distinguishable marks or tattoos?"

Amy's eyes narrowed in keen observation. "Um...both had to be around thirty or so, give or take a few years. The guy had a tiger head tattooed on his neck. It appeared as if it might have continued past his collar. Why? What's wrong? Is this official police business?" Amy rushed, as if a light bulb went off in her brain. Her blue eyes lit up with interest.

"Go get the camcorder, Ames, we've got to document this!" Tom sprang into action.

"No," Wulf cut in. "Do you remember anything else about them?"

"They had a nice car. A Mercedes AMG, dark gray, nice chrome," Tom added with a nod.

"License plate?"

"Nah, sorry."

"Names?"

"Uh...the lady's name was Soledad," Amy said with a confident nod. "At least, I think. When the guy called her that, she got really mad. Maybe it's some type of nickname."

"Okay, anything else you remember?" Wulf asked, stopping Amy's chattering ways.

"Nope." Tom shrugged.

Amy shook her head.

"Okay, thanks. Once she comes home," he felt stiff making the statement, "we'll invite you to dinner." He turned to leave, heaviness weighing him down, since he was always a man of his word.

Amy gasped. "Oh, Mary Jane did leave a message for you!"

"It's probably inconsequential now. But what was it...?" Tom chewed his bottom lip.

Amy said, "Something about her cooking. Uh, she'd gone fishing and marinated salmon—or was it bass? Mary Jane was so serious about it, I swear. I can't believe we forgot to tell you then. She'd said lunch would be ready when you got home."

Wulf gulped down the notion that he'd failed Mary Jane. *Just like Gracie.* He was reliving the day he'd told the girl's social worker he didn't have enough time to become a caregiver.

***

Wulf turned down the street he grew up on and honked

his horn at Bryan and Ryan who were coasting past him on the sidewalk. While his own stomach rumbled for dinner, the boys seemed like they could run the summer away without so much as stopping for nourishment. He managed a tight smile despite the uneasy tightness in his gut, seeing them turning at the end of the cul-de-sac and heading back toward him. He parked on the sidewalk and stared out of the window for a moment. The suburb faded away as Wulf thought about catching the first flight back to Mexico. With the Feds after Jake and their interest in tying him to Mary Jane, he didn't want to alert them with using his debit card. He sure as hell didn't want to make any wrong moves. Because right now, Wulf only had Amy and Tom as witnesses to Mary Jane's disappearance. He'd have to use resources and be smart about finding her.

Rubbing the back of his neck, Wulf determined his game plan and got out.

Brenda sat on a lilac colored wicker chair with fresh snipped roses in her lap as she watched Bree. Wulf put his hands in his pockets and watched her from the gate. The tot rode leisurely around on her Big Wheel, making a wide turn at the porch then coming toward him.

"Uncle," her shy voice was drowned out by her loud brothers'.

"Dylan, Dylan," they said in unison. Questions flew around him about playing catch and basketball.

He patted both boys on the head as Bree methodically moved out of the bike.

"Oh, so I'm on babysitting duty tonight," he replied, tossing Bree into the air. She gave a tiny little shrill. "Girl, we have to toughen you up." He caught her and placed her down.

"Yes, you have to watch us," Bryan cut in.

Ryan piggy-backed with an upbeat response, "Our parents are going to a party. So what are we gonna do?"

Wulf rubbed a hand over his face. He needed to focus and ask Quincy to use his resource of the LAPD database about Mary Jane's abductors. The children followed him up to the porch where he planted a kiss on his mom's head.

"We're on diaper duty?" He barely managed a joke.

"Not me." Brenda grinned. "You've got some catching up to do, and my DVR is filled with every episode of *Law and Order*."

"Sometimes Grammy recites the words." Bryan chuckled.

She reached over and grabbed his cheek, smacking it with a kiss. "So what? It makes me feel younger, recalling the words. Okay?"

"Okay, tonight we'll have some fun," he said. "I'm going to head in and get cleaned up."

Inside the house, Shelly walked down the steps in a simple white dress and strappy high heels. "Hey, before I forget, there's a package in the hall for you. What happened with the infamous Mary Jane?" Though Shelly's voice sounded encouraging, her eyes warmed with worry. "Were your mutual friends able to help?"

Wulf's eyebrows furrowed, ignoring her question. He'd been ready to address Quincy and beg for his help in searching out Mary Jane's abductors, but he went to the accent table in the hallway. Wedged between a vase of faux orchids was the family's junk mail, but at the edge of the table sat a small brown box. He plucked it up and headed back into the living room to sit down.

Shelly stood at the ornament mirror, placing a ruby red chandelier earring into her ear. "C'mon, spill, I need to know what —"

"I haven't given anyone this address." He glanced at the official USPS stamp then at the sender. Linda G. Curbelo from San Francisco.

"You haven't?" His adoptive sister mumbled, slipping on the second earring.

"Should you be opening that?" Quincy speculated as he ambled down the stairs in a white linen suit. "D, who is it from? Do I need to call in the bomb squad?"

He put it down, grabbed his cell phone, and Googled her name. A hunch made him add "+ Grienke." Instantly, various articles popped up with divorce settlements and claims that Linda had helped Grienke create a revolutionary facial product but she did not get the credit.

"She's Peter Grienke's ex-wife."

"D!" Quincy's vein pulsed. "You're telling me that crazed sociopath, Peter Grienke, has his ex-wife working for him? That he possibly knows where *your entire family lives?*"

"I don't think the package is a threat," Wulf barked. "Listen, I have never given out this address. And, Quincy, I haven't left L.A. to unlearn everything." He held up the package. "It's probably some mind-fuck or taunt about Mary Jane. She's missing."

"Quincy, we have to help." Shelly came to sit down beside her adoptive brother.

"I need to ask you a question, Quincy."

His friend's chest deflated as he leaned against the doorframe.

"Mary Jane left with two people," Wulf said. "A male, around seven feet tall, with a tiger tat, possibly traveling from his neck and downward. A woman with—"

"You want me to run their description through the database. Why would I do that?" Quincy crossed his arms. "Why would I help you, D, put yourself in further danger for that crazy bitch?"

Shelly cleared her throat. "Quincy, if you don't help my brother, I will."

He cut her off with a raised hand of defeat. "The Feds are handling it, Shelly. And if something happens to your brother, then you're in my face, harping another tune. So I'm out of this. And, babe, your supervisor's annual summer fling is tonight. I don't want to go, but I'd prefer it to whatever suicide mission Dylan is on for some girl he hardly knows. Hell, she doesn't know herself."

"Quincy!" Shelly snapped.

"No, the two of you went behind my back earlier to figure out my password. Just do it again."

Shelly glared at her husband's back and then gestured for Wulf to open the box. Too anxious to sit, Wulf took a wide legged stance next to the fireplace and worked his finger into the adhesive. A letter was tied around a leatherbound notebook. He started there, placing the notebook onto the coffee table.

Hello, Officer Dylan Wulf. I can only assume that your first intention was to disregard me as you've previously done while screwing MY wife. Before you allow your impulses to take control, it would behoove you to continue with this letter. The package includes the contents of my journal, which outlines the few precious years I've spent with my sweet honey pot, Mallory.

Now as to why you've been included into the equation, it is obvious.

At the current time, you are alone. That should be insufferable enough, right? Having loved Mallory and her leaving you. Yes, I know your plight. Isn't living without her unbearable? I'm not sure how I sent her away for memory extraction without my heart breaking for good.

I've been told Mallory is now referred to as Mary Jane "Doe"? Our sweet Mal has declined my name. I hear she's also declined her maiden name (for logical reasons). Please excuse the ramblings—

"IT TOOK all of my strength not to devour her at first sight." Shelly scoffed.

Wulf glanced away from the delusional asshole's letter to see his sister holding the journal and reading from it.

"This sick fuck probably has a healthy diet of his own urine." She continued to scan.

Bile burned at his throat considering how Grienke and Mary Jane crossed paths. "What does it say?"

"*The young Miss Portman, with her pristine education and numerous accolades, was not as I'd anticipated when she came for an interview. Her demeanor soft and polite to the point of being weak. When I stated my interest in another laboratory assistant, she came to life with a vigor that prompted me to act. Without another thought, I gave Miss Portman the job.*" Shelly pushed the book across the table. "I can't read any more of it. Okay, I literally hated her for taking you away from the family longer, then for leaving you. You're my brother. I have to look out for your best interest, but—you must find her."

Wulf shoved a hand through his hair. "I'm working on it."

He scanned over the concluding remarks of Grienke's letter: *Dylan; my objective is to bring you up to speed which is why I chose to include this letter to prompt you to continue on with reading my journal. Therefore, allow me to get back to the topic. Mary Jane is gone. – Peter Grienke.*

46

"I'M NOT A BIG FAN OF BEEF STROGANOFF," JAKE GROUND OUT the words as he sat at the kitchen table. He glanced to his left where Tom sat and received no response. The man was bad company, but not as bad as his wife. Her throat had been slit as she sat tied to her chair straps. She'd been the one with a mouth. He'd smiled earlier, as the three sat around the table and enquired about Mary Jane. *Talkative, just like my MJ.* However, as his knife coasted along her jugular she'd tipped her chair backwards and gone falling to the floor, still tied to the chair. As Amy lay dying, her head lolled and her cheek kissed the floor. She bled out on the travertine tile.

But Tom had only been beaten with a meat tenderizer to the abdomen. And so he was better company when Jake decided to eat the dinner Amy had prepared for them.

"Well, I reckon I'd rather eat my meal with a lovely woman," he told himself, grabbing Amy's chair from the floor with her in it. He picked up the chair with her dead weight. Her body slumped, blood drying in her hair that was draped over her shoulder. . Almost satisfied with her positioning, Jake pushed her in and on second thought, snatched a bright yellow towel from the counter behind her, and placed it around her neck.

"Better, don't you think?" His southern twang would've been soothing had Amy not been a corpse.

Five minutes later, Jake had warmed the beef stroganoff on the stove. He then sat with Tom to his left, Amy across from him, and steaming plates of food before them all.

"Y'all gonna bow your heads?" He chuckled. He knew they couldn't respond. He was just excited about completing his mission so that he and Mary Jane could start their lives.

He prayed to his God, thanking Him for keeping Mary Jane safe wherever she was, thanking Him that she'd always been such good company. "Unlike you motherfuckers," he finished off and began to shovel food into his mouth.

"Wowwwwy!" Jake hooted. "I have never had food so good. And I have never really liked stroganoff."

Music from his iPhone broke through Jake's happy mood. He picked up his cell phone and placed it on speaker. "What?"

"Don't you fucking *what me*, Jake," Linda Curbelo growled.

"All right, bring that ass here, sweetheart. I'll do it to your face. How 'bout that?"

"Have you found her?"

"Have you?" he shot back.

"As a matter of fact, I've found another MJ for you. You'd like that wouldn't you, Jake? What do you do after you kill them?" She gave a sinister chuckle. "Fuck them?"

"Free 'em," he mumbled. Desire began to consume him; he glanced at Amy's lovely face and said, "Tell me about this MJ. Where can I find her?"

Linda sighed through the phone. "I'm not sure if Peter wants that, Jakob—I mean, Jake."

Jake's eyebrows pinched together. Words began to formulate in his psyche. *Jakob. Jakob... Jakob W...* Something in his mind was triggered and for a second, Jake attempted to recall just what kept popping into his brain. It was no use. Concentrating on the present he asked, "Where the fuck is Mary Jane, lady?"

"Listen, I haven't been able to speak with Peter to gather more orders. And when you headed down to Mexico, he was so pushy, I had to tell him that she'd been found. He's gotten obsessed with her and that damn cop."

"Fuck the cop."

"I agree. Peter was overzealous and prematurely wrote Wulf a letter and sent it to me. He was fixated on having us kidnap Mary Jane to screw with Wulf's mind. For now, continue watching Wulf since he returned to Los Angeles. Those idiot agents are hounding him. But we have to stay a step ahead of the game."

"Roger that." He shrugged, shoveling more food, half listening.

"Jake, we have a great life ahead of us once we find Mary Jane and return her to Peter. My ex stated he's willing to give me the computer codes to take over his share of our company. I just mailed him proof of sending a package to the girl's cop friend. To all intents and purposes, Peter should receive proof that the package was mailed to Dylan Wulf, at which time he will believe you have Mary Jane. Maybe that will suffice, and we'll be done with Peter altogether and get what we need from him. If not, we just have to figure out a plan to get you to take her to Peter or break him out to get to her—whatever. He's a dog with its tail between its legs. And I suppose, being in prison, he has nothing left to live for. Nevertheless, this entire scheme to ruin the woman's life is beyond me. I don't care as long as we get the computer codes, and then we can be done with Peter and his little puppet."

Jake laughed. *Right, return her to Peter.* Linda Curbelo was confused. Did she really think Jake worked with her because Peter said so? Now, since Peter was locked up, the bitch thought she was calling the shots—well, she had another think coming.

Linda wanted to use Peter's obsession with Mary Jane for her own gain. She assumed Jake worked for her but, no, he still worked for Peter Grienke albeit he was compromising the task since he had an allegiance with Mary Jane as well. He allowed the woman to continue chattering while scarfing down food.

"I cannot use the system without him, Jake. Hopefully, the FedEx shipping proof will be enough for Peter to provide me with the codes. If not, I need you to continue searching for her and working harder to find her, because as soon as Mary Jane is in his hands, Peter will give me the information I need to continue running our billion-dollar industry. We've got a buy-in in the Middle East but I don't fully trust the guy, so I'll need you to assist me with running the deal. You'll be promoted, like Lyle. You'll get to help make the world a better place. You'll assist in teaching chosen people to be more compliant. How does that sound?"

Jake was a loyal man, through and through, but that loyalty ended the second his eyes set on Mary Jane. No one in this universe loved her as much as he did. "Whatever you say, honey. I'm gonna go fuck with the cop, see what he knows."

"But the Feds are watching him, Jake. You've been told to watch from a distance. Use those good recon skills."

"Whatever you say." He clicked the off button. There was one last order on the table. Peter Grienke wanted him to do the unthinkable. Jake wasn't quite yet ready to follow through, and he sure as fuck wasn't following Linda's orders.

The music rang out again. Linda was calling back. He pressed the away button and concentrated on eating. After a good nap, Jake had a bull to wrangle with.

47

20 YEARS AGO

Seven-year-old Canelo pushed his nine-year old brother out of the way as his mama marked his height on the clay wall next to the tiny kitchen door.

"Oh, Canelo," she chided. "No mango for you, my son, if you don't play nice." She put the black marker in her apron.

"I'm taller?" he asked, his eyes wide with hope. Canelo loved sweet fruit, but nothing meant more to him than his desire to grow an inch or three.

"You are...smarter, my son." She chuckled softly and continued to help two preteen daughters make masa.

"Mama," he implored, "did I grow?"

"No!" One of his sisters laughed while placing rice into a serving bowl for dinner.

Before he could push her, the front door opened. Three older brothers strolled into the house with their father. They placed their boots by the door and closed it, taking a seat at the table. His sisters set utensils on the table for dinner as his father popped the back of his older brothers' heads.

"You just came from the field! Go wash!" he ordered, following them into the only bathroom that the family of ten owned.

As the nine of them sat down for dinner, the front door burst open. The intruder interrupted their prayer. A young Canelo sat in shock, gawking at the richest man on the entire universe. In his short life, he had never seen someone dressed in a suit that wasn't frayed. This man had on gold rings and a necklace. The man had big, mirror sunglasses. Canelo admired the Mexican's white suit and cream shoes.

"Get out of my house!" His father took a stand.

"Have you taken into consideration our business proposal?"

"No!" Mama stood. Her wood chair fell back and tumbled to the floor. Her hand went to the gold cross around her neck as she spoke, "We will plant food and only food!"

The dignified man picked up her chair slowly. "The entire town is complying with my wishes, so allow me to be foolish enough to provide you with one more chance."

His smile indicated for her to sit. Canelo looked at his father. For a moment, Papa's head dipped into a nod, but Mama frowned and voiced, "No!"

"All right." The man gave a whistle. Two armed police officers swarmed into the tiny hut. The well-dressed man circled his finger in the air and the two cops took action. One kicked the dinner table. It flung into the air, sending food and dishes crashing to the floor. Canelo and his younger brother pushed their chairs back closer to the walls, since there wasn't much room. A cop slid the table out of the way. Now the family of two daughters and five sons faced each other.

The man in charge picked up a gasoline can from near the front door.

"Call me crazy, but I forgot your answer." The wealthy man, with a determined expression, calculated his movements as he went toward Canelo's father.

"Juan Junior." He smiled at the first-born son. "Please tell me what your father and mother have decided?"

Juan Junior's head was held high, eyes tearing up, but he said not a word.

"Look at those strong legs." The man signaled and the two cops poured fluid onto Juan's lower body. Toxic gas began to clog the room.

"We—" Juan Senior began in a voice of defeat.

"We said no!" Canelo's mother argued. She had more convictions in her pinky finger than he had bones in his body.

The man pulled a small silver case from his pocket. He unlatched it and pulled out a cigar. He let it dangle between big, white teeth. While one officer tied Juan Junior to his seat, the other swiped a match, holding it up for him. "Thank you." He nodded, while taking an inhale of the sweet concoction.

"Juan Junior, I'm nervous. Very nervous. Are you?" he asked, worried mocking expression of concern on his face as he puffed on his cigar.

"Mama!" Juan Junior screamed as the lit match fell onto his left leg. The orange-blue and red flames instantly engulfed his body. Fire licked around him and his upper body wriggled with agony. An ear-shattering cry tore through the tiny home.

Canelo's eyes were glued to Junior's. There were flames in the black depths. Fear clamped his throat, his tongue glued to the roof of his mouth.

"Forgive me, Maria," the man shouted over Juan Junior's sobs. "You are a close family. I should include everyone in the festivities. Where is the baby? There are eight children, no?"

When Maria didn't reply he told the cops, "Tie and gag everyone but Mrs. Maria," as he disappeared down the hall. He came back with four-month-old Bernice who was cooing innocently.

"You are the devil!" Maria spat just as her husband cried for her to agree.

Canelo's brothers and sisters quietly sniffled, each one trembling in their chairs.

"Then where is your God?" The man sneered as he continued to hold the baby in his arms. "Oh, the baby, pretty girl. You're hungry. Pray to your God, Maria. See who the provider is. Me or Him," he said, pulling out his gun. Maria broke down crying, yet he placed the tip of his Magnum in Bernice's mouth. "No worries, Maria. Let me see if the baby's hungry."

"Stop, please, we agree!" Juan Senior shouted.

"We will not." Maria shook with rage. "Our God will avenge us."

The sadistic man ignored her and chuckled. "Well, she is sucking. Rather a bullet than..." He sat the child in her mama's lap. Maria held the baby tightly, whispering a prayer in Bernice's ear.

Canelo finally looked back at his eldest brother. He hadn't noticed the cries die out. The noise still rung in his ears, but as he stared at Junior, his brother's eyes were closed, mouth shut, all so peacefully despite the charred lower half of his body. Canelo's ears would forever be tormented by the sound.

The entire family was doused in gasoline. Canelo stared across at his mama as he choked on the bitter taste when he went to scream. His eyes snapped back to the man.

"Now, being that I'm a fair man, who shall we save, Maria?" the man questioned, walking around between them. He stopped to eye each child intently. "Maria, you were so vocal a minute ago. Which one of your children should live?"

He nodded for one of the two cops. The butt of a shotgun went to Maria's mouth. She held the baby tightly as she fell to the floor.

The rich man stopped right before her. As blood and spit was spewed in his direction, he backed away for a second. He pulled *out a handkerchief and handed it to Maria. "Wipe your mouth. Since you've been so persistent, please inform me as to who of your children you wish to spare?"*

Juan Senior shook his head 'no' as Mama's eyes held the first glint of hope. Her eyes connected with Canelo's as she struggled to get up to her feet.

Before he knew it, his mom screamed his name.
***

"That sick bastard could've saved your baby sister." Mary Jane rubbed the tears in her eyes, sitting Indian style on her bed.

Canelo continued to pace back and forth.

"So, your tormentor had mercy?" Mary Jane held in her emotions as he told his story. At first, she searched for a connection. Something to manipulate him, probably not on the level that Hurricane was molded, but something. Now she was engrossed in the life that had been wrenched from him.

"*Mercy*? A lifetime of torment is more like it," Canelo replied. He nudged his square chin to the oily bag he'd placed on the tiny bedside table. "Now eat your dinner."

"I'm not hungry."

"Aye, Dios!" he snapped. "You promised to eat if I told you how I know so much about nightmares."

Sympathy and trust were on two different playing fields for Mary Jane. She asked him, "Your abductors let you live. I've asked you a thousand times what you want from me, Canelo. Why you and Soledad abducted me. You won't say a thing. So now, I'm beseeching you to allow me to live."

Canelo stopped right before her, yet his eyes didn't meet hers. "They won't kill you."

"They? Who is they? You're lying to me!" Mary Jane shouted. He ignored her and walked out of the room.

48

THE POLICE DATABASE SYSTEM DID NOT PULL UP ANY
information on either abductor's identity. Quincy and
Shelly reluctantly left that night, since she was a fron-
trunner for the Chief Nursing Officer position at the
hospital where she worked; but they promised to be back in
a few hours. Wulf did his best playing with Bryan and Ryan
to wear them out to the bone, so he could return to the
journal to see if it would provide more information. Bree
had gone to sleep promptly at nine.

But it was almost a quarter to eleven and the boys
weren't having it. "How long can you stay up again?" he
asked them while his thumbs worked the PlayStation
controller. He was so totally and utterly consumed with the
journal and with Mary Jane's safety that it almost hurt. With
each play, Wulf concentrated on any clues Peter's words
offered.

Ryan said, "We can stay up till—"

Bryan elbowed him.

Wulf's eyes narrowed as he paused the game. "What
time are you supposed to go to sleep in the summer, guys?

Because I know for a fact that heads would be rolling if this were a school night."

"Midnight," Bryan said.

Wulf was up in seconds, Bryan over his shoulder, as his knuckle ground into the kid's ribs. "Midnight? You sure?"

Bryan laughed and screeched at the same time. "Tha-that hur-hurts!"

"What time!"

"Ten!" Ryan caved.

He tossed the oldest son on the couch. "You, I'm going to punish you more tomorrow."

Bryan held his side, his face a mixture of pain and excitement. Ryan ran up the stairs as Wulf turned to him and Bryan took off like lightning after his little brother.

Wulf checked the locks and went to the downstairs bedroom. A blue light was aglow. Wulf tapped softly on the door. He entered when he heard no sound. Brenda was propped up on feather pillows, the remote nestled at the tip of her fingers. She slowly opened one eye.

"Mom, you should turn off the television."

"But I'm not sleepy." She sat up.

"You're not sleepy?" He cocked an eyebrow.

"No. This is the good part," she mumbled as he gently shut the door.

***

In the boys' bedroom, championship snore-games were going on in the top bunk. Wulf shook his head at how quickly the kids had gone to sleep. He settled in the bottom bed, pulled out the journal and the flashlight on his iPhone. *Give me a clue, you sick fuck,* he told himself. Tomorrow, he'd head back to Mexico. He'd search for a clue and that clue would lead him to Mary Jane, and he'd kill any man in his path to keep her safe. She deserved it.

Today I sat and watched Mallory through a one-way mirror in the laboratory. As of recently, I'd spent much more time in the States than usual, intrigued with a woman for the first time since Linda. She worked on a set of compound functions for the newest facial cream; and stopped to answer her cell phone. Thinking everyone was gone for lunch, she put her sister on speaker phone.

Megan attempted to interest her in coming to dinner with her parents. Her father did not agree with her choice of fiancé. It curdled my stomach as Mallory mentioned requesting time off from her internship for marriage and possibly for pregnancy. That beautiful mind of hers deserved more than being entrapped with a disgusting disease. People call children bundles of joy. I call them useless parasites.

As they giggled and chatted, Mallory paused mid-conversation. I heard the sound of a printer and became infuriated. She had crossed the line. The chem interns had signed a contract. No Grienke materials were to leave the office without being signed off —which would never occur. Just as Mallory told her sister she'd have to give her a call back, I stepped out of the private room.

The beautiful bird trembled when she saw me. Schemas firing off in her brain as she worriedly attempted to explain that there were vast errors in one of my chemical compounds. Little did she know, that day, I had specifically exchanged the interns' usual curriculum for that of an older model compound for my beta brain blocker.

I explained to her my brilliant plan and how I'd rewritten the formula which initially caused cancer. She did not understand when I mentioned that the decreased timeframe I now used on humans was a lot safer since its invention.

Wulf stopped reading.

Skin cancer.

He continued to read each word of Peter's convoluted story. If Mallory hadn't the intelligence to understand the dangers of his initial brainwashing program, Peter would've never seen fit to make her his wife. The man spared no expense with detail. Making it seem as if he were saving Mallory by brainwashing her. They were supposed to run his empire without the assistance of his silent partner, Linda Curbelo. He anticipated that her ability to make said inferences meant she could assist him in creating an even better version.

However, Peter's Mallory became depressed after her so-called drug addicted sister continued trying to see her. The beautiful wife that Peter had groomed became unwanted. He sent her to Beasley, the man that orchestrated his entire scheme of brainwashing affluent women. This time the genius thought he'd eradicate all her memories and save her from Beasley. Mary Jane never gave her husband the chance to screw her over again.

But, all things considered, Peter Grienke had ruined her entire life.

***

It was a little past midnight when Wulf's cell phone buzzed. He knew he needed to stop reading the journal for the night and prepare for a drive down to Mexico. He got out of the bed quietly so as not to ruin the boys sleep, and then answered it while checking in on Bree.

"What's up?"

"We're stuck in traffic. Been about an hour," Quincy grumbled.

Shelly chimed in, "You know how the construction workers like to further convenience people in the day. Well, they chose to shut down the entire freeway connector tonight, so we're taking the streets."

"All right, everything's good here." Wulf closed the door to Bree's room and finished sweeping the entire upstairs.

When he ambled down the stairs, he noticed the light was on in the kitchen. Brenda's bedroom door was cracked, the television still on. Maybe she'd had a late night craving. He remembered how uncomfortable he felt each time he went to a stranger's home as a child. She'd been the only foster parent to actually not argue with him for staying up. She'd warmed him milk as he regarded her with an attitude.

"It's a given that you couldn't keep MJ safe," Jake said, placing Brenda's homemade cookie back onto the napkin as he sat at the breakfast nook. He rose from his comfortable position. The blood splatter on his boots told its own story.

"What the fuck are you doing here, Jake?"

Jake shrugged. "I've decided to tie up some loose ends before saving MJ."

"And what makes you think she needs saving?" Wulf asked. On the inside, he was trembling with a plethora of emotions. Did the blood on Jake belong to his mom, Brenda? He warned himself to distance any emotion and use strategy. He'd go the old question 'em route. The shorter man was of a stockier build but Jake had the upper hand by being fully dressed. Those boots were a weapon in their own right. Jake could possibly have concealed weapons too, while Wulf was in basketball shorts and a wife beater.

Jake shook his head. "My Mary Jane. She was just foolish enough to run off with a man who couldn't save her. How the heck did she end up with those two fuck-offs?"

"Who?" Wulf growled. *The two people who abducted her?*

"Tommy boy and my girl, Ames."

Tiny ants swarmed over his body. "Where are they?"

"The more appropriate question is where is MJ? At the moment, the Blackwoods are being processed in the county morgue. I have three minutes."

Three?

When Jake lunged at him, Wulf grabbed the wood dough roller off the table. He hadn't even laid eyes on it in Jake's presence. Knowing the crazy psychos Beasley had on payroll, Wulf had to stay one step ahead. He bludgeoned Jake over his left temple. A blow that would send any normal being unconscious. The roller broke in half and only angered Jake. The stocky man bent low and went in for a body shot, ramming Wulf into the countertop. He railroaded into the edge of the granite, which sent a spasm of fire down the nerve endings in his spinal cord. Wulf double-fisted Jake against his lower back.

They separated, catching their bearings.

Fist met fist as Wulf's right knuckle slammed against Jake's left. Pain radiated through Wulf's fingers. Jake wrung his left hand with the same bone crushing sting.

Wulf went in for a power kick that dropped Jake to his knees.

"Wow, this motherfucker is getting active!" Jake laughed, holding onto his gut. Blood spat from his mouth as he winked. "Is your motivation the fact that MJ is mine, or are you fighting for your old Mama in the last room on the left?"

"What did you do to her?" He lunged toward Jake's throat. At the sound of sirens, they both turned around and when he turned back to go in for the kill, Jake was slipping out the back door in the kitchen.

Wulf ran out and down the two-step porch. His hands slammed against the cinderblock wall and he was over it in seconds.

Bright lights lit up the place and flashlights, laser beams from rifles pointing at him. The defense team was more than professional and accompanied by LA's finest.

His hands went up. It was dark enough that they couldn't see him clearly, probably mistaking him for Jake.

"Stand down," came the soft and commanding voice of Special Agent Ariel Juarez. "I take it Jake got away."

Wulf finally slumped, feeling like he'd been run over by a semi.

"Search the fucking perimeter, guys," Agent Robertson ordered. He then flanked Ariel's left as their unit retreated to search for Jake and the LAPD officers slowly observed the surrounding areas.

"Congratulations, Wulf," Robertson said. "You've fought with Jakob Woods and lived to tell the story."

"Yes. Tell *us* the story?" Ariel asked with a raised eyebrow as she followed him toward the backyard door. They entered the grassy area and up the porch steps, back into the kitchen.

"Wulf, you need to sit with us and talk!" Robertson shouted.

Now, Wulf was not only plagued by tiny little, flesh eating ants, but a sinking feeling clinging to his gut. Images of a lifetime with his foster mom flashed through his mind as he hurried down the hall. The day he'd committed the ultimate no-no and he'd assumed she'd tell him to kick rocks... Tears formed in his eyes thinking of that day. He couldn't care less that two FBI agents were trailing him as he turned the knob to her bedroom door.

"Don't ask me what I was doing. You know I was getting ready to steal your money, Ms. Miller. You going to send me back now?" Thirteen and reckless Dylan asked. All he wanted to do was go to the group home, but his social worker continued to refuse.

Brenda stared at him as he stood next to her purse on the nightstand of her bedroom. The clouding of her eyes, he'd never seen before. It finally registered; Brenda looked at him with disappointment. He'd never seen it before.

Shelly stepped into the room. "Brenda, please don't send D back."

"We are having a discussion, Shelly. Leave the room please," Brenda finally spoke, never turning around or taking her eyes off him.

Wulf's other foster brother shook his head as he and Shelly made their retreat.

Chin high, chest puffed out, he was ready to tell her he didn't give a damn where she dropped him off. His lips bunched together as Brenda's eyes watered.

"Dylan, I apologize that you even think you'd need to take without asking. Son, how much money do you need?"

"What?" Dylan asked.

"You heard me correctly." She took the purse from his waiting hands and pulled out her coin pocket. "How much and what for?"

"Nothing," he hastily replied. Yeah, he'd seen this before. One of the foster kids at a few placements prior to Brenda's told him the game about the foster parents that played nice. They'd turn right around and accused her of stealing money. "Man, I don't need anything from you."

"But that is where you are wrong," Brenda said, looking him straight in the eye. "You need money for the football team. I've been waiting for you to ask. Next time you will, won't you?"

He glared at the money that she tried to hand him. Brenda knew the exact dollar amount for new cleats. Still his face was hard with disinterest. Why did she care?

She cleared her throat.

"Thank you," he mumbled, taking it and shoving it into his pocket. He turned to pass by her, but she stopped him with a hug.

"More than money, you need to know that you are cared for and you are loved, son. You can't give out any more love than you've received... I plan to change that."

Wulf's heart raced. He pushed the door open. Every

fiber in his body screamed to murder Jakob Woods as he looked inside. Seated in a rocking chair, Brenda gave him a look that could kill.

"How many times do I have to tell you to knock before coming in my damn room! Oh," she paused. "I thought you were Bryan. Ryan learned his lesson one morning before I had put on *both* my bras. But we both know that you know better, Dylan. And who are these people?"

"I'm sorry, Mom." He quickly closed the door.

She continued to gripe as he escorted the two back into the kitchen. He took a seat on the booth at the breakfast nook, trembling like a boy.

Juarez snapped, "We have a situation, Mr. Wulf. You and Ms. Portman-Grienke were to keep in touch. Now—"

Wulf asked, "What happened to the Blackwoods? Jake said he had approximately three minutes."

"Jake called the cops from outside of this house and said he'd murdered them. He has this fetish with being truthful to dispatch. Now, where is she?"

"I don't know."

"Woods has killed six women with the given name *Mary Jane*. Each murder has escalated. There's only a matter of time before he strikes again. Why don't you tell us what happened to her?" Juarez asked.

Wulf glared at her. While he felt sorry for the other women, something in their demeanor wasn't right. They planned to feed Mary Jane to the ex-militia wolf to stop the bastard from killing more women, with her given name. Feigning disinterest, he mumbled, "We parted ways."

"We have *six* Mary Jane deaths on our hands. Should the next Mary Jane's death be on your hands, your conscious? 'We parted ways' is not going to cut it, Wulf," Robertson warned. "The Blackwoods just came home from Mexico. I'm betting that is where you and MJ were on a short honey-moon of sorts. Pardon me for coming up with my own conclusions. Oh, let me warn you. If I have to resort to figuring out everything on my own, this team we have going won't be a pretty one."

"Team?"

"You're coming with us." Juárez nodded.

Before his brain had a chance to formulate a reply, Shelly's screaming broke through the night as she shouted for her mom and children. "Where are my kids? Where is my mom?"

She, along with an arsenal of uniform cops and Quincy, came through the door.

"Touch me and I'll beat your ass," Shelly screamed at the officer who wanted to keep a barricade.

"It's all right." Ariel nodded to the cops.

Brenda appeared at the kitchen doorway. "What the devil is going on?"

Shelly ran to her mother.

Wulf turned to Quincy, since his sister was still over-whelmed with emotion. "We're leaving now."

Quincy gave Wulf a look that only he could read.

"Dylan," Brenda began, worry lit the depths of her dark brown eyes. "Why are you leaving with these people?"

"I have to find Mary Jane. These agents have come by for my assistance," he said, looking at Robertson.

"I-I don't like this," Shelly murmured.

"Your brother knows how to watch his nine." Quincy gave his wife a confident smile.

"Shush, Shelly," Brenda said. She nodded for Wulf to come give her a hug. She said a few parting words in his ear before he left. Words that would stay on his mind for a long time.

49

"Why would I stay at a place that we planned to make our home?" Wulf glared at Robertson who sat in the back seat beside him. Agent Samuels was driving the unmarked Suburban, and confirmed to Juarez, who was in the front passenger seat, that he'd personally made an attempt to find them at Wulf's home in Claremont while they were in search of him. Wulf had bought it after making lead in the LAPD Gang Unit. Yet, Wulf spent more time at work, and often even stayed with Brenda, before Shelly and Quincy moved in due to her bad hip.

"Like I said," he stuck to his guns. "Mary Jane and I planned to settle down in my house. That was before Linda Curbelo paid some goons to kidnap her. My old partner has been assisting me with trying to get her back. Curbelo said no cops, no Feds, nothing."

Robertson glared him up and down. They didn't have to know Curbelo had sent him the package. He determined that they weren't as dumb as they appeared, seeing that they also knew of her.

"So you're telling us, when Ms. Portman-Grienke was

taken in Mexico, Curbelo gave you a note to return to Los Angeles? No ransom?"

"Why would she need to ransom MJ? Peter is obsessed with her. They're fucking with me, because I'm aware of something they don't know."

"What's that?"

"Mary Jane only married Peter because he took her. She was his intern. She found out about the cancer in his facial products," he paused, searching for any cue from the half-lie he'd just told. "Okay, so that lack of response on your end signifies that you guys don't give a fuck about that. That you just want Mary Jane for—"

"The Grienke products are no longer on the market, Wulf," Robertson growled.

Wulf laughed as Samuels sped down the 10 freeway.

"What's so funny?" Ariel snipped out each word.

"You guys. Covering up everything, I see. Mary Jane would often feel so much guilt over not saving the women who were left stripping at The Petting Zoo. What did you all do? Erase their minds again, make them forget that fat fuck?"

Silence.

"You did. Mary Jane's memory is coming back. Her true memory. That's how I became aware that Peter wouldn't let her go that one evening when she was interning. She'd been brainwashed, then she'd been his good wife. Now she's remembering shit. Just like the women I'm sure you've fixed. Fixed like fucking animals. You people are ridiculous!"

The ride was long and quiet. Wulf calculated how much money he had in his pocket. He almost laughed, recalling how Mary Jane bashed him for not wanting to hotwire Pastor Tobias's truck a year back. He'd have to do that tonight to get away from these idiots.

Wulf spouted off the key code for the gated community where he lived. They began to pass by the stucco homes of various shades of beige, each with neatly kept yards. Samuel pulled into the driveway, and Wulf got out. As he anticipated, Robertson followed him to the front door. He opened up and the fresh scent of Pine-Sol keyed him to the fact that his once-every-two-weeks cleaning lady had made a recent trip. Wulf started down the hall toward the alarm.

"Get the letter," Robertson ordered.

"I am." Wulf continued down the hall, mentally counting down the moment until the alarm would go off. He went into his home office, picked up a Dodgers' baseball cap from the back of the chair and opened the French doors. He paced the length of the backyard and prayed his neighbors didn't have Dolly—their Pit bull, out. Wulf was over the wall and running around their lap pool when the alarm whistled into the sky.

In this neighborhood, cops would be surrounding his home by the time Samuel could circle the block. He hurried along the side of the house and unlatched the gate. Eyes narrowed, Wulf glanced down the street, searching for the best car to lift.

50

Wulf left the old Acura he'd hot-wired at a gas stop at the tip of San Diego. He'd gotten onto one of those cheap sight-seeing buses that took him into Ensenada, Mexico. From there, he'd stolen yet another car. On the long ride to Generosa, Wulf thought about how Mary Jane had transformed. The Arizona Mary Jane versus the one he grew to love in Mexico were so different—she'd become compassionate and loving. Though he'd planned on coaxing her to return when they started their lives together, Wulf determined that he could live in the world that they'd made forever.

It was midday when he found Tito, the kid Mary Jane once paid for newspapers. He was on a street corner in Puerto Vallarta, selling traditional handcrafted toys. Since the area teemed with pedestrians, Wulf slowed down and honked. Tito glanced over from a family of four and glared. Wulf honked again.

"Excuse me," Wulf spoke out the window, so that the family could move along.

Tito hopped into the front passenger seat of the car and

sniggered. "Where's the Chica? I like her. Besides, I've been busting my ass on the street corner since the two of you left!"

"That's why I'm here. Did you happen to see her leave?" Wulf drove slowly, searching for a coffee shop or somewhere else they could chat.

Tito smirked and rubbed his hands together. "I see everything."

Wulf pulled out his wallet. He didn't have much cash to give the little shit. He handed over two twenties. "Tell me what you know, and I need a phone."

The boy crossed his arms, considering the deal.

"I need a smartphone, and don't act like you aren't sure what one is. You've been lifting off the tourists since you could walk."

"*I've* been lifting off tourists since I was in my Mama's belly." He pocketed the money. "Oh, before I forget, when I was blindsided by you leaving without a goodbye, I had grabbed your mail with the newspaper. I have a letter from Mary Jane's friend back at my home. Regardless of how rude you two were for not saying goodbye, I knew how happy MJ was when I'd bring by her letters. I'd hoped she might come back."

"Okay." Wulf nodded, aware Glenn had sent her yet another letter. "We'll get it from you later. Tell me about the people she left with."

"So, the guy's name is Canelo and the woman is Soledad...fool, are you stupid? *Soledad!*"

"Don't know of them."

"The first lady of El Toro cartel. Well, one of Hector's favorite *putas*."

"El Toro cartel?" Wulf hid his concern as he bit his lip though repeating the words. He recalled some of what he'd

337

found out about the El Toro cartel when he'd been back on the force: gruesome grisly murders; cocaine kings; paid-off Mexican officials... Wulf held in a sigh. "Okay, what happened on the day she went with them?"

"One of your neighbors said they came into the house. She grabbed her luggage, and she left with them."

"Who's the neighbor?"

"I can't tell."

"Tito, I don't have time to run around asking everyone that lived nearby," Wulf spat.

"And I'm telling you that I cannot tell! I mentioned El Toro cartel; you need to be glad I got that information out of the person. Since you two had so much money at the beginning, I assumed you were rich, bad people like them."

Wulf's chest deflated. "Did Mary Jane appear to be upset?"

Tito put up a hand. "She was okay, I guess."

Wulf continued onto a street that headed west to the coastline. He told himself to just focus on finding Mary Jane and concentrate on the promise he made to her father.

51

TWO DAYS LATER

MARY JANE TUGGED AND TUGGED AT THE SHEETS UNTIL THEY shredded apart. The latest nightmare roamed through her mind and she couldn't see another way out. Peter still tormented her night and day.

Premonitions of her horrible past with him tormented her while awake.

Night terrors that broke her heart in half when she slept.

Seated on the mattress, she started knotting the sheets together. This was her way out, she determined as she looped one side of the homemade rope over the wrought iron light fixture. Canelo still refused to tell her why he'd abducted her, so ending her torture of an existence was the only solution.

Canelo and Soledad would lose.

Now, she pondered the same depressing thought she had while Beasley's patrons leered at her: *Why live?*

She pushed the bedpost over until it was almost level with the Spanish wrought iron light fixture then looped the rope around her neck.

No regrets, she sighed to herself, and stepped one foot

off the edge of the bed. The pressure on her throat was so unbearable that she almost considered pulling back, but she fixated on sorrow.

"Peter, please, you're making a mistake. I just wanted to show you the miscalculated computations is all," Mallory said, as he came into the basement of his mansion. She'd said the same line over and over for three days, maybe four; time seemed to have merged together. "I won't tell anyone, I promise. I'm getting married in a few weeks. I am in love...I won't tell..."

"No, you won't tell," he said, opening a small pill bottle. He held out the red capsule to herbut she didn't want to take it. She'd had one before and it had made her head hurt. "Please." She pulled at the chain around her leg.

"Don't worry, Mal. I won't hurt you any more than I already have." His hand went out to her, but when she tried to lunge at him, Peter pulled back. "The computations that you went over are for a brain processing program that I have. They're not for a facial product. Thus, the reason why the stats didn't add up. There'd be no lawsuits for skin cancer, because this process only takes a few weeks. Not long enough for those extreme UV rays to have such a dire effect. I've worked the math and gotten my system to fix a person's cognition within a month. So my current test subjects are safe."

"What are you talking about?"

"You are so beautiful, Mal." He rubbed a hand over her cheek. "I told myself not to get married again after my first wife took me for half. Nobody knows it, albeit she literally gets half of my money from work that has nothing to do with the Grienke Laboratory. That's where the real money is, sweetheart."

Mallory's face blurred in confusion. Peter's ramblings made no sense.

"It's all right, Mal. I understand that you're confused. We'll have a lifetime to get it right. But let's say I offer a service for the

wealthy, using the very compound you tried to compute. Do you know Senator Riley?"

She knew of the man whose political campaign just skyrocketed after a speech about his wife dying in a fire.

"Whitley Rodgers was baking a cake for her dear husband while he boarded a plane from D.C...but that's a lie. His wife is living in Arizona, without her inheritance of course, because the good senator needs it for when he runs for presidency. Money is required for those types of things."

"You're crazy!"

Peter's words made no sense. Whitley Rodgers had died horribly. Half the state had mourned the rich woman's death because Whitley had been an advocate and not just a silent force at the senator's side.

"Don't worry, Mal, I would not condemn you to the same lifestyle as Mrs. Rodgers. You're too beautiful for a place like that."

She stopped listening as he told her a story of chemical neuron blockers. Peter was mad! He seemed to think he knew how to erase memories and present new ones. Her eyes grew brighter. "But...but...I'm, I'm pregnant," Mallory whimpered. She'd been so moody as of late. Arguments with Dad escalating. Arguments with Keegan too. All because he wanted her to quit the internship. She'd finished the hours, their wedding had the possibility to be "quaint" instead of more extravagant. Honestly, she only wanted to invite so many guests just to goad her dad, which meant she spent more time at Grienke's making money. Now... "Peter, please, Keegan and I are getting married soon. We're having a bay-baby," she sobbed.

That sparked Peter's anger. "That, my dear, can be taken care of!"

Peter didn't want children. The "Mallory" who became his wife was meant to believe that her womb could bear no fruit. Mary Jane's eyes popped open. She attempted to push her fingers through the rope around her neck.

What if I'm pregnant? With her memory slowly returning, she recalled the tiny pill Peter gave her every day.

Her eyes brightened to the dark of the night. She'd thrown up a few times after being abducted, but thought it was nerves. The way Mary Jane had suddenly decided she wanted pickles, and Wulf went searching high and low for them a few weeks back. All the mushy talk with Amy added up. Mary Jane tried to scream, but the confinement around her throat didn't allow it. Slowly, a deep need to sleep took over.

52

CANELO'S EYES BUGGED AS HE TOOK IN MARY JANE'S ASHEN skin. Truth be told, the light that shone behind her brown eyes had waned long ago but he hadn't expected it to come to this. He'd been the same way in the days following the horror of watching his entire family burn to death. He knew that the only thing left was hopelessness. He went to her body and lifted her up, arms around her hips, quickly pulling the rope from around her neck.

Canelo placed her on the bed and closed his eyes quickly to the tears beginning to burn. He snatched the rope, mumbling profanity as he shoved it into the wastebasket and turned back to the beautiful creature before him. Telling the story of his nightmares wasn't meant to leave her feeling hopeless. He hadn't expect her to attempt suicide. An urge compelled him to grant her some type of sympathy, but to cross Soledad? Even worse, to cross Hector?

Slowly, his hand went to her forehead and he gingerly brushed the strands away from Mary Jane's face. He sat at the head of the bed. Laying her head in his lap, he leaned back against the headboard and serenaded the woman with a song his mother had once soothed him with. The Mexican melody wove through a cracked voice, sending tears streaming down his puffy pocked cheeks. After a few minutes he stopped. His head fell back, and he took a deep breath, still rubbing Mary Jane's hair.

***

Eyes closed, Mary Jane gulped a few times. The tenderness of her throat made the job uncomfortable but being parched and bruised, she continued to gulp. She kept very still as Canelo sang a melody, her heart hardening as his bled for hers. The hate, the self-preservation she once thrived on while determining her identity began to stir within her abdomen.

What about my baby?

She felt her heart tremor within her chest. She'd almost killed herself and her unborn child. If her premonition of the past with Peter was correct, her husband had fed her birth control pills, calling them "anxiety" meds, during their time together to ensure she wouldn't become pregnant. She had to believe it was true, although it didn't make sense given that he brainwashed her over more important matters.

Mary Jane set her thoughts aside, baby or not, blood veiled over her eyes. The death of Soledad and Canelo were inevitable. As if on cue, the man softly removed her head from his lap and got up. Still pretending to be unconscious, she felt his warm, callused hand go to her neck.

When he walked out of the room, she allowed sleep to claim her. She needed time to recuperate. She'd dream about the self-defense skills her father taught her and the lack of emotion she'd been gifted with while being brainwashed. The character, Agent Anya Randolph, had instilled in her a need to survive, and Mary Jane would survive.

Wulf was gone. Either he wasn't aware that she had been

taken, or heck, he had returned to live his life. She did not need him. This time around, Mary Jane would save herself. And her baby. *Fuck everyone else.*

***

It was late in the evening when Canelo entered the bedroom with beans and rice. He pulled a spoon from his back pocket, took a big scoop, and ate. Noticing Mary Jane's interest in the food, he set the plate on the bed along with another spoon.

"And the water." She nudged her chin.

He grumbled before holding the cup a few inches above his mouth and gulping it down. "No drugs."

Canelo gave her a look of remorse and left the room, closing the door behind him.

While eating, Mary Jane concentrated on the fact that she hadn't heard the lock click. Gulping down the food in her mouth, she rose from the bed, took off her tennis shoes and tiptoed over to the door. It wasn't locked.

Her thoughts rocketed. *Is this a trick? He's always locked me in.* She stepped outside of the room into an arch-shaped hallway where dim sunlight shone through the dark-wood framed windows on the left side of the hallway. There'd be no sneaking through a window. Besides, these two deserved to die. Even after Canelo saved her life. In doing so, he'd only condemned her to another hell. She still didn't know their intentions, but whatever they had in mind, death had to be more pleasing.

Mary Jane slipped down the stairs, ears perked, certain that such a large villa would be teeming with house staff.

A vase of wildflowers was on an accent table in the foyer. She turned and walked down another set of stairs and a hallway even longer than the one above. Passing by a cream-colored living room, Mary Jane's feet padded soundlessly against the clay tile. She stopped when the hallway turned into a sunroom of sorts. The entire area was encased with glass, and she could see Soledad swimming in a turquoise oasis outside.

With mermaid like skills, she glided back and forth. The greedy woman craved attention as she showed off to Canelo who sat on a patio chair near the door, his back to Mary Jane. His head was down as if he were busy.

Mary Jane inched along, fully exposed, and saw that he was fiddling with his cell phone.

"Canelo!" Soledad's tantalizing voice echoed through the open sliding glass door.

Mary Jane's eyes narrowed. The way Soledad spoke, they didn't appear to be a couple.

"What?" Canelo barked.

"I need it," she pleaded.

"Hector will be home tonight!"

"So!" Soledad snapped. Her body lunged up out of the water and onto a seated area in the pool. She leaned over the pool's edge, folding her arms, staring at the man who gave her no attention. Mary Jane's body shook in sheer repulsion.

"Come here, Canelo," Soledad implored.

"What are we going to do with the girl?" he asked.

"Offer her to Hector. I've said it a thousand times."

"But she's not Lalina!"

"How do you know she's not our enemy's daughter?" Soledad had a playful grin on her face.

"This woman just isn't her. I can feel it." Canelo scoffed. Mary Jane listened intently.

"The bitch is playing you, so, who cares?" Soledad's finger trailed in a figure eight, skimming the surface of water. "Canelo, listen to me, honey. Her father, Escobar, is fucking with our U.S. boarders. The Colombians have always claimed more airways, but we have our mules."

Mary Jane could only hear bits and pieces of Soledad's argument since the wind carried some of her words.

"Sales have decreased in all the cities bordering Mexico," Canelo said. "We both know that, Soledad. None of those fucking Colombianos are fessing up to trying to seize El Toro's passageways. I've told Hector that they're putting much of the blame on the Puerto Ricans."

"So what? You could be right." Soledad shrugged. "But the head honchos of a Colombian cartel are hiding in Cuba. One of those damned Colombian underdogs is helping Escobar, Lalina's father. So we need her!"

"We don't need her. Escobar is disgusting. He isn't even a real threat! He's a politician playing a game," Canelo scoffed. "Five years ago, that *cabron* siphoned money from outreach programs in *his homeland*."

She shook her head at him. "Doing so, he made enough money to play poker with the Colombianos, Canelo! Escobar wanted in. He got it. Since we can't get to the Colombians, we will teach that *hijo de puta* what it means to be in the business."

Mary Jane silently fumed at that. Canelo defended her when he shouted, "She isn't Lalina!"

"If we can scare Escobar with the death of his daughter, then he will surely know that we mean business. We know how much you like to be the good lil' dog for Hector. I'll say this was *your* plan."

Canelo took a deep breath as she got out of the pool, sauntered over to him and straddled him, water dripping off her skin. "Hector will be so happy with you," she purred in his ear.

Mary Jane put her ear to the glass door, as Soledad's voice became softer.

"And if he finds out that this woman is not her?" Canelo asked as his hand snaked around Soledad's neck.

"If he does?" Her voice quivered with each word, but Soledad's eyes sparkled as she reveled in the tightening of his hand on her neck.

Mary Jane's eyebrows rose together as she heard feminine laughter. When Canelo yanked Soledad's head back and kissed her harshly along the jaw line, Mary Jane saw the crazy woman's grin of satisfaction. His large hands seemed abrasive from Mary Jane's line of view as he tore the string from Soledad's shoulder. Disgusted by their barbaric display, Mary Jane walked away. Even when she and Wulf played dirty, it was never like this.

Taking a deep breath, she allowed her heart to calcify. *No more thinking about him.*

Canelo and Soledad would finish soon, so Mary Jane rushed around the house, feeling a lonely presence as she went door to door, opening each one. A smile lit her face as she opened the door to the cleaning supply room. Chemicals.

Mary Jane had a flashback of Dr. Kohl's class in high school. She'd literally created a bomb. Her mom had built good rapport with the principal over the years, but Mom was on vacation. That meant her dad was going to murder her when he arrived. Only Dad didn't get mad. He didn't rigidly reprimand her at school. He ruined his daughter's lives by making them spend half their waking time studying self-defense.

In the maintenance closet, Mary Jane found hydrochloric acid in the form of Lime-Away product. Her hand then skimmed over a more concentrated form of the chemical in Lysol disinfectant. She grabbed a few more bottles of bathroom cleaner that would make for a rather distracting explosion then headed for the kitchen.

She quickly surveyed the expansive room for a refrigerator since it was surrounded with glass doors leading to a portico. She then went to custom-made cherry wood doors, opened the refrigerator, and grabbed a few bottles of soda. Quickly, she opened and drained them into the stainless-steel sink. Grabbing a bag from under the sink, she placed the empty bottles inside and picked up her cleaning supplies. Bypassing the stainless-steel cutlery on the counter, she sifted through drawers and found another set of knives scattered about. It wouldn't do for anyone to notice a missing knife from the block. She grabbed the largest butcher knife. Picking up her bag of items, she paused at the sound of voices.

On her tippy toes, Mary Jane scurried for the kitchen archway. The exit was right in the line of the sun area near the pool. Reminding herself to breathe, Mary Jane peeked just outside of the kitchen to see Canelo buckling up his pants. Soledad was already at the door, fully naked, her hair a modest cover to her tiny breasts, but Mary Jane saw more than enough. Eyes wide she froze, knowing she'd been caught, but Soledad turned around and shouted back at Canelo.

Mary Jane slipped out of the kitchen a fragment of a second before Soledad's head turned forward. She ran up the stairs with her toes softly padding against the ceramic floors. Hearing Soledad heading up the stairs, she knew it would take too long to get back to her room so she slipped inside the first door and stood behind it, slowing her breathing and listening to Soledad's footsteps.

The echo seemed to stop right outside the door.

Seconds later, the footsteps continued. Leaning against the door, Mary Jane inhaled a deep breath. The all-wood room had a two-monitor computer. More importantly, there was a printer. Her eyes locked onto the HP Laser Jet and Mary Jane placed the bag onto the floor next to the desk.

She pressed the button and it started up. The sound made her grimace. She pulled up the top and detached the imaging drum set. The aluminum in this product would be the perfect match to the hydrochloric acid in the cleaning supply. Closing the compartment, Mary Jane lifted her plastic bag. She pushed open the door slowly and with her back against the wall, she moved cautiously toward the office door.

When Mary Jane didn't hear a peep, she stepped closer to the center of the large hallway and from the corner of her eye noticed the top of Soledad's head as the woman headed up the stairs. She dodged back into the office.

"Canelo! Canelo!"

"What the fuck, Soledad?"

"She – she's, damn it!"

Mary Jane pulled the knife out of her bag.

"I told the chef to be home by now. She's late. All the housekeepers are late!"

With a lump in her throat and heartbeat pounding in her ears, Mary Jane listened as Soledad mentioned how a man named Hector would complain. Once the coast was clear, she finally left the office and went back to her room.

She considered her choices. Hector seemed important. She could try to kill the two of them now, but she'd have to hurry with her diversion.

The door opened. She plopped down onto the edge of the bed, sitting in front of her bag.

Canelo entered with a half-smile. "I'm going to help you, Mary Jane. I just spoke with someone who can help you."

Mary Jane didn't blink as he came closer. He usually sat on the bed next to her. She leaned back and deftly pushed the sheet up over the bag. After hoping it was fully masked by the rumpled covers, she rose as he placed the plate on the foot of the bed.

He sighed. "I know you're not talking to me. When Hector arrives, I will speak with him about you. I know you're not Lalina."

"Huh?" Standing there feeling useless, Mary Jane's nervous gaze found the tiny lump on the bed. She tried to concentrate on not being caught.

"I'm going to talk to the boss," he said, starting to sit exactly where her bag was hidden.

"Thank you," she said, coming to stand before him. She patted his shoulder. Canelo arose and the air in Mary Jane's lungs evaporated as he towered over her.

"No more hurting yourself." He reached over and brushed her hair over her shoulder.

Attempting to keep her concentration on Canelo and not the task at hand, she nodded, licking her lips. "Thanks for earlier," she mumbled.

Canelo's mouth descended on Mary Jane's before her brain registered what he'd done. He'd completely misunderstood her appreciation.

Bile slammed up her throat at the thought of him having just had sex. She gulped it down, pressing away from his chest and forced herself to look at him with kindness, when all she wanted to do was pull out her knife and defend herself.

"Thank you, thank you," she said breathily.

The lust in Canelo's eyes struck her hard, pinning her in place.

"I'm sleepy." She yawned.

Canelo paused, then nodded as if realizing that he shouldn't be touching her. He smiled and backed out of the room, closing the door behind him. Mary Jane sank down onto the very spot of the sheet which was covering her bag and laughed at herself as she hopped back up. She moved to a seated position next to her explosive chemicals. That moment taught her one thing. Canelo would be easy to trick; Soledad was another issue.

53

AFTER A FEW HOURS OF FORCED SLEEP, WULF HIT THE ROAD again. Tito's directions hadn't been entirely specific but driving inland and south was the gist of what the kid knew. Three hours later, tumbleweeds and sand had transitioned to a smog-filled city, then finally opened to a beautiful lush green land. Tito had said once he passed the agricultural town of Juero, Mexico, he'd travel up a windy mountain further into the emerald green mountains. Through the thick of vibrant trees, Wulf first noticed the red clay tile roof that seemed to extend for ages.

The mansion popped into view. As he drove past, he noticed the dirt terrain showed signs of less traffic. At a rest stop about a hundred miles back, Wulf had grabbed a map of the area, since his iPhone might fail him for potentially unused roads. There was a trail leading up into the windy mountain and he had a hunch they might have to use it.

About a quarter of a mile north of the mansion, Wulf placed his right shoulder on the passenger seat headrest and reversed into the thicket, preparing for a covert escape if necessary. He got out and shut the door.

Taking in the scenery, he moved toward the mansion and found security lacking. He took a swift survey of the home before nearing a window. Just his luck, he looked into the kitchen and saw Mary Jane.

She didn't look like an abductee, digging around the refrigerator and grabbing a bottle of soda. She looked like this was a leisure Saturday with Netflix.

He ducked down when he heard noises.

I'm going to talk to her.

What the fuck!

I'm risking my life for a chat with a woman who left me.

A war raged within his psyche. When he looked up, he saw a feminine frame in the upstairs window across the courtyard. Wulf zipped toward the cherubim water fountain in the middle of the courtyard, but the woman was gone. He knelt for a few moments until he noticed Mary Jane again, in what appeared to be an office upstairs, but a few doors down. He was unable to get a close view of her face. Again, she moved around entirely too freely. Someone who had been abducted wouldn't meander the kitchen and various places around the house, back to a room where they should no doubt be confined.

Someone abducted would run once they broke out of their room.

Peeking around the statue, he noticed a balcony and hurried out in the open toward it. At the base of the balcony, Wulf jumped. He gripped the ledge and grunted while pulling himself up onto the floorboard of the iron balcony. He leaned his legs over the railing one at a time. It was diagonal to the room he'd seen her in.

Wulf cursed himself for being on the balcony out in the open for any of Hector's goons to see. All he needed was one thug to unexpectedly step out of the house or drive up, and that'd be the end of his life.

He cursed the feelings he had for Mary Jane because just being hear her felt closer to home. That was not a good response to have with regard to a woman who'd left him for this extravagant existence. A frigid feeling clenched at his heart as he watched Mary Jane kissing a man. Not just any man.

Canelo.

It had to be him.

I'm a fucking idiot.

After a minute, he peeked back up and couldn't see anyone. Maybe they'd laid down on the bed. Wulf climbed over the side of the railing and jumped down. He ran toward the forested area.

Just within the safety of the trees, Wulf slammed his fist into a cypress. Searing pain shot down his forearm, but it didn't compare to the tearing of his heart. The ripping in two. There'd be no dying for love today—a love that didn't love him. He silently hurried back to his stolen car.

Void of all emotion, he got in and closed the door. He lay his forehead on the steering wheel for a few minutes as he took in the drastic change he called life. This person that he'd become was an old recycled version of his younger self. Foolish and dumb. A life of stealing and fighting was exactly how his father raised him.

Biting his bottom lip, Wulf put the key into the ignition. He determined that the private security job would do. At least he'd make a shitload of money, and there'd probably be enough beautiful women who would help him drown his sorrows.

"Shit, that's why you fell so hard for Mary Jane." He laughed bitterly at himself.

Boom!

An explosion drew his attention back to the house. After the loud blast, an eerie silence followed for a split second, and then he heard a woman scream.

54

THE SHRILL, OPERA-LIKE SCREAM SHRIEKED THROUGH THE house. The moment Soledad appeared at the door to bring her a provocative dress for Hector's arrival home, Mary Jane attacked. She threw the smoke bomb at her face. The chemicals combusted, splashing against her skin. Soledad's cry delayed her reaction time. Mary Jane needed to get out now. A slight inhalation of the chemical would be enough to make her lungs cave.

She covered her face with her shirt and moved around the side of the door, leaping over Soledad as the bitch went crumbling to the floor.

Every fiber in Mary Jane's being was on fire the instant Soledad entered the room. She had seen Wulf heading back into the forest—a vision that seemed so real. Now, she hurried down the hall, wielding the butcher knife as Soledad rolled on the floor with respiratory failure and chemical burns bubbling the skin of her neck and face. Mary Jane's lungs burned when she sucked in a breath, and she hadn't even taken a breath since tossing the bottle at Soledad's face.

"Lalina!" Canelo called as he headed down the stairs. Mary Jane took her last step and sprinted toward the front door. Shadows of large men moved behind the frosted glass and wrought iron wood double-door.

Hector was home.

She skidded on the hardwood floor and started to turn, but a clicking sound stopped her dead in her tracks. The cock of a shotgun's safety.

"Not another move!"

Before her, Canelo stood at the end of the hallway. His eyes wide with concern for her.

Hands ascending slowly, Mary Jane dropped the knife. Her only other form of defense went clanking to the floor.

"Turn around," he ordered.

Mary Jane completed a slow about-face. The expansive room grew crowded as seven Mexican men in shiny suits ranging from black to gray glared at her. All except for man in charge who wore a posh white suit with a black rose in the lapel.

"And you are?" The boss, with his salt and pepper slicked back hair, stared at Mary Jane.

She managed a gulp, eyes widening at just how menacing he appeared.

"Hector, she's a gift." Soledad's cracked voice traveled down the stairs. They all looked up to where she leaned over the balcony, holding a wet rag to her face. The men's expressions contorted. She was no longer a captivating beauty, but just as ugly as her heart. One of those dark soulless eyes was sealed shut. Soledad's face and hand had blotched red spots as she held onto the railing of the stairway above.

"What the fuck happened to you?" asked one of the goons in Spanish.

"Lalina did it!" Soledad used both hands as she came down the stairs. Her breathing rasped with each step. She stepped in front of Mary Jane. With force, she slapped her.

Mary Jane went sprawling to the floor. She bit her lip and growled, "Fuck!"

Staying on the floor for a death that was sure to come seemed the most obvious of choices. Giving up without showing fear to these heartless bastards was better than begging.

Hector hiked up his pants and knelt. "Who might you be?" he inquired again, this time in English.

"Mary Jane."

"Pretty little thing," he said, wiping the blood from her lip with his thumb. "Mighty nice gift, but I prefer my gifts to not harbor malicious intent."

"She'll be the best gift you've ever received." Soledad's lips trembled into a grin, causing her cheeks to crack and deepening the lines of her chemical burns. "She's the Puerto Rican's daughter."

"She? *She's* Lalina?" Hector's eyes locked onto Mary Jane as if she were the rarest jewel as he helped her up.

"No, she's not," Canelo spoke up.

"Yes, she is!" Soledad exclaimed, staring at Mary Jane.

Every eye shifted back and forth between the two.

"She does look just like Escobar's youngest," one observed.

"But she's not." Canelo shook his head. "I have a friend that works at the resort in Generosa. Lalina stayed there at the same time this woman did and—"

Soledad shouted, "Shut the fu—"

"Quiet!" Hector ordered. The force of his voice made Soledad's shoulders quiver, her body freeze. "Speak!" he commanded Canelo.

"Fernando, a valet at the resort where this girl also stayed, says a Jag blew up a few weeks ago. I just got off the phone with my friend. We can call Fernando back if you want. The police are keeping quiet. They're afraid Escobar will..." Canelo paused, as if embarrassed about mentioning something, then he shrugged and said, "You know, retaliate. So they haven't said anything. The Jag wrecked in a canyon, inland and away from where the *puta* was vacationing. Two women were found dead. One of them had a license for Lalina. Escobar's kid is dead."

Hector seemed to be thinking as he pinched the bridge of his nose. Mary Jane recalled Soledad and Canelo arguing about Escobar. This enemy of his was becoming a thorn in his side.

"If Soledad's right, then having Escobar's baby girl would put the El Toro cartel at the top of the totem pole," one of the other men mumbled. A few nodded in agreement.

"She's his daughter," Soledad said, obviously trying to justify any fuck-ups quickly.

"And if she's not?" Hector's right-hand man questioned.

"Beat her black and blue and barely recognizable. We can send him photos of his daughter's *death* afterward. But with Escobar not aware of his daughter being dead, he'll make deals. We just won't be able to keep them. Not that we've ever given a crap in the past," Soledad assured him.

Hector smiled, and in Spanish said, "Just knowing his daughter has been marked by Devil's Blood is enough for me."

"Yes," Soledad said. "And with Canelo's news. If the cops have Lalina's body, we can go get it–"

Soledad's body dropped swiftly and smoke fizzed from the hole in her forehead. The chrome Desert Eagle in

Hector's hand dropped back to his side. There were tiny blood spatters on the sleeve of his suit jacket. He removed it, saying, "Now that we've talked business, where is dinner?"

A maid skulking near the door spoke up. "Please, this way."

The men headed toward the dining room. Hector took Mary Jane's hand and retrieved her from the floor. Apparently, he didn't know she understood the language. He smiled at her.

"You are our guest. Please sit." Hector held out a camel-hair-dining chair for her to sit at. He retired at the head of the ten-seat table. "Canelo," his eyes stopped on the man, "please take the head opposite me." He pointed across from him.

Canelo's face glowed. Each goon's eyes latched onto Canelo as he claimed the coveted seat. Chandeliers twinkled above as well as the crystal glasses before them. This was a celebration and she was their fearful guest. Mary Jane kept quiet as she watched the look of satisfaction on his face. A maid placed tortilla soup on the gold charger before him. Well-seasoned bowls were then offered to the rest of them. Without words, everyone began to eat.

"My dear, dig in." Hector patted Mary Jane's hand.

She looked at him, still unsure of what to do.

"The maids were arriving just as I did. The kitchen seems as if it hasn't been used for days," Hector said in between bites of food. He spoke in Spanish, apparently trying to keep his conversation private from her.

"We've been in search of Lalina since you left," Canelo replied.

"I see. Soledad advised of your return a few days ago."

"Ye-yes," Canelo said.

"You've been in my home with my woman all this time. No other guards? No other maids?" he asked.

"Well, no. Because we had the girl here too." Canelo placed his spoon back in his bowl without taking another sip. "We cannot trust everyone. I didn't want it to get out that we had the upper hand with Escobar."

"Makes sense. Who can be trusted these days, eh?" Hector placed the cloth napkin in his lap. "I've had security cameras installed."

The color drained from Canelo's face. Mary Jane glanced back and forth between the two. The intensity of the silence made it hard for her to breathe.

"Hector...I – I can explain!"

"You've been in my bed," Hector murmured.

Canelo slammed his hand on the table. "I didn't want to sleep with her!"

"I said, *you've been in my bed!* Is it not apparent that I don't give a fuck about Soledad? Wasn't it evident a few minutes ago?" Hector stopped to take a sip of his wine. "There are some things we haven't been eye-to-eye about, Canelo."

"I'm – I'm sorry," Canelo replied. His hands went to the Mother Mary medal around his neck, and he spilled an arsenal of repentance, begging for mercy.

"Shhh!" Hector commanded. The room became deathly quiet. "When I started my business, I economized on very small towns and readymade farms. *I* saved you from a life as a little beggar!"

Canelo's fleshy face softened. "For that, I will always be grateful."

"I turned you into the man you are today. Put more money in your pocket than you'd ever see where you came from." Hector pointed a stiff hand at him.

"And I appreciate it," Canelo spoke sincerely.

"You are a very big man. Yet, I've come to understand to be patient with you, Canelo. See, it takes time for your brain to catch up," Hector said in annoyance as he tapped an index finger to his forehead. His lips curved into a smile, framing expensive veneers. "Treated you like a son all along."

"Thank you, Hector," Canelo practically spat the words, the sorrow for his misdeeds written all over his face.

Hector glanced around and laughed. "I said I've been patient with you. Fuck, I've wagered with a few of these motherfuckers here... That you'd find out a long time ago, though you didn't." He paused as more of his men tuned in with laughter. Hector picked up his bowl and slurped up the last bits of creamy soup. He turned to Mary Jane and in English said, "Eat up, please. You are my guest."

Her eyes cast downward to the full bowl of soup as Canelo appeared to be swallowed up by guilt.

"Still he doesn't get it?" Hector spoke in Spanish. They all shook their heads *no*.

"I," Hector replied, standing. He dabbed his lips with the cloth, then let it float to his empty bowl. "Requested the death of your family. The man and police who invaded your home, killed your family and set it all on fire, work for me."

"You," Canelo whispered, beginning to grip a fork in his hand. He twirled the handle in his thick, sweaty palm. "You...you..."

"*Si.*"

"But," Canelo stood, and then they all did. "But you're my family. You've been like a father to me!"

"Yes." Hector shrugged. "I've done my best raising you."

"Raising! Me! You–raised–me!" Canelo stabbed himself in the chest with the fork. With each word, spots of blood dotted his light gray button up. "You took me out of the home with my Madre and brought me here. Motherfucker, *you* raised me!"

Mary Jane looked back and forth between them. Canelo crying and stabbing himself made her mouth drop open. Guns were raised at the snap of a finger, all pointed at Canelo. The fork fell from his fingers in a nano-second. He whisked out a snub-nosed revolver and pointed it toward Hector.

Mary Jane reared back in her chair as shots fired. On hands and knees, she slithered toward the door to the kitchen. Pushing it forward with one hand, she quickly crawled inside as a frenzy of fireworks went off.

The sound of a hammer cocked back on a Winchester rifle brought her back to her knees before she could even make it to her feet.

"Make a move, I'll blow your fucking head off!" said the cook in broken English.

She closed her eyes at his words and nodded her head then took a deep breath.

"Up!" he announced. "Slowly, very slowly, Lalina!"

Mary Jane cried, "I – I'm not—"

"Shut up!"

She stood, eye-level to his gnarly yellow teeth.

He grabbed a knife from the rack. When he lashed out with it, Mary Jane jumped back. He gripped her wrist and yanked her body towards him. Her hand went out to hit the chef, but he turned her quickly and pinned her back to him. The knife chewed softly at her neck.

His sweaty body molded to her behind. "I wonder how Escobar will feel, receiving a call while I rape every orifice of your body."

Mary Jane whimpered at the callous beast. He pulled

her against his body, his member hard and poking harshly against her bottom. The chef wrapped a large arm around her throat, putting her in a headlock. "Do you think Escobar will stay on the phone long enough to hear his precious daughter take her last breath?"

The cook's fat sausage fingers groped at her breasts. The slob became a wild animal as he struggled and concentrated on undoing the button of her jeans.

In that exact instant, Mary Jane hauled back her head and slammed against his fleshy nose.

"You bitch!" he screamed. The knife flew from his hand and his squinty eyes narrowed even more until they seemed to be swallowed by puffy skin. She kicked him in the crotch, and he fell to his knees.

"Now, Mr. Cook, that's never been my favorite word." She smiled.

"Yeah, but now this knife gets to have some fun with you." He grinned, grabbing a serrated utility knife from the rack. The blade was semi-hooked and had a jagged edge that matched the sharpness of the chef's smile.

"Not gonna happen." Mary Jane grabbed the wood chopping block as he lunged toward her. The sound of it smacking his forehead sent shimmers of happiness down her spine. His large body fell back and hit the floor, knocking him out cold.

Taking a quick breath, she stood up as the side door flew open. Her eyes widened. "*You!*"

55

Wulf's heart began to beat once more as he took in Mary Jane, a disheveled mess. He thanked God she was alive. The mansion had been surrounded in chaos while he strategically moved throughout it in search of her. He'd feared the worst.

Wulf sidestepped the large cook. He quickly scanned across the room for more threats. But the shootout in the dining room still rang loud and clear.

"Mary Jane, we have to go," he ordered. Though getting out of the house was paramount, he reached out to embrace her. She pushed him. "What did I do?"

"You bastard!" Mary Jane screamed.

"Shhh!" He put a finger to his lips. There had been more movement in the house when he scoped out the place. He'd run through the kitchen entrance upon seeing her through the window.

On instinct, Wulf knelt.

"Lalina." The voice was soft, sincere, and held a hint of madness. The kitchen door swung open again. Wulf reached for Mary Jane to yank her down, but she stood rooted in shock.

Hector held a bloody hand to his chest but smiled at her. In his other hand was the shiny, pearl handled Desert Eagle. The barrel of the 44 magnum gun was at her heart. "Sorry about your last meal; my team can be a bit overzealous at times. There's nothing like seizing the moment when shots are fired. Let's take this party into the office, shall we? I have a camcorder to set up."

Wulf looked up as Mary Jane nodded. He almost rose but at his angle noticed the gun in the man's hand and couldn't risk her life by lunging at the man.

Mary Jane argued, "Oh, I get it. You plan to record my death? A few hours ago, I was really thinking about dying... about the man I care for with every bit of my heart and soul, and *how he abandoned me*." She gritted her teeth, the tremble of rage in her voice was enough to make Wulf grimace.

Hector chuckled. "You're chattier than before. I enjoy a laugh."

Wulf attempted to catch Mary Jane's gaze. All he needed her to do was get down as swiftly as possible. But instead, she started out of the kitchen with Hector. In a crouched position, he moved toward their voices.

The dining room was a massacre. Riddled bodies slumped over tables, on the floor, and in seats. He traded the knife for a nine-millimeter, checked the clip and continued to follow the sound of their voices. They were heading up the stairs and he could hear their seemingly friendly chat as they climbed.

"Please have a seat while I ready the camcorder," Hector ordered Mary Jane.

"Okay." Mary Jane was so complacent that, although he could not observe them, Wulf had a hunch she had something up her sleeve. *Don't get yourself killed, MJ*. He fisted the gun in his hand as he turned the corner, coming closer to the room where their voices traveled from.

Wulf peered into an office. Hector was an easy target, but he still held his gun on Mary Jane. She caught Wulf's gaze as she sat on a chaise near the cherry wood desk. She was pulling something out of her pocket, behind her back.

"Get down," he mouthed with tensed lips. She shook her head no.

The minx was unpredictable, and Wulf feared shooting a man with his finger on the trigger trained at Mary Jane. Especially if she refused to cooperate.

"I'll have more help in a few minutes," Hector warned, "but I need you to cooperate and not try to run. If you do, realize that this property is surrounded. My men will be on you before you can make it off my land. Got that?"

"Sure." Mary Jane shrugged as Hector turned around to look in the drawer of the desk. Wulf ducked out of the doorway as the man rustled around. The moment Hector turned back around, Wulf glanced inside to see Mary Jane stuffing something into a bottle behind her back.

"Did I say you can move?" Hector faced her.

"Not even for a better backdrop?" Mary Jane held a throw pillow in front of her.

Assuming she was harmless, Hector turned around to check another drawer.

"Ah ha! Here we are." Hector grabbed a camcorder. The instant he glanced Mary Jane's way, she swung her arm forward, the chemicals in the bottle soaring out and spraying his face.

"Hold your breath!" Mary Jane shouted to Wulf as she ran toward the door. Just speaking sent fire racing down her throat and lungs.

Hector reached for Mary Jane as she darted past him. Wulf took the shot. A bullet pierced straight through Hector's right eye. The drug lord fell backward into a clay statue that fell and shattered alongside his dead body.

Wulf and Mary Jane's hands connected, and they ran downstairs and out the door. Heavy exhaust sounds sparked through the air. As Hector had said, there were more men coming. SUVs were packed with armed men ready to strike.

"Wulf," she gasped the words, voice hoarse.

He tugged her hand.

"But that's the way down—"

"Trust me," Wulf barked.

They sprinted toward the thicket, lungs working overdrive.

Hard voices shouted words in Spanish and footsteps pounded the pavement as men got out of cars behind them, but Wulf and Mary Jane escaped into the foliage without being noticed.

***

The sun had fallen, but the stars had yet to reign. And it was an hour into driving before Wulf realized Mary Jane hadn't said a single word to him. He'd just pulled back onto the highway after navigating rocky, curvy terrain. He rubbed a hand along the back of his neck and then shook his heavy arms. While taking the road at about five miles over the speed limit, he contemplated their interaction after the explosion. *Fucking ironic. She hates me like this is day one.*

"I thought you left me, MJ," he said, the sorrow woven into his tone.

"Good thing you've vowed your love to me, Wulf. You promised to me on countless occasions that you'd never leave me as I *lay in your arms crying about stupid dreams*." Her voice raised with each word. "You made promises! Now, was it my imagination? I could've sworn I saw you earlier today, after that nasty motherfucker wedged his tongue down my throat. You left me."

A heavy grumble vibrated through him. "I apolo—"

She cut him off in a monotonous voice, "We're both alive."

The tires screeched and Wulf jerked the wheel to the right. They went swerving onto the gravel. Mary Jane's beautiful brown eyes glowered at him, and she held a hand against the dashboard.

"Fuck that, Mary Jane!" he shouted. "You don't get to turn off, okay? You don't have the right. We've been through too much shit together."

Her steely gaze slid away from his and to the open road. For a second, Wulf noticed a softness in her eyes, but the rest of her was like a detached shell. She said, "Drive."

Adrenaline washed through his veins at her flippant demeanor. *I keep fighting for this woman and she doesn't give a fuck.* But what he'd said was true. After all the crap they'd gone through together, he'd be forever loyal. Wulf's head dropped back against the headrest as he breathed heavily. "I fucked up. I thought you left with Keegan and Megan."

Mary Jane sniggered, still glaring out the window. She was pulling even further away from him than they'd been in the past few days. "Why the fuck would I leave with those people?"

"*Those people?* They're your family!" Wulf reached over and grabbed her chin. He forced her to meet his gaze, and her lips trembled in indignation. "I went to see Amy and Tom after I learned that you hadn't run off on me."

Mary Jane silently stared out the window.

"After I left, they were murdered. The only man in this entire world that you never get a fucking attitude with—he did it." His gaze latched on to hers again, searching for a shred of humanity. The grit of her jaw was all the emotion he'd see. Wulf let her chin go. Again her gaze went to the road. This time, she turned her body away from him, lifting her knees onto the seat and positioned herself along the side window.

Wulf pulled back onto the road. "They were our friends."

The blood in his veins boiled. Mary Jane was being seriously callous, and he'd just risked his life for her.

He drove in silence; his jaw clenched. He heard a muffled sob coming from Mary Jane. Not sure if he should strike up another conversation, he reached over to grab her thigh. Her hand went to the top of his and the only sign that she gave a damn about Tom and Amy was a soft squeeze.

"Thank you for saving me," she mustered after a few more minutes.

"I'd do anything for you, Mary Jane."

56

AFTER A FEW HOURS OF DRIVING UNDER THE CLOAK OF NIGHT, Wulf traded in cars. Mary Jane returned to the passenger seat and gulped back the lump in her throat. She'd cried and cried already. Amy Blackwood's death had hit hard, but Mary Jane had a set of skills provided by her brainwashing: she clung to the "drug addicted Megan" who rarely exhibited any grain of emotion. Strangely, a part of her felt an urge for a hit—some hardcore shit that would cut through the loneliness.

Wulf's large, muscular frame was tense in the driver's seat. With the sporadically placed lights on the freeway, shadows cast along his angular face. It made him less approachable, which was all wrong since she was truly the asshole. They'd been through so much shit together he'd said.

Wrong. She'd ruined his life and forced the shit upon him. It was the same thing Peter had done to her and she hated Peter. Why didn't Dylan Wulf want to be a million miles away from her?

Out of the blue he spoke. "We're going to have to drive to the airport in Le Quela."

Mary Jane's eyes closed as she listened to him. She pretended they were back in the villa they'd rented where they were happy and life was good. A small seed churned in her gut, warning her that no matter what, her life ultimately sucked. No need keeping Wulf around. *People around you die; just push him away.*

"How do you know about Jake?" she finally asked, after guilt had all but eroded the lining of her stomach.

"Juarez and Robertson."

"So Jake and the Feds are searching for me?"

"The Feds want to sacrifice you to Jake. He's murdered half a dozen women named Mary Jane."

"Oh," she mumbled as his words just solidified the fact that she was toxic. Faces flashed before her gaze. The elderly Protestant couple, the Blackwoods, the women Jake murdered, even some of the idiots who worked for Beasley had to have families that would miss them.

"Stop," she said.

"Why?"

"I'm feeling queasy." Her hand planted against the dashboard again, but this time Mary Jane's vision began to swim before her.

"I told you that I'm getting you home to your parents."

Her voice was devoid of its commanding nature, almost alluring as she pleaded, "Okay, but not tonight. Can we stop? I need a hot shower and a good night's sleep." *I need to save you from me. Being around me is a death sentence.*

"All right," Wulf replied. "Just a few hours' sleep, then we will head home."

An hour later, they pulled into the parking lot of a two-story motel. When he said he'd check in and wanted her to stay in the car, Mary Jane saw that as the prime opportunity to hit the road.

To save Wulf's life.

To save him from her.

But she couldn't leave him without a note and a quick check in the glove compartment showed only old, frayed insurance documents and nothing to write with.

At the sight of his thick silhouette leaving the motel lobby, Mary Jane groaned. It was too late.

***

The hotel room was a blur of tans and browns with the typical two wooden tables and two chairs by the window. It also had double queen-sized beds. A rush of relief flooded through Mary Jane. She'd leave once Wulf was asleep. Her eyes skimmed across the room where there was a Gideon's Bible along with a token pen and tablet that had the motel insignia. Her body tensed further, plans ready for fruition.

Wulf came up behind her and skimmed a hand down her shoulder. She bit down harshly on the inside of her lip, warning herself not to cry, needing the pain to remind her that he deserved better than all of the craziness she could offer. One foot before the other she subtly moved away from the caress.

"Don't do this!" He yanked her around. "Don't allow yourself to just shut the world out. I told you in the car not to fucking do it, and right now, I am telling you *that it is not allowed.*"

She took calming breaths. Being good to her shouldn't have been allowed. Wulf deserved better than Mary Jane.

"Peter had a means far beyond any man should. He's tossed a wealth of curveballs at you but concentrate on what you have. Your family cares. MJ, I care. Don't shut me out. Talk to me."

Digging down deep, Mary Jane clung to the despair she'd felt when Canelo and Soledad abducted her. There were so many emotions churning in her soul. Raw anger radiated through her, though her heart cried for *him*.

She pointed a stiff finger at him and channeled the actress Beasley's goon had unknowingly gifted her with. Anya Randolph was so angry at Trent Winehouse for failing her. Mary Jane felt like shit for using the lines, but she needed Anya's words. Anya's actions. Anya's broken heart. "Let's talk!" She shoved her index finger against his chiseled chest with each statement. "So, you said you care. I *waited* for you, just knew you'd come. Put my trust in you."

"And I fucked up. I love you, Mary Jane. I'm fucking crazy in love with you, but I fucked up."

No, Wulf, you didn't! It felt like a shot to the heart, her being unable to say it back. But Mary Jane had to stay strong in order to save him, give him the better life he deserved.

This next part was all her own but made Mary Jane's guilt grow exponentially, because the man she loved didn't deserve it. "And then when I figured you wouldn't arrive, I almost ended my problems myself." She nodded, tears in her eyes. The hatred Mary Jane had for herself—for being manipulated by Peter Grienke—was directed toward Wulf. "Yeah, Megan and Keegan came along and presented a good enough past. I can return to the life they've offered me, Wulf. I'll give you that. But in the company of those crazy fucks we just left, I realized something. I'm kind of getting used to the bullshit. I put too much faith in you, Wulf. No more putting faith in you."

No more putting your life on the line.

"Yes, I've disappointed you, Mary Jane. Yet, you'd

conclude that not one person in the world gives a damn? Set me aside." He gestured with his hands. "Reminisce on your family. Somewhere in your mind you remember them. I'm sorry about all the crazy shit Peter put you through. Man, I can say that until my face turns blue. Somehow, you recall your mother, your father, your sister. And, damn, I told you I made a mistake, but your parents haven't. Your mom—"

"So, I tried to kill myself," she said, not wanting to hear anything he had to say about the Portmans. Every word he spoke was like shit slinging against her face. Wulf was a good man, and he deserved better than her guilt trip. Mary Jane spoke again—no compassion, no empathy, just strings of coherent words, "I took the bedspread and cut it up into strings then tied it together."

"Oh, baby." He tried to wrap her in his arms but she pulled away. Needing his pain to lift herself up. She had to be on her toes, ready to abandon Wulf. Didn't he understand that he deserved a better life?

"So I tied it to the light fixture, stood on the bed, and let go. Wulf, I let go."

"What happened?" He breathed heavily.

Her eyes cast downward.

"What happened?"

"I..." Her hand went to her belly. "I might be pregnant."

Mary Jane's body shook. Tears coursed down her cheeks. Why had she spoken those words? Telling Wulf that she was pregnant was counterproductive to pushing him away. She was a walking plague and a baby would only compound matters no matter how dreamy the thought sounded.

"But how? You said Peter was outraged when you couldn't have children?"

"That's all a part of the deception, Wulf."

He engulfed her in a hug before she could even push

him away. The pure strength of him pacified her heart, calming the erratic beat. "You're pregnant?"

"Wulf, once we confirm if I'm pregnant or not," she began the ultimatum. He pulled her to arm's length, giving her all of his attention. At the mere thought of it, she just couldn't finish the sentence.

57

Keeping Mary Jane safe was Wulf's primary goal and not for the sole reason that she was bearing his child but because things were different now. The long ride and their arrival at the motel had been marked with Mary Jane pulling away from him. The woman he was madly in love with had lost all hope in him.

Wulf lay in the bed nearest to the door. Glancing at the popcorn ceiling, he ruminated over the conversation they had about ten minutes ago as the sound of the shower droned on.

"Once we confirm if I'm pregnant or not," she'd said. Her tone had fluctuated with emotion.

"If she's not pregnant, there's no us," he spoke the words into existence. The shit didn't sound right exiting his mouth, albeit instincts told him she'd been inferring to them parting ways.

"Wulf," she called out.

He was at the bathroom door in a flash. He'd seen and still went crazy with arousal over her body, but he averted his gaze to the glass door. He gave a nonchalant, "Yeah?"

"Can you wash my back?" Mary Jane whispered, her voice fighting with the sound of the water.

He raised his eyebrows.

"Please," she replied. No matter how tomorrow played out, with her being pregnant or not, she was out-of-this-world attracted to him.

Wulf slid the door to the side and grabbed her lathered towel. There was no nurture, no tenderness in the movements, not as he'd done in the past. She wanted to leave. A part of him was just as jealous and mad as Beasley had been, wanting to keep and claim her. His heart desired the best for her, and before the past few days, Wulf had assumed that was him. Her head dipped as he deftly worked over her back muscles and neck.

"MJ," he said, his voice reclaiming that uniformity she'd been used to when meeting him as an officer in New Mexico. "My arm is getting wet."

"So? I'm all wet." She gave a half-smile.

Their eyes connected. And Wulf became as greedy as he'd been the first night they'd screwed. He undid the clasp of his button up and slipped it over his head, then his pants.

She moved over in the shower. The confines of the area had shrunk tremendously and his cock was at attention, further taking up the space between them. He clasped a hand behind her neck and his mouth claimed hers. Those curvy, creamy golden thighs of hers slid around his waist.

"Oh, fuck," she sighed against his ear as his manhood fit her like a glove. Her mouth was titillating, soft against his as he began to pump in and out of her. Mary Jane's hands wrapped around his neck. His legs planted wide. and he hit home with each thrust, sending her screaming his name.

Then he sank deep into her core, harder than he'd ever been.

"I won't let you go, Mary Jane," he growled in her ear. They both understood. Baby or not, she'd unlocked this animalistic hunger in him.

"Wulf, please..." Her voice was hardly audible. "Please just fuck me, just fuck me."

His eyes met hers, his gaze hard and unyielding. No other words were necessary. His biceps bulged as he continued to thrust inside of her. With each force, Wulf recalled the shit he'd do for her. Every muscle, tendon. and bone in her body mellowed in serenity as he worked his cock inside of her. They were unconventional and more than dysfunctional, but out of all the chaos, this single moment was a driving force.

An eruption, so strong his toes clutched under, took hold of him, and Mary Jane burrowed into the crook of his neck. She eternally belonged to him.

58

WULF FLEW TO A SEATED POSITION IN BED BESIDE MARY JANE. Her eyes had just adjusted to the light of morning when she noticed he was holding a gun. With a huff of relief, he lowered it. Her line of vision focused in on Agent Robertson who was seated with a bag of Starbucks and a four-holder set of coffee.

Ariel stood at the edge of the bed, hands on her slender hips. "Good morning, Mrs. Portman-Grienke."

"Mary. Jane. Doe," she corrected, sitting up with the sheet around her.

"Did you enjoy your rest?" Ariel asked.

"The mattress could have been asphalt; I slept like a rock either way."

"Very well," Ariel said. "I was in the room right across the hall. Robertson and I took turns so I would have to say the night wasn't a bust. Now that we've had enough sleep, Miss...Doe, I need you to come with us."

"Over my dead body." Wulf broke into the girls' conversation with a growl.

"The ladies are chatting," Robertson quipped, taking a sip of his coffee. He held one out for Wulf.

"Where are the harem of abused women who made it away from Beasley? The last time I asked that question, the two of you looked guilty."

"Oh, don't act like this is a conspiracy." Robertson stood up and dropped a plane ticket on the frazzled bed comforter. "And no need for threats. *Over your dead body*, Dylan Wulf. There've been enough deaths. We want Mary Jane and request that you go home. How about, we also give our word not to advise local authorities that you carjacked a 93' Honda, nor your pending felony for—"

"I'll go!" Mary Jane shouted. "Leave *Dylan* alone."

Wulf looked at her. She cracked a smile. Robertson and Ariel didn't have to know that she only called him by his first name when she was angry or to manipulate. But in this case, Robertson had just provided Wulf with his way out. The edge in his broad shoulders disappeared. She smiled, glancing away because in this case, the only person being manipulated was the man she loved.

"Get dressed." Robertson dropped a bag of clothes on the bed. "Wulf, your plane leaves shortly so we have to get you to the airport."

The agents stepped outside, allowing them a few minutes to dress.

Wulf spoke, "I take it you're using my first name is a sign of a plan? You don't have to do this."

"Yes and yes." She smiled. "But, I have a feeling Robertson will add all kinds of felonies and knickknacks to your name if I don't assist them."

"What's your plan?"

She tugged into the new jeans. "Let's just get to the airport."

"But what's your plan?" he asked more insistently.

Mary Jane smiled up at him before shoving a touristy Mexico shirt over her head. "You'll know it when we get to the airport."

"MJ." He shook his head.

She snatched off tags and dressed in clothes that fit comfortably. If these FBI agents knew nothing else, they knew her and Wulf's sizes. She gave a thankful chuckle while tugging on a brand new pair of socks and boots. Then she headed to the bathroom to brush her teeth.

"I don't see anything comical," Wulf retorted, taking the toiletries the agents had brought as well.

"Really? Have you forgotten how I feel about clean undergarments? Anyway, I see something cute." She pulled him into a hug and kissed his lips.

After they both took a deep breath, Wulf looked her straight in the eyes and said, "They are going to give you to a maniac killer. I'm sure you remember Jake as helpful, but do you recall in the late 90s? Jakob Woods?"

Mary Jane glanced away. There was no deterring Wulf as to how dangerous this situation was, so she gave a half-smile. "No, I don't remember him. I was just a kid."

"This is no joke."

"No. It's not. I'll just see what they have to offer," she replied, combing her hair back with her fingers.

"*You* are what they have to offer."

"They'll let you tag along, okay? You will get to rescue me. Isn't that what you want?" She winked.

"No, I want you to be safe and sound, so I don't have to rescue you. It makes life easier."

"For the sake of women who unfortunately have my name, will you compromise?" She held out her hand. He took it, and they walked out together.

***

They traveled in the navy blue unmarked SUV to the airport. The moment they entered the terminals, Mary Jane complained of a parched throat. They stopped inside a shop with Robertson muttering all the way. While the two Feds headed toward the checkout line, she slipped away from Wulf. Pretending to glance through a few gossip magazines, Mary Jane snuck over to the medicine aisle. She took a quick sweep of the shop as she grabbed a pregnancy test, stuffed it in her pocket, and pulled down her shirt.

"What are you doing?" Robertson questioned in a sharp voice.

"Can I have a headache in peace?" She snatched up a bottle of aspirin and tossed it to him, then stepped toward the exit where Wulf and Ariel seemed to be having a heated conversation. The chatter ended as she appeared.

"I need to use the restroom," she said.

"No stalling," Juárez warned. "If you're not out in three minutes, Robertson will escort Officer Wulf to the terminal." She stared at Robertson through the glass partition of the store as he finished making Mary Jane's purchase.

"All right, I get it. I'll hurry," Mary Jane replied.

She rushed into the bathroom and tried hard to pee, but anxiety made it difficult to do so. This was the defining moment. If she was pregnant, then she'd beg and plead the agents to allow Wulf to stick around as they dangled her before Jake like a piece of Kobe beef.

If she wasn't pregnant...

***

"Keegan," Mallory called, leaning against the granite counter in the en-suite bathroom. She could see him sitting on her bed in the apartment she shared with Megan.

"Are you pregnant?" He hopped up.

"No, I can't." Mal bit her lip. *Dad was going to kill her.*

"You just drank a gallon of water." He folded his arms and leaned against the wall, but she could feel his elation shot down by a good dose of terror.

Her USC doctoral program flashed through her mind. The internship at Grienke's would be lost to her, pending the pregnancy news. She whimpered, *"Help me."*

"Do you want me to hold your hand while you do the deed or something?"

His light laughter made her smile. *"Ha, ha. I'm thinking more along the lines of help me figure out how to get out of this—"*

"If you're pregnant, the baby is a blessing, Mal."

A few minutes later, Mallory washed her hands. They stood over the marble countertop, glancing at the test, waiting for a sign. Her lips tipped upward into a smile as Keegan's hand sought hers. The seconds ticked by a little faster with him being her teammate.

"Uh oh," Mallory murmured as a blue 'plus sign' bled into the small white screen.

Keegan's hands went behind his head, kneading his neck. *"Your father is going to kill me, and I'm pretty sure he's going to be harping about his army accolades as he chokes me to death."*

"Man up." She kissed his mouth.

"You're having my baby." He pulled her into a hug. *"A wedding and a baby."*

***

This shouldn't have been a ritual that she completed on her own, not while she had a willing partner. While waiting for the sign to appear, Mary Jane had a vision of herself with Keegan. Although she hadn't been ready for a child, there had been a raw goodness to that moment. It had been over-shadowed by her despair while in Peter Grienke's basement when he'd gotten rid of her baby. She'd bled and he'd been disgusted about it. Though her memory seemed to be grabbing fragments and not in any sort of chronological time, Mary Jane knew that not much time had elapsed between her spontaneous abortion and her marriage to the wrong man.

Mary Jane bit her lip, scanning the pregnancy test results. She opened the stall door and chucked it into the trashcan, washed her hands, and then stepped out.

Robertson handed her a brown paper bag with the useless Tylenol. Wulf came up to her and placed a hand in her hair, pulling her to him. He kissed her. "MJ, we don't have much time left," he whispered against her lips.

She smiled, staring straight through him. Licking the kiss from her lips, Mary Jane regarded Ariel. There was no time to catch her bearings. She shoved a hand through her hair and said, "Um, I need a few things in writing before we leave."

"What now?" Robertson commanded.

"Stipulations of sorts. Wulf gets his job at the LAPD."

"I don't want my job back," Wulf cut in.

She continued over his voice, "Maybe not head of the Gang Unit but somewhere up the totem pole."

"You're not in the business of making commands, *Ms. Doe*." Ariel smirked.

Mary Jane smirked. "Yes, I am."

"You are not." Robertson stepped closer to her and not a moment later, Wulf stepped forward and stared him down.

"I've got this." Mary Jane softly patted Wulf's shoulder and continued. "If we're measuring balls, Robertson, mine are bigger than yours, baby. I've literally taken a pair, and I've been through so much that neither your demeanor nor Ariel's demands will persuade me. You *will* let Wulf return home safely with a damn title parallel to his previous position *or* I refuse to help you take down Jake."

"Listen, you little shit," Robertson commanded. "We can erase Wulf's LAPD pension in the snap of a finger. Oh, and not only that, I'm thinking about pinning all kinds of cases on Dylan Wulf."

"Fuck you!" Wulf said.

"No, a bunch of Mexicans will take that honor when your ass lands in jail for murdering a cartel king!" Robertson assured. "I'm sure the local authorities don't take kind to tourists committing crimes."

"Let's just take it down a notch," Ariel said in a calming voice, watching travelers pass by. "Look around you, Wulf. I'm sure your extensive vacation has you believing that we're incompetent. The little game you pulled while returning home the other day, that was amusing. We're over the entertainment."

"Oh, trust me." Wulf's fiery gaze turned from Robertson to her. "I know there are agents surrounding this place. Black suit left corner, sipping a drink at the coffee station. Please don't fucking insult me. Side right corner standing near the second terminal with no luggage in a business suit and no briefcase. Kiss my ass, Juarez. If that idiot's not the Feds, then by all means you win. Shall I continue?"

"No, that won't be necessary," Ariel retorted. "Your plane is scheduled to leave the terminal in five minutes."

"And he'll be on that plane," Mary Jane assured. "Let's just walk Wulf toward it, leave all the bullshit here."

Robertson and Ariel nodded.

She took Wulf's hand as they proceeded toward his departure area.

"I didn't think this was your master plan, Mary Jane," Wulf growled.

Mary Jane gave his hand a gentle squeeze. "I've been told that I'm a selfish one."

"Then be selfish, MJ. Your safety is key."

"No. It's time that I stop putting myself first. We spent a year in Mexico because reality and *life* scared me. This plan works for you. Okay?"

"I don't need it to work for me," he replied through gritted teeth.

"Remember the man you were. Rules and regulations. You've broken a lot of them since we've met. Go home."

"I will not leave you." He stopped walking and stood in front of her.

"But I'm letting you," Mary Jane replied. Her eyes brimmed with tears as she searched Wulf's hard glare for agreement. Tears trickled down her cheeks. Throat clogged, Mary Jane felt the words ready to leap from her mouth. She loved him.

Ariel and Robertson stepped back when Mary Jane's hand went up, though Robertson pointed to his watch.

"Go home. Live your life. Get your job back. Clean the streets of LA."

"You're not that optimistic, MJ."

Her hand went to the stubble on his jaw. "Nah, never. But I have faith in you."

"What about our baby? And your family? I won't allow it."

Gently, she pushed away from his caresses and embraced her womb. The vocal cords in her throat tremored as she spoke, "I just took a test, okay? So, no worries about putting our child at risk, because I'm not pregnant."

Those gorgeous eyes of his roamed over her. He wasn't

letting go. "What about your sister, your mother? You haven't seen your mom in—"

"God, Wulf, you're making my cry," she said, placing her head against his chest. "Stop the madness. Or just tell...my... family I'll be home shortly." Sensing his defiance, she kissed him softly on the lips. Mary Jane recalled Amy's words while they were seated on the beach after dinner. Amy had known Wulf loved Mary Jane when she hadn't the slightest clue. As soon as her lips parted from him, she murmured against his chest, "I love you. I love you too, Dylan Wulf."

She cupped his jaw and told him again. "I love you, but you're gonna have a good life. No drama. No bullshit."

59

THE LINCOLN PULLED INTO QUINCY AND SHELLY'S DRIVEWAY. The agent who babysat Wulf during the plane ride and escorted him all the way to the door gave a quick bid of good luck. Clutching the manila envelope that he read during the airport exit traffic, Wulf got out of the car, ruminating over the incentives Mary Jane had secured on his behalf. More money in his pension than he'd recalled and a note from his old Chief of Police welcoming him back come Monday morning. It was safe to assume that Mary Jane's presence meant volumes to the FBI. Just that realization burned in his gut and began a tormenting churn.

He'd abandoned her, yet again. Left her in the care of agents whose concern was "the greater good."

The tiny gate creaked as he opened it and strolled through the garden. Shelly came rushing out the door.

Her joy faded a notch. "I thought I'd meet the chick. I'm sorry."

This was far from a fairytale ending.

Wulf's gaze didn't even meet hers as he shook his head.

"Maybe later you'll meet her." *If you don't, I'll hunt down Jakob Woods myself!*

Shelly's brow rose, catching the deadly undertones in his voice. Her own held a note of trepidation. "See, prayer works. You're home safe. Quincy got in a few hours ago from an overnighter. He hasn't even been to sleep and is so happy. So, a *Starsky and Hutch* reunion is on its way!"

The agent's promptness made Wulf's worry amplify. "Good," he said as they climbed up the steps.

Bryan and Ryan flew into his arms next. "Uncle Dylan, you're back."

Bree grinned, fidgeting with her fingers.

Though he was having a crummy day, he squatted down.

"Oh, beautiful, you always bring a smile to my face."

The tot said not a word as she let go and ran back to her father's lap. Quincy sat in his favorite recliner.

"I'm back." Wulf found himself at a loss for words.

Quincy said, "You need a beer. Let's get one and talk."

"And you don't sound grateful about it," Brenda retorted from behind them, then she grumbled something about alcohol in the morning.

"Mom." He gave her a hug, a tight long one remembering Jake's words. It made his blood boil, but he had to stop thinking about Jake because it only brought worry about Mary Jane's situation.

"Well now, you're hugging me like we haven't seen you in years."

"Hmmm, it might have something to do with those El Toro boys in Mexico," Quincy said.

"*What*?" Brenda sat down on the couch. "Is that why the police are keeping an eye on us?"

"Bryan, Ryan, take your sister into the kitchen and... make her a peanut butter and jelly sandwich," Shelly said.

"Awwww." They whispered about having just eaten breakfast and hopped out of the room.

Wulf told the story of what happened.

"Wow, your crazy chick isn't that crazy! Sounds smarter than anything," Shelly exclaimed. "Mary Jane made some type of chemical bomb?"

He nodded.

"Well, wherever she is, with a brain like that, she can keep herself safe." Brenda patted his hand.

"Daddy!" the boys called in unison.

"What?" Quincy shouted.

"It's Bree!" Their voices held urgency.

Quincy and Wulf bolted toward the kitchen, Shelly on their heels and Brenda not far behind.

The back door was wide open.

"Wh-where's Bree?" Shelly clutched her heart.

Quincy already started for the back door.

"She went with the soldier. We told her not to."

Shelly slapped Ryan in the face, and Wulf held her back from slapping her other son.

"Where is my daughter?" she screamed and Brenda wrapped her in a bear hug.

Wulf hurried out the door. Quincy was already hopping over the wall to the left.

Wulf gripped the cinderblock and bounded over. He saw Quincy standing with hands on his head. Quincy slammed his fist into the wall. "Fuck!"

"We will get her back," Wulf began.

As Quincy pulled out his cell phone and heatedly called dispatch, Wulf heard Bryan calling out to them. He hurried back over to the other side.

"Uncle Dylan, here...the soldier left this." Bryan held out a piece of paper.

Now that I have the closest thing to you, in regard to an immediate family, it's time to return what's mine.

—Jake

60

THE FIRST THING SHE NOTICED WHEN STEPPING INSIDE THE visiting room was Peter's eyes. They were a slate gray today, mimicking the cement walls. Those piercing eyes appeared to be glued onto a marred, plastic face. Beasley's Rottweilers had shredded every bit of his lips, leaving a flat effect between his weak chin and nose. He sat in the corner near the back of the empty room as if observing something from a ghost's perspective. His catatonic demeanor came to life once Mary Jane sat across from him.

"I assumed Dylan Wulf was here to visit me." Peter's mouth dipped into a gnarled smile. "I'm truly delighted that my dearest wife has paid me a visit."

She sat down across from him. Ariel had let her listen in to a message from dispatch: Jake had called in threatening to murder another Mary Jane within the next twenty-four hours. However, he hadn't provided any information as to his whereabouts. A bud was wedged into her ear, and she was awaiting Ariel's prompt since none of the other agents had gotten a word out of Peter.

"You deserve to die." She made the statement, no dose of

maliciousness riding along in her tone, but just offering facts. "You deserve it, but not as much as you deserve to live. As your assistant, I grew to learn how prideful you were. I know the power, the confidence that consumed you once your next facial product hit the stands and you were revered," Mary Jane paused.

"You must be angry with me, eh? My beautiful wife? No divorce but death? You want your husband dead?" he taunted.

"Laugh now, Peter, but I hear that you have...what was it? Thirty consecutive life sentences? This is a cage; it's the type of place that will consume a man like you, a man that needs to rule. It has, hasn't it?" She smirked. "The hours upon hours of solitary confinement. Nobody to praise your latest genetic discoveries. It's already fucking with you, right?"

He held onto the frown that itched at the corners of his mouth.

"You've screwed with my mind, made me afraid of *me*. Afraid of my own thoughts! Can I trust myself?"

"What is it that you want?"

"Nothing, Peter. I have something for you." She licked her lips. "I can make you feel better."

The light danced in his eyes. He was intrigued.

She pulled out a Glock. "There's statistics on the affluent, how they fall, how they aren't resilient and commit suicide once the power they held is gone. Do you mind if I ask, is it better to have had said power and take your life, or just live life like commoners?"

A crazed chuckle licked annoyingly at her ears as Peter shook his head. "You were such an intelligent woman— when you were Mallory Portman, of course. We could've gone far as husband and wife, the two of us. If only you had taken the story I gave you. Stayed away from your family."

She contemplated his words. "And followed your orders."

"Yes. That's true. Albeit, two heads are better than one, but it would've been lovely, just the two of us. Taking over my businesses."

She inched the Glock closer to him. With his wrists in shackles, Mary Jane could taunt him more. "Let's return to the present. Too late to speculate on our perfect life together," she spat the words. "You're drowning here. No more students to revere you. No computer in solitary, right?"

The tendons in his jaw constricted. "What the fuck do you want, bitch?"

"Tell me about Jake."

He sniggered. "I've been told he's acting up."

Juarez: Good, now ask him who has given this information to him.

"Who told you?"

"My ex-wife, Linda. A few months after that whore and I split ways, she got nosy about investors seeking information in Grienke Pharmaceuticals. I didn't know that vindictive bitch was searching for a paper trail, something to say I'd already signed deals before our divorce. She found out about my dealings with Beasley. That's a more lucrative business, sweetheart."

Mary Jane asked naturally, "So you can't do anything without her?"

Juarez: Good job.

"She actually assisted me with the computations in order to cut down on the length of time it took for the brain to become more malleable. We both have key codes."

"And—"

"Tsk, tsk, we're being listened to, my lovely wife. That's all I'll say."

"Oh, really, you'd rather let her run rampant taking over your business. That's not your style, Peter."

"Tell me, *Mrs. Grienke*, have you begun to dream of Wulf's death at the hand of Jake?"

She gulped down the rock lodged in her throat. The night Mary Jane had been so spontaneous, wanting to go out to dinner and the subsequent dining with Amy and Tom had begun with a torturous dream. The dream had started coming to her a few months before, and it clung to her for hours in the middle of the night. She'd be too afraid to wake Wulf, too afraid to say something for fear that it would come true.

"Keep fucking with me, Mrs. Grienke, and—"

"Fuck you!" Mary Jane slammed her palm down onto the table.

"You are an adulterer. You disgust me."

"Peter, you stole me from my family and the man I was to marry!"

"Tough shit," he snarled. "You left Keegan for me, like a common whore. Then you ran off on me with that..."

Juarez: Pull back a little. He's getting angry. We don't have time to bait him.

"You're just like Linda."

"So we screwed you over, Linda and I? Is she calling the shots for Jake?"

Juarez: Great.

"Jake has literally lost his mind—aside from the cognitive conditioning," Peter huffed. "I paid him in full to murder you if you didn't cooperate with Beasley. That idiot is—was—the dumbest person ever, but greed is the one caveat that made me utilize Beasley's resources. He would be loyal for the money."

She inched the Glock forward, just out of his reach. "How can I find Jake?"

"He's got a tracker, sweetheart. A chip in his brain. Give me the gun."

Juarez: We need all the details we can get on that tracker, please.

"Since we're both aware that the Feds are listening, tell me more, Peter. Just get it over with." Mary Jane shrugged.

"You'll give me the gun?"

"I promise."

His pearly white teeth came out and bit down on the plastic-skin of his top lip. Peter caved. He told her about how to find Linda and even gave the password to one of the firewall systems that had not shown up on the computer systems the technical team had worked on in the past.

"Don't insult me, *Mrs.* Grienke! Give me the gun!"

Mary Jane waited until Juarez's voice chimed in her ear. They had a moving location on Jake. She gasped, standing to her feet.

"The fucking gun, bitch! I look like a chew toy. I want out of this stupid place one way or the other."

She headed toward the door with a smile, then at the last second tossed the gun back toward him.

Mary Jane's eyebrow arched as he pointed the gun at her instead of his own cranium. Water spouted toward her.

"Funny story. The Feds had to personally speak with the warden to agree to that *illegal* water gun, Peter." Mary Jane curved her lips slowly into a smile.

The guard shut the door and *boom* the automatic lock confined Peter in the nightmare of his own making. She leaned against the wall, closed her eyes, and took a deep breath. Crossing paths with the man who'd ruined her entire life *and not murdering him,* well, that had been the hard part.

Ariel offered a look of sympathy. "We found Woods, as you know, but there was a call from LAPD. Looks like we're going to need you after all."

Mary Jane's heart sank.

"I wasn't going to put you in jeopardy if I didn't have to; however, Woods has Officer Jones's daughter. We will do our best to—"

"Just take me. I'll do whatever needs to be done," Mary Jane said.

She and Wulf didn't do much talking about his nephews and little niece in the past, but she'd heard him on the phone with each of the three kids during their subsequent birthdays over the year. He loved them, and so she'd do whatever she could to save his niece.

61

AFTER A SHORT HELICOPTER RIDE, THEY LANDED IN THE middle of mayhem. Law enforcement swarmed an abandoned factory in South Central Los Angeles. As soon as they climbed out of the helicopter, the Chief of Police introduced himself. Robertson blew him off swiftly, but Ariel Juarez could see the look in the Chief's eyes.

Not only was the Chief of Police invested in the welfare of one of their own—Jones's daughter—this was the end of the line for her and Robertson because the Associate Deputy Director of the Federal Bureau of Investigations flanked the Chief's left. The two men mirrored each other's rigid, angry demeanor and with the Chief glaring through Ariel and Robertson, it was unmistakable that they'd be scapegoats.

Which made Ariel being ousted even worse. Her eyes locked onto the Caucasian man with pinched eyebrows. Before she could speak, he said, "Juarez, you and Robertson —you're both *liaisons* now." That meant only speak when consulted with. The big boss shoved his chin toward the FBI trailer that was about thirty yards away and surrounded by other police cars and a SWAT bus.

"Wulf?" Mary Jane asked.

Ariel licked her lips. Casually, she undid her ponytail and tied it into the most severe bun she'd ever had in her entire life. "I'm sorry," she mumbled. Truly she was sorry. From the start, Ariel intended to feed Mary Jane to Jakob Woods.

If one sacrifice meant that others survived, so be it.

Mary Jane seemed to understand as well during their short time of being reacquainted, and while traveling to Peter Grienke, the women had bonded over this understanding. Ariel knew about Mary Jane's dreams where Grienke threatened of getting rid of Wulf, and so, on the ride here, they'd both agreed that Mary Jane could assist in deescalating the issue. Which was not to be the case with the Associate Deputy Director here. While Ariel had a subtle approach, The Director would utilize all the tactical resources. And with such a narrow mind, his only resource would probably be SWAT.

Now she repeated herself, "I'm sorry, Mary Jane. I know that Wulf cannot be here." Her voice tapered off. Ariel had never held so much power in her life since the Tiana Clement case. She sighed heavily. This was no longer about bringing down the biggest, baddest terrorist turned serial killer. This was about her broken word.

Mary Jane glanced at her and then at the Associate Deputy Director, who was silently conversing with the Chief of Police, and then back at Ariel again. "I thought – I thought... I agreed to go in and talk to Jake. There's no need for guns and... and scaring Bree."

Ariel held her hand up to calm Mary Jane's hyperventilating. She was numb about the entire ordeal. The young woman was in love with a man, and a bunch of bad dreams continued to tell her that Peter would break her apart from Dylan Wulf for good. She couldn't help but try to explain. "Mary Jane, before it came to a hostage situation, using you to bait Woods was a risk I was willing to take. With a minor abductee, there's no way my boss will allow you into that building. I appreciate your willingness to place your life in jeopardy, but it is literally out of my hands." *All we have now is prayer. My mother would want me to pray.*

The heartbreak that pierced Mary Jane's eyes and gave rise to an onslaught of tears made Ariel feel even worse. She needed a double shot of whiskey.

Robertson explained, "In a matter of minutes, the plans have changed, Mary Jane. We can't very well have you playing hero with a kid's life at stake."

Animosity rode in his tone, so Ariel spoke up, "The captain of the police force is best friends with someone in the FBI's chain of command, and he's been given a level of control in the situation. We're going to get screwed in the ass since I just heard that Curbelo has successfully fled the country. Now, we've got a little kid's life on the line."

Mary Jane scoffed, "But—"

"Trust me, I don't like it." Ariel placed her hand on Mary Jane's shoulder. "And I haven't forgotten what you said about the dreams and Jake murdering Officer Wulf, but neither I nor Robertson are calling the shots anymore."

The barracuda stepped up to Ariel again. "Are you deaf? You are now a liaison, Juarez, Robertson. Get 'er out of here, now!"

The only association he had with Mary Jane was a frown. He did an about-face and headed toward the FBI trailer with his friend in tow.

"Wait." Mary Jane followed his retreat. "I have to go in and talk to Jake."

His pale blue eyes turned in her direction for the first time. Ariel took a gulp. She'd just been demoted to 'liaison', which meant she could only give intel when spoken to. Yet, Mary Jane had the balls to make an order.

The Assistant Director growled, "Not today!"

Mary Jane started after him. Ariel grabbed her arm.

"I can make him listen, Ariel. I can make Jake listen. Can you get that asshole to stop for a second, so I can tell him?"

Robertson smiled faintly. "There is a four-year-old girl being held hostage by *your friend*, *Mrs. Grienke*."

She and her partner exchanged glances. Ariel shook her head. He'd always thought that the Mary Jane angle wasn't a good one and Ariel knew it was off with her head when all was said and done, but Robertson was taking it too far.

"As a liaison, I'll try to mention that, Mary Jane. I'll be back in a few minutes. Stay by the chopper."

Ariel moved with purpose toward the trailer. She held her head high, though her fellow agents probably were highly aware that she had been dismissed. This was by no means the end of her on the Grienke/Woods case.

There was a young girl that needed to be saved, and Ariel wasn't counting another body today—not unless that body was Jakob Woods.

There were women around the world whose minds would be slowly transitioning as they recalled where they came from. *All this 'sweep it under the rug' bullshit was going to come back and bite us in the ass.* And she'd be there to fix things. The stakeholders were going to follow her lead once she told them exactly what mistakes they'd made in brainwashing the girls again.

A million women...yes, that number was outlandish, but the truth was just as dire. And she'd given her all from the start. For Tiana Clement. For Whitley Rodgers. "I'll be damned if I'm somebody's fucking liaison."

She gripped the handle of the FBI trailer and entered.

62

Mary Jane started after Ariel, but Robertson grabbed her arm and yanked her back. "We're not on the case anymore, Mary Jane, since we spent half our manpower and time searching for you."

"Please, understand that Woods is a very bad man. I know we haven't gotten along," Mary Jane spoke to Robertson before he could slip inside the camper where Ariel had followed the boss. "Please, if he sees Wulf, he's liable to kill him and the little girl. I had a dream about it. Let me go in first!"

"There's nothing I can do. Now, listen to Juarez and don't move a single muscle." Robertson started for the stairs of the trailer.

Eyes wide, she stared at the back of his head.

Everyone had blown her off. Everyone except for Ariel. Mary Jane had gotten the feeling that the agent had to prove herself as a woman.

Mary Jane bit her lip as she passed one zig-zagged cruiser and then another. She fidgeted with her fingers as she moved around the SWAT bus.

Then she ran.

"Ma'am!" The shouting came a split second later.

A slew of officers tailed her to the barricade. A few yards away from the building, they fell back in order. There was no time for her to rationalize why they chose not to continue after her – it was either because of the imminent danger or they were under orders. She hurried toward a rusted door and crept inside the abandoned factory.

It was dark inside. Her eyes widened then squinted, and her vision adjusted to the lack of light.

Mary Jane took a deep breath of air that was moist with contaminants. The faint sound of water dripping slowed her heart down, and Mary Jane tiptoed toward Jake's voice.

Her eyes widened in horror when she spotted Bree. Rope engulfed and bound the child around her chest and legs, and was thicker than her little arms. Bree sat on the floor in the middle of old bins and other factory equipment. Mary Jane hurried over without a thought besides helping her.

The girl's eyes were wet with tears, and her brown irises held no glimmer of hope.

Intuition caught up with Mary Jane and she put a finger over her lips and finally looked around her. Jake was nowhere in sight. She bit her lip and ducked around the bins and crates littering the room, bending down as she moved toward the girl.

"Bree," she whispered in a soothing voice as she reached her and knelt beside her on the floor, "I know your uncle Dylan." Mary Jane smiled as hope washed over Bree's face. Hope which instantly vanished. "Do you like ice cream? How about Dylan and I take you to get some ice cream after you see your parents?" she asked, trying to get the little girl to reclaim just a seed of faith. Just a smidgen made all things possible, and she needed Bree receptive to orders if need be, not hollow and timid with fear.

The sound of a gun being cocked back close to her ear made Mary Jane flinch. With a heightened level of awareness, she cautiously slowly looked over her shoulder and saw Jake. He wore army fatigues. *He's ready for war.*

"Hello, Jake."

"Hello, Mary Jane." His voice reminded her of sweet tea and a summer breeze. His gun never left the back of her ear as she stood straight, arms up. "What are you doing?"

Though she looked dead ahead, Mary Jane gulped. "I just want to get this little girl to safety. That's all."

"Where's Wulf?"

"I don't know."

"I have to kill him and the kid," the gun went back to Bree, "or you, Mary Jane. Let me kill them, please. And we can go."

"No!"

"Don't do this." His honey-brown eyes warmed over once more as he glanced at her.

"It's the dreams, isn't it?" Mary Jane slowly reached out to touch his shoulder. It was a calming movement but the gun went to her chest. Keeping the focus on her and not Bree was exactly what Mary Jane needed so she held her composure.

His voice was filled with regret. "The dreams won't stop, MJ. You...you're supposed to be my target."

She thought of the right words to say. The dreams had taken root into her mind, making it so much easier for her to leave Wulf last night. That was, until she told him she might be pregnant.

"You don't have to kill anymore, Jake." She needed him

to remember the man he'd been for her very own sake while saving her from Beasley and Peter.

As her hand caressed his cheek, Jake's eyes stopped on hers. Dark eyes consumed with death, he uttered each syllable slowly, "I – refuse – to – stop. It's the kid and Wulf or you. MJ, I swear, I refuse to murder you, unless you force me to!"

The gun left her head. Mary Jane stumbled in front of Bree. With as much conviction as she could muster, she shouted, "Listen here, Sergeant Woods, you've been reassigned!"

He didn't seem convinced.

"Sergeant Woods." She spoke with the force she remembered her father using, his words coming automatically to mind. There had to be some truth in them when he'd jokingly ordered Elena around before she went on vacation and became timid. Or the stories of war he'd tell when Mom wasn't around to complain. Mary Jane knew some soldier lingo. She knew how to use certain words to her advantage. "Your mission is over, Sergeant! Stand down! Do you understand?"

Something in his stiff mannerisms indicated that she'd gotten through to him, that maybe whatever curse or scientific spell Peter put on Jake had been tampered with. The brain is a flexible and strong muscle, but how was it that she so easily learned about her past? Mary Jane didn't know how many years Jake had been under the influence of Peter but she determined that the length of time had something to do with it.

"Listen to me, Sergeant!" she barked.

Bree had further retreated into a shell. Her lip quivered and there was not an ounce of hope in her big brown eyes.

"No." Jake shook his head. He clutched a hand at his forehead but held his gun steady at her chest.

Mary Jane drummed up more of her father's old war sayings. The crude jokes that many army men knew became second nature as she spoke of the enemy. She willed something, anything to switch his mindset, but in the end, Jake held steady.

"Just kill me then," Mary Jane said, as simply as that. There'd be no assistance from a sniper since the building had no windows. At that very moment, she knew breaking through his resolve would be two steps past impossible. He'd been fucked with for too long and Ariel had explained that Jake had never been a good guy to begin with.

"Kill me." Her voice rasped. "Just me. Nobody else has to die but me."

"No." He shoved Mary Jane so hard she fell.

"You want to kill me, Jake, do it." Her voice faltered as Jake pointed the gun at Bree. Tiny sobs made her heart crack even further. On her hands and knees she crawled. For the first time in her life, Mary Jane desired to be happy, and even more, she longed for a future, but she took Bree's hand and they both stood there as she concentrated on a small dream of happiness. Wulf was outside, probably trying his damnedest to get inside. To save Bree and *her*.

"Close your eyes," Mary Jane spoke softly to Bree, and then she stepped in front of her again.

Bree's sobs became silent. Her tiny body vibrated against Mary Jane's back. Mary Jane gripped the barrel of Jake's nine millimeter and planted it squarely in her chest. Eyes glossed over, she said, "Do it. Complete your mission. The dreams will cease once you finish your assignment. My bad dreams will stop too."

She'd dealt with Peter Grienke's dreams for long enough

—the hold he had on her was already more than she could bear. If her death meant Wulf, and Bree who'd just started to live, would be safe, then she readily agreed.

Jake took a deep breath.

*Don't sleep. Don't sleep. Don't sleep. Don't dream. Don't dream...*Those thoughts plagued her again, making it easier for her to goad Jake.

"Pull the trigger, soldier!" Mary Jane screamed at the top of her lungs. "Complete your fucking mission!"

Bang!

63

ONE WEEK LATER

T HE SWEETEST AROMA WAFTED FROM THE KITCHEN. Cinnamon, vanilla, and pure sugar interwove with the sound of humming. Brenda placed another piece of French toast on the tall stack as she hummed an old hymn.

Wulf leaned his shoulder against the wall, legs locked about the ankle, and took a sip of freshly brewed coffee. His demeanor was detached, though he did his best to be appreciative. He had lots to be content about, such as Bree's smile as she and her brothers took turns licking the batter for the cinnamon buns.

"Big brother," Shelly said from behind him. She came up beside him, placing her arm around his waist. "Don't come over to my house with such an ugly mug for a face."

He chuckled, shaking his head. "Better?"

"He is so nonchalant about everything," Brenda said. "Well, I'm going to feed you breakfast and send you on your way."

Today, Wulf planned to visit the Portman home. When he'd mentioned it to Brenda the other day, she'd told him to come by for breakfast with the family first. Wulf slid into the breakfast nook with the first family he had ever known.

***

Elena stood at the screen door of her house. Today, she looked Wulf in the eye. "Good morning, Mr. Wulf." She offered the faintest smile as she unlatched the lock. "Please come in."

"Thank you." He stepped inside, feeling self-conscious for towering over her in such small confines.

"Mom, who is at that door?" a familiar feminine voice called out from down the hall. After a few seconds of light footsteps, Wulf stood face-to-face with one of the most beautiful sights he had ever seen. Megan Portman was just as gorgeous as his Mary Jane, yet her eyes didn't light up.

"Oh, Dylan. You're here," she said.

Wulf wasn't able to discern her feelings because Mary Jane's father stood in the hallway.

"Wulf, step into the kitchen with me," Vincent commanded. The thinning hair on the back of his head became Wulf's instant line of vision, prompting him to follow.

Down the hall Wulf went. The white walls were covered with family photos. He stopped in front of one of Mary Jane at a chess tournament. She wore a denim button-up, like one would in the nineties. Two long, thick pigtails lay over her shoulders, and her eyes made Wulf fall in love with her all over again. Confident, twinkling dark brown eyes.

Feeling Vincent's stare, Wulf turned to walk again. They stood in the kitchen. The door to the backyard was open, and bright light streamed in through it and the windows.

Vincent gestured for him to have a seat but didn't sit himself. Therefore, Wulf didn't sit.

While Vincent stood against the dining table, Wulf leaned against the counter in front of the dishwasher.

Vincent rubbed a hand over his mouth before meeting Wulf eye-to-eye. He folded his arms to stifle some of the emotion he was feeling, and then said, "I misjudged you. You're all right in my book."

"Thank you," Wulf said, knowing full well that they'd gotten as close to compliments as they would go as far as Vincent was concerned.

"Now, what are your intentions?"

Laughter blossomed from the back door, washing away the sound of Vincent's interrogative demeanor. The sun beaming inside the windows and door added an effervescent glow to the kitchen. Magnetized by the sound, Wulf stepped toward the door. His breath caught as he watched Mary Jane. She stood in soot-covered overalls that almost masked her voluptuous curves in front of the open hood of a '67 Mustang. A smudge of dirt coated the slender angle of her jaw.

Wulf's gaze narrowed as he saw Keegan leaning against the side of the car. His smile mirrored hers. They were so happy together.

Setting aside his broken heart, Wulf turned to Vincent and said, "Looks like MJ is doing well here."

"Mallory," Vincent corrected.

"Yes. Mallory. I have a few of her things in my trunk. Anyway, here's a letter from a friend of hers in Arizona."

"And that's all?" Vincent asked.

He gave a curt nod before turning on the heel of his boots and stalking toward the front door.

He couldn't hate Keegan Little as the memory of Mary Jane and Bree coming out of the warehouse dashed before his face. A lone sniper had finally infiltrated the air shaft and taken the final shot that murdered Jakob Woods. All in all, Mary Jane was the hero. Who didn't love a hero?

That night, Agent Juarez allowed Mary Jane to leave her sight with a damn near blood oath that she'd stay in the general vicinity. Mary Jane had asked Wulf to take her *home*. There were no words exchanged regarding what she meant by home, and the timeframe of how long she meant to be home. Well, the sight he just saw confirmed that this was where she planned to stay. He'd been a pussy, just bringing the letter from Glenn into the house, hoping on a whim that she still loved him.

Granted, he'd left the boxes in the trunk in hopes that they'd take them to the home he longed to share with her. When Wulf had reached out to Tito about Glenn's letter a few days ago, Tito said he'd have an older cousin drop off everything. Little did Wulf know but Tito had felt remorse about taking the knickknacks he and Mary Jane had left at the villa since their purchases blended in with the rented furniture. If Tito hadn't mentioned the letter in the first place, Wulf didn't know how long it would've taken him to come by. Shelly had forced him to search for *closure* when he thought Mary Jane left with her sister and Keegan. Of course, he had questions. Well, just one question.

Was she really happy here?

All he had to do was see Mary Jane's face to know. He stacked two of the three boxes and was prepared to grab the third one as Megan came to his side.

"Let me help you with those," she said, pulling it into her arms.

"I've got it."

"I see. Looks like you have one foot on the race line already." Megan started toward the porch. "Mom makes the best chicken enchiladas in Southern California. You're welcome to stay."

They glanced toward the kitchen. From this distance, Wulf couldn't hear the cheerful banter between Mary Jane and Keegan. "No, thanks."

He made a quick trip into the house and when Megan dropped the box by the couch in the living room, he placed the other two there. Their 'goodbye' was awkward as he reached out a hand, and she gave him a quick hug. In seconds, Wulf was outside closing the trunk of his car.

"Wulf, you idiot!" Mary Jane shouted. Arms folded, she stood on the top of the patio.

"Me?" he asked bitterly.

"You just dropped off my shit—"

"Watch the language, young lady," Vincent snapped. Wulf hadn't noticed the tiny man had taken a seat on a chair at the furthest end of the porch, cigarette in hand.

"C'mon, Dad, like father like daughter. Close your ears if you need to."

"I will not." The sides of Vincent's mouth creased a tad. He was secretly delighted by the quip.

Wulf cut in. "I'm an idiot because I didn't make it into the building to save you and Bree?"

She bit her lip. "It's..."

He rubbed a hand along his face in defeat. "I tried my best to make it to the two of you, and with the Feds holding the perimeter too—believe me, I tried."

She snorted.

He grabbed the door handle. "What happened? You saved yourself! Bravo, MJ."

"Mallory," Vincent interjected.

Mary Jane scoffed. "Fuck that, Wulf. Fuck 'bravo!' And

fuck the fact that you think you can be an asshole to me right now."

"How am I being an asshole? My tone was congratulatory." *I'm being an asshole because you should be my Mary Jane, not Keegan's Mallory.*

"Hello! You just dropped off my *shit*, and then ran with your tail between your legs."

His eyes widened. Jaw clenched, he regarded Mary Jane in the same manner as he once had. The thorn in his side. They were arguing across a lawn anyway. A flat effect marbled his face; his tone became emotionless. "I returned the rest of your things. Most women would say thank you!"

With an eyebrow raised, Mary Jane turned around and stalked back into the house.

Lava boiled through Wulf's veins.

"That's all?" Vincent sat high in his chair.

"Yes." He turned away only to see Keegan at the end of the driveway, placing a few quarts of oil into the big dumpster.

Keegan nodded at him. "Mallory is about as stubborn as Vin. You are aware of that, right?"

"I am." Wulf regarded him while searching his cargo pockets for his car keys.

"So you're leaving? Drop of her stuff, adios, end of story?" Keegan slowly stepped toward him.

The sudden urge to punch the man's face in took over. Wulf hadn't been so angry since accusing Brenda of tricking him into taking her money when he was a teen.

"End of fucking story," he said, opening the driver's side door.

"Hmmm, that doesn't sit right with me." Keegan's soft voice deepened. "I know Megan doesn't want you around.

Meg's happy that you brought Mal home, and that's all. Under any other circumstances, she's truly the nicer of the two. Megan just sees you as a part of Mal's nightmare, though she is grateful. She wants all sorts of therapeutic services for Mal and for her to shed this part of her life. You included."

Hardly listening, Wulf slipped into the seat, noticing his keys in the cup holder. He scoffed at himself, having never made this mistake and snatched them up.

He had another problem now. Keegan continued to chat and he was standing behind the car. "Mal never gets what she wants. She's too much like Vincent. Too stubborn to speak from the—"

Wulf leaned out of the window. "Move."

"Nah, I'm not moving."

Wulf got out of the car. He walked around to the back of it and glared down at the man. "I will move you."

Keegan placed his palms up. "Look, Mal is my best friend. You can't leave, not until you go inside. Talk to her, tell her you love her."

"Yes, fucktard, tell her that you love her," Vincent spoke up from his reclined position on the porch chair. "I do believe I was wrong about misjudging you because you're still the dumbest motherfucker I've laid eyes on. Keegan no longer counts. I've known the little pansy too long."

Keegan rolled his eyes at the snub, but glared up at Wulf.

"Why would I tell Mary Jane I love her?"

The neatly dressed man shook his head.

The back door of his car opened. Mary Jane placed a box into the back seat. "Keegan, he thinks he can get rid of me easily, well, he's got another think coming." She turned around and stalked back toward the house with Wulf on her heels.

"What the hell do you mean, I intended to get rid of you!" He grabbed her arm.

"You just drop by, drop my shit off, and poof! You're done with me?" Mary Jane argued through gritted teeth. He just stared at her like he did when she was at SCPD.

But Wulf was bitter about loving her. "You haven't answered my calls in a week. You wanted to go home. Now you have Keegan back. Your entire family, MJ!"

Mary Jane rubbed the back of her neck and smiled. "Damn, I had such an enjoyable conversation with your mom a few days ago. Brenda told me how hard it was to get through your head that she loved you."

Wulf's eyebrows scrunched together. "You spoke with my mom?"

"I know your sister's family lives with her. I called around at the police station. Quincy gave me her number and invited me to dinner, and she answered. It was the first of what I *assumed* would be many chats with her."

He gripped her arms and felt like rattling her, instead spoke sincerely. "But why did you just shut me out after coming home?"

"Before Juarez allowed you to pick me up, she explained that the women who were brainwashed all chose locations. Live by the ocean. A small town. A big city. They chose places and were given money to start over. Juarez asked me where I'd like to 'start over.' Those words sounded so good. Start over. It's the same thing I forced you into doing when leaving Santo Cruces. She showed me a bank account that many men would kill for, just as each other woman had received. I declined."

His knuckles caressed her shoulder as he listened.

"The women are getting their memories back. The moment I said no, Ariel gave me another opportunity, even greater than the last. She said I could be an advocate for the women. There are so many of them, Wulf," Mary Jane's voice quivered. "Knowing that I'm capable of helping others, I decided that I can't be afraid of reality." She snorted and added, "I have to keep in the loop too, since Linda Curbelo is out there somewhere living the good life."

Wulf admired her gumption and the slight pursing of her lips as she mentioned Linda Curbelo. He loved the life in her eyes when mentioning justice.

Mary Jane chewed on her bottom lip and added, "Juarez said the bitch dropped off the grid in Italy. What a better reason to be grounded in reality than hopefully being the first to know about Linda's whereabouts and helping other women who suffered more than I have.

"So in order for me to be the best version of myself for us and for the women that I plan on helping, I had to come home. I had to right my relationships with my parents, my sister, and Keegan. I learned that Peter gave me a pill to abort my baby with Keegan. It was hard to handle. Keegan is my best friend, so we're pushing through that now. But you and I have gone through hell. Will you let *us* start fresh in the real world?" she begged. "Wulf, I had to do this by myself for a while, but it's always been us, and I love us."

He blinked, letting her story simmer in his brain. He saw a future with her.

"Dammit, Dylan," she said through gritted teeth.

"You never call me *Dylan*," he growled, pulling her towards him by the waist.

"I need your attention." She locked her arms around his neck and rose to her tippy toes. "Wulf, I love you. Don't make me find Peter's brain scrambler because I don't want to change you into my robot. I love you as you are, but I refuse to let you go."

THANKS FOR READING

Click on the image to join my Mailing List for information about my upcoming BWWM Romantic Suspense and a #Free Summer Read

ABOUT THE AUTHOR

Mother of two. Wife of one alpha. And alpha to his alpha.
   Lover of thrills and enticingly sexy chills.

Okay, so I thought that sounded like an interesting way to sum up who I am. But the quick, punchy line didn't allow me to add how much I love Taebo (hey, I have been kickboxing with him for almost two decades), movies, movies, movies, and I love Christmas. I can be so goofy and at other times I will focus on my darker persona where I bring to you dark action thrillers. I attended Azusa Pacific University graduate program. I received two Bachelors and a Masters in Counseling. And as you may have been able to tell, I have a fondness for the mind of a psychopath.

Did you forget to join my newsletter for a #free book . Also, the readers in my Facebook Group Amarie Avant's Aroused love saying which characters they miss ... big hint, I keep hearing that Victor D'Ross needs another book.

Alright, before you go, I beg of you to leave a review on Amazon. I'd also like to interest you in my upcoming Romantic Suspense "August" that includes two parts alpha. I thought of the bajan heroine while listening to singer, Rihanna. She's not an easy girl to wrangle for the cowboy, August. So turn the page for a sneak peak.

AUGUST: A ROMANTIC SUSPENSE

AUGUST
Texas

"WE'RE SITTING outside a convenience store, in the middle of the night, to grab KY-Jelly for ..." Addy gives an infectious giggle, glancing out of the window of my Chevy Silverado. It's the dark of night, but those old-school, big-bulb Christmas lights twinkle from the roof of the Lone Star Convenience Store before us.

"KY-Jelly for your parents," she finishes with a chuckle. A red warmth creeps over her cheeks due to 'sex'; sex and my crazy ass parents – or highly intelligent and sexually enlightened parents, if I must.

My father is a gynecologist and yet the only pussy he enjoys belongs to none other than the woman he has been married to for almost thirty years. My mother is a therapist, by way of centering and elevating a person's sexual appetite. And to round off the family tree, I'm a hitman for hire, while Addy is the sweetest thing I've ever known in a world full of corruption. She's a kindergarten teacher at a swanky private school. We met while I was assigned to murder the father of one of her students—fucked up, I know—but it was the best thing to ever happen to me.

Addy's porcelain skin is glowing from my proposal of marriage earlier this evening, and she can't quite keep her gaze off the princess-cut diamond sitting high and mighty on her engagement finger.

Her brown eyes sparkle as she tugs her bottom lip through her teeth in embarrassment. "Are you gonna drop me off at home first? We should..."

"Addy, they're aware we live together—but, if you insist."

"Very southern gentlemanly of you," she says, smile bright "While you drop them off, I'll have your surprise waiting ..."

Her voice is as light as a feather with anticipation. My good girl wants to be bad for me, but my train of thought is on my parents. I'm watching them, and I can't tell where one of their limbs or where the other's begins, and not because it's midnight. An aura of laughter surrounds the tipsy pair as they walk down the aisles of the store in search of KY-Jelly.

The Middle Easterner who is manning the station looks like he could use a cold beer.

"Look at them, glued together like flies to a pig's buttocks." I shove a hand through my tuft of dark blond hair, though I'd rather pull the tie away from my Adam's apple. Jeans and t-shirts suit me the best. It also feels weird when I'm not wearing my cowboy boots; I've taken many lives with my steel-toe bad boys. "Grammy didn't have on her daggon glasses when she spiked that Eggnog tonight."

"And you just did a good deed, offering to drive your parents' home. You also have the cutest grandma ever, Auggie. Stop being so hard on everyone."

I shake my head, wondering how I ended up with my eccentric parents. "Wait a minute, you talk structure in your classroom. Well, I command it in my life."

"A routine for five and six-year old students is to raise their tiny hands when asking a question and not run down the hallway, so your analogy isn't working for me, buddy. You just got engaged, try to smile." Her tiny fingers weave through mine.

As she talks, I glance at my parents and a rush of adrenaline prickles in my veins. Eyes narrowed, I survey the various large windows, sweeping the entire scene in an instant. A kid with a baseball cap slung low and a hoodie is standing near the cash register and keeps shifting around. His back is toward me, and I can't quite make out why he's hesitant.

"Addy, when I get out of the car..." I say, and the hardness of my voice jars her shoulders and steals the sparkle from her gaze.

Now my glower alternates between the kid at the cash register and another teen, wearing the same high school hoodie, who just entered.. reach past her to the glove compartment and command, "Lock the door and—"

"What are you doing?" she squeaks out the words as my forearm grazes across her knee. I undo the latch of the glove compartment and pull out my .9-millimeter.

"Addy, listen to me. Lock the door and don't open it!" This is the first time in our relationship that my voice has raised. Addy's light, airy laughter falls dead the instant I break it to her that I have transitioned from my position as bounty hunter to hitman. And after it sinks in, she cries some, too.

"Wha-what?"

Eyes enriched with sincerity, I hold her gaze and say, "I love you, Addy." This instant declaration steals the fear and fretting, which is enough to gather her attention again.

I growl, "Now, do it!" and she jumps just about out of her seat. "Do it now Addy," I order, getting out and slamming the door behind me in an instant.

I'm heading up the curb as the two hoodied teenagers one is hold up a gun to the cashier. High beams brighten behind me. Before I can turn around to see if it's someone giving a warning to the patrons or to the robbers, the gun is now pointed to my dad. All the years of combat training flash before my eyes.

The fight has never hit home

Not until this very single moment

"Dad!" My voice pierces through the night. "Dad, *look out!*"

I burst through the glass door as a fragmented bullet blows a hole through the cashier. And then the second teenager, the one nearest my parents, aims for my father's chest and pulls the trigger. Two slugs pierce through my father's heart and another shot pierces my mother in the middle of her chest. Taking aim, I squeeze the trigger and a shot fires through the back of the gunman's head.

A needle of pain plunges into my bicep, courtesy of the gunman near the cash register. The left arm of my suit jacket is instantly warmed with sticky, red blood and I turn, quickly. A bullet that was meant to take me out pummels through a litre of Coke. My shot slams right between the guy's eyes. The pocket change he'd just grabbed from the cash register is clutched in his hands as he falls to his knees. Postmortem eyes on me as he slowly slumps to the floor.

I'd kill him again.

My world stops as I step toward my parents. Though I've seen the streets rain with blood, my eardrums almost burst as I head over to their lifeless bodies.

"*August!*"

Addy!

I stand. Addy's no longer in the car. She's standing outside of the truck, arms awkwardly tensed at her sides, fingers trimbling. There's a figure behind her.

The man in a ski mask is about two inches taller than her; five seven, stocky built. He's standing just behind her and to the side. There's a spider tattoo on his neck, in blue ink. His arm is draped over her shoulder as if they're friends. The barrel of the Smith and Wesson in his hand taps, ever so softly, against Addy's heart.

And then he takes the shot...

THANK YOU, I hope you enjoyed the preview. Now, I beg of you to review Killing Mary Jane on Amazon, Goodreads, tell a friend, tell two friends...

WHILE YOU WAIT FOR AUGUST...

While we wait for August to go through that final proofing processes, I would like to introduce you to my alpha, Evan Zaccaro. This cover is just so fucking hot, it's ridiculous!! But I can promise you that the book is filled with sex and action and sex and... well you get the point. Check out a sample and I dare you not to grab it for free off Kindle Unlimited!

Chapter One

Detective Valentino Evan Zaccaro

"What the fuck are you doing, Evan? Evan?" My partner, Tyrone, snaps in the tiny bud connected to my ear. "*Zaccaro,* do not engage. Don't fucking en–"

Tyrone's cussing me out is doused into the piss-temperature beer where I just flicked the tiny bud. He's sitting in an unmarked SUV about a block away from the dive bar I'm currently darkening a corner of. The owner allowed us to tap into the cameras all over this shitty ass place, so Tyrone is viewing the beginning of a shit storm.

Across the room is my mark, Riker. He's built like a linebacker, and doesn't have an ounce of respect, not even for his own. It curls my insides, knowing that Riker murdered his own biological mother in cold blood after a few rookie cops attempted to question her a few years ago for calling emergency services. His crew had been cooking meth in the basement of her house which started a fire. This was before he'd acquired land and placed a chemist on the payroll.

Since I am a narc detective, Riker is at the top of the list of fuckers that I need to put away. But here I am, about to break protocol for another reason.

Riker's sitting at the bar with a young woman dressed in yellow. The tart came into the bar about twenty minutes ago with another friend, dressed in red. While the broad in red appeared to handle her own, I noticed Riker taking a liking to the one in yellow. He just slipped her a fucking mickie.

My eyes narrow as he touches her shoulder. I start over to the bar, and it's as if my presence has been made. At least by the females who begin to eye-fuck me, mentally undressing my all black tailor suit. They hadn't noticed before, and their greedy eyes say as much.

On a mission, I step toward the unknowing young woman. Riker is going to make me, I've hauled his ass into the precinct on a few occasions, and he's not your average dumbass criminal. Hence, his ability to walk freely.

"Sweetheart," I turn to The Lamb. She pauses, toxic drink at her lips, and hasn't yet taken a single sip. Our eyes connect. For just a nanosecond, strategy isn't second nature. Yes, she had a great ass when I watched her walk in, but I assumed Riker chose her over the big tit one in the red dress because this one seemed too innocent.

Mocha eyes. Big, mocha eyes that warm you to the core. Plush, pink lips with a hint of gloss, and this sheer innocence. A bad ass shape fills out her yellow dress, which makes the dark golden complexion of her soft skin pop. I almost call her Lamb. "Lam–Come on, sweetheart, it's time to go home now."

Her pearly teeth scour over her bottom lip, and my cock knocks against my pants as if to retort, 'Hello, Dumb Fuck, let's screw her.'

As a behavioral analyst, it takes even me by surprise when *The Lamb* murmurs, "Okay, babe."

Her gaze sears me with questions. Instead of inquiring who I am, she places down the spiked drink, and then holds out a hand. My rough, callused fingers wrap around her tiny, soft ones. It's as if her single touch has made me lose my fucking mind. Riker makes no move to engage, and take back his treat. And I am more interested in escorting her safely outside, than keeping an eye on my mine.

We get outside. A salted, Venice Beach breeze feathers her long, thick hair, and she has to push away a few kinky strands from that huge, innocent gaze.

I place my hands on my head, letting it all sink in, the fact that this warm, soft body before me will breathe another day. The smoggy, dank Los Angeles breeze has brought her closer to me, her sweetness.

Before I can speak, the tart's voice damn near blows me away. Her tone is a sensual rasp, but the pitch is increased with interest.

"So, what was that all about?" Those gorgeous eyes twinkle as if she's a fan of playing games. "I read people. The two of you have some serious hate for each other. He stole your chick, you wanted to extract revenge?"

A scoff hardly exits my mouth when she begins to play out the entire scenario. "No, better revenge would have been to take off the *suit* jacket and get your hands dirty. I honestly walked out of here on pins and needles hoping that one of you made the first move. Granted, I'd have to step away from you rather hastily, but a good bar fight, is in fact a good bar fight."

I glance back at the bar. Riker is no doubt leaving through the employee exit. And *suit*? Her tone fluctuated in a particular manner.

I hold out my hand. "Evan Zaccaro, and you are...?"

The energy in her tone takes it down a notch. She glances at my hand and then folds her arms. "I'm not telling you. For all I know you could be some creep. I came to the bar to be entertained, guess I fell into the 'assumption' trap by *assuming* you and that guy in there had some sort of problem. Tell me what this thing was between you and..."

"You don't even know his name? But you allowed him to buy you a drink," my eyebrow rises.

"Sure. Look, Evan, it's been a crazy damn week, you can bet your ass I was gonna milk a few more drinks out of him. As far as entertainment, I had my bets on The Hulk in the bar wiping the floor with your white ass." She pauses to point to herself, and says, "But *I*, being the unfortunate person I am, have a load of shitty luck. I thought; why not help out the underdog. You looked desperate, and I needed to tip the scales of karma." The woman ceases her theory, and starts for the parking lot. It's almost comical when she begins to cuss under her breath. "Shit, Sandra left me here for Mr. Tubs!"

She mentions some person named Jamie, who'd never leave her at a bar. I put two and two together. The broad in red, has to be Sandra, wasn't accompanying the bartender for a marathon fuckfest the fat-ass must've clocked out instead of taking a quick break.

"Come with me, Sweetheart."

"I'm not some slut that can't handle herself. I'm going back inside to call a taxi. And despite the *sweetheart* face, I had no problem stepping outside with you. I know Taekwondo in case you have any bright ideas." Those hips of hers begin to sway as she plants one foot behind the other. She begins to back toward the front door.

One stride to her three, and I'm right in her face. I take her forearms and allow my thumbs to softly rub. The passive assertion often helps anxious persons.

As expected, her pupils dilate, I've arrested her attention. *Do not confuse my kindness for weakness, Lamb.*

Tone authoritative, I reply, "No taxi. I'd prefer taking you home instead, *sweetheart*." I add emphasis to the nickname which I assume would hold more weight than dominating her. Those plump lips of hers sneer as I add, "I'm a cop."

Just the mention of my occupation sets her off. Normally it provides a safety net... for law-abiding citizens. Now the Lamb's hands rise in the air as if this situation has become too dramatic for her. "Oh, dang, you're a cop? You know what, this just became highly amusing. For a moment there, I was second-guessing your little ploy."

"No ploy at all." I stop myself from addressing her mention of me being desperate and say, "I truly am a cop, a Narc detective." I begin to take out my badge.

"This isn't a cop bar. And you look a little too spiffy..."

Her voice trails off as she observes my Los Angeles Police Department badge. My instincts are on alert. No, this isn't a cop bar. How would she know?

There's a sliver of a moon above us and the lights are dim. Reese squints. "Detective Evan Zaccaro. Zaccaro, that Italian?"

I nod.

"Hence the suit, I see. So you were staking out the place, Mr. Hot and Buff on your radar, eh? That why you'd prefer I didn't go back inside?" The interest begins to twinkle in that gaze again.

She must have a cop boyfriend or something. I nod. "Sort of."

"Alright, my momma didn't raise no fool. I've got a photogenic memory, Evan Zaccaro. Reese Dunham. But I need a drink, first. A real man's drink. You can drop me off at the next bar, whatever suits you."

~~

There was no fucking way I'd drop the lamb off at another bar. We'll end up at my place. Not that I was hypnotized by the sultry rasp of a voice, or those innocent eyes. I just needed a real drink too. That is before I tell the captain I possibly blew my cover for a woman that isn't even my type. I prefer blondes. And I also prefer women at a distance, in my own timing who also don't remind me of *home*. While we headed over in my Porsche, I almost closed my fucking eyes with just the image of being back at home, twenty years ago, as a little-ass kid while sneaking into my mom's fresh baked brownies. This woman makes my stomach tingle with thoughts of sweets.

Reese steps onto the white limestone of my four-thousand-square-foot penthouse apartment. Her eyes sweep over the all-white studio which is all open spaces but designed in sections. There are splashes of color, where antiques and statues are situated throughout. But besides that, the entire living space is all white.

From the state-of-the-art kitchen to my Cal King bed, her narrowed gaze lands back on mine. Before she can speak into existence my own thoughts about this not being a hookup, not in the least, she silently moves past expensive artwork. Those ample hips sway, not in exaggeration as I'm used to viewing, but Reese is in a class of her own as she saunters to the floor-to-ceiling window.

In the ultra-bright lights of my studio, I'm at war with

myself. I've fallen even harder for her. There's no dim bar lights, no smoky hazed curtain to mask her view. Outside it was dark, but here, bathed in light she's an earthy-golden with a certain bloom about her, like a delicious ripe fruit.

As if on cue, Reese does another three-sixty in slow motion. "Damn, I'm speechless," she says of the million-dollar view of Los Angeles below.

I'm fucking speechless too. My eyes tear away from her giving proportions, though she's preoccupied anyway. I step over to the wet bar, grab two glass tumblers. My index finger skims over the various alcoholic drinks. There's a toxic persuasion for any event. I pick up the fifth of Wild Turkey. The amber liquid splashes over the rocks. Recalling the undertones of sadness in her voice as she mentioned it had been a long day at work on our ride over, I give us both a generous amount. I didn't ask her to elaborate, usually talking about the job when off just puts you back in the mindset anyway. With that in mind, and my own botched case, I add a bit more Wild Turkey to both drinks.

"If I squint just a tad," Reese's voice is a sexy slur, from the shots her friend gave her, "I can see the tiny speck... my apartment is way across town."

"That so," I respond crossing the room.

I hand her the glass.

Reese nods her thanks, and sips a good amount of it. And my own drink burns down my throat.

Her nose wriggles, ears perked as she takes the pain. Then Reese shakes her head. "Wow! You weren't kidding. This will clear the flu up for ages to come."

A flurry of red creeps up her neck, and Reese's plush lips purse just a tad as if she's used to chatting and regretting her words. I smile at her first case of verbal diarrhea. Then Reese licks her lips, while gazing at the city lights once more. Peace takes over, and her mouth is just ajar, those perky breasts rising and falling softly.

What is she thinking? I have no problem sifting through a person's thought process. After all, over ninety percent of communication is non-verbal. There's something behind those eyes that tell me Reese is looking off into the distance, and the little tart has become a ball of doubt.

Then I realize that whatever reservations she has, has nothing to do with me. And she smells so fucking sweet. Something in me needs a small taste.

I stand behind Reese. Instead of relaxing into me, her entire body tenses. She downs the rest of the drink and is back to biting her lip again.

So unsure.

My rough fingertips leave a trail of goosebumps up her arm. I push her lustrous hair over her shoulder and bestow the nape of her neck with a kiss. That enthralling, saccharine scent of Reese once again takes me back thirty odd years to when I was a child, sneaking into my mother's kitchen. And I'm not a man who delights in sweets. My nose nuzzles the back of Reese's ear as I breathe her in.

"Evan, this isn't a good idea," she murmurs. She's woozy and it's not because of the drink. My hand dominates her flat belly, pulling her back to me rather abrasively. Her mouth drops open, somewhere between a sigh of desire and shock.

Reese turns around. Wedged between myself and the glass wall, she has nowhere to run. Though every bit of her body is melting for me, there's a bit of resolve in the way those lavish lips set just so. Her hands press against my chest at an attempt to deter what I want. What she wants.

There'll be no second-guessing this attraction between us, as I immediately take one of her wrists. The pulse at her palm is beating wildly against my thumb. I massage the anxiety from her soul, all the while holding out her palm, and bring it to my lips.

Doubt crashes from her shoulders. This is my incentive to hike a succulent thigh over my waist. The magnetism of our mouths meeting is instant. My hand claims her jaw, deepening the kiss. Her leg clenches tightly around my waist.

The warmth between her legs is bewitching. My other hand stakes claim to her toned flesh, and my thumb kneads the soft skin at the inside of her thigh. Sin sparks through the innocence of those big, brown eyes, begging me to do very bad, bad things.

My lips scour the corners of her mouth yet again, taking her breath away. Kissing a trail from her lips to her jaw, I press her against the cool glass.

In an instant she tenses up again.

"Look, Evan, I don't screw cops."

My eyebrow hitches but Reese doesn't strike me as a criminal. I want to devour every bit of her tonight. Although honestly, it's unnecessary for me to be made aware, protocol trumps desire. I ask, "You some sort of outlaw?"

Chapter Two

Reese

He has these Mediterranean eyes with the sort of eyelashes most females would die for. Evan's smile is this extraordinary grouping of confident and cocky, which is the reason why I followed the cop out of the bar. And another thing, he was good. Genuinely good for a cop. And coming from where I'm from, I can peg dirty, lowdown motherfuckers. Shit, I was drawn to honey before I even knew he was a cop. That smile made his stone, chiseled face seem more approachable. Gone was my mantra of running in the opposite direction of men who wore tailored suits.

He needn't say a word, just the command of his touch was enough to compel me to drop to my knees or do *anything* he craved. Evan was all over me, and then he plastered me against the wall. The cold glass snatched away my confidence, and I said the damndest thing.

A second ago, Evan asked if I was a criminal. My father wasn't good at much, let my momma tell it that all men aren't good. No matter their race: black, brown, white. When I was a kid, I was a mutt, with only the sordid roots my father offered. Milo Gianni Benincassa always said: *'The truth's all in the eyes. Never take your eyes off of your opponent for guilt, and that, doll, is how shit works in your favor...'*

And shit, I want Evan badly. But I don't screw Italians, my mom would slap the taste from my mouth. Evan Zaccaro is truly my opponent. My teeth comb over my lip, gander locked onto his. "No."

Again my body is plastered against the wall, with him all over me. Now, it's as if our heat has scorched the freezing glass. I want to forget the woes of my life. I refuse to believe my bakery might not be my own in the near future or that I have a next to non-existent sex life. In fact, I haven't been touched in almost a half a year, let alone kissed.

Never have I ever been kissed like this. My body literally aches for Evan to do with it as he so pleases.

Evan takes to my neck again. His eagerness is exhilarating as it is arousing.

"You smell so fucking sweet." His deep voice coupled with the way his nose nudges my neck has my core aching.

The sensation of his fingertips scorching across the

sensitive skin at my hips makes my sex tighten in anticipation. My brain is beginning to divide against itself. Logic and desire are in an internal battle, as one hemisphere of my brain keeps registering that Evan is a *COP*, and the other can't get passed his smoldering, brown eyes. My hands weave through his hair, massaging the chocolate-brown tresses. "Evan, fuck me now! Please," I gasp.

His low laugh is warm against my collarbone, and it sends a riot of chills throughout my being. Once again a spurt of wetness catches me by surprise. I play with the silk buttons of his shirt, but am too feverish to unclasp it. Evan places a hand over my shaking fingers. With one hand, he pulls at the Italian silk shirt. Buttons clatter onto the floor.

We're both just a little bit drunk, but I rest my hand on his firm pectorals imagining licking each chiseled muscle. Each one has been cut from the finest stone. There is only the faintest flurry of dark hair below his navel disappearing beneath his tailored pants. The rest of Evan is taut golden skin.

Though I'm still dressed, Evan says, "Fuck, you are a sight, Reese, I can't take my eyes off you." His tone has an edge to it. I have a feeling he can detect the finest hint of my body trembling. He feeds off my innocence. He sets me down on solid ground, and his thumb caresses the pulse at my wrist. Then Evan spins me around in one debonair, agile move. My palms plant against the glass as he unzips my dress. It falls to the floor, and he gasps at the sight of me as I take in the city lights below.

The kisses at the back of my neck force my knees to cave. "I gotcha, beautiful," Evan says reverently. He's more attuned with my body than I am, and I've been stuck with myself for twenty-six years. He turns me back toward him, undoes the front clasp of my strapless bra.

In total silence, the lace bra falls to the floor. I don't have the biggest breasts in the world, but the sex in Evan's eye has me alternate from drawing my hands over myself to standing tall in confidence.

He closes the space between us again. His presence consumes me. I tell myself to breathe. The silence is everything, yet my mind was made to gravitate toward my flaws. Without a word, Evan's hands cup my breasts, brushing his thumbs across my tingling, hard nipples. The sensation erases all thought from my cognition as it propels a sharp shot of pleasure straight to my nether regions.

My feathery lashes kiss against my cheekbones as he bends down. His mouth lowers onto my right nipple, and I moan. He licks and flicks at the hardened bud, sending my desire in a tailspin right down to my pussy.

My breath flows softly over my parted lips. I pant and beg, "Fuck me, Evan..."

He groans into one breast while applying pressure to the other nipple. The pleasure and pain concept forces my body to waiver with desire. Because my brain is now defective, I don't even argue about him not listening. Once more, I purr, "*Please* fuck me, Evan..."

Paying me no heed, Evan's warm breath caresses against the curve of my breast. Though he is oblivious to my verbalization, he attends to my body in ways I'm not even aware to ask for. I am weak, he holds me up.

Out of nowhere, my cell phone vibrates. The old ringtone—my best friend Jamie's ringtone—is loud and clear. My eyes close tightly as the friend-anthem song clashes with the moment. *Damn you, Jamie,* I wish I could say, but know this is for the best. Since junior high school, Jamie and I have looked out for each other more than we look out for ourselves. It takes sheer willpower for me to utter the word, "Stop."

Instantaneously Evan stops. This isn't like before when I put my foot in my mouth mentioning not sleeping with cops. He seems aware that this is the end of the line.

Evan embodies the ultimate gentleman. He stands to his full height. A coldness clings to my body, and it seems he's taller than before, taller, sexier, or my senses are amplified, and bruised with desire. I'm eyelevel with his taut chest. That Mediterranean gaze searches my wayward one as he softly bites the nail of his thumb. Without words, Evan beckons me back to him. And, oh boy, it takes every inch of my willpower to tear my gander from his enthralling one. The lips of my pussy quiver and I force myself not to stare at him.

Drenched in silence, he reminds me of a lion stalking his prey, calmly waiting for me to react. A piece of my soul dies. I lean against the window, attempting to catch my breath. *I'm not a fucking one-night stand type of girl. It'd be more embarrassing completing the walk-of-shame after giving himself a cherished piece of me. Leaving now is easy-peasy.*

"Th-thank you, f-for the drink." My eyes flit over the man I should have never taken a ride with. I take a breath, hoping I haven't been the tease of the century. "I'll call a taxi when I get to the lobby downstairs."

Evan nods, rubbing the back of his neck as I kneel to grab my dress and bra. I'm passing the large, deconstructed dining room, while shoving on my bra, not sexy like at all. On a mission to hightail toward the front door, I make the ultimate mistake of looking back. He stays planted. Why does the pit of my stomach clench in disappointment? Upon turning forward, I almost topple over one of the marble statues.

I wonder the price of it, and then the weight. Can I get this thing downstairs and to the bank? I'm sure it could pay the back-due mortgage at my bakery 'Flour Shoppe' and then some. Zipping up the back of my dress, I step to the side and back away from what must be a Greek marble piece.

A loud crash, behind me, cuts the monotony of stillness. My eyes close momentarily. It's an automatic thing I've done since I was a child. Dad beat goons to within an inch of their life before my eyes, I was never physically punished. Not sure if I thought closing my eyes meant I was invisible, or I'd go unnoticed from my latest gaffe.

The air escapes from my lungs as I turn slowly. There are pieces of broken clay all over the floor.

I give a huffed breath as Evan starts toward me. "Take it easy, Reese. Watch your st–"

"Damn, I am so sorry," I begin. "Look, how much did it cost? I'll pay for it." *One day, within the next millennium...* God, why didn't I turn around and flee as soon as Evan showed me his badge!

"Reese, stay put," he orders. As my mouth moves a mile a minute offering to once more pay, Evan adds, "It was one of a kind. Aztec. My mother... gave it to me."

"Look, I... I..." Shit, I can't replace it. And as he steps toward me with more concern for my well-being, I blurt. "Oh, my goodness. Your mom..."

Yeah, I've seen lots in my lifetime, which normally makes me perceptive. This is one of those times where being ditzy is best. My throat clamps. There's a connection here. And it's not the fact that I should steer clear of the cops because my father was *murdered* by one. But the fact that he's grieved a mother just as I have grieved my father.

Evan nods, finishing my sentence, "My mom's deceased."

"Sorry." A breath sucks into my throat, filtering through my lungs. My body is still geared toward fleeing. "I'm so… very sorry."

"Please, don't move," he holds out a hand. Then Evan steps over to me, careful to sidestep some of the larger pieces. My bottom lip begins to tremble, and I want to abuse myself for this blunder, but he has me in his arms in one quick swoop.

"Evan, I am sor—"

"No more apologizing," he issues a soothing command. As Evan sets me down near the window again, the hot zone, my mouth opens for another round of apologies. My father was taken from me way before his time, and I have one single item of his.

"Shhhh," Evan's fingertips graze from my temple down my face. The upsurge anxiety attack which threatened to overpower me vanishes. "Wonder why I have so many statues?"

His question further erodes at my guilt. My eyebrows knit together, and I realize this is a touchy subject as we both stare at the fragments of broken clay. The art pieces do make the place eclectic, disjointed even. If it weren't for the various statues, there'd be no color in this place, no color what so ever. The place would be cold, lavish but lifeless.

Perceiving my humiliation, Evan speaks, "My mom, she was a curator for one of the top museums in New York, and then she headed the expansion of the museum in Los Angeles when I was about nine or so. If word got out that there was an original Picasso at the edge of the world, you could bet your ass my mother dropped everything to investigate."

"Oh God," I whisper. A terrible sinking feeling rushes over me as I comprehend that what I had broken was truly priceless. Tears burn my eyes, but my throat is clamped, and my usual arsenal of apologies for being clumsy is stuck down my windpipe. Again my eyes close, the useless defense mechanism does nothing because Evan continues to speak.

"Most of her findings are in the museum in Downtown Los Angeles. Shit, I'm not even aware as to why I've decided to mention this," Evan pauses though it's obvious he wants me to stop apologizing.

Biting on my bottom lip, I gesture for him to continue, "She was on the board at the Smithsonian. When mom died my father couldn't bear to look at the few–and I say that lightly–pieces of art she chose for home instead of selecting to have on exhibit."

I can't look away from the man I shouldn't even be having a general conversation with, let alone converse about something so intimate.

His story is full of emotion, yet pride resides there too. "They were married eighteen years. I was twelve when my father lost my mom, but I knew love. That good Italian love where nothing could tear it apart. The happily ever after stuff. But cancer nipped that shit in the bud."

Why me? Why is Evan being so open with me? Set aside the fact that my mother has made me shun the Italian half of my heritage. But, Evan is entirely too open. And then says he's never talked about this with another woman before. There's a connection between us, built rock-solid. But I can't just divulge *how* my father died. Blood flashes before my eyes each time I blink, yet I've never told the story. I surely never intend to, least of all, to a cop. I'm the daughter of a slain drug lord, at the hand of LAPD's finest, no less. Yet, I'm drawn to Evan in ways I never imagined were possible.

Chapter Three

Reese

The sky is a flurry of turquoise and lilac as dawn takes hold. A cool morning breeze cuts into the warmth of the hearth burning before us. Tiny embers float into the weak morning light. We've been lying here on the wicker loveseat outside on Evan's veranda. Somehow, this stranger before me has me wide open. Not sexually. But we have talked the night away. There's something erotic about being in our undies, simply chatting.

"So, you used to be a homicide detective?" My gaze meets Evan's, as my index finger swirls languidly over his rock-hard chest. Soft, silk to the touch, yet powerful, hard, steel beneath my fingertips. Though I can't bring myself to fully divulge the dilemma of my business or otherwise, I don't want him to see straight through me. Might be ridiculous, us being strangers, yet this uncanny connection forces me to desire more about him, hence my asking a personal question when, so far, we've kept the topics general.

"Yeah, I was the walking cliché," he replies, voice a lazy dream. "My job consisted around advocating for the dead. They can't talk, I talked for them."

"I bet you were a hero to their families." I lick my lips so as not to leave my bottom lip dropped, so in awe of him. Evan's like the savior I never got the day I watched my father be gunned down. "Why become a Narc detective?"

A tension thickens between us, but whereas some would turn away, Evan's eyes meet mine. "People say there's nothing as sinister on this green earth than the murder of a child."

"Oh God," I wince, hands raised to the heaven. "You officially win, with regard to worst job ever. I would break down and attempt to murder all the potential suspects just at the thought of them..." I pause, skin crawling.

He downs whiskey on the rocks. That soft, mesmerizing laughter wraps around me.

"I suppose you wouldn't make a good cop." Evan elaborates, "But I caught him. He's on death row. Let's not get into a debate on the procedural safeguards for those on death row." Evan gives another wry smile, similar to the one he offered after I apologized profusely. "The investigation was probably the longest time I went without sleeping, though. Prior to that case, I felt such a sense of accomplishment when working out the clues, putting the puzzle together in order to give rest to weary family members. Now your turn, Reese."

I toss my drink back. Like the little chickenshit I am, taking a sip of this rather good wine has become my ploy. It's the same thing I did about an hour ago when we were unable to agree about the best underrated rock band. My brain doesn't comprehend 'agree to disagree' and my brain surely doesn't comprehend the ability to trust. I place the empty wine glass onto the side table, and shrug. "I really don't have that interesting of a job..."

"Don't downplay yourself, Reese," Evan adds, reading me full well.

My mouth hitches upward. *Fuck, I am. Telling you about me, is just as intimate as sex.* Instead of admitting the truth, I say, "I'm not. Although my work isn't nearly as dangerous, I'm just frustrated with myself." Instead of telling Evan the name of my business, I toss the ball back in his court. "Back to this 'Who done it?' stuff. Heads up: dumb question here, so you caught the child..." I pause, even the words give me the creeps, "The child murderer, right? Why quit doing what you love? I can see the pride in your eyes that being a homicide detective and putting the pieces to a puzzle together had to be..." *Kind of like the finished product of my latest, greatest cupcake recipe.*

Those warm brown eyes darken as Evan says, "I didn't quit."

My eyebrows rise. So far, Evan has been mellow, I sense that having the notion he quit is hard for him.

"I still help families, and the general public live in a safer environment. Now, there was a long, lengthy court battle. That bastard got death row, but what does that mean in California? Yet and still, he's sitting behind bars, with men who will live long lives and die on death row. Him too. In my opinion, the motherfucker hasn't truly paid. My apologies for my language."

Evan stands abruptly, the tension is dead. His eyes twinkle as he picks me up and into his arms in one quick swoop. I laugh at his spontaneity.

"We've been outside long enough, Reese. If someone were to observe this gorgeous body of yours, I'd have to retaliate." Evan carries me past the sliding glass wall.

"Mmmm, retaliation?" I joke, "I knew sticking with you would be entertaining."

"Oh yeah," Evan says. My body goes sailing into the air. I shriek in laughter when physics forces me to fall, sinking onto the plush mattress of his bed. The feather duvet puffing around me. Though I traded Wild Turkey for a clean, crisp wine a while back, I giggle incessantly.

Evan grabs my thigh, his large fingers, enveloping around the curviness of my flesh. "Besides," he says, dragging me toward the edge, "you've damn near killed me half the night, with those tantalizing, big brown eyes..."

"I think I can live with that," I retort, all smiles. Try as I might, I can't pull away from his hold. He mumbles about how good I smell, and I make a mental note to thank Jamie for his perfume.

"Turn over," Evan orders.

In another life, I'd question him. We've known each other for a mere moment in the span of a lifetime, yet the motion is as automatic as inhaling fresh ground coffee on a Sunday morning, I roll over to my stomach.

As I lie across his bed, Evan's large hands knead into my back. He'd tossed me over with so much strength, my entire body is aching for him to take me. My fingers instinctively cross, my God, my luck has changed. At least for tonight while in the company of a man I wouldn't dream of being with.

My voice is somewhere between a rasped croak and grumpy cat's purr, yet I am not self-conscious as I ask, "Were you a masseuse in another lifetime?"

From deep within the rock-hard planes of his six pack, Evan gives a boisterous laugh. He has a knack for not responding, and I'm learning the art of silence as his knuckles work wonders at the top of my spine. Evan truly is a mind reader, in some aspects, because my eyelids flutter before closing as he begins to rub my lower back. Then his large hand and fingers expand.

"This ass is the first thing I noticed about you." He says, cupping one of my butt cheeks.

The anticipation is at its peak. On impulse my back arches for him. Once more, a thrill of laughter coming from the body etched in Italian gold marble behind me. I almost frown, yet the sides of my lips twitch before curving upwards. He. Knows. Exactly. What. I want. And I *refuse* to beg again.

Evan's fingers slip past my thong.

Take it off! I internally grumble, yet I've learned so much of this man in such a little time. He's smiling at my expense.

My lungs fill with fresh air as Evan presses a thumb into my wet slit while he continues to rub my ass. My mind is washed away of my business woes, the only thing left is the memory of his touch. His touch from thirty minutes ago. An hour ago. Two hours. Every stolen caress as we talked, the expectancy. He skillfully strokes the sensitive flesh at my clitoris until my lungs force me to take a breath.

"You want me to fuck you, don't you?" Evan's deep voice is heavy with pleasure, smooth and sensual.

"I won't beg," I respond tersely, and then bite my lip as his thumb continues to coax my honey.

"No? But I'm entertained. Your pleading has *entertained* me."

My eyes narrow slightly; Evan is goading me with that damn word. I flip this around on him, "Whatever! You want entertainment, I'll sashay my ass right out that d—"

SMACK.

The sound of Evan's bare palm against my buttock reverberates against my ears. Now he delicately rubs at the pain. My eyes widen in shock; I glance back at him. He becomes aware that I've never been hit before. There's a cocky grin that comes along with his dominating demeanor too.

"You're tense, Reese, let me finish."

"Oh, 'let me?' No, 'do this, do that?'"

"Lie down."

And I do. Evan climbs on top of me, the hard slab of his chest against my back. His whiskey-peppered breath roams trickles over my neck and the back of my earlobe, sending a ribbon of ecstasy down my spine. Once again, pleading is on my mind.

My mouth waters as the tip of his thick cock probes at

my entrance; my fingernails begin to sink into the feather pillowcase as I lift my ass up more.

"Easy, Reese," Evan says, his hand spanks the very same spot as before. He then caresses the pain away and inches his cock into my tightness. He grabs my wrists, and captures them at my back while my walls stretch to accommodate his heavy cock. I have not a zilch of control, as his hand clasps mine and he thrusts against me.

Evan brings his other arm around to my front. He palms my breast and tweaks my nipple with the rough padding of his thumb and forefinger. It's as if a button has been pressed, a river rains down on his dick as he continues to thrust inside of me.

His hand sneaks down the slimness of my tummy and works its way toward my clit. All the while, Evan's other hand holds me steady. I bite my lip from gasping as he fucks me.

Something in me sparks, coming alive. I want to touch him, see him, feel him.

"Trust me, Reese, we'll get around to you touching me too." Evan's masculine chest leans forward, my body stretching even more for his length. He nips at my ear and tells me, "A baker, of all people. You're in for a real treat."

***

Suit. Custom suit pants are my line of vision upon waking up. For a moment I'm transported back into the past. My ex- fiancé owned an entire arsenal of tailor-made suits. I blink away the image.

I'm delirious. Not hung over delirious with a massive headache, but it's as if my mind needs to enter the current century and catch up. My body is infused into this bed of clouds as anxiety creeps in.

My eyes bug out from the sight of a friggen badge. I. Do.

Not. *Screw*. Cops. The salmonella is less contagious than Los Angeles finest.

The digital clock on the nightstand reads one forty-one in the afternoon. I cringe while rolling over to look at the man beside me. Evan's skin is a warm olive, glowing under the sunlight. Oh, and I recall pulling the heck out of that wavy, dark hair at the crack of dawn. Lucky him, it's still perfect in his sleep. Those eyes were a caring brown. If I blink, they flash before me.

I mentally take a note of his features: thick, perfectly arched eyebrows, faint lines of wisdom on his forehead. That fucking mouth. Exactly how long did God take sculpting his distinguished jawline and cheekbones? For half the night, Evan conjured feelings I never knew existed. And I bite my lip wanting to bask in the way he took so much thought into pleasing my body.

But in this moment, I've failed the memory of my father. Jesus, it's time to exit stage left–STAT. I glide out of bed, moving quietly and with a side of sultry if he does happen to wake up to a vision of the full moon.

I consider nabbing his linen shirt just to take one last whiff of his intoxicating cologne. Yet, him catching me in this position might elevate me to creeper status. I step past the no-no suit and grab my yellow dress.

Where are my panties and bra? This place is huge. The night lasted forever, unfortunately for us, forever had to end. I sift through my mind from all the crazy sex positions to a vision of me tossing those suckers. Then my gaze glances toward the living room section of his place, and as naked as I came into this world, I scurry over there for it.

I stop short of breaking a very odd, yet manly statue. An imaginary vice grips at my heart while Evan's story about his mother sifts through my mind. Something tells me Evan understood that we're more alike than I'd verbally let on.

He'd told me all about her. As a devout Catholic, he still prays for his mother. I said zilch about my father's death, and I'd be too afraid of thunder and lightning to pray for Milo Benincassa's soul. Or is it laughter? Would the clouds open up and Almighty chuckle at my expense?

Don't look back, I tell myself. He's everything that I steer clear of.

A Beyoncé song rings out loud and clear; it's the ringtone for my mother. Now why hadn't I turned the darn thing on silent last night after Jamie's call almost bailed me out? This is proof that some people never learn—me included. I fumble getting one foot into the panties, press the away button. My mom needs to learn how to be patient anyways.

I glance back, the detective has stirred but still slumbers peacefully.

I quickly begin to pull the smoke-infused dress over my head. Why do bars always smell like stale cigarettes?

BEYONCE!

I answer. "Yes, Mom?"

"Why are you whispering, girl, and cut that bite from your tone, Reese's Pieces. I'm married!"

"You're what!" I scream. Who the fuck did she hypnotize? My mother is hot as sin, but she's missing a few marbles in that brain of hers. And when I mean a few, it's all niceties on my part because we're blood related. After my dad's horrific murder, I visited my mother at the psychiatric ward in Torrance at the age of eleven and a handful or more times so I've observed all sorts of craziness. "Mom, you've never gotten married in Vegas. You've done it many times but not *Vegas*," I reprimand her as usual.

"I know," Lolita simpers. "Hey, don't mention my

marriages in that fashion. Look, I'm going to hang up with you since this idiot cell phone provider won't allow texted photos to transfer while we chat. Soon as you see these gorgeous pictures, call me back!"

Mouth tensed, I glance back. Evan hasn't moved a muscle. So I stalk toward the door without breaking any of his expensive items.

Just as I gently press the front door, my cell phone pings.

God, say it isn't so. I lean against the door and look at the photos. Low and behold, there's mom. She's popped up married before. However, in her defense, I've gotten a few foreign vacations out of some of her hasty nuptials. A wedding in a small French village, a weekend in Tokyo, a husband she swore was a Nigerian prince, one hubby in Brazil I swear had to be dabbling in some sort of illegal activity to afford to have our family attend, no matter how tiny the Dunham family is. But Vegas. Lolita Dunham is too snooty to marry men in Vegas.

Then I notice the ring on her finger. A full body shot of her and an old geezer, yet the damn diamond is almost as flawless as Lolita. Sheesh, I see why she's holding onto the stiff, the damn ring has to weigh a ton and she needs the support. Lolita's got some new perky boobs and not one wrinkle on her dark skin, and I doubt Lolita will get wrinkles anytime soon. She's pushing sixty but hasn't had a job since my father died.

The man beside her is Italian. I cringe. Learned racism from her. My father was full-blooded Napolitano. He was no good per Lolita. So all Italians are no good. Hence, another reason why I sort of attempted to run away from Evan.

Evidently mom has switched up the motto because this Italian man is hubby number… six or seven. I've lost count.

She just got a divorce a few months ago. That's the

reason why Flour is behind on everything. In between her marriages, I front the bill for her lavish lifestyle. I'm too chickenshit to tell a grown woman to grow up.

Glaring at the photo, I search for a flaw. I can't tell if he's new money or old money in the cream-colored linen suit. It's snazzy vacation attire. And he's a hefty size, broad shoulders, stocky build. I gnaw at my bottom lip, realizing I won't know if hubby-number-so-and-so is a bad guy until I hear his accent.

I glance back at the door. The *Suit* inside strummed my body like his personal guitar. But my mind has been shaped and molded by a bipolar woman who had frequent bouts of verbal and auditory schizophrenia when I was a child. I can't do mainstream guys. I can't do cops. Nor Suits.

"Goodbye, Evan," I murmur, palm planted against the door. Last night my body shattered into a million pieces with just his touch. There were tears in my eyes before sleep snatched me away from him. My eyes close for a second, and I bite my bottom lip.

Evan Zaccaro. I will never forget the name. Maybe I'll send him an anonymous 'thank you' card one day. This was about the oddest one-night stand. But I reluctantly step away from the door. Surely he has no intentions of setting eyes on me again either.

Grab Zaccaro now!!
    And don't forget to review Killing Mary Jane

CPSIA information can be obtained
at www.ICGtesting.com
Printed in the USA
LVHW04s1928260918
591451LV00021B/389/P